I have written this story as a tribute to my lovely mum. I don't want to forget her character, how she spoke, and the key events which shaped our family life growing up in the north-west of England from the 1970s onwards.

It is based on my own recollections and perceptions, which may be different from those of others. I have changed people's names to protect their privacy and imagined some characters. Some places, events, dates and times have been similarly modified or created.
My mum was good at telling stories. I've tried to be like her…

Helen Birchill, 2021

FOREWORD

S quabbles without spite, courage without cruelty, loyalty without question, and sturdy professionalism, define all four members of this family coming to terms with the loss of their mother who made a home for them throughout their childhood despite all that her married life threw at her. When you read this moving tribute by her daughter with a keen ear and a prodigious memory for dialogue, you will marvel at how she raised caring, capable children you know you could trust with your life. Just as I marvel to this day at how my grandmother did the same in the early 1900s, my father having been one of a coalminer's family of eleven children raised in a town centre slum.

Jenny Martin
Member, The Society of Authors

EIGHT

A MEMOIR OF MUM

Helen Birchill

ISBN: 979-8-4873974-3-0

First edition. Printed 2021

For Jaine and David - who always make me laugh

INTRODUCTION

I always thought number eight belonged to my brother. It was his number. The one he always referred to.

"That's the equation, our kid," he would say. When faced with any numbers, he would always try to show they added up to eight or were divisible by eight or were a factor of eight.

He was born on the 2nd of April .

"Two times four is eight," he'd say. "April is the fourth month."

In later years, he had four children - half of eight- who were each born either on 28th of the month or the 26th.

"Two and six add up to eight."

And further down the line, he predicted that his future grandchild would be a boy, as

"G. R. A. N.D. S. O. N - eight letters, our kid!"

He lived at house number 206 - "Cos two plus zero plus six equal eight." Obviously.

But actually it wasn't his number at all, but, rather, my mum's. He just inherited the fascination with it.

Mum was born on the 8th of October. She met my dad, Len, who was born on the 18th of September. My eldest brother was also born on the 18th of September. When my sister and I arrived together - one baby more than expected - that brought her total children to four. Half of eight. And so it went on That was the equation for everything that mattered to her. I didn't really notice it at the time, but key events continued to play out in this way.

When I told her I was getting married on the 18th of April, she asked, "Why that date?"

I told her I had no idea. It was just the date the registry office was available. That's all it was. But she saw it as some kind of sign. A destiny of some description.

Unfortunately, though, the number wasn't always associated with good fortune. Diagnosed with lung cancer on the 8th of March 2015 - two plus one plus five is eight - she passed away on the 8th of September of the same year, after just a couple of weeks or so in hospital. It was a date of which she would have approved and probably engineered - just to make the point it happened at 9.18pm. This is the story of those times.

CHAPTER 1

Freda awoke. It took her a moment to remember where she was. The smell of disinfectant and cleansing wipes, masking an underlying smell of urine, soon reminded her. The hospital. Or, more precisely, the Chest Ward. She had been in here almost a week now - since the 8th of August - having been rushed in in the middle of the night with breathing difficulties. It had been a terrifying experience which she hoped not to have to repeat. She felt much better having staff around. Safe.

She'd been dreaming again of the kids and what it had been like when they were growing up. She chuckled at the memories. Only she could have a dream involving chips and Mr Kipling! She remembered how she used to stand on the top step outside, shouting them in from across the road where she'd sent them off from under her feet to play out with their mates.

"Jean! Anna! Peter! Michael! Your tea's ready!"

It was a scene reminiscent of something from an old *Tarzan* film, Freda with her hands cupped around her mouth, bellowing out the names of her four children. You wouldn't do that today of course - you'd just text them, no doubt.

How she wished she could do that now - bellow, that is, not call in children. She struggled to even speak, let alone speak with any kind of volume. Lung cancer was stealing away her one pleasure in life - talking. It was cruel. But, as her mother used to say, there was no use crying over spilled milk. She'd just have to make the most of whatever time was left.

It was the unmistakable snoring of her youngest son, Michael, who was asleep in the armchair at the side of the bed, which brought her back to reality. Having been assigned the responsibility of staying with her through the night, on account of the fact she had recently been waking up experiencing panic attacks, Freda marvelled at his efforts.

Typical! she thought, laughing. *He's nodded off! He's neither use nor ornament!*

She smiled at the thought that if she had woken up, he would've been none the wiser. Stretched out, legs akimbo, mouth open, snoring loudly, he was totally oblivious to any of the goings on around him.

She didn't blame him, of course. The poor sod had just done a full day at work, finally getting to install the curved oak bannister he'd spent weeks crafting. Then he'd dutifully turned up to do his shift as assigned by Jean, who had organised a full round-the-clock rota of all four of them to ensure Freda was never on her own.

She should've known he wouldn't be able to stay awake. He'd no sooner sorted her bed out for her the night before - taking great delight in using the remote control to adjust it and throwing her left, right and centre in the process - than he'd settled down in the guest armchair. Indeed, he had only just uttered, "I'm just resting my eyes, Mum. Shout up if you need owt," when he fell into a deep sleep. She hadn't had the heart to wake him up and remind him that he was supposed to be looking after her. Instead she took out her iPad and took note of the status of her games from last time she had been online.

I wish I could play on Castle Story, she thought. *Our Jean's going to get well ahead of me now. I wish there was WiFi in here.*

She'd become quite competitive in recent weeks and, unbeknown to her daughter, had been buying extra coins so she could improve the grounds of her estate more quickly. It saved having to wait ages to win the currency to get what she wanted. This was in addition to the coins she'd been gifted by people on Facebook. That had been a good tip from Jean. She didn't do social media as a rule, preferring to chat on the phone to people, but she'd set up an account anyway and was happily reaping the rewards. As a result of getting in touch with random strangers, she had managed to plant a whole new field of crops and buy some much-needed stock.

She had caught up with Jean. Of course, this wouldn't have been necessary if her knights had been a bit better at their quests.

"How come you send a knight out on a quest, Jean, and he comes back with a cow, and I send one out and he only brings me a bowl of soup?" she'd complained. "It's just not on! I want to get what you get. A bowl of soup's no use to me. I want animals. Your castle grounds look far better than mine. What are you doing that I'm not?"

"Well, you've either got it or you haven't Mother," Jean had quipped, tongue in cheek.

Then there had been the episode with the magic tree. She had spent hours solving puzzles so she could earn a star for that tree. And what had happened to it? One minute it was there, all glistening and sparkly on top of the tree in the courtyard and the next day when she'd gone online it had vanished! It just wasn't right! Of course, Jean's tree hadn't gone, as she was quick to keep reminding her.

Well, she wasn't having it! There was no way she was letting all those hours go to waste. Not when she'd worked so hard. So, she'd googled the phone number of the company who produced it and phoned them up.

5

"What are you playing at taking away the star on the tree in my courtyard?" she'd demanded of the rather shy-sounding lad on the other end of the line. "I've spent hours working hard to get that tree. There's a fault on the game. What are you going to do about it?"

"It's the fairies," he'd explained.

"What fairies?"

"The woodland fairies! They'll have stolen it when you weren't looking. You have to be more attentive."

"You're having a laugh, aren't you? I didn't even know that there were any woodland fairies, let alone that they nick stuff! What kind of a game are you running?"

"It's a new feature," he'd said, "designed to keep you challenged."

Challenged! She'd give him 'challenged'!

"I've been swizzed, more like it! Never heard of such gobbledygook. Bloody fairies!"

Her blood was boiling. Well, they wouldn't get the better of her a second time! No, she'd buy more guards to put on duty. That's what she'd do.

She'd slammed down the phone and got to work on it straight away. What's more, she'd made a 'to-do' list. That reminded her, she'd better write down instructions for Jean. She was due to take the iPad home tonight and complete the tasks on her behalf. There was the top field to weed and some carrots to pick. Oh, and the roof on the barn needed mending. That'd do for now. Keep the place ticking over for a while 'til she was able to get home. She'd be able to manage that much in an evening. And it'd stop her spending time on her own game. A win-win situation in her opinion. She put the pen down and smiled with satisfaction.

Freda turned her attention to the locker at the side of her bed, hopeful of finding a drink to quench her thirst. Her eyes glanced over the card from Anna, complete with tooth marks from where her Jack Russell, Bobby, had got to it first. A baby meerkat toy sat grinning at her - a gift from one of her grandchildren. Then, there was the inevitable piece of wood brought in by Michael on her first night in hospital. Something he'd acquired years ago when he was first apprenticed as a cabinet maker.

It was called lignum vitae and was the strongest wood on the planet and extremely rare. In fact, it was a protected species. Michael treasured it as a lucky mascot and rarely let it out of his sight, so she was honoured to have been allowed to keep it by her side.

"It needs to breathe, Mum," he'd said.

She laughed at how she'd scolded him the day after since she had had difficulty breathing that same night, and had remarked at how "when the wood was breathing, I wasn't!"

Of course, she didn't want to hurt his feelings by rejecting it, so she'd relented and let it stay, assigning it to a less prominent position at the back of the cabinet, alongside the plastic tub which contained her false teeth.

She spotted a carton of blackcurrant juice and hastily picked it up. Inserting the straw, she took a few sips, noting how it was becoming more difficult to breathe and drink at the same time. "Bloomin' lungs!" she cursed.

It was remarkable how you only really noticed the benefit of something when it was disappearing. Freda had always taken her health for granted really. As long as she could get up every morning to walk Niko and Mollie, she was content. She'd gone for miles with the German Shepherd and Cairn Terrier, accompanied by her friend, June, thinking nothing of spending all day out of the house in the fresh air. Even when suffering with pains in her knee, she'd still continued to take them out every day without fail. Nothing gave her more pleasure than to see them enjoying themselves, sniffing and snuffling about.

Of course, it was Sod's law. The doctor had been wrong. That marked the beginning of it all really. It wasn't her knee that was the problem but her hip. Embarrassed by her mistake, Dr McGuire had fast-tracked her to a consultant who, shocked by the almost complete lack of cartilage, and surprised that she could even walk, put her in for an immediate hip replacement. That was two years ago. Without this error, she was convinced the operation would've been sooner and not as traumatic. She wouldn't have got blood clots and she might have noticed the breathing problems before they advanced to a point where they could not be rectified. It was one thing after another, numerous trips back and forth to the hospital, endless blood tests, the painful injections of blood thinners.

It was a good job she took after her father in that respect. Bert had put up with numerous incidents and accidents in his life that might have floored a lesser person and so must she. Resilience was bred into her. No! She wasn't 'mard'. She'd not only borne four children, the last one delivered breech, but she'd also experienced at one time or other having a needle through her eye, her foot stitched up without anaesthetic, and the top of her finger chopped off in a doorway whilst learning to roller skate.

She smiled as she remembered this. It had put her top of the league tables against others of her age. Having had it stuck back on without any kind of an operation, for years there was no feeling in the end of it. Triple Sewing Class on a Friday afternoon took on a whole new focus! She thought about her peers desperately trying to embroider flowers into the end of their fingers in the way that she could. Of course, they couldn't do it. Mind you, she'd received the cane for that little stunt.

Freda winced now at the very real pain in her chest, caused by something as simple as sucking on a straw. How life had changed!

"Hiya Freda! How are you feeling today?" enquired the staff nurse, Michelle, who had just come on duty.
Freda liked her as she was always cheerful. *Not like that miserable bugger she got yesterday. What was her name? Maureen? Yes 'Miserable Maureen'. If she had smiled her face would've cracked*

for sure. Very prim she was, a proper Miss Starchy Knickers! Everything done by the book – "Swallow your meds! Drink your water Eat up your breakfast!"

"Oh, I'm not too bad," Freda replied. "A bit fed up but there are them worse off than me." As she said this, she looked over at the bed across from her. In it was a girl who could've been no more than fifteen years old, lying prostrate, attached to an oxygen cylinder. Periodically, she would begin to choke and would have to be suctioned. Poor sod.

Noticing this, Michelle distracted her.

"Look what I've got for you today! Liquid medicine, no less."

"Aw! You're an angel."

"Well, I can only do my best. Can't have you suffering trying to swallow huge pills each day. I collared the doctor this morning and made him write you up a chart for this alternative. Now, open wide."

Michelle proceeded to take the spoon of liquid she'd prepared and fly it, plane-like, towards Freda's mouth, making a silly swooshing noise as she did so. This reminded Freda of being a toddler. She smiled warmly at the memory as she dutifully swallowed the liquid.

"There! That didn't hurt, did it? Another satisfied customer!"

"Thank you. You're a star!"

"Well, only the best for my favourite patient!"

"I bet you say that to all the girls!" Freda laughed.

"Course I do! Anyway, I've another treat for you."

"Really? What's that?"

"I've only gone and got you some physio booked in this morning to help you deal with all that gunk on your chest."

"Oh." Freda looked devastated. She hated doing breathing and coughing exercises.

"Don't pull a face. You'll enjoy it. Mark's great."

"A man?" Freda's ears pricked up. She'd always assumed that physios would be female, though she didn't know why.

"Yep! And not just any old man either. He's tall, dark and handsome. And young. You're in for a treat!"

"Oh no. But I'm not wearing a bra! I've got no bra on!" Freda remarked, looking down self-consciously at her chest. She hadn't worn one for weeks now due to the discomfort it caused.

Michelle laughed, signed the chart on the clipboard at the foot of the bed, then winked cheekily. As she headed off, she turned around momentarily. Freda was sitting up straight and adjusting herself, no doubt in anticipation of the arrival of Mark. Michelle smiled and proceeded towards the next patient.

Just then, like a whirling dervish, Jean, the elder of Freda's twin daughters, breezed in.

"Morning ladies! How are you all? Has my mother kept you up all night with her snoring?" Her unmistakable voice boomed across the ward as she placed a large tray of chocolate muffins on the nursing station as she passed by.

"There you go girls, something sweet to keep you going! You can't beat a chocolate muffin, and these are 'très delish'! I would've made them myself, but I've been a tad busy sorting out kids and Mother's dogs! Anyway, why do that when Morrisons do them so well? Enjoy!"

Then "Hey up! Has he been asleep all night instead of looking after you, Mother?" - directed at her brother, along with a sharp kick to his shins.

"What's happening? Where did you come from?" remarked Michael, all bleary eyed and disorientated.

"The land of nod, where you've just been by the looks of it!" she replied. "Honest to God, have you been looking after our mother or what?" she demanded to know.

"Oh, leave him alone, Jean," Freda said defensively. "He only shut his eyes for a moment! Give the lad a break!" she pleaded, winking at her son.

"Right. Well, I'm here now, our kid, so you can update

me on how it's gone and then bugger off home and come back tomorrow for your next shift. You'll be pleased to know you're here during the day so there'll be less chance of you falling asleep! Our Anna's coming over at two and then Peter and Janice at nine to do the night shift, so they'll expect you to be here no later than eight on Thursday morning. See if you can manage to get here on time."

Michael got up, put the chair back in its upright position and gathered his wallet and keys. Planting a big kiss on his mum's face, he squeezed her hand and wished her a good day, before exiting the ward.

Left in charge, Jean immediately rearranged the table, replenishing the water jug, rinsing out the dregs of the cup of tea, and tidying away a magazine, before proceeding to take out her phone, switch on her data and settle down to do some much-needed weeding on her game. Not wishing to be outdone, Freda picked up her iPad again and resumed her list of chores, determined to beat her daughter. And so, the morning proceeded, two figures perfectly at ease in each other's company, totally engrossed in their efforts and oblivious to the outside world.

CHAPTER 2

Mavis, the auxiliary picked up a photograph of Freda's dogs from off the bedside cabinet.

"Aw! Who's this then?" she enquired.

Sitting attentively in a garden was a large German Shepherd and a small Cairn Terrier. Freda looked up from her iPad, breaking her concentration and returned to the reality of the hospital ward.

"Aren't they gorgeous?" she beamed proudly. "They're Niko and Mollie."

Anna, her daughter, stopped reading her book and rolled her eyes. Trust her mother to have put a picture of her dogs on display! Everyone else, of course, had framed photos of their family at their bedsides. She smiled as she knew what was coming next...

"Have you got a dog?" Freda asked.

Bingo! She'd uttered the words which would ensure she could keep the unsuspecting nurse talking for a good few minutes longer. Once she got going there would be no stopping her! Anna sat back to observe the proceedings, marvelling at her mother's ability to chat away non-stop and enjoying the nurse's futile attempt to get a word in edgeways or escape from the bedside.

"Isn't he handsome?" Freda remarked, commenting on the German Shepherd, who had always taken priority in the pecking order of her dogs. Indeed, if the truth be told, the smaller dog had only been bought to keep Niko company and do a favour for her friend who'd wished to re-home the bitch.

"Geraldine said she was useless as her teeth are wonky," Freda explained to Mavis. "She wanted to show her, you see, and she wouldn't win any prizes like that."

Poor dog! Fancy not being deserving of a place in a home on account of such a basic attribute. It was all so wrong, thought Anna. Fortunately, her mother was a dog lover and one for a sob story, so couldn't bear to see any animal unloved. She had immediately offered to take her in as a companion for Niko.

Of course, it wasn't the first time she'd ended up with a dog she'd not planned on having. Years before she had accompanied her friend to the dogs' home which resulted in her bringing back what she thought was a cross-bred Jack Russell as company for her previous German Shepherd, Shona. Thinking that a small dog would be ideal and no trouble, she had quickly been proven wrong. 'Ben' turned out to be a proper handful, chewing up slippers, shoes, the grandchildren's toys - just about anything he could sink his teeth into.

Also, he kept growing and growing until he was just as big as Shona. Lacking the discipline Freda always associated with dogs of a high quality, Ben ran rings around her, refusing to come when called and frequently running off in the opposite direction whenever he heard a train, which was more often than not.

Freda had never been one to give up on a dog, but she was tearing her hair out, worrying how she could keep him under control. So, just as her trial period with him was coming to an end, she reluctantly telephoned the dogs' home with a view to arranging his return. She was horrified to learn that he had first been taken there as one of several pups left in a bag at the side of a railway - hence his understandable fear of trains.

Furthermore, she was alarmed to discover that he was actually on his 'last chance'. Unbeknown to her when she had agreed to take him, he had already been returned by two prospective owners. This was it now. Three strikes and you're out! If he returned to the kennels, he would be put to sleep. Freda just didn't have the heart to do this to him. She could never have lived with herself knowing that she had signed his death warrant. So, she had hung up the phone and resigned herself to keeping him. That was when she had joined the dog training club.

All of this history and more was related at great length to Mavis, who, try as she might, could not find a way to make her excuses. Anna grinned as she listened to her mother who, in spite of her obvious breathing difficulties, was continuing to tell her story. Talking was her passion and she could talk to anyone and everyone. Even better was to reminisce about her beloved dogs. Anna knew that there would be no stopping her now, so she didn't even try to interrupt. She continued to quietly admire her mother's efforts. She was on form today and it was nice to see her so happy.

Freda was now in full flow and missed nothing out: how she'd grown up with Samoyed dogs; bought her first German Shepherd, Sheba, when she got married but lost her to stomach cancer when her four children were small; 'showed' her next dog, Shane, across the country and even qualified for Crufts (but didn't go as she knew the judge didn't like his particular 'type'); bred from her son's bitch, Zaer, providing yet more dogs for the family; lost Shona to a mystery illness; and bought Niko with money from her son, Peter, to fill the empty space caused by the loss.

Niko was something special, of course. Freda had wanted a bitch when she went to look at the litter, as you 'shouldn't really have two dogs in the same house', but the last bitch had literally just been sold as she got there. She'd been resigned to going home, having wasted her journey. But then Niko had chosen her! He'd come right up to her on her arrival and had followed her down the long path to the gate when she departed. Jean had accompanied her and, five minutes down the road had pulled the car up.

"You've got to go back, Mum," Jean had said. "You know you want him."

Freda had 'Ummed and ahhed' but then agreed.

"Ok then. In for a penny, in for a pound."

They'd returned to find him still waiting patiently at the gate where they'd left him.

"It was a sign! It was meant to be. Best dog I've ever had!" Freda beamed now as she told the nurse.

Mavis, having been brought fully up-to-date with the family tree of the lives of Freda's dogs, next listened to her regale tales of 'The Dog Club', 'Programmes I have watched about dogs', and, finally, 'Walks I have been on'. Anna had heard all this before, several times over. She chuckled as Freda talked of 'The Canal Eight'. This was a group who met every morning to walk along the local towpath with their various breeds of dogs. Anna thought it was a name which was more in keeping with a group of thugs or murderers rather than a collection of ageing pensioners who shared an interest in 'man's best friend'. Freda knew the background and details of every dog which formed part of the group, as did Mavis by the time she'd finished...

Of course, it was a very biased version of events which Freda recalled. As Anna noted, she was careful to miss out any detail which made hers or anyone else's dogs look anything less than saintly.

Freda neglected to mention how destructive the German Shepherds had all been. As a child Anna had witnessed them chewing up just about anything and everything. Her mother's dogs didn't just go for small items such as dolls and the inevitable pair of shoes. No! They went way beyond these! Two settees, a bed, and 'the pièce de resistance' - the Renault 20 family car.

People didn't want to believe Anna when she informed them of how, having left three German Shepherds in the car whilst the family dined in a pub during a holiday, they had returned to find that what they thought had been Zaer 'sleeping' in the front of the vehicle, had actually been Zaer biting her way through most of the instruments around and about the dashboard. Gone was the middle portion of the steering wheel, the knob off the gear stick, the end of the handbrake and lastly, and most importantly for the driving of the car, all of the indicator, light and windscreen washer levers. 'Happy' (the nickname for her dad, Len) had gone apoplectic when he discovered what had happened!

How was he supposed to drive them back to their chalet? And, even more importantly, how on earth was he going to afford to have the damage rectified?

Freda had been at pains to excuse the unruly behaviour of her perfect 'never-do-anything-wrong' dogs, shifting the blame onto the kids who a) had taken too long to eat their food (so condemning the dogs to spending too much time alone) and b) not done their duty of checking at regular enough intervals that they were ok.

"Had they not been 'so bored'," she had insisted, "it would never have happened!"

Needless to say, their dad had not been listening to anything their mum had said. As usual he had switched off. Luckily, Michael had come up with a solution to save the day. As a joiner, he could craft the pieces from wood and paint them, so they looked the part. Of course, this wouldn't happen until they had somehow got home, but at least it was promising and managed to placate their father.

It was the same when they chewed up things at home. It was always a case of "Well, you shouldn't have left them where they could find them!" The fact that the dogs were always on the hunt for something or other to destroy was ignored. The dogs were never told off - just the kids - for potentially causing injury to the treasured beasts. Like the time one of the pups, Kizzy, ate a pair of tights. This was only discovered after she vomited them up. How anyone could have been expected to anticipate that a dog would eat such a thing.

Anna decided that it was time for her to intervene and let Mavis off the hook. She'd been more than dutiful in listening to all of Freda's tales. So, she picked up the newspaper from the bed and hurriedly pointed out the TV listings for the night - *Paul O'Grady's For the Love of Dogs*. Her mother instantly took the bait. Mavis didn't need telling twice. She quickly seized the opportunity to scarper, hastening off down the ward, only stopping briefly to give Anna a surreptitious wink in thanks

CHAPTER 3

Peter was sitting at his mother's bedside, engrossed in checking his emails from work.

"Nurse! Nurse! Get me a commode quickly!" Ethel balled from the bed opposite.

Peter looked up from his iPhone, glanced at his watch, and rolled his eyes. "Right on time again!" he muttered under his breath.

Just as the evening meals were being dished out and the staff run off their feet, Ethel had decided she had to 'go'. And, just like every other evening so far, it wouldn't be just a quick wee she needed but a full-on bowel evacuation! Great. Just what everyone wanted - the noise of someone 'thrutching' and breaking wind whilst everyone was trying to eat! Just because there was a curtain around the bed, didn't mean nobody could hear everything going on.

The auxiliaries were straight onto it, of course, wheeling in the chair and plonking her on it, handing her a remote buzzer so she could signal them when she had 'done'. Peter watched with interest, observing the lack of hand washing afterwards as one of them proceeded to make each patient a hot drink. He squirmed at the thought of what germs might be lingering on her hands.

"Would you like a nice cup of tea or coffee?" the auxiliary asked him, adding, "I know we're not supposed to offer visitors drinks, but I'll make the exception for you as you've been here all day."

"You're all right, flower." Peter replied politely. "I'm not thirsty," he lied.

"Ok. If you're sure?" she replied.

"Yes," he responded, "but thanks anyway."

He turned back to his phone, relieved that he'd escaped the dreaded drinks trolley. Truth be told, he'd had an upset tummy all week which he put down to his previous adventure with the hospital coffee. Dodged a bullet, he had. He wasn't going to be contaminated again - 'once bitten' and all that.

He looked up to check on his mum who was engrossed in an episode of *Coronation Street* on her iPad, oblivious as to what was going on as she had her headphones in. Jean, his sister, had spent hours sitting in front of the TV this week, holding up the iPad so she could record their mother's favourite soaps. There was no Wi-Fi in the hospital of course so this was the only way she could ensure their mum kept up to date. That took some effort, that did. There's no way he could've held up an iPad for that length of time. Must've made her arms ache something chronic. He knew she'd roped the kids in too, which made it even more commendable as they didn't even like the programme and usually went upstairs to play on the X-Box when they heard it coming on. He had to give it to them, they could be very thoughtful when they wanted to be.

He smiled and wondered if Jean had really thought about what she'd committed to - *Emmerdale*, *EastEnders*, *Casualty* and *Holby City* were all on his mother's weekly list of 'must watch' programmes. Rather her than him.

He didn't understand why she didn't just watch them 'live' on the ward TV, but, then again, considering the hustle and bustle of activity it was unlikely anyone would get to see what was going on, let alone hear the dialogue. His mother was the worst one for gabbing all the way through something anyway! She frequently phoned up his sister, Anna, to inform her of a programme which was about to come on, then proceeded to talk for so long - "Oh, let me just tell you this!" - so that she invariably missed it anyway. *It's a good job someone had the sense to invent catch-up TV,* he thought.

Freda suddenly started to laugh uncontrollably.

"What's up?" Peter enquired, not recalling anything in this episode that warranted such a response. (Indeed, *'Corrie'* was never anything less than doom and gloom in his opinion.)

"Have a listen," Freda said, pausing it briefly whilst she pulled out the headphones.

She pressed play, to reveal the unmistakable sound of a howling dog. Niko, her German Shepherd, was belting out the theme tune to her favourite Soap. He did this regularly and Jean had thoughtfully recorded it for her mum's benefit.

"Aw! Bless him!" Freda exclaimed proudly, dabbing her eyes with a tissue.

She really missed her dogs who had been her life for the past few years. She hadn't seen them since she'd been rushed into hospital.

"Yes, Mother. Very good," said Peter, not lifting his eyes from his emails.

Dogs didn't hold the same level of interest for him as they did for his mother. Obsessed she was. He still hadn't got over the fact that she'd refused a third round of chemo and, instead, taken her dogs on a holiday.

"Aw. But they've never been to the seaside before," she'd explained. "I've always wanted to take them away, but I've never got round to arranging it. Our Jean's found us a lovely cottage in Cemaes Bay. It's big enough that you can all come down and stay."

Peter had no intention of joining his siblings on a holiday of any description, never mind one revolving around dogs. He'd quickly made his excuses and tried not to show his disappointment in her decision. It worried him that she was putting herself at risk of contracting an infection, for the sake of a week away. He never really took holidays himself.

The only good side to all this, as far as he could see, was that she'd delayed giving the consultant an answer as regards radiotherapy. He'd not met one person for whom that had proved successful and was adamant that she should avoid it, even if the experts were marketing it as a 'last chance'. They were wrong. Chemotherapy mightn't have shrunk the tumour in her chest, but it had stopped it growing at least. That was good news. A third bout of the stuff would do the trick, he was sure.

Of course, his attempts to persuade her of this had come to nought. She'd had enough of sitting in The Christie, week in, week out and she'd gone for the radiotherapy anyway, regardless of his opinion on the matter.

He could recall her saying, "In for a penny, in for a pound."

Well, he'd been right, hadn't he? Here she was, less than a week after treatment, suffering in hospital. He blamed Anna for this state of affairs. It was her hand in all this. She naïvely believed it would do some good. No doubt she schemed with Jean to take the dogs away too. Well, if his mum didn't recover, it'd be entirely her fault. He was the eldest. His opinion should've counted for more.

As if reading his mind, Freda chirped up.

"Aw! I do miss Niko and Mollie. I'm so glad I got to take them on holiday. It was a lovely week. It's a pity you didn't get to join us."

"Well, some of us had to go to work, Mother," Peter said.

There was an obvious bitterness to his voice, as he realised he'd missed out on a full family get together. Jean and the kids had gone for the week; Anna and the girls joined them for the first weekend, along with Michael's eldest daughter, Melissa; and Michael had turned up for the last couple of days. A full turn out, but for him.

"They had a marvellous time," Freda continued. "The weather wasn't perfect but there was a lovely conservatory on the back of the house, planted with flowers, where we could sit out each night, even if it rained. The kids were great too. I never wanted for anything."

Peter found this hard to believe, given the way Jean's kids usually behaved, but he resisted the urge to comment.

"You know what? They never went on their phones either! Melissa brought some embroidery things and the girls all sat there sewing. It was lovely. They played cards and noughts and crosses with paper and pens. They even played board games without arguing."

Now he found that last point even harder to believe. His memories of family board games almost always included a row over one or other of them cheating. He recalled that on the very rare occasion that 'Happy' played Monopoly with them, he had exercised his authority by demanding Michael "give him Park Lane and Mayfair or get to bed!" There must have been one hell of a transformation in attitude amongst his siblings and their offspring, that's all he could think.

Freda was now in full flow, waxing lyrical about the care she'd received from them all.

"They even helped carry the mobility scooter over the sand dunes so I could get to the sea. That takes some doing. We weren't allowed the usual way there on account of the dogs being forbidden on some stretches of the beach."

Bloody dogs again, thought Peter.

"It's not an easy task to lift the scooter with me on it. But they insisted. So, we made it! I've never seen Niko so happy. He chased a ball and paddled in the sea - only up to his knees, of course. It was lovely to see him enjoying himself."

"What about that other dog of yours - Mollie - didn't you take her?" said Peter, a note of sarcasm in his voice.

"Yes, of course I did! You can't take one without the other. That would be unfair. Mollie is just Mollie. She plodded about and sniffed a lot. We couldn't let her off 'cos she runs off. Jake had her on the long lead for me. He's always had a soft spot for Mollie."

Unlike you, Peter thought to himself.

"The kids all played too. Jessica and Emily built a huge sandcastle and Melissa and Ava went in the sea with their clothes on. It was cold you see."

"And I suppose you bought them ice creams too?" Peter asked.

"Of course! You can't go to the seaside without having an ice cream, Peter!"

"And did Niko and Mollie like their ice creams?" he grinned.

"Wha...oh, I see...cheeky sod! I meant the kids all had ice creams, not the dogs."

"Well, everything else is about the dogs, Mother. I wouldn't be surprised."

"Well you obviously don't know much about dogs, Peter. You shouldn't give them sugary things. They're bad for their teeth. And Mollie's teeth are bad enough already."

That said it all really. No wonder they'd all had to have teeth pulled out as kids. Evidently, it was perfectly all right to feed sugary things to your children but not to your dogs. Talk about getting your priorities right...

"Did you feed them all chips and doughnuts too?" he asked. Then, tongue in cheek, "The kids of course, not the dogs."

"Yes. We had 'the works.' Fish, chips, doughnuts and loads of fizzy pop. It was great." Freda smiled proudly. Having sensed Peter's objection to the holiday, she was keen to paint the best picture she could of the week. And, indeed, those parts were all true. She chose to leave out the other parts.

The week had gone well but had taken its toll and she'd noticed her deterioration. She'd got progressively more tired as the days wore on, choosing to stay indoors rather than venture out. They'd had the log burner on all day even though it was summer since she'd just not been able to feel warm enough.

That had been great. Fire had always fascinated her, and she smiled as she remembered how she'd taught Jean how to twist up strips of newspaper to get it going - 'spells' she called them. This had been one of her jobs when she was a girl growing up after the war. As soon as she returned from school, she would set to work making them to save money on coal.

"We had a log burner in the holiday home too," Freda recalled. "Our Jean really got into it. It was funny. She sent Jessica out to buy a newspaper just so she could burn it. She came back with *The Angling Times*! She couldn't have bought a thinner newspaper if she'd tried! Jean went spare, since it was also the dearest one."

Peter raised his eyebrows. His ten-year-old niece always was a bit dipsy.

"But you know why she bought it, don't you?" Freda looked directly as Peter who lifted his head to pay attention.

"I've no idea, Mother. Why?"

"Well it was the only one not written in Welsh!" she cried.

Freda was chuckling good and proper now. "Priceless!"

"Well, there's a logic to her argument, I suppose," Peter said. "I'm surprised she even went on an errand for anyone without getting paid for it. She's very enterprising that one."

"Aw. You know what? She was lovely that week. Really attentive. She ran me a bath and organised all my night things out on the bed for me. She even helped me get in and out of it. I wouldn't normally let her see me naked, but she wasn't bothered. She was a little angel."

Bloody hell, thought Peter. This didn't sound like the relatives he knew.

"The only downside was that it passed so quickly, Freda said. "Wish we'd gone for a fortnight, but they were all on half term which only lasts a week. I had a lovely surprise when I got back too. Did I tell you?"

Peter knew all about the surprise since she'd told him more than once already. However, he decided not to say anything since she was enjoying talking. He hadn't seen her this animated in a while. It made him think that perhaps he'd underestimated the power of good a holiday could do for a person.

"Our Michael and Anna had been to my house on the days they weren't in Anglesey and given it a makeover. The kitchen had been de-cluttered and decorated and the rest of the house had been 'bottomed'. It must have taken ages! Our Penny and Barry had been round too and sorted out the garden, so, now I've got somewhere nice to sit whilst I watch the birds."

Penny was Peter's cousin; Barry her husband.

"That was nice of them," said Peter.

"Yes, it was," said Freda. "Penny promised Aubrey she'd look after me when she'd gone. She's kept to her word."

"Well it won't be long 'til you're out of here, and then you can watch all the birds you want," said Peter. "All you have to do is take your medicines, eat your food and do your exercises. Your infection will go, and you can get back to normal life at home. Watch your soaps, eat cake and have as many cups of tea as you want whilst talking to dogs."

If only thought Freda.

Freda hadn't told anyone, but life hadn't been 'normal' for a good while now. Despite all the home-made meals Peter had lovingly prepared for her so she could just microwave them, she found herself living on build-up drinks, and, when allowed, soft boiled eggs. That's if she bothered to eat at all. Invariably, she had no appetite. Her taste buds were 'shot' after the chemotherapy so nothing ever tasted as it should anyway. Of course, she could never let on to him as this would hurt his feelings, so she went on with the pretence and accepted the food parcels each week without a word. Jean would call round each evening to give her a blood-thinning injection and boil her an egg, believing she had eaten a proper meal at lunchtime. And she let her go on thinking this.

As for drinking tea, she hardly did this either. Drinking tea meant having to go to the toilet. That required the gargantuan effort of having to mount the stairs. The stairs in her house were steeper than most people's - even the dogs wouldn't tackle them. There was a bannister, of course, but that was difficult to reach from the kneeling position she inevitably had to adopt in order to be able to climb and breathe at the same time. She had to claw at the edges of the carpet trying to get any kind of purchase so she could drag herself upwards.

It was a good job I'd lost weight, she thought.

Sixteen steps it was - she'd counted them of course - but it felt like far more. By the time she reached the top, having already had to stop several times to recover her breath, she felt utterly drained. She just didn't have the energy to keep that up throughout the day, so it made sense to keep her drinks to a minimum rather than having to ask for more help.

Freda didn't want to impose on anyone any more than was necessary. They all had such busy lives and were already doing a lot. Peter prepared her meals and did her shopping every week, Michael took the dogs out every evening and Anna, who lived much further away, drove over every weekend to take the dogs out on a proper big walk and do all her housework. Jean came round at least twice a day, before and after work, to administer her injection of blood-thinner. Poor sod had never coped with needles but had forced herself to do it since the community nurses had been so off-hand about having to come round to do it.

"You should be able to this yourself!" they'd complained.

Of course, it wouldn't have bothered her if she was doing it to someone else, but it was a bit different trying to administer an injection to yourself, especially when it had to go in your abdomen. But Jean had been a star, asking the doctor for a 'masterclass' on their last visit to the hospital.

"I'm not having my mum feeling uncomfortable because of those nurses," she'd told him. "So, you'd better show me how it's done then I can sack them two off."

It hurt like hell, of course, when Jean did it, but 'beggars can't be choosers' and she was grateful for her efforts. She was always undertaking jobs for her and running errands. Nothing was too much trouble. She even helped her with her games on the iPad.

All of them took turns running her to The Christie too, so she felt she couldn't ask for anything more. Determined not to be a burden, she continued living like this for weeks, hiding the weight loss under baggy clothes.

In the end she succumbed and asked for help only because of one thing. Fear. Having awoken in the early hours of the morning, sweating profusely, she'd been unable to get her breath. And it had frightened her. Massively frightened her. She could cope with the prospect of dying – "when your number was up, it was up"- but she wanted to just fall asleep and not wake up. She didn't want to gasp and struggle. Clutching her crucifix that always hung around her neck she had prayed more fervently than ever and made a promise to God that if he helped her now, she'd make the necessary phone call. After several minutes which felt like hours, she had managed to calm herself down and regulate her breathing to the point where she could pick up the phone. And within minutes, responding to her prayers, like the cavalry, her family were there for her.

Freda looked at Peter now. Her first-born son had returned to working on his phone oblivious to what was really going on. But she wasn't going to tell him the truth, which, deep-down she'd known for months. She wasn't getting better, and she wasn't going to get better either. There wasn't going to be a 'normal life' for her at home, and she wasn't prepared to live one where she was bedridden and dependent on others. But this was not yet a secret to share. She picked up her iPad and clicked on her farm game, content to escape from the reality of her situation.

CHAPTER 4

The ward was peaceful at last. Anna was sitting by the bedside as her mother slept, carefully sorting her holiday photos into a logical order ready to put into an album. The only sounds were those from the generator which was keeping the special mattress pumped up. Freda had struggled to walk to the toilet recently so had been confined to bed so this latest contraption was a godsend. Of course, there were the usual very loud snoring noises emanating from Ethel but Anna had got used to these by now and had all but filtered them out.

As she glanced up, she smiled at the sight of the old lady. Having been moved from her bed to the Parker Knoll chair, she was now slumped backwards and had dropped the blanket which covered her undressed lower half, so revealing her rather ample lady-bits to all and sundry. Grateful that this was an all-female ward and wishing to spare her the indignity, Anna wandered over and carefully placed the blanket back over her, making doubly sure to tuck it right in so it didn't happen again. Ethel stirred only slightly, shifted her large bottom a little and grunted loudly before continuing her sleep.

"Is she showing her flange again?" joked Michelle, the

staff nurse, who was entering the ward to begin the morning drugs round.

"Good job your brother's not here!"

She continued, "That's not a sight for a fella!"

"Well it's not a sight I want to wake up to either!" interjected Freda, who had awoken just as Anna had got up and moved. "It's enough to put anyone off their breakfast!"

"Aw bless!" said Anna sympathetically. "It's not her fault. It's that short nightie she's wearing which keeps riding up. They don't let her wear knickers in here 'cos she's always needing the commode or a bedpan and she can't really stand up and adjust things so she's frequently exposing herself!"

"Well, it's fortunate you're here, love, to keep sorting her out," chuckled Freda, "or else I'd be looking at that view all morning!"

"Yeah right, Mother," replied Anna. "As if you ever look up from your iPad long enough to notice anything!"

"Don't be cheeky! It's our Jean who's always on her games, not me! She used to come round to my house every night just to do so."

"I think you'll find she was coming round twice a day to give you injections, walk your dogs and make your tea, Mother," Anna retorted.

"Well...yes," Freda conceded. "But she always stayed longer than she needed to in order to play her games without the interruption from the kids. She'd rather be building her farm than interacting with that lot! Not that I blame her, of course. It'd do my head in living at her house with all the arguments They're always fighting and falling out. And as for Gary! Well, don't get me started on that one!"

This was true, thought Anna. He would've been under the patio by now if he was her husband. She wouldn't put up with his mood swings and all. It was funny really as her dad, Len, had been just as bad and Freda stayed with him for years, only plucking up the courage to leave home when she, as the youngest of the four kids, had completed her 'A' levels. Talk about the pot calling the kettle black.

But that was water under the bridge now and it wasn't the right time to bring the subject up. Once her mother got started, she knew, she could go on for hours. She smiled as she thought about what she'd just said. Her mum secretly loved the company of Jean and looked forward to her frequent visits. It broke up the monotony of some of her days. Since she'd been ill, it was difficult to go out without support and she missed the outdoors. It was lovely to see the obvious excitement of the dogs when Jean arrived - especially Niko who went mad, jumping up and whining, fetching his lead in anticipation of a walk.

Freda enjoyed hearing of where Jean had taken them and who she'd bumped into on the way. Knowing all the people who regularly walked their dogs round her area, it was nice to keep up-to-date with what was going on in the world of dogs.

And, far from her twin, Jean, being the one prolonging the stay, Anna knew it was her mother, with her "Let me just tell you this!" routine, who would keep her there longer. She imagined Jean - coat on, handbag on her shoulder ready to leave, door open at the ready - trying desperately to escape and get home to sort tea before the soaps all started, but being kept there by her mother's endless conversation.

Her thoughts were interrupted by Michelle enquiring as to where the photographs, strewn across the bed, were taken.

"Mexico," said Anna. "We've just had a family holiday there. Treated ourselves to an all-inclusive deal in a large hotel. It was fab - had a swim-up bar; a room full of optics and a fridge full of mixers. What more could you want?"

"Oh, that's not my type of holiday," remarked Freda. "I'm not a drinker. I'd rather have a nice cup o' tea. It cools you down, you know? It's a fallacy that you should drink cold drinks when it's hot. It's hot drinks that are best."

This had always been her mantra. Anna remembered

how she and Jean had accompanied their mother to Tenerife, which she had paid for, very kindly, with her divorce money. They'd never been abroad before and this was a treat. Freda had taken a shedload of teabags and a kettle! She'd loved it when she discovered the local supermarket sold Jaffa Cakes and immediately bought a box, despite the hefty price tag. They were at least three times the price of a packet at home, but "they go just right with my brew," her mother had exclaimed.

"It looks lovely." Michelle continued, "Look at those beaches! They're beautiful. All I get is a week in Wales where it usually pees it down!"

"Oh, I've had some lovely holidays in Wales," said Freda. "Don't knock it. I've always said that if we got the weather over here, nobody would bother going abroad. Only just recently I went to Cemaes Bay in Anglesey. The kids took me with the dogs."

Seizing the opportunity to stop her mother from launching into another rendition of her dog trip, and allow Michelle to get back to her dispensing, Anna switched the conversation back to a previous holiday in Wales.

"Do you remember when dad took us all to that caravan at Aberdasach?"

"Oh yes," Freda chuckled. "Elaine Smith recommended it. Mrs Evans rented it out to people and your dad agreed we could all go as it was a bargain. She said it was right near the beach and there was a shop on site. It sounded just right."

"Yes. It was a bargain all right!" Anna recalled. "It didn't even have a toilet! We had to use an old one outside in a shed. I was terrified at night 'cos it was pitch black and there were snails and slugs everywhere! Peter or Michael had to come with me and shine the torch so I could see where they were and remove them. They were all over the seat!"

"Yes! And all your dad kept saying was that you should think yourselves lucky because French people ate snails and would think it a great opportunity!" laughed Freda.

"I know! He was crackers," said Anna. "He seemed to be under the illusion that you could just pick random snails and boil them up like we did with mussels from the beach. But we refused to even try – thank God! He'd have had us all poisoned! And the 'shop on site' was a counter in someone's living room! They only sold about four things! We cleared them out of sweets in the first night. They must've thought we were a dream. Bet they'd never made so much money out of one family."

"Your dad was determined to catch something to eat that week," said Freda. "He was up at six every morning, armed with one of those fishing nets on a bamboo stick which people buy for their kids. He'd cut it in two so he could use the stick to poke under the rocks in the rock pools and then used to try and persuade the prawns to skip into the net."

"I know. I got up early one morning too and he let me go with him. We must've spent two hours ferreting about until the tide threatened to cut us off and we had to abandon the mission," Anna laughed. "We came home with a small handful. He insisted on cooking them straight away. Atlantic prawns they were – identifiable by their striped legs apparently. By the time we shelled them, there were just enough to cover a tiny cracker. Well worth the effort!" she said, rolling her eyes.

"But you all enjoyed doing it," Freda said. "And it was the only time 'Happy' actually did anything with any of you."

"Well there is that, I suppose," Anna admitted. "Although he only came out at the crack of dawn before the pubs opened. Outside of those times, we just all played together. I admit we had great fun competing against each other to see who could catch the most and then watching them go pink in the boiling water. I think we had about a saucer full by the end of a full day."

Anna reflected on how her dad, having passed out after his afternoon session at the nearby pub, had awoken to learn of their adventures. He had promptly requisitioned the prawns and made himself a prawn omelette. They all just had to sit and watch him devour it. It was like something a pack of animals might do – relinquish the spoils of hunting to the pack leader.

"He didn't just go prawning though, did he?" Freda said. "He also took the lads sailing their model boat on the sea."

"Oh my God. Yes! I remember that now you've said it," Anna said. "*The Sea Queen*! It was about two or three feet long and he'd spent hours doing it up and putting an engine in it. He used to take our Peter down to the model shop in Ashton every week to get bits and pieces for it."

"Oh yes. Poor Peter!" Freda looked sad as she thought about it. "He so looked forward to building that ship but your dad never gave him a look in. He had to sit and watch him putting it all together. It used to upset me watching him observing him and so longing to have a turn."

"With hindsight he'd probably have been better off letting Peter put it together," said Anna. "When he finally put it into the sea for its maiden voyage the rudder wouldn't work."

Freda started to laugh. "The ship set off heading for the oceans and your dad thought it was great. Then he tried the remote control to make it turn around and nothing happened! On and on it went!"

Anna joined in the laughing as she pictured the scene – her dad going berserk and screaming at her two brothers to get the ship back. Adamant that it couldn't possibly be his fault that the rudder didn't work, he insisted that they clambered into the sea to retrieve the model.

Envisioning it going on and on forever, they'd dutifully obliged, jumping in fully clothed and racing hell for leather to catch it before it disappeared from view altogether, cheered on by her and Jean. Arriving in triumph back at the beach, mission accomplished, they'd not been greeted with a round of applause or any praise but instead faced a grumpy father with no sense of humour. He'd immediately snatched it from their grasp and in an action reminiscent of a small child taking his ball back, had stropped off up the beach and back to the caravan on his own. Needless to say that was the one and only time it actually got used. Thereafter it would be confined to a box in the garage with previously abandoned projects.

Freda's eyes twinkled as the laughing increased and tears began to roll down her face. Anna was just as bad, giggling like mad. She dabbed at her eyes with a tissue as her mum continued to double up with laughter at the memories.

"You'd best stop talking about him now!" Freda shouted. "Or I'll wet myself!"

Having heard the conversation as it had developed, Michelle now looked up from the medicine trolley and shouted up.

"Keep the noise down over there! You're not here to have fun. I've got poorly patients in this unit!"

She then winked at them both conspiratorially and continued with her jobs. It was nice seeing Freda enjoying herself and looking so full of spirit. Laughter was one of the best tonics in her opinion and not to be discouraged. Life was hard enough for these patients and a little laughter went a long way.

Michael arrived then.

"What have you got the giggles about then? I can hear you from right down the corridor!"

"We were just reminiscing about our holidays in Wales," Anna answered. "We were saying about that time dad launched *The Sea Queen* into the sea and it wouldn't come back."

"I remember that well. Happy wouldn't go and get it and insisted me and Peter went in after it. I had to swim like mad to catch up with it. Got soaked, I did."

"We were commenting on how ungrateful he was," said Freda. "You would've thought he was the child not the other way round."

"Well, he was the same with the kite, wasn't he?" said Michael. He continued, "Bought it for our kid so he could learn stunts, then wouldn't give him a turn. We sat all morning watching him making it swoop and turn. We were gutted."

Freda conjured up the picture in her mind – Michael holding the kite aloft as commanded whilst Len teased out the strings; a dejected-looking Peter quietly observing and secretly longing to play with what was, after all, his birthday present. Typical Len: "Watch and learn!" He'd been like a man possessed, throwing and hurling it across the sky. The only saving grace was that it was approaching lunchtime so they'd not have to wait too long for him to surrender it up. Soon enough, the call of the beer gods would start, beckoning him away to the pub. They'd get to spend the afternoon as usual with just each other for company – four kids, a mum and two dogs. This was their typical family unit which they'd got used to. She'd resigned herself over the years to the fact that Len was never going to change and become the father she'd always dreamt of for her kids. At least they could relax and be themselves when he was out of sight.

"Remember that Saturday he came home in his usual drunken stupor from the pub saying we were going away the next day?" Michael had got himself a chair now and joined his sister at his mother's bedside. "Some bloke at the pub had been telling him about a beach on the way to Conway."

"I'll never forget it!" acknowledged Anna. "Not for us some beautiful golden stretch of beach we could play on! But some large expanse of pebbly terrain and rocks!"

"Well that was typical of your dad," Freda chipped in. "No buckets and spades for you lot to have fun with."

"Not even a bucket!" laughed Michael. "We got a carrier bag each!"

"Yes. Along with strict instructions to go foraging for mussels and winkles," said Anna. "Under no circumstances were we to come back until we'd filled them all up!"

"Free food!" mused Freda. "He neglected to factor in the cost of all the petrol getting there!"

"Wasn't it peeing it down too?" Michael smiled. "So we all got drenched whilst Happy sat in the car reading his *News of the World?*"

"Yes it was. He was all dry and warm in the car and we were wet and miserable."

"Yes but at least that meant he didn't venture out to join us! That would've been worse," Anna commented. "He'd have been shouting out commands and telling us to hurry up all the time. Do you remember his face when he looked up and noticed we'd downed tools to go off skimming stones across the sea?"

"His eyes were like organ stops!" Freda added. "He was bibbing the horn on the car to get your attention and you all just ignored him! He wasn't best pleased."

"Served him right! We knew what he'd do next. He would've just made us get in the car and driven us home, then told everyone at the pub how he'd taken us for a day out to Wales. At least we were having fun of a sort." Michael was quite animated now.

"Our Jean wasn't throwing stones but chucking the dog in the sea to watch her swim!" Anna noted.

"Poor sod!" Anna and Michael exchanged a grin as Freda empathised with the dog as usual. The Jack Russell had never liked water so they all got a good laugh out of making her go in the sea. Her legs would start the swimming actions even before she was plonked in. They thought it hilarious and would keep on chasing her, cornering her between them and repeating it over and over again. Freda had reasoned that they had to do something to keep themselves amused and it did the dog no harm.

Michelle returned and paused by the bed. She scanned Freda's notes to check on her medication. Not on tablets anymore, she poured her out a small tumbler of liquid.

"There you go, sweetheart," she said. "This'll make you feel a bit better."

"You're an angel!" Freda said gratefully.

"Down in one! Down in one!" chanted Michael, laughing.

"What're you like!" smiled Michelle. "Anyone would think this was a social club not a hospital, the way you all carry on!"

"What? You mean it isn't?" mocked Michael, winking. "That's what you all need around here. A bit of laughter. Does you the power of good."

"I'm only teasing you!" Michelle replied. "We love having you all here telling us about that no-good dad of yours! We haven't laughed so much in ages."

"Well at least you have some funny stories to regale courtesy of dad, Mother, if nothing else," Anna quipped.

"There is that," Freda replied.

"And four lovely kids!" This was from Joan who shouted up from her bed across the way. "You're a credit to your mother. I think it's really nice how you've all given up your time around the clock to look after her in here. You should be proud of yourselves."

"No more than she deserves," Anna and Michael piped up simultaneously.

"It's on account of her that we all grew up so normal!" Anna said, tongue-in-cheek.

"Well I wouldn't go as far as that, our kid!" Michael joked, pulling a funny face. They both started laughing again. Michelle clipped the pen back on Freda's clipboard then returned it to its position at the bottom of the bed. She exited the ward, happy that all was well in the world.

CHAPTER 5

Freda suddenly shouted out.

"I don't believe it!"

Peter looked up, having been absorbed in his emails from work once again.

"What now, Mother?"

He sounded exasperated as his concentration was broken.

"Look at this!" she cried, pointing to a photograph on her phone. "Our Michael's gone and bought Georgia a dog! And after everything I said to him about not getting one. He never listens."

Peter glanced at the image, feigning interest. Small eyes peered out from under a ball of white fluff on the screen. To him it looked more like something you'd wash your pots with rather than take out on a lead.

"Very good, Mother. So what?"

"Well, he asked my advice and I said 'No. Them kids will never look after it. And *she* will only have bought it 'cos it's clean and small.' "

'She' referred to his ex-wife, whom Freda disliked intensely.

"She'll think it won't take much looking after but even

small animals need a lot of attention. Mark my words! It'll be gone by Christmas. As soon as it poos on her cream carpets it'll be down the road!"

"Well, that's our kid for you, isn't it?" Peter replied. "Always gives in. She'll have guilt-tripped him into it and made him look like a bad dad again."

"Umph!" Freda retorted. "They're an ungrateful lot as well. He only sees them when they want something. Bet he's paid a few hundred quid for it too - they don't come cheap those Pomeranians!"

"Well, that's his business, isn't it? Best keep out of it," Peter replied.

This was Peter's answer to everything, thought Freda. *Anything for a quiet life.* She let it drop but made a mental note to have words with Michael when he next came to visit.

Having been disturbed, Peter now took the opportunity to observe what was going on around him. The old lady across the way - Ethel he believed she was called - was quietly folding pairs of large knickers into smaller and smaller parcels; placing them neatly in a row on the bed; then shaking them out and starting over again. Mesmerised, he wondered what motivated her to keep on doing this over and over again. If he ever got like that he hoped somebody would have the good sense to put a pillow over his head and have done with it.

The teenage girl in the bed near the window looked in a bad way too. She was unable to keep still and kept slipping down the bed and then struggling to breathe. Fortunately, her mother was keeping a constant vigil by her bedside and alerting the staff to her needs. She required frequent suctioning to remove fluids from her throat which compromised her breathing - something which you had to be trained properly to do. The mother had taken it upon herself to perform this action, much to the annoyance of the staff on duty.

"Well what am I supposed to do?" she had argued when told off yet again. "She's entitled to one-to-one care and you're not providing it! I'm not going to sit and watch her choking whilst waiting for you to turn up! It's ridiculous!"

"But what you're doing is dangerous!" the nurse had protested. "You could cause more damage."

The mother wouldn't listen of course. To her, it looked like a small vacuum cleaner so must operate in the same way. She'd hoovered her living room carpet loads of times so how hard could it be? Anyone could do it.

Peter had kept out of it. The mother was a very large woman, bedecked in tattoos and didn't look like the sort you wanted to argue with. Indeed, she'd already been causing controversy by smoking in the patient's toilet. He'd not inherited his mother's genes. She always spoke up in the interests of people, whereas he kept his mouth firmly shut. He smiled as he remembered the times she had interfered in things that had nothing to do with her. Times when she could've easily turned a blind eye and saved herself the hassle but chose not to. All in the interests of standing up for those who couldn't help themselves.

Peter settled back in his chair and replayed an incident in his head. It was the one where his mum had been driving home from grandad's, having just been round to give him his lunch.

Freda spotted a gang of teenagers in the middle of the school playing field all pushing a small lad around. Standing in a circle, they were passing him from one side to the other, jeering and shouting at him. His bag was hanging off and he fell to the floor, scrabbling around for his glasses.

Freda screeched to a halt, shot out of the car and marched across the field, shrieking at them to "Leave him alone!"

Like Attila the Hun, she rampaged towards them, determined to give them a piece of her mind whether they liked it or not. She was taking no prisoners.

The teenagers were so shocked by the sight of an elderly lady 'tear-arsing' towards them in full combat mode that they immediately stopped what they were doing. They might have been forgiven for imagining that they were being confronted not by a five foot one pensioner at all, but rather a six foot four warrior. She had absolutely no intention of losing this battle.

Being in no doubt as to the extent of her wrath, they began to move away from the scene.

"That's right! You go off!" she hollered. "I've got a big German Shepherd in my car and I won't think twice about setting him on you!"

The boys, looking beyond the edge of the field, sought out the car from which she had emerged. True to her word, there on the back seat was a huge black and gold German Shepherd. Such was its size that it filled the entire window. Its eyes locked onto their gaze and it began to snarl viciously, curling its lips to reveal huge incisors. The boys recoiled in fear. This woman meant what she said.

"Come on! Let's get out of here!" they chorused. Then they turned and scarpered, shouting "Leg it!"

Freda reached the boy and offered her hand to help him up, assisting him in straightening his coat and picking up his bag.

"Thanks missus," he said gratefully.

"You're welcome, sweetheart," she replied.

"You touch him again and you'll have me to deal with," she shouted at the backs of the lads who had by now put a good distance between her and themselves. "And him!" she added, pointing to Niko.

"Yeah right! Whatever!" they called back.

Always having to have the last word she added, "I pass here every day. Don't think I don't know who you are!"

And with that, she turned and walked back to her car, satisfied with her victory. She was a tough old bird, his mother. The older she got, the more 'bolshy' she became. Peter smiled with pride as he remembered all of this.

Mind you, spending over twenty years with Happy had probably made her toughen up. Having been oppressed and unable to do anything about it until the kids grew up, she'd felt empowered once she'd left him. It gave her an inner strength.

It was a long time since Peter had thought about his dad. He'd died at the age of only 58. Funnily enough, although divorced, it had been his mum who had alerted the relevant authorities to this. His friend, Terence, had called to see him and found him dead in his chair. It had really shaken him up and he'd called straight round to Freda's to ask for her help.

That was twenty years ago. Everyone was always telling Peter how similar he was to him, both in his looks, and, sometimes, his mannerisms. He didn't like to hear this. Though he shared the same birthday – the 18th of September (*Why did all significant dates in their family always have an eight in them?*) - that was enough. His mum always used to say, "They broke the mould when they made your dad!" and Peter had always thought, *Jesus! You wouldn't want another one like him!*

The kids who lived down the road had nicknamed Peter's dad Jesus. Rather like a scene from *Whistle Down the Wind* ("We've got Jesus in our barn!"), they had come up to Peter on one occasion when he was visiting asking how he knew this man who, with his longish grey hair and beard, was marked out for the role of the son of God. Clearly, they were overlooking the brown fingers and yellow stains in his hair caused by the nicotine from his endless smoking. Peter was pretty sure that Jesus didn't use Brylcreem on his hair like his father did either.

Mind you, the formal way in which he conducted himself certainly marked him out as different to other people from around there. He never abbreviated words like 'didn't', 'shouldn't' or 'wouldn't' but always spoke them in full, such as "Did you not hear me, son? Should you not be in your room now? Would you not like to know?" Peter thought 'Victorian Dad' was more fitting a description: always sensibly dressed, expecting high standards of behaviour from his kids. If he needed the toilet in the middle of the night, he got fully dressed to do so. He'd gone mad at their mum once for stripping down to her bra and knickers in order to bath the dogs. Michael had been assisting her and it was "totally inappropriate for her to dress like that in front of him!"

One would imagine that if he ever did go swimming - which of course he never did - he would be seen sporting a full-piece all-in-one and emerging from a carriage strategically placed in the sea for the purpose of hiding him from view. Peter remembered how his great gran had remarked at how much Len, when he first grew his beard, reminded her of her own father who was, indeed, from the Victorian era. She begged him to shave it off, such was the resemblance, but to no avail. Her interest had only served to make him more determined to keep it, so stubborn was he. Peter had never seen him without a beard, except in old photographs. He grew so thin that he needed it in later years to disguise this fact and make him look less like someone from Belsen.

Peter's thoughts now turned from the past and focused on the present. His mum would never be left alone like his dad had been. He'd make sure she was always comfortable and had everything she needed. She'd suffered enough in her life and he just wanted her to be happy. The iPad had been a gift from him and he'd been slipping her money for years to help her out. Which reminded him...

He reached down into the bag at his feet and drew out a tartan flask.

"Here you go, Mother!" he called out. "Get some of this home-made soup down your neck. You're not eating any more of that hospital crap! We want you better so you can come home where you belong!"

Freda smiled at her son. He'd remembered how, just the night before, she'd said she'd hated the meals on this ward.

He didn't leave until very late - gone ten - and he'd been back by breakfast so he must've wasted no time in gathering the ingredients and getting to work on the soup. Personally, she hated cooking and had never gone to the trouble of making anything which could easily be got from a tin! He might come across to some people as a very matter-of-fact person and sometimes grumpy, but he was a softie at heart and she knew he would always be there for her when she needed him. She didn't have the heart to tell him that her complaints were just a front for the real reason why she ate so little. She dutifully poured some of the soup into the cup, keeping her fingers crossed that it had no lumps in it.

CHAPTER 6

Freda was sitting upright in bed, pointing at the television screen on the wall of the ward.

"What do you mean you haven't seen it?" she said. She was incredulous.

"You must've done!" she continued. "It's been on the TV all week for the anniversary of the sinking of the *Titanic*. This girl lost her dad on it and she's wandering around Liverpool with the dog. You must've seen it!"

"No, I haven't. I don't watch much TV," said Anna.

"But they're big mechanical puppets. It's been on the news all week. Look! They're amazing. Surely you've come across it?" Freda was not going to let this drop.

"No. I haven't had time to watch TV," Anna replied.

"But everyone knows about it. I can't believe you missed it."

"Well, obviously, I have." Anna was getting annoyed.

"But it's even been on *Granada Reports*. Don't you watch *Granada Reports*?"

It should have been pretty obvious to anyone by now that Anna didn't watch *Granada Reports* and hadn't seen this particular piece of news that her mother found so interesting. It was also clear that she wasn't going to see much of it either by the time her mother finished talking.

On the screen, a gigantic freaky-looking mechanical girl moved slowly and laboriously around the streets of Liverpool, operated by a large number of Eastern Europeans. A mechanical dog also began to move to join its owner. A myriad of impressed Scousers looked on.

"What are you watching?" Jean had arrived now. Plonking her bag on the bed and drawing up a chair, she stared at the screen.

" Oh I've seen this! It was on *Granada Reports* last week. That girl lost her dad on the *Titanic* and now she's looking for her uncle with her dog. It was all over the TV every night. Look! There's her uncle now!"

She pointed as an even larger puppet began to emerge from the River Mersey dressed in an old-fashioned diver's suit. The crowd of people gawped on.

"It's amazing isn't it, Jean?" said Freda. "I told Anna to watch it. I can't believe she didn't see it on the news last week. Everyone saw it."

"I can't believe you missed this, our kid. It was on every night," Jean said.

"Well I don't have time to watch the news," Anna replied. "There's too much else to do."

She thought about her daily routine - getting up at 6:30, walking the dog, making sure the girls were up and fed, preparing packed lunches, then off to work teaching in a high school. There was always something to prepare or mark as well as meetings to attend. She wondered how she managed to fit it all in as well as run the household. She'd recently gone back full-time after several years on four days a week, taking advantage of an opportunity to develop a new course. The girls were old enough to take more responsibility for themselves - one doing GCSEs and the other A levels - so it made sense to do it now. No one could have foreseen that her mum's health would suddenly decline in the way that it had. Sod's law.

"Is this that thing that was on in Liverpool last week?"

One of the nurses chipped in now.

"Yes. It was on *Granada Reports*," said Freda and Jean simultaneously.

"Our Anna hasn't seen it before though," Jean remarked.

"Really? I remember it," recalled the nurse. She turned to Anna. "Don't you watch *Granada Reports*, love? I thought everyone around here watched *Granada Reports*."

Anna rolled her eyes. She was clearly outnumbered. No amount of explanation was going to placate them.

"I live under a rock," she offered. No reply. "In the back of beyond. We don't have televisions, or the internet. We still communicate in the old fashioned way by talking to one another. News travels by word of mouth."

No-one took any notice. Glued to the screen, you'd be forgiven for thinking that they'd not seen it several times before. Various 'oohs' and 'ahhs' accompanied the footage emanating from the three women who seemed transfixed by the whole spectacle. *Well, each to their own.* Anyway, it was nice to see her mum grinning away and sharing a common experience. Took her mind off the reality of the situation - that she was actually very poorly in hospital. She was on form, commanding the conversation as she gave a running commentary on the whole thing. She loved nothing better than talking!

Such a difference from when she'd first been brought in! Freda had been terrified. Unable to catch her breath at home, she'd got Anna to ring for an ambulance as a last resort. She didn't like putting people out and worried how they'd react. *Silly sod! That was their job.*

Anna re-played the scene over in her head:

Two paramedics had arrived on the scene and quickly got to work with nebulisers and oxygen.

"You should never feel that you can't ring for an ambulance," the first paramedic said. "Especially when someone is struggling to breathe," the other one added.

"But you're in safe hands now, Freda."

Anna remembered the look of worry on her daughter's face. Ava had come over to stay and help out for the night. Only hours before she had been keeping her nana company watching *Les Misérables* and now she was seeing her struggling to even breathe normally. How quickly the situation had changed!

Usually Freda would've relished the opportunity to travel at speed in an ambulance. Indeed, when Anna had been hit by a car at the age of thirteen, her mother had been ecstatic at the prospect! It was a story on which she 'dined out' for weeks, working, as she did, at the local shop. Any mention of an accident or a hospital and she was off with her "Let me just tell you this!" routine.

But this occasion had been all rather sombre in comparison. Only Anna had chatted on the way, trying to take her mind off what was happening by talking about anything else that sprang to mind. Like how she used to work at this hospital many years ago when she was a student; how much it had changed in those years; how she had only been to the outpatients in recent weeks with her mum and how expensive the parking was.

She'd managed to get hold of Jean to tell her they were off to hospital and she had been waiting for them when they arrived. Accident and Emergency was, surprisingly, not that busy, so they were soon being seen by a doctor who basically told her that she had all kinds of infections on her chest.

"That's what happens after radiotherapy, I'm afraid," he'd explained. "The treatment kills off some of your good cells as well as the bad ones, so your resistance is low. Your chest is like one big picnic for germs. We'll have to do some tests to see just what you've got so we can target the treatment appropriately. In the meantime we'll throw some of our strongest drugs at it."

Jean had said just one thing – "Bugger!"

Anna knew that Jean, like herself, had been secretly

hoping that the radiotherapy had been worth it. Her mum had always said she would go ahead with it and it had been her own decision, but Peter's objections remained. He'd argued that everyone he knew who'd undergone the treatment had died within weeks. No one knew whether this would have happened anyway, but they both prayed that their mother wouldn't be another victim. It hadn't helped that Peter had persuaded her to forestall the treatment by a month instead of going for it straight after chemotherapy as advised. They'd decided to take a leaf out of their mum's book. She had always said. "When your number's up, your number's up!" Of course, at this particular time this was little consolation. All they could do was wait to see if things would take a turn for the better.

After a few moments of silence, ever the optimist, Jean had chirped up, "Well I bet you never thought you'd be described as a picnic, Mother, did you? Don't worry, here's your chance to get loads of drugs for free! They'll be giving you morphine and everything! You pay a fortune round near me for stuff like that!"

This had lightened the mood.

"Yes in every cloud there's a silver lining!" Anna added. "When I was in labour they gave me some kind of heroin substitute. It was amazing! I only knew I was having a contraction 'cos the machine I was wired up to told me that I was! I was too busy giggling to be bothered. Make the most of it while you can!"

"You'll have to have another baby, our kid - see if you can't get some more of it!" Jean joked.

"Not likely!" Anna replied. "That was fifteen years ago. Two kids and two Caesareans is enough thank you very much. I've done my bit for world population!"

"Well I'm not surprised you had to have a C-section, our kid! How big was Emily again?"

"Ten pounds, fifteen ounces. They wouldn't weigh her until they'd all had a bet on how much she'd be! I was mortified. The nappy wouldn't even fit her and she had to wear one of their baby outfits 'cos none of mine were big enough. I felt like a right scrounger!"

"Thank God they cut her out then! You'd be walking like John Wayne now! Having a natural birth isn't all it's cracked up to be anyway. You've not missed owt! I'm just glad my babies were all so small - Jake was the biggest at six pounds and that was bad enough!"

Their mum had joined in then,

"My friend Judy was only four foot ten and she had a fifteen pounder! And she gave birth to it naturally!"

"Jesus!" Jean winced. "It doesn't bear thinking about. Bet her husband was pleased - not! Must've felt like going in a cave, if you get my drift!"

"Jean! Don't be so crude!" Freda shouted. "Trust you to lower the tone!"

"Well you were all thinking it! I was just the one to say it! Like mother, like daughter," she jested.

"Don't think you take after me you cheeky sod!" Freda retorted.

After this, Anna had decided to take a turn at winding up her mother.

"Weren't you the one growing cannabis on your front window sill when we lived on Corporation Street?" she mocked.

"Give over! I didn't know what it was, did I?" Freda blushed. She had been cleaning out Jean's bedroom after she had just left home to go and work at Pontins and had found a single plant growing in an empty wardrobe with a bulb directly above it. All she'd done was move it so it could get some proper sunlight. Anna and Jean laughed uncontrollably.

"Did you not think that it was a bit strange that our Jean was growing a plant in the wardrobe, Mother? Our Jean, who never had the slightest interest in gardening. Was it not a bit odd?" Anna said, winking at Jean.

"Well it sounds so now, yes. But I didn't think anything of it. I just wanted to look after it for her whilst she was away. It would've died in there by the time she returned. It came on a treat with a bit of TLC."

Anna laughed at that. "So there it was," she said, "out on display for everyone to see! And you living on a main road as well! You were lucky you weren't shopped."

"Treated like a shop more likely," Jean joked. "I'm surprised no-one knocked on to ask for one!"

"Aw yes! Just think. Our mother. The drug grower! You get years for growing cannabis!"

"Give over. Just for growing a plant? I don't think so!' said Freda. 'It's well known you can buy cannabis seeds."

"That's true," Anna said. "But the irony is that you're not allowed to actually plant them. Some flaw in the law."

"Well that's a load of bunkum!" said Freda. "Whoever made that rule wasn't thinking straight."

"Neither were you when you breathed in the fumes from Jean's cigarettes!" Anna recalled.

"Oh yes. Do you remember, Mum?" Jean added. "Me and Melanie and Tracy were all smoking weed in the living room and you were trying to knit a jumper. After a while you kept missing the stitches and you didn't understand why. We were killing ourselves laughing at you!"

"Well how was I to know what you were up to? I just presumed you were smoking ordinary roll-ups."

"Really?" said Anna. As a non-smoker she had always recognised the smell of tobacco straight away and Jean's smoke was very distinctive. It was nothing like a normal cigarette.

"Yes. Really." Freda was getting defensive. "I don't condone drug taking."

"No. Just drug cultivation!" Jean and Anna both started giggling again.

"Well you know what it smells like now, Mum," Anna said. "Our Jean's smoked that much of the stuff! She even took it when she was in labour with Jessica."

"Well it worked a treat. I didn't have one of those fancy TENS machines like you had. Smoking a joint took the labour pains away. Made the trip to hospital more bearable too. What with Mum being the driver!"

"Oh God, I remember that!" said Freda. "Joe had been out and got tanked up and you were at home on your own. You phoned me up when he came in. You gave him the kids and let me drive you to the hospital. I'd always wanted to see a birth in real life."

"You've had four kids, Mother. I think you could say you've seen a live birth!" said Anna.

" You know what I mean! Someone else having a baby. It was fantastic. I would've liked to have been one of those people who volunteers as a birthing partner to someone. I would've loved that."

Anna thought about the reality of that. Her mum would be like a pig in mud supporting a new mother. She'd certainly keep her mind off the pain by talking to them incessantly!

"Well I nearly had her in the lift. Do you remember, Mum?" Jean continued.

"God yes! It was a bit hair-raising!"

"That's what you get for being so last minute, Mother!" Anna said, remembering how she was notorious for always turning up late. Whenever she invited her over she gave her a different time to everyone else to allow for her tardiness.

"Yes but on this occasion I wasn't to blame. We couldn't leave the house until Joe returned to look after the kids."

"Well I'm sure it made all the difference, him being so drunk. I bet he did a great job caring for them all," said Anna. The sarcasm was noted.

"It didn't help that Mum went the wrong way up the road to the hospital," said Jean. "I was on all fours in the front seat screaming at her! She had to reverse back down whilst we found our way in. I only just made it!"

"Well it all turned out well in the end. You got the baby girl you always wanted."

"Yes. Even though she looked like a cabbage patch

doll!" laughed Anna. She conjured up the image of a wide-mouthed baby and smiled to herself as Jean prodded her in the ribs.

Anna felt herself being prodded again. A strong nudge on the upper arm. She lifted her head and blinked her eyes to re-focus them. Awakened from the depth of her private thoughts, she found herself looking directly into the much-older face of her mother. She registered her look of concern.

"Penny for 'em!" said Freda as she gently stroked Anna's arm.

"Sorry, Mum! I must've drifted off!" she lamented. She remembered the mechanical puppet show they had been talking about and turned towards the television to see that it was no longer on. Jean was rummaging in her bag and the nurse had gone back to her duties.

"You need more sleep, love. That's what you need."

Jean produced a roll of sweets from her bag.

"What's up our kid? Tired? I forget you're on a different clock to me and Mum. You're an early bird who goes to bed before most people. We're used to staying up late," said Jean.

"Never mind. See how you fare tomorrow tonight when you're on the late shift. There's a challenge for you!" She prised a fruit pastille out of the packet and popped it in her mouth, then offered one to her sister.

Anna, feeling in need of a sugar rush, took one gratefully before passing them back, then continued, "Well I can't be any worse than you were when you looked after Mum just before she had to come in here! You took a sleeping pill, didn't you?" asked Anna.

"Oh God! Yes I did. Out of habit. I totally forgot. It was a good job Jessica was with me. It was she who heard Mum banging on the wall. I was out for the count!"

"Well, neither of you were much cop as I recall," chipped in Freda, shaking her head at Jean's offer of a sweet.

"You gave me that stick so I could bang on the floor when I needed you. I was banging it like mad and you didn't turn up! I could've died and you would've been none the wiser!"

"Aw yes, I know," apologised Anna. "We both had our headphones in."

"Yes. We only got up 'cos Niko was pacing up and down!" said Jean.

"See! I told you. Dogs are more use than people," Freda quipped.

"Yeah right, Mother," replied Anna. "He came straight upstairs and calmed you down after your panic attack, didn't he? Got you breathing regularly again."

"Yes. And helped take you to the bathroom,' added Jean. "He's a proper angel that one!"

"And all the while Mollie was downstairs in the kitchen making your tea for you," said Anna. "Speaking of which, Mum," she added, "I'd better get back to yours."

"Yes. See if Mollie's cleaned the kitchen whilst you've been out," laughed Jean.

"Aw! You know what I mean, girls," said Freda. " I am really grateful for what you do for me."

"We know, Mother," said Anna. "We're only pulling your leg! I'll be off now and see if I can get a nap in. Recharge ready for tonight."

"All right. See you later, our kid," said Jean.

Anna planted a kiss on her mother's cheek.

"See you later, love," said Freda. She waved from the bed as Anna left the ward.

CHAPTER 7

It was mid-morning on the ward and the auxiliary was doing the rounds.

"I'll have a coffee, love, please," said Michael.

The ward had been a hive of activity that morning - first the drugs round; then the daily session with the physios; then the doctor's round. Michael felt tired just watching them.

"You need to eat something, love," suggested Freda.

"I don't do breakfast, Mother. A coffee and a cigarette - that's me."

"Except there's no smoking in here," Freda said.

"That's why I've been outside. Full of smokers out there it is! There was even a guy in a wheelchair this morning who was attached to an oxygen cylinder. His helper took it off whilst he had his fag. It was surreal."

"Blimey! He's lucky he didn't blow up!"

"I know. He looked like he didn't have long."

"In for a penny, in for a pound," said Freda. Then, in a resigned tone, "That's what got us all in here in the first place - smoking. It'll be the death of us all. You should give up whilst you can and improve your chances."

"I know. I know. But it won't be happening. I drink

too much and I smoke too much. That's the equation. Gets me through the day."

Freda worried about Michael all the time. He'd moved in with her when he split up from his partner, Lydia, and she'd seen first-hand what he was like. He was in the pub every night after work, only coming back to watch *Coronation Street* or *EastEnders* or *Emmerdale* with her. Even then, he drank a can or two whilst watching the TV then promptly returned to the pub. It upset her to see him like this. It reminded her of what her husband, Len had been like.

The landlord at the pub around the corner had opened a tab for Michael so he could drink as much as he wanted without worrying and pay at the end of each month. It annoyed her that he facilitated his drinking in this way. She believed you should have to pay or do without. This would stop excessive drinking and cut down on all the broken relationships which occurred as a consequence. Anyway, who knew that he wasn't just making up a figure at the end of the month? Freda didn't trust anyone. Also, she knew what Michael was like - very generous. He'd buy anyone a pint if they were civil enough to him. No wonder he was always in debt.

What was it with her sons? Peter was the same, always buying rounds for people he barely knew. Mind you, he took it to another level. He'd started ordering takeaways at the end of the night for everyone in the local bar he frequented - Chinese; Indian; kebabs - you name it. Some people only went in at last orders because they wanted free food. They could've bought their own as they all had good jobs. It saddened her to see him taken advantage of in this way. Nobody ever offered to buy him one back.

"Give over, Mother," he'd say when she pulled him up about it, "it's only money!"

But he worked really hard to earn it, she thought, *and it wasn't fair. He didn't need to ingratiate himself with people in this way.*

His dad had been the same. He'd do anything for

anybody, even if it meant his own family went without. Having spent months persuading him to install a dimmer switch in the living room, he finally got around to doing it. She was chuffed to bits and told everyone in the local shop about it. Then, they went out with Reg and Maria one night - a rare occasion where Len didn't just go out on his own - and she told them all about it. Maria lamented that she hadn't got one of those (she was the type of woman who had everything else). Next day, Freda got home to find the dimmer switch had gone and an ordinary switch was in its place. Len had not only given it away to Maria, but had even installed it for her!

Similarly, when Terence's wife, Bet, broke her iron, Freda's was promptly given to her. The worst was when Len was working away in Ireland. Manchester United were doing well and had brought a single out. Michael had saved his pocket money and had been lucky enough to get hold of one before they sold out everywhere. Len phoned home and ordered him to post it to him so he could give it to a bloke he'd met who was a fan. He promised he'd replace it. Of course, Michael did as he was told, and, of course, Len never kept his promise. Michael was gutted. Typical of Len to let his kids down. She wished her sons hadn't inherited quite so many of his habits.

"So, what was the doctor saying to you at the ward round this morning?" Freda enquired, abandoning her thoughts and turning to her son once more.

"I don't know! I didn't understand it," said Michael. "Something about blood counts. He said something about the numbers that you ought to have."

"Well did I have the right numbers?" Freda asked.

"I don't think so. But it doesn't matter. It is what it is. You're still here aren't you? That's what matters. Just keep concentrating on getting better and doing what you do. Take your medicines and do the exercises Mark gives you for your breathing. That's the equation."

Freda thought about how hard it had been to do the exercises this morning. She persevered only because Mark was so lovely. Some people might have judged him as a bit of a lad on account of a large tattoo on his arm, but Freda knew that this was actually a picture of his grandad, whom he missed. Like all good northerners, she had wheedled his life-story out of him and she really warmed to him as a result. She wanted to please him, so, despite the pain it caused in her chest, she had done as she was asked.

She'd been worn out and had had to resort to a nebuliser straight afterwards. She was becoming more and more dependent on these. She knew she was getting worse, not better. The nurses had stopped getting her out of bed to use the commode too, insisting it would be easier to lift her onto a bedpan.

And now, here was another challenge arriving - lunch. It seemed like they'd only just had breakfast and yet here they were again, doling out more food. Anna had got quite frustrated yesterday when filling out her meal forms for her since she'd not been able to make up her mind. Sandwiches were out of the question as they were too difficult to swallow, as was salad. Anna wanted her to have a full meal since she thought she needed the calories. It was available as a 'soft' option so she should be able to manage it. *But who had a cooked dinner? That was something you had for tea. And who wanted something resembling baby food anyway?* In the end, much to Anna's annoyance, she had circled soup and yoghurt.

"Are you going to eat that, or what, Mother?" Michael asked.

"Yes, in a minute!" Freda replied. "You sound like our Anna! 'Just eat this! Just eat that!' I'll eat when I'm hungry."

"Well you left your breakfast earlier and now you've eaten two spoonfuls of soup. It's not exactly going to fill you up, is it?"

"Well I'm just not hungry, am I? I'm lying in bed all day

doing nothing. I don't need much food."

"I'm not a doctor, Mum, but even I know that you need to eat even if you're not doing owt. That's how you get better. Your body uses it to repair itself. If you want to go home soon, you're going to have to cooperate. That's the equation."

Just then, Michelle, the staff nurse, appeared with another round of medicines.

"Bloody hell! Not more medicine!" Freda groaned.

Freda wasn't one for swearing but the routine was getting her down. It'd taken all her energy this morning to swallow it all and it had hurt her throat. She didn't relish taking any more.

"I'm sorry, darling," Michelle apologised then stood by the bed. "Tell you what. I'll make it easier!"

She promptly took out a syringe, filled it up and gently placed it in the corner of Freda's mouth.

"You blink when you're ready and I'll squeeze this in. It'll take seconds."

Freda did as she was told. Four syringes later it was all over.

"See! Job done! Would you like me to get you some pain relief? I can get it in the form of an injection?"

"Drugs, Mother! Take them! Don't look a gift horse in the mouth!" Michael started laughing.

"Go on then!" Freda said. "You've twisted my arm!"

"You know it makes sense!" Michael said in a cockney accent, mimicking Del Boy from *Only Fools and Horses*. This had been a catchphrase of his for years and always made her smile. "Lovely jubbly!" he added.

Michelle grinned. "I'll get the doctor to prescribe you some morphine."

"Even better!" Michael playfully dug his mum in the ribs. "Can I get a bed in here too, love? Sounds like my kind of gig!"

"Sorry love. Only women in here! You'd have to change your sex."

"I think that could be arranged if necessary!" Michael continued, "I look quite good in a frock even if I say so myself!"

"Well you wouldn't be the only one," Freda acknowledged. "It seems to be the 'done' thing these days. You can be what you like - LWT or something it's called."

"I think you mean LGBT," said Michelle. She grinned.

"You're confusing it with London Weekend Television, Mother!" said Michael.

"Oh aye, I am," she laughed. "Hasn't some big star just become a woman? That family that's always in the news. Thingamabobs. Oh, it's on the tip of my tongue. Our Emily watches programmes on them all the time. What're they called?"

"Don't ask me, Mother. I don't watch TV often. Haven't the time. I sit in the garden most nights burning wood," said Michael.

"You mean the Kardashians." It was Michelle again. "Bruce Jenner recently changed to become Caitlyn Jenner."

"That's right! Looks nothing like a woman though! Got six kids by three different women, I think. I wouldn't be changing to a woman if I was a bloke. I've always said I'm coming back as a fella! They have it far easier than us women."

"Me too!" Joan spoke up from her bed across the ward. "They don't do owt. My husband thinks if he does anything beyond going to work, I ought to be grateful. Lazy sod! I told him he should try childbirth and see how he copes."

"That'd stop the population rising, wouldn't it?" declared Michelle. "They'd only do it once!"

"Yes. Wouldn't have four like I did," said Freda. "I always wanted one of each, but I got two lads. Tried for a girl and ended up with twins. Told my husband that that was it. Once they start arriving in twos, you have to stop before it gets out of hand!"

I didn't even know I was having two babies until I'd given birth to our Jean. I said to the midwife that I still looked pregnant. She agreed, examined me, and said I was right. There was another one in there! Really strict she was too - Matron Tully. Said they didn't deliver twins and I'd have to go to another hospital. I told her! Not blinking likely! I'm not having one in Glossop and another in Ashton. No way! Luckily, I delivered Anna just as the ambulance arrived."

"Goodness," said Michelle. "I know they didn't have scans back then but you would've thought your doctor might've noticed. Women are usually a darned sight bigger when carrying twins and he should've noticed two heartbeats."

"You obviously haven't met my mum's doctor," said Michael. "He's useless. She's been with him for years too. I went to see him once 'cos I was really down. For twenty minutes I poured my heart out to him. He was writing stuff down when all of a sudden, he said 'Four by twos, Michael.' I said 'What?' 'Four by twos,' he repeated. 'How many do I need to build a shed?' I couldn't believe it! Turned out he'd been drawing a diagram all along. He didn't even apologise. All he could say was that he thought I was a joiner! I told him that, yes, I was, but I thought he was a doctor! Then I walked out."

"You see. That's men for you!' said Joan. "They can't even do their jobs either! So, Freda, how did your fella take to finding out he'd got two babies and not one?"

"Well he was a bit shocked to be honest. Caught him off guard. He got flustered and messed up telling the relatives the news. Then he complained about where we would put them. We only had one of everything. Our Michael was still in the cot too as he was only eighteen months old so that left us with just the Silver Cross pram which could be used as a carry cot. We just had to make do as we had no money for another one."

"Didn't you have it converted?" Michael asked. He recalled going out for walks as a child, with him sitting in the middle of the top of the double-ended pram and Peter holding onto the side. Obviously, there was a German Shepherd on the other side...

"Yes. I had to have another hood put on it," Freda recalled. "Luckily prams were bigger in those days so there was room enough for two babies."

"I don't envy you," said Michelle. "Four kids! That's hard work. I only have two and that's enough."

"Well I didn't have a choice," said Freda. "I just had to get on with it. I could've done with our Michael learning to walk a bit sooner, mind! He was still shuffling along on his bum when the girls arrived! He's always been a late developer!" She nudged him playfully.

Michael winked back at her.

"Well there's no use putting effort in if you don't need to," he said. "I could obviously get from A to B without needing to walk."

"You certainly could!" replied Freda. "Myrtle next door once found you at the bottom of the drive! Another couple of minutes and you would've been on the main road. I dread to think what would've happened if she hadn't been looking out of her window!"

"Good old Myrtle," said Michael. "There's something to be said for being a nosy old crow!"

"Well yes. She was a star that day. She spent the whole afternoon with me after that. Between us, we got you to walk."

"You need eyes in the back of your head when you've got kids," said Joan.

"Yes. I was only hanging the washing out. One minute he was there and the next he was gone. Like Jack Flash he was! Our Peter was playing in the garden and didn't say a word."

"Well he wouldn't," said Michael. "He was more interested in toys than us lot. He was probably constructing an engine or something - clever clogs that he is!"

"Give over, Michael! Don't be mean. He was playing with his Tonka toy. He had a big digger and was always digging up the garden and moving it about."

"Sounds about right for our kid. He always did stuff on his own."

"Well your dad never played with him so he learned to amuse himself. In fact, your dad never played with any of you. It was a good job he had a sister; I tell you. I know you never really took to Aunty Paula as you always thought her a snob, but I have to admit that she helped out a lot when you were all little."

She turned to Joan: "You should've seen the state of the boys when Len brought them in to see the twins for the first time. I was really looking forward to seeing them. They kept you in for ten days then, remember?"

"Yes I do," replied Joan. "It was the same when mine were born. None of this six-hour nonsense they have today."

"Well. He turned up with the lads and I could've cried! Peter had Michael's trousers on, which only came down as far as his knee; their clothes were dirty and both of them had odd socks on! They looked a right pair of ragamuffins!"

"Aw bless!" said Michelle. "Well at least he turned up. My husband went off when I was giving birth to our second child. I thought he'd popped out for a cup of tea. But he didn't come back. So, I guessed he'd gone to get our Aaron. Turned out I was wrong on both counts. He was with his brother putting up a fence!"

"That's my type of bloke!" said Michael. "You always need a handy man about the place! You women always moan when jobs don't get done then criticise when they do. We can't win!"

"I wouldn't have minded so much if it was our fence," said Michelle. "But it was at his brother's house!"

"Well I suppose that's a bit different," said Michael. "I didn't know the equation. I'll concede you that one. One nil to you."

"Right. Well I'm off to chase up that prescription for you, Freda," said Michelle.

"Thanks Michelle. See you later."

"Well I'll just go and give my legs a stretch, Mum. You give your vocal cords a rest and try and have a nap. I won't be long." Michael picked up his cigarettes.

"Thanks, love," said Freda as he turned to exit the ward.

She decided to take advantage of the peace and quiet to reach for her iPad.

"Now. Let's see what jobs Jean's done on my farm. Hope the crops are all right," she said to herself.

CHAPTER 8

Anna stood outside the door of the main ward, waiting for a member of staff to let her in. Usually she only had to wait a couple of minutes but today it seemed to be taking an age. She peered through the glass panel of the door. No wonder! Inside there was a hive of activity, as doctors and nurses raced about. There was definitely an air of urgency to their movements and they all seemed to be heading towards the same place - her mother's unit. She felt the colour drain from her face and her mouth went suddenly dry.

Oh my God! What if something's happened to Mum? she thought. She remembered the words of the doctor when they'd first admitted her – "Of course we won't be doing any heroic measures should it come to it."

"What do you mean?" had been Jean's reply, instantly on the defensive.

"He means they won't resuscitate her if she has a cardiac arrest," Anna had explained. She was familiar with this, having worked in the Care of the Elderly unit as a student. Jean was appalled. His dismissive tone irritated her. It was as if he placed no value at all on their mother. To him, she was just another patient he had to deal with, taking up a bed in his precious hospital.

"You needn't worry, doctor. She's not planning on being in here for long. She's got over worse than this," Jean had replied as she looked him straight in the eye. Taking heed of the warning, his face flushed, he had turned and walked away, offering to complete the paper work immediately so she could be transferred to the chest unit, as advised. Just as he thought he was safely out of earshot, Jean remarked quite deliberately and loudly,

"Let's hope we don't meet him again, Mother! I thought doctors were supposed to be positive - Hippocratic Oath and all that malarkey. I'll be having words with the hospital about him!"

He had paused momentarily, contemplating whether to say something but evidently thought better of it and proceeded to walk off briskly. He'd decided that it wasn't the day for battling with relatives.

One-nil to Jean. She thereafter referred to him as Dr Death, making sure everyone knew of his reputation.

Panic struck Anna now and she began to pace anxiously up and down, wringing her hands. Presently, a doctor approached to exit and she took the opportunity to enter, thanking him profusely. Nervously, she hurried towards where her mother's bed was, dreading what scene might confront her.

What she saw was Jean seated by her mother's bedside, iPad in hand. She was encouraging her to complete a jigsaw of some dogs in a vain attempt to distract her from what was going on all around her. Across the ward, the curtains were around the bed of the teenage girl and doctors were running in and out. Freda was clearly flustered. Anna hadn't seen her mum so pale in a good while, and she noticed that her cheeks were tear-stained. Jean put a brave face on it.

"All right our kid? Here for your night shift?" she laughed, trying to keep spirits up. Anna kissed her mother on the forehead and drew up a chair.

"How are you?" she asked.

"All right I guess," she whispered. "I'm just a bit shook up. Chloe went into cardiac arrest earlier. It was all panic-stations. The staff were brilliant but her mother was, understandably, hysterical. Poor woman! A nurse had to take her away whilst they tried to revive her daughter. The curtains were around but we could hear everything that went on. It was awful."

"Yes," agreed Jean. "It was like something off *Casualty*! I honestly thought she was brown bread."

Freda frowned. "Jean!" she chastened.

"Well. I'm just telling it like it is, Mother! You saw the state of her. It's a miracle she's still here."

Just then, the curtains were opened as the final doctor moved to leave. A nurse was tidying up the bed. Chloe was sitting upright, an oxygen mask in situ. Another nurse led her mother back to the bedside.

Freda nodded almost imperceptibly at Barbara - a shared acknowledgement of what she'd just been through. Barbara held her hand up to let on then immediately threw her arms around her daughter.

"Poor sod," said Jean. "That could've gone either way tonight. I know it's her daughter and all but it wouldn't have been that disastrous if she'd gone. She's no quality of life sitting in a bed all day, has she? She can't even have a conversation with anyone. They spend all day lifting her up the bed and suctioning her out. And she's always flashing her bits at everyone!"

"Jean! Don't be so rude!" said Anna, trying to shout in a whisper.

"Well, I'm only saying what others are thinking," she said defensively.

Freda was unusually quiet. No doubt she was considering that that could've been her. Anna saw that she was genuinely frightened.

Aiming to take her mind off the present situation, Anna

sought to engage her mother in a different conversation.

"You'll never guess who I've just seen down town?" she ventured. "That woman who used to come round to Jean's all the time flogging shampoo and stuff."

"Belinda Bentlegs?" said Jean.

"Yes. That's the one!" replied Anna.

"What was she stealing this time?" asked Freda. "Something big?"

She recalled how she used to shoplift to order. She'd once legged it from Morrisons with a gigantic packet of Pampers, a security guard in hot pursuit.

"What? Like a telly?' laughed Jean. She turned to her mother.

"Do you remember helping her to make a getaway?" she asked.

"Aw! Don't say that, Jean! I didn't know she'd nicked it! I just saw her struggling with it and thought she needed a hand. How was I supposed to know she'd just stolen it?"

"Well who do you know that carries a telly down the street?" asked Anna. "Surely it's not rocket science to work that one out!"

"No! Come on now, Anna! To be fair, she might've been moving house," said Freda.

"Yes. One item at a time,' joked Jean, "You know what people are like around there. They can't afford removal vans!" she mocked.

"So they walk? Who moves house at nine o'clock at night anyway?" Anna continued.

"Just think, Mother. Some poor sod was probably out at the pub when his telly got taken. There's just a bare space in his house now where it used to be!"

"Yes and you aided and abetted the criminal!" Jean was enjoying winding her up now.

"What do you get for that these days, our kid? Five years?"

"Probably. It's almost as bad as nicking the stuff in the first place isn't it, Jean?" Anna said.

"Yes I think so."

"Well nobody would know that I wasn't just offering her a lift, would they?" said Freda, not convinced. "Anyhow that was ages ago. They'd have been round to mine by now if they had any evidence."

"Aw! Leave her be now, Jean," said Anna. Then, to her mother, "You know we're only kidding, Mum. Everyone knows you were only doing her a favour. You weren't to know she was dodgy."

"Anyway. What were you doing down town, Anna?" said Freda.

"I called in at Asda to get you a new nightie and some stuff to do your toe nails," she replied.

"What? Like a pair of industrial scissors?" mocked Jean. "Have you seen our mother's toenails recently? Rather you than me..."

"Well that's why I got the stuff," replied Anna. "We were sitting on Mum's bed the other night watching *Les Misérables* and Ava wanted to take a photo of our three pairs of feet - three generations - but Mum wouldn't let her 'cos her nails looked so bad."

"That's right," added Freda. "So, our Anna said she'd sort them out, didn't you love? She always used to do my dad's for him."

"Ugh! Grandad's feet were horrible," said Jean. "His nails were all yellow and crumbly. Yuk! I don't know how you did it our kid."

" It doesn't bother me. I got used to it after working in the hospital."

Anna turned to her mum.

"I'm surprised really, Mother. You're not squeamish about anything else. You've a strong constitution as a rule."

"Yes you have," said Jean. "It gets me how you can watch all those hospital programmes with operations and stuff in them. You know what, Anna? When I called round the other night she was watching this massive fat guy getting huge lumps of fat cut off him and all the while she was eating her tea!"

"It was fascinating!" said Freda. "I've always loved programmes like that."

"They make me feel sick," said Jean. "Probably because I imagine the pain. I don't do pain myself. When I had my kids I took everything they gave me. Just upset that I was too last minute with Jessica so I didn't get any morphine. Had to make do with gas and air. But, you, Mother, you don't seem to feel anything! I remember you standing on that knife our Michael left on the floor in the kitchen and it going through your foot. You never even cried."

"God, that hurt!" said Freda. "Especially when they stitched it without any anaesthetic!"

"See what I mean, our kid? She's made of strong stuff, our mother!" said Jean.

"I take after my dad in that respect," said Freda. "He was as strong as an ox."

"Didn't he fall in a stone crusher?" asked Jean.

"Oh yes. Up at the quarry where he worked. I remember that night well. He hadn't come home from work and my mam had a strange feeling. She was psychic, your nana. Said something had happened to him. She got in the car and went up to the quarry and found him in the machine. He was lucky to be alive. A large stone had got trapped and stopped him going in completely but he still got a crushed knee. She brought him home - he refused to go to the hospital."

"Why was that?" asked Jean

"Well it used to be the workhouse before it became the General Hospital and in his mind it still was. He was adamant he wasn't going anywhere near it."

"Well how on earth did he get treated, then?" asked Jean.

"My mam gave him a chop on the back of the neck to knock him out whilst she looked at it," replied Freda. "Then she got his friend who was a vet to X-ray it! A proper mess it was - his knee was broken in several places. But he just left it to heal on its own! Don't you remember his knee?

It was huge."

"I remember," said Anna. "He looked like he had bandy legs. He always used to complain about it hurting."

" Yes. People used to laugh that he couldn't stop a pig in a ginnel!" Freda recalled. "He was a proper old type. They don't make 'em like that anymore." She smiled broadly.

"It was the same when he was younger. He turned his lorry over at Stanage Edge and tore off some of his scalp."

"I remember him telling me about that," said Anna. "Apparently, there was a large tree which broke its fall. Otherwise the lorry would've careered down the edge. He went to hospital for that one though. They put a metal plate in his head didn't they?"

"Yes. He was lucky," said Freda.

"Lucky?" said Jean. " He got scalped, broke his knee and on earlier occasion, I believe, broke his back in a Speedway race. That's not my definition of lucky! I'd say he was very unlucky myself!"

"Well I guess that's one way of looking at it," replied Freda. "But on each of those occasions he could've died and didn't. That's what I mean by lucky."

"Each to their own," said Jean. "But wearing a back brace; having bandy legs; a metal plate in your head and looking bald from the age of twenty five is still a tad unlucky by my reckoning. What do you say our kid?"

"He was a bit of a rum 'un I guess," replied Anna. "But as Mum says, he just got on with it. Quite inspiring really when you think about it. I did an assembly at school about him to motivate the kids."

"Really? How did that work then?" asked Jean.

"Well I told them about all his misfortunes but emphasised how he had no regrets in life because nothing stopped him doing what he wanted. He achieved everything he wanted - or so he told me - and lived until he was ninety four. Not a bad innings."

"And how did that go down with the kids at school?

Jean asked.

"Really well. They gave me a standing ovation!"

"Blimey. You must've made an impression then," said Jean.

"Probably. Although some of it might've been guilt from my form 'cos they were supposed to deliver an assembly and they refused to do so. Left me on my own and I was well- nervous. Mind you, I got a bit of street cred from it. I had kids coming up to me all week asking if he was really ninety four and if I had any more stories to tell. They found him fascinating."

"Well he was a character, I grant you," Jean said.

"Didn't you do a history lesson on him as well, Anna?" Freda reminded her. "Our Aubrey said you rang her up to ask her some questions."

"Yes. I was teaching the Second World War and I wanted the kids to do some research on a family member so I used him as an example. It was funny 'cos I started with a montage of pictures of famous people like Anne Frank, Churchill, Montgomery and the like, then put in a random photograph of grandad and asked them to spot the odd one out. Surprisingly, not all of them spotted it! Mind you, it was that one of him in a red French beret taken at someone's 18th when he was messing about. One of the kids thought he must be a famous French man!"

"I remember that photo," said Freda. "Daft sods!"

"So what did he do in the war then?" asked Jean. "Surely he wasn't a soldier? Not with all his injuries!"

"No he wasn't," said Anna. "They wouldn't let him volunteer for any of the services even though he tried for all three. He ended up working for the military though, delivering supplies all over the country. He was often also first on the scene when a plane landed and his job was to get them back off the ground."

"Yes, imagine that!" said Freda. "And driving in the blackout too. You were only allowed a small chink of light on your headlights."

Jean laughed. "I'm surprised he still had his eyesight. I was expecting you to say he got his eyes poked out in a freakish accident or something."

"Like *The Six Million Dollar Man*," mocked Anna. She mimicked their opener. "Albert Edward Kendall, a man barely alive. Gentlemen, we can rebuild him. We have the technology. We have the capability to make the world's first bionic man. Albert Kendall will be that man. Better than he was before. Better...stronger...faster."

Then, to Jean, "Do you reckon they were his real eyes?"

"Definitely not! They were transplanted by the vet!"

Jean was on a roll. "That'd explain that glazed look he sometimes had. When you didn't know which way he was looking! You know like that lion - what's his name? Off that programme we watched as kids."

"Oh I know the one! Clarence. But I can't remember the programme," said Anna.

"Yes that was it!"

"Hang on! That was cross-eyed!" said Freda. "My dad wasn't cross-eyed! He was actually a very good driver, I'll have you know! He was an excellent mechanic too. He modified many of the vehicles to enable them to run on alternative fuels since there were so many shortages." Freda spoke defensively. She had always been proud of her dad.

"Of course! That's the only reason we won the war!" Jean was off again. "He got the Victoria Cross and everything, our Anna. The queen even invited him to Buck Palace. Said he was a credit to his country."

"Yes. That's what I told the kids at school," said Anna. "Just think what he achieved, kids. Imagine how much more could've been done with a full head, strong back and straight legs!"

"And a pair of eyes!" added Jean.

"Oh, and don't forget a full set of teeth," said Anna. "He only had the one. Remember?"

"Oh yes. I'd forgotten that! He used to suck polo mints until they were really thin and hang them off it. Right at the front it was," said Jean.

"No doubt they got knocked out in some major incident!" laughed Anna.

"Working undercover for MI5! That's how he got his medals!" Jean was creased up laughing now.

"Come off it now!" Freda said. She'd cheered up no end.

"Well, on that note, I'd better be off," said Jean, "or else I'll no sooner be home than it'll be time to come back again. I'll love you and leave you, Mother. Oh, and I'll make you some Angel Delight and bring it in. What flavour do you want?"

"Oh anything. I don't mind."

"A bit of each!" laughed Anna.

"Okay doke. See you later, our kid."

And with that Jean gathered up her bag, kissed her mum and took off.

"Right, Mother!" said Anna. "Let's see what we can do to those toenails of yours..."

CHAPTER 9

E thel was shouting again.

"Nurse! Please can you switch the light off? I want to go to sleep."

"Of course, sweetheart," said the auxiliary. She added, "Sorry! It's really late. You should've asked earlier."

"I know you're all busy, love," said Ethel. "Thank you."

"You're welcome. Sleep tight."

Anna looked around her. She'd forgotten how busy hospitals were, and appreciated her mother's complaints that she was getting no rest in here. After Jean had left, there'd been the evening meal, visitors' time and two drugs rounds. Her mum had had two nebulisers and, true to her word, Michelle had got her written up for some morphine which she'd injected into her about a half hour ago. She'd had to wait for another staff nurse to be free as it was a controlled drug, needing to be witnessed. Freda had been knocked out by it and was happily snoring now.

At least the activity had helped to keep Anna awake. She was usually tucked up in bed by ten at the latest so this was, as Jean had predicted, a challenge for her. She'd filled her time quite easily, mind you. There was always one of the patients in need of something, so she'd become an unofficial auxiliary nurse, fetching and carrying for them. Ethel, no doubt tired of folding and unfolding her knickers all evening, had assumed Anna was a nurse and asked her to get her a magazine from the drawer at her bedside. She'd dutifully presented each one in turn, only to be told 'No! I've read that one, love.' Anna had smiled at the way she did this - her nose was systematically pressed up against the glossy front cover of each whilst she scoured them hoping to identify something of interest. It was evident that the woman couldn't see, which was confirmed when she finally plumped for the first one she'd been shown and proceeded to read it upside down.

Aw bless! thought Anna. Ethel never seemed to have any visitors and she felt sorry for her.

Meanwhile, Barbara had drawn the curtains around Chloe's bed, indicating that she wanted to be left alone. She was spending the night here too, providing the one-to-one care that her daughter needed and which the NHS didn't seem able to provide.

Sylvia, in the end bed, had chatted to Anna for about an hour about what it was like to live in Bollington. She'd overheard her talking about where she lived and had remembered that she'd read about it in *The Sunday Times*. Apparently, it was in the top ten of places to live in Britain and the number one village to bring up children.

Sylvia had enjoyed having someone to chat to. Her husband visited every day - twice a day in fact - but never seemed to speak. He just sat at the side of her bed like a stone statue. Other than "Hello, love" and "See you tomorrow, love" he never uttered a word. *It was strange*, thought Anna, *how some couples behaved*. She'd like to believe in the romantic notion that they'd been together so long that they were content to just sit side by side, perfectly happy in each other's company. But she knew from her chat with Sylvia that this wasn't the case - unlike her mother, who really wanted to get home - Sylvia dreaded it.

"Can you imagine what it's like?" she'd asked. "He drives me mad. Just mopes about like he's waiting to die! He's been like that since he retired. He's always been a bit of a miserable bugger but I thought all that would change once he left work. I dreamed of a fun-filled retirement. How naïve was I? People don't change just like that. I spend my days clearing up after him and preparing his meals. He can't even boil an egg! I should've listened to my mother years ago. When I think of the men I could've had.'

Anna hadn't really known what to say to this so had just made comparisons with her own family.

"My dad was like that," she'd recalled. "He hardly uttered a word to anyone at home, except when ordering his meal, or a brew or demanding one of us turn the telly over for him. Made our day when they started making televisions with a remote-control! You know what? When he lived on his own, the TV that he had was on the blink and the colour was all wrong. All the pictures were shades of pink! We got him another but it didn't have a remote. He ended up using the pink one just because he couldn't be bothered to get up each time he wanted to change the channel. I wouldn't mind but he was sitting less than three feet away from it! Lazy sod!"

"You wouldn't think that, would you?" said Sylvia. "Your mum's so talkative! I never imagined she'd be married to someone like that."

"Oh aye! My mum's a proper gasser! She can talk the hind legs off a donkey. She'll talk to anyone and anything! She drove us mad when we were growing up 'cos she was always on the phone. She'd spend hours on it - and I mean hours - then she'd wonder why the phone bill was so huge. We always got the blame for it." Anna smiled thinking about it.

"You know what? She was once on the phone for an hour and a half, and, when she got off it, we were curious as to who it was. Turned out to be a wrong number! The guy had been so interested in her that he asked if he could call again sometime! She'd regularly stop people on the street to ask about their dog or their baby just so she could engineer an excuse for a conversation."

"Well, that's quite a skill to master," said Sylvia. "Not many people can readily talk to anyone like that. I find her fascinating to talk to. It doesn't matter what the subject is, she always has something to say."

"You're right there," said Anna. "But it can be annoying sometimes. I can't tell you how many times I've seen people trying to get away from her 'cos she can't shut up! They've even got in their car and started the engine in the hope of a getaway. But they've always made the classic mistake of winding their window down - out of politeness - which gives her another opportunity to talk. She leans in with her 'Just let me tell you this!' routine and that's them trapped for a good few more minutes. The worst case was when she offered to give my best friend, Danielle, a lift home. She doesn't drive so was grateful when mum offered to take her. She arrived promptly outside her house and switched off the engine but then proceeded to go into full flow. An hour and a half it took Danielle before she finally managed get a word in edgeways and then was released from the vehicle. It was the middle of winter too. She was frozen! Her husband couldn't believe she'd been outside all that time."

"I've enjoyed nattering to her," said Sylvia. "I don't get much opportunity to talk to people at home. My kids have grown up and don't live nearby. They've got kids of their own now. We only really see them at birthdays and Christmas. The neighbours are young and still go out to work. The days can drag a bit sometimes."

"Was that your son who came round earlier?" Anna had asked. The one in the nice suit?"

"Yes. That's our Darren. He's got a degree and he works in finance. He lives in London but he had a conference in Manchester so called in to see how I was. He's not a bad lad. Wish I saw more of him, though."

Anna had smiled. The way Sylvia talked about him was exactly how her mother would present her to people when she first met them . She always introduced her by what she'd achieved. First it was "This is our Anna, she's just passed her 11+ and is going to Grammar School" then, "This is our Anna, she's at Manchester University" and subsequently, "This is our Anna, she's a school teacher." Having lived in Mottram village for years, where many people with money looked down their noses at people with no money, Freda took every opportunity to brag about what her four children had achieved. It was a classic game of 'one-upmanship', necessitated by the desire to prove that just because she had twice as many children than other people there (something which always surprised people since two was 'the norm') this didn't render her in any way inferior.

Working in the local shop, she had ample chance to hone her skills in this respect – "Our Jean's running a bar in Bognor Regis, you know and our Michael's just set up a carpentry business. My eldest lad, Peter, well he's not just an electrician anymore but he's a water treatment specialist. He passed the exams without even attending his day release course. Passed with flying colours!"

Freda had quite a reputation. Everyone knew and respected her and would deliberately call in the shop to buy something so they could ask her advice.

She always put them at ease and had a laugh with them. Like the time a man came in asking for pepper – "Would that be writing pepper or drawing pepper?" she joked. He didn't know whether to take her seriously or not. Another time she held someone up with two bananas, shouting 'stick 'em up!' Her best was when she had Michael paint false eyes on an old pair of glasses. She went into the back room to get something for a customer and exchanged her specs so she emerged wearing the false ones. The customer nearly wet himself laughing at the joke.

If anyone was deserving of attention when she needed

it, it was her. She'd put herself out for others for years and no one begrudged devoting time to her care. This was why her four kids were rallying around now. She'd earned every moment of their time.

Anna's thoughts were interrupted by the distinctive rattly cough of Chloe. She looked across to her bed, fully expecting to see Barbara spring into action behind the curtains. But there was no sign of Chloe's mother moving. *Strange. Why wasn't she doing anything?* The coughing got louder and became more persistent. Anna stood up. What should she do? She didn't want to impose but she couldn't just stand by and do nothing. She stood still and held her breath as she listened intently. As well as the coughing, she could now hear another distinctive sound. Was it snoring? Anna noticed that the curtain was lifted up near the back of the Parker Knoll chair which was pressed up against it in a reclining position. She moved nearer to the gap, got down on all fours and bent her head in an attempt to see what was happening inside the bay. Barbara's two bare, fat feet were splayed out beneath the chair and one of her arms was hanging loosely by its side. She was most definitely asleep! Anna got back up and began to carefully draw back the curtain. The woman, oblivious to her surroundings would need to be woken gently, not surprised. She gathered the bulk of the curtain in one hand and lifted it up to train it over the chair and back towards the wall.

"Aargh!" Anna screamed and jumped at the sight which confronted her. Barbara was lolling in the chair, wearing only a pair of knickers and a vest and, what's more, she was bald! Anna barely recognised her, so different was she from the usually well-coiffured mother of the teenager.

"Jesus Christ! What's happening?" shouted Barbara. She instinctively grabbed at a blanket to try and cover herself up whilst also reaching for her wig which was sitting on the bedside cabinet.

"I'm sorry," said Anna, "but Chloe has been coughing

and I was scared she was going to choke. I was trying to wake you up."

"Well, you certainly did that, love," shouted Barbara.

"We'll sort this," said a voice. Arriving on the scene like the cavalry, were two staff nurses. They ushered Barbara to one side, and went straight to Chloe's aid, taking care to draw the curtain back round to maintain her privacy.

Panic over, Anna went back to her seat. She could hear the suctioning machine being used. Chloe was soon stabilised. Relieved, Anna was finally able to relax once more and concentrate on her own issues.

Freda was still asleep so Anna let her be. Positioning her chair in an upright position to avoid the temptation to nod off, she took her mother's hand in her own and carefully stroked it. It had been a long time since she'd held her mother's hand - in fact she'd probably not done this since she was a small child - but she felt it was important to do so now. Her skin was warm and comforting and evoked memories of her childhood, being accompanied to school, being reassured when she went to the dentist to have a tooth taken out, being taken to hospital in an ambulance that time when she got hit by a car. Her mother had always been there to guide her - the one constant in her life, unconditionally supporting her through thick and thin. These were no longer the strong hands she recalled – "Look at me, I've got hands like a navvy! I should've been a fella!"- but were far more fragile looking. It was as if they'd been swapped with those of somebody else. Somebody far older. The skin was more translucent, revealing the blue of her veins beneath and here and there were small brown liver spots. On the back of her hands were the puncture marks left by the various cannulas which had been sited there over the past few months. Evidence of blood tests, chemotherapy, and, more recently, a saline drip. Anna winced as she thought about the latest attempt to find a vein. One of the nurses had tried unsuccessfully before calling the doctor who only managed it on her third go. Her mum had clearly been in pain but demonstrated her usual stoicism. Having completed the task, the doctor had waltzed off, leaving the sheets splattered in blood, passing on instructions to a nurse on the way out to "Get that cleaned up!"

Anna reflected on how her mother had changed over the last six months. Fluctuating over her lifetime between a size twelve and a size sixteen, she was a fraction of that now, reduced to a size eight, if that. The weight had literally fallen off. There didn't seem to be an ounce of fat on her. Her previously strong arms and legs lacked any muscle or tone. Her chest bones protruded from underneath her nightie. It upset Anna to see her mother reduced to this state.

Weak. That's what she had become. And vulnerable. Anna felt like she just wanted to wrap her up in cotton wool and protect her as she had protected them all throughout their lives. Her marvellous, strong-willed, feisty mother was now but a shadow of her former self, viciously attacked by the cancer which had invaded her lungs and chest.

Suddenly, the silence was broken by Ethel, shouting loudly. "Get me my bloody shoes! I'm going home! Get me my bloody shoes!"

Two nurses quickly arrived just in time to stop her getting out of bed.

"You can't go home, you're in the hospital, Ethel. Get back in!"

"I shan't!" she screamed. "I'm not stopping here! Get me my bloody shoes!" She flailed around, arms going in every direction, narrowly missing hitting one of the nurses in the face as she was wrestled to the bed.

Then, from behind Chloe's curtain came the unmistakeable voice of Barbara,

"Shut the hell up! People are trying to sleep in here!"

Anna was incredulous. It was one thing a patient complaining but Barbara was just a visitor. In her mind, she had no place to comment and certainly not so aggressively. Still it continued as Ethel shouted more loudly, over and over again.

"Get me my bloody shoes! I'm going home!"

Barbara reacted with "Shut it!"

Now there were three nurses all attempting to deal with the situation. One was trying to calm Barbara down as she ranted and raved, whilst the other two, having pinned Ethel to the bed with one arm each were frantically pumping at the pedal on the bed, trying to raise it to a height at which Ethel would deem it too unsafe to try and get out. However, finding that this wasn't working, they then resorted to tipping the bed backwards, knowing that she wouldn't be able to lift herself up. Another nurse then arrived with some cot sides to keep her fenced in. But now there was the danger of her not only trying to clamber out - something it seemed she was hell-bent on achieving - but of her falling even further to the floor, risking a serious injury. The solution adopted was to send for reinforcements. Five staff duly positioned themselves around her bed, taking turns to push her back onto the bed whenever it looked like she was going to succeed in escaping.

You have to credit the woman with spirit, thought Anna. *God knows what triggered her to behave like this, but she's single-handedly managed to disable the efficient management of the whole ward by commandeering every member of staff to her bedside!*

Whilst this might have been manageable, as it was indeed the middle of the night, it was entirely impractical. The staff had plenty more to do than just write up notes. There were at least another thirty patients in need of periodic attention, some of whom were very seriously ill. And there was still the added problem that Ethel (and, by turns, Barbara) was still shouting. *It's a pity they can't just gag the old woman!* thought Anna.

Finally, one of the nurses had a brainwave. As a last resort, they decided to move her away from everyone. Unplugging her inflated mattress, they chose to wheel her into the space outside the bays where the nursing station was situated. And hey presto! It worked! Without an audience, and by pretending that Ethel was just going to be waiting there until such time as the transport to take her home arrived, the old lady shut up, rolled over and promptly fell asleep. Job done, the nurses took a collective sigh of relief and went back about their business.

Freda continued to sleep, totally unaware of all that had gone on and Anna went back to watching the rise and fall of her mother's chest as she laboured to breathe steadily.

"Thank fuck for that!" Barbara's voice boomed from across the way. "Maybe a person can get some sleep now!"

Clearly, she was doing a grand job of the one-to-one care...

CHAPTER 10

Freda awoke to find Anna with her eyes closed. "Aha! You too!" she said.

It was seven thirty in the morning. Anna had literally just closed her eyes to give them a rest. Having been awake all night, her eyes were aching but she had achieved her target. The nurses were just changing shifts and were meeting for the handover at their morning briefing at the nursing station. Ethel's bed had been wheeled back to its usual space and plugged in. Its height was once again level with all the other beds and Ethel was fast asleep, as if nothing had happened.

"Mum! I've been awake all night!" Anna protested. "I closed my eyes just a minute ago 'cos they hurt!"

"Likely story!" Freda laughed. "And you called our Michael a lightweight! There's only Peter who's managed to stay awake all night."

"Mum! That's not fair!"

It riled Anna that Peter was yet again being given such an exalted status. As first-born son, he could never put a foot wrong. Everything was "Our Peter this, our Peter that." He was 'The Chosen One.'

Anna sat up in her chair and arched her back then

stretched her arms wide as she took in a big lungful of air. Then continued, "If you want, I can give you chapter and verse of what happened during the night, Mother. I can tell you, I'm surprised anyone sleeps in here. It's been non-stop! I couldn't have slept if I'd wanted to! Ask the nurses if you don't believe me! Or ask Barbara. She'll confirm that I was up all night." She turned around towards the far corner.

Freda glanced across to Chloe's bed. Barbara was just emerging from the toilet. Thankfully, she was fully clothed, sporting a blonde wig. A definite smell of cigarette smoke trailed behind her and Anna made a mental note to report this when she got chance.

"Good morning, Barbara," said Freda. "How's Chloe?"

"She's stable, now. Thanks for asking," replied Barbara. "She had a bit of a do in the middle of the night, though. Good job I was here to sort it out."

Anna looked away and rolled her eyes, but kept her mouth shut. There was no point saying anything. Instead, she turned her attention to her mother.

"Well you slept well at least, Mother. You didn't wake up once. That's good. I'm glad the panic attacks seem to have stopped."

"Must've been that injection they gave me," replied Freda. "Fair knocked me out."

Just then, Michael arrived for his morning shift. Anna wasn't used to seeing him looking so dishevelled. Keeping up with visiting as well as working full-time was beginning to tell on him. Dark circles were forming under his eyes.

"All right our Anna?" He made an effort to sound chirpy.

"You got the short straw last night then did you? I thought it'd be our Peter again. You're not a night person, are you?"

"No she isn't, Michael," Freda interjected. "She was asleep at the side of the bed when I awoke!"

"Mum! I told you I'd just that minute closed my eyes!"

"Not that old chestnut!" mocked Michael. "Come on, the truth! Were you asleep all night or what?" He drew up a chair as he spoke.

"Was I heck as like, Michael. It never stopped all night long in here!"

She proceeded to fill him in on all the antics of the night before.

Michael took off his coat and placed it over the back of the chair.

"Same with me, Anna. Everyone assumes I was asleep but it's not possible in here. There's always something going off."

He rummaged in the pockets of his hoodie and drew out a bunch of keys. He placed them on the bed in front of him. His cigarettes he deliberately left in there.

Freda looked at both her children and rolled her eyes. Anna and Michael exchanged knowing glances.

"You'll never beat our kid, Anna, so there's no use trying to," advised Michael. "Peter can't put a foot wrong in Mum's eyes. He could've been asleep all night but she'd tell us something different. The golden child."

"Aw give over, Michael! I treat you all the same." It was Freda's turn to be defensive now.

Anna made to leave. She moved her chair back to its usual position against the wall adjacent to the bed.

"Anyway, on that note...I'm off back home now," said Anna. "I'm going to have the kip you all seem to think I've already had. Penny will be visiting you later. She's offered to bring Ava and Emily to see you."

"Ok love. When are you back?"

"Tomorrow, I think. Jean's updating the rota."

"Yes," said Michael. Then, laughing, "She's putting our Peter on all the night shifts since he's the only one good enough to do it. Make sure you have a rest, Anna, you're looking tired." He lent back on his chair.

"Will do. Is there anything I need to do at Mum's house on my way?" Anna yawned.

"No. You're all right, our kid. Jean stopped there last night with the kids. She'll give the dogs their breakfast and take them out."

"Are they all at my house?" Freda sounded worried. Jean's kids weren't the tidiest of individuals at the best of times, least of all when she wasn't there to keep them in check.

"I hope she's feeding Niko properly." Freda sounded anxious. "He has to have a glucosamine tablet every morning and he needs to have some water sprinkled on his biscuits. He doesn't like to eat them too dry."

"Yes. I hope she's warmed the dog meat to an ambient temperature and stirred it properly too," added Anna. "Oh, and remembered to feed that other dog you've got too - you know the one you never seem to mention, Mother!"

Freda looked embarrassed.

"Aw, I know I always talk about Niko but he's getting on a bit now - he's an old man - and he's set in his ways. Mollie will just eat what she's given, no trouble. I don't need to remind anyone about her. I just hope Niko's eating properly as he frets easily, that's all."

"Mother, they're fine! Stop worrying.' said Michael. "They were scoffing Go Ahead biscuits like there was no tomorrow when I called yesterday and Jean was stocking up on KitKats for Mollie,' he mused.

Michael always knew how best to get his mum going. She was very particular about what she gave her dogs and would never dream of giving them anything with dried fruit or chocolate in it. He winked at Anna conspiratorially awaiting his mother's reaction.

"Wha...?" Freda stopped mid-sentence, realising they were just winding her up. She knew Jean loved Niko like he was her own. These past few months she'd been the one taking him for walks mostly - first on account of the hip operation and then after she was diagnosed with lung cancer.

She cursed that doctor every time she thought about it.

For over two years she'd been telling her she had a bad knee. She'd even had two lots of cortisone injections into it. Over and over again Freda had asked, "Are you sure it's not my hip? It really hurts." and time and again, the doctor had replied, "No. It can't be."

It was after Freda had been on holiday with Jean and her friend, Christine, that year, and had had to hire a mobility scooter so she could go out shopping for souvenirs to take home for Anna, that she finally put her foot down and insisted on further investigations. And, of course, she'd been right. She needed a hip replacement as a matter of urgency. Seven hours it had taken, not to mention several months of recovery. The kids had all stepped up to the mark to help her out, of course.

And now here they were again, looking after the house and dogs. Freda enjoyed hearing tales of where they'd walked and who they'd bumped into. Complete strangers were always stopping them to remark on how gorgeous Niko was. It was only last year that she'd been asked by a photographer who was shooting a calendar down by the canal if Niko would pose with his two female models! That had made her day. She was grateful for the way the kids prioritised the dogs. Jean, in particular, living nearby, was an angel.

She wasn't one for cleaning, of course, but this was as Freda expected. You only had to look at her own house to see that. With three kids making a mess all the time and not cleaning up after themselves, and Jean at work all day long it was hardly surprising. But she made up for it in all other areas and nothing was too much trouble. Anyway, she was fortunate in that whatever Jean didn't do or didn't like doing, Anna did. That was the beauty of having twins who were like chalk and cheese.

"Anyway, I'm off, Mother!" Anna had spent the last five minutes packing up her stuff and tidying round, wiping down the table and putting things away which weren't needed today. This was her second attempt at a get-away.

She picked up her bag and approached the bed.

"Okay doke. See you later, then," she said. She kissed her mum and departed.

"Can you just sort this bed out for me, please, Michael? I seem to have slipped down it. I can breathe better when I'm more upright."

Freda shuffled in the bed as she tried to make herself comfortable.

"Course," he replied. He leaned over and gently lifted her up to where she wanted to be, rearranging the pillows for her. Disturbed by how little she weighed, he tried not to let her see this but instead made light of the situation.

"Blummin' 'eck! Get any lighter and they'll be having to tie you down, Mother! Do you want me to make you a contraption to stop you floating away? Wooden of course."

"Of course!" she replied. "I'd expect nothing less."

Michael was a master craftsman when it came to fashioning things from wood. He could turn his hand to anything. Like that fantastic wooden playhouse he made for his daughter, complete with shutters at the windows. Visitors to the workshop waxed lyrical about it, offering him hundreds of pounds. But skint as he was, this was a one-off made just for her - he never made two things the same - and no-one else could have one. She was chuffed to bits with it. It broke his heart when his ex-wife didn't look after it and left it out in the garden to rot. Melissa was all grown up now and more recently he'd spent an entire weekend with her making a giant birdcage as the centrepiece for her degree show exhibition. This was something which her tutor had said was beyond the skills of their resident joiner. But Michael had enjoyed the challenge, not least because he got to design and make it with his daughter.

"Will this contraption have eight in it somewhere too?" Freda asked. She and Michael had always shared an interest in the number eight. She'd been born on the 8th of October, Len and Peter both had their birthday on the 18th of September, Anna had got married on the 18th of April

18. Michael's four children ("Half of eight, Mother!") had all been born on days with an eight in them or whose units added up to eight - the 28th of July, the 26th of April, the 28th of February and the 26th of December. The connection, unwittingly, was always there.

Only three years ago, for her seventieth birthday, Michael had made her an octagonal coffee table out of solid maple. Even its base had eight sides. There was a hollow in the middle, about a foot high, where something could be stored or even hidden. She'd joked with him at the time about whether it was for all the precious jewellery she didn't have, and, quite seriously, he had replied, "No. that's for you, Mother."

"Yes I know it's for me, Michael, but what's it for?" she'd asked.

"For you!" He had raised his voice.

"Yes. For me. You've said that once." Freda had raised her voice too. "But what is it for?" she said, getting frustrated.

Michael had just raised his eyebrows. Surely he didn't need to explain?

She had thought hard and then the penny had dropped. He actually meant to put her ashes in there when she died.

"Well what else would you use it for?" he'd replied when she'd worked it out. He didn't crack a smile, and, for once, she was speechless. Finally, she'd responded, clearly offended, "Well I'm not bloody going yet, Michael! I'm only seventy! Don't wish me dead yet!"

And that was that.

Michael now fiddled with the table pushed by her bedside, designed to go over the bed so she could take her meals when needed. It was always in the way and never quite lifted up properly so her knees frequently caught on it.

"Plastic!" Michael commented like it was a dirty word. "This could do with redesigning too."

Freda smiled.   She loved it when Michael talked about making things. He got that from his dad. Despite his faults, Len had been a very creative person. When he put his mind to it, he could do incredible things. He'd made his own pinball machine when they first got married, and had gone on to make, at various times when the kids were little, sledges from bread trays and carpet runners, a 'bogey' from an old three-wheeled bike and some bits of wood, and two skateboards for the lads. The latter had been particularly inventive, made from two children's ironing boards and a pair of roller skates. Of course, the twins hadn't been happy about him requisitioning their favourite toys... He'd even made tin soldiers out of the silver paper found in cigarette packets. Saved them up, melted them down and poured them into moulds. Mind you, it had taken hundreds of packets of Benson and Hedges to make a division. But at forty cigarettes a day, he soon had plenty. Was to be death of him in the end, mind...

Just then, the young girl who gave out the drinks arrived.

"Your usual coffee?" she enquired.   Freda only ever drank tea in the morning. But, of course, she wasn't looking at her. She was looking at Michael when she asked.

"Yes please, love," he smiled. "Two sugars."

Typical thought Freda, *Just who's in hospital here?*

CHAPTER 11

Penny arrived like a whirling dervish, going straight to Freda's bedside.

"Hiya Freda," she said, planting a big kiss on her cheek.

Ava and Emily queued up behind her, then did the same, whilst Penny commandeered chairs for them all.

"How are you?" she asked, not really expecting an answer as she went on to explain why her husband, Barry, wasn't with them.

"Now I know you're expecting Barry, Freda, but he's just not well enough, so I banned him from coming. I told him you've got enough germs to deal with without adding his into the mix."

"That's a shame," said Freda.

She always looked forward to seeing Barry. He was one of those people who was easy to get on with and he usually gave her lots of cuddles. It was unusual in her family for anyone to hug anybody else - Len had been so Victorian in his ways - so he was like a breath of fresh air.

"What's up with him, then?" Freda asked.

"Oh the usual," replied Penny. "Bad head, snotty nose and all that lot, man flu basically. You'd think he was at death's door, the way he goes on. He was upset he couldn't come though, so he's made you a video."

She proceeded to get her iPhone out of her bag and set up the video so Freda could watch it. The girls smiled as they watched their nana interact with it like she was having a conversation with him. She could talk to anything!

"Bye. Love you!" Barry finally said as the video ended.

"Yes. Love you too," Freda answered, as if he could hear her. "That was nice," she said.

"Well it won't be long until you see him again," said Penny. "We're taking you to that restaurant in Manchester, remember? For some seafood. San Marino's. You said you've never had lobster so you can give it a try. They do a fabulous lobster ravioli."

"Oh yes. But I thought you didn't like seafood? I remember our Aub telling me that."

"Me mam? Well yes and no really. I don't do prawns 'cos they look like little embryos swimming around."

Freda grinned at her niece. Penny continued, "But I like lobster. I've never had crab so I can't say what I think of that."

"You've never had crab? I'm surprised," said Freda. "Mind you you'd have to buy it dressed. If you can't cope with looking at an unpeeled prawn, you've got no chance with a crab! They can look quite menacing. I remember our Anna buying one when she shared a house with that vegetarian girl I didn't like. She left it sitting in the fridge on the shelf staring out. You could hear the screams down the street when she opened that fridge door!"

"I'm not surprised." Ava was speaking now. "I'm vegetarian. I'd hate to find a creature like that parked in the fridge. It's bad enough seeing parcels of meat in ours at home. I reckon if everyone had to see what they were really eating then more people would refuse to eat meat."

"I wouldn't," said Emily. "I love steak. Don't know how you can live on just vegetables - carrot sticks and spinach - it's well boring!"

"Yeah, well that's you, Emily!" said Ava. "You've got

no principles. You just follow the trend. You only went vegetarian for a short while and only then probably because some celebrity did, like the Kardashians or something."

"Oh shut up, Ava!" replied Emily.

Freda chipped in to stop the bickering, "Crabs are difficult to prepare if you don't know what you're doing, Penny. They have poisonous bits - dead man's fingers - that could kill you. Len brought one home once from a fishing trip and it was still alive. Expected me to cook it. It was walking all over the place. The kids thought it was great. They were getting it to race up and down the kitchen!"

Freda looked at Ava apologetically, then continued, "I'd never cooked one before, so I phoned me mam up to ask her how to do it. She said to boil it for 10 minutes or so. Well you've never seen anything like it, Penny! I got a big pan of cold water and put the crab in, then switched on the gas. But it was clambering up the sides trying to get out! I had to stand there shoving it back in. So, I put a lid on it, but still it was pushing on it. Had to weight the lid down in the end with a brick. I tell you, it was horrible! I told Len I'd never do it again!"

"Oh my God!" exclaimed Penny. "That's horrendous! What did Nana say when you told her?"

"Well she played bloody hell with me!" said Freda. "I told her what I'd done and how upsetting it was and she said 'You cruel bugger! You're supposed to boil the water first then drop it in so it dies instantly!' Well, I didn't know that, did I? I said to her 'You said boil it. You didn't say owt about boiling the water first!' She said she assumed I wouldn't be so bloody stupid!"

She looked at Ava again who looked, understandably, horrified.

"Sorry, Ava!"

"God, I don't think I want to try crab now you've said that," said Penny. "That's put me right off."

"Well you wouldn't see it if it was hidden in pasta or in a sauce," said Freda. "You'd be all right. It does taste really nice. Richard made it for me as a starter last Christmas when Anna invited me for dinner. It was mixed up with apples and celery and tomatoes. It was lovely. He did it with scallops and pea purée."

"Yes, that was Ava's favourite starter before she became vegetarian," said Emily. "It made dad cry when she ate it all up and told him how lovely it was. He was well chuffed."

Then she looked at Ava adding, "You can't eat it now that you're veggie!"

"I wouldn't want to!" Ava retorted. "Anyway, dad makes a vegetarian version which is just as nice, and no cruelty in sight!"

Emily pulled a face. Ava poked her in the ribs.

"Will you two pack it in?" said Penny. "Honestly!"

Chastened, they both went quiet, turning their attention to their nana once again.

"Anyway," Penny continued, "as I was saying, me 'n' Barry are taking you to that restaurant when you get out of here so you can finally try lobster. You can have it any way you want - in sauce, in pasta, or just boiled to death!"

"Aw, I still feel awful about it," Freda said. "But I'm not that bothered about lobster now anyway. Our Jean got me one from Cemaes Bay. I was disappointed. Don't know what all the fuss is about."

"What? You've tried it? When you went on holiday the other week? I didn't know you'd been out to any restaurants when you were there," said Penny.

"Oh, we didn't go out for it," replied Freda. "Jean picked one up from a restaurant on our way back home along with some scallops for her kids to try since they'd never tasted one and I'd said how nice they are."

"How did she manage that?" asked Penny. "They don't usually let you have it to take home."

"Well that's right," said Freda. "They said 'No' at first, but Jean managed to persuade them."

She looked sheepish as she added, "She played the 'C' card. She told them I was dying."

Penny looked shocked. Freda noticed that Ava and Emily had their eyes downcast.

"Oh! Well that's your Jean for you! She'll say anything to get what she wants. It obviously did the trick," said Penny.

"Yes," Freda replied. "She said once she'd told them, they said she could have anything she wanted!"

"Well you've got to admire her cheek!" said Penny, making light of it.

"Yes. Don't know where she gets it from. Glad I was outside in the car though so I didn't have to witness it.'

"She's always been good at acting," said Penny.

Freda looked momentarily away, avoiding eye contact.

"Well I've tried it now. I can tick it off my list."

"That's true. In every cloud and all that lot," replied Penny.

"So, what's next then? Are you going to be like grandad and aim to try everything you've never had before?" Penny jested.

"God no! You're joking, aren't you? He ate anything and everything. I'm not a fussy eater but I draw a line at some things. He ate hedgehog, you know? There was always a touch of the gypsy in him, me mam reckoned!"

"Hedgehog? You're pulling my leg now, aren't you? How on earth would he have eaten one with all those prickles and that lot? And there'd be nowt on one of them anyway! Did he use one of the spines as a toothpick?" she laughed, then added, "Oh, wait a minute, he couldn't have could he? He only had one tooth!"

They both laughed. It was true, of course, but it hadn't stopped him from eating what he liked. He regularly gnawed at chops and bones. But he'd not always been that way, of course. It was just how Penny remembered him.

"He had it in Australia, he said, when he was doing speedway over there. Reckons they wrapped it in clay then put it in a hot oven in the ground. When it was cooked, they peeled off the clay and all the spines came off, leaving just the meat," explained Freda.

"Well it's to be hoped they killed it before they put it in the oven!" Penny looked at Freda playfully.

"I wouldn't want to try that either. Yuk!" said Penny. "Hedgehogs eat all sorts of rubbish - slugs, snails and all that lot."

"I've eaten snails!" Freda boasted.

"You never have!" said Penny.

" I have! I had one when I was over in France visiting Anna and Richard when they did that year abroad."

"Yes, and so did I," said Emily. "And Ava did!"

Emily shot a triumphant look at her sister, like she'd just reported her for a crime.

"Emily, I was seven! I wasn't a vegetarian when I was seven! God. You're ridiculous, do you know that?"

"Yuk! You wouldn't catch me eating snails, either," said Penny. "They look like balls of snot! What was it like eating one of them?"

"It was horrible, actually - really chewy," said Freda. "It looked like one of those whelks Len was always bringing home, only smaller. Made me gag! But I didn't spit it out!" She smiled proudly.

Freda shifted on the bed, now. Sitting in one place soon took its toll on her bottom, making it feel numb and she had to take care to keep moving about to prevent any sores developing. She'd heard enough about the horrors of bed sores from when Anna used to work in the Care of the Elderly Unit years ago. She dug her heels in and pushed herself up, using her hands against the side of the bed to lever herself. Instinctively, Penny got up to assist, rearranging her pillows for her, then, noticing her lips were dry, passed her a carton of juice.

"Thanks, love," Freda said. She caught her breath back then took a long sip of the juice, before continuing.

"It was over there that I had the best burger I've ever had in my life." She paused and looked ahead longingly, as she remembered. Automatically smacking her lips, she went on to explain how they'd been to a festival where they were cooking them to order.

"Luckily our Anna was able to translate and tell the chef to cook it really well," she explained. "You know what the French are like - they don't cook their meat properly. Took ages but it was well worth it. Tasted gorgeous. Not like the beef we have over here which seems to taste of nothing."

"Yes, it's to do with the cows they have over there - Charolais," said Ava. "It was weird since they had the cows in pens for you to look at and then, right next to them, they were frying up minced bits of their friends and family!"

"Yes that's right!" chuckled Freda. "Beautiful animals they were. All cream and filled out. Not like the bags of bones you see in the fields over here. But the French aren't noted for hiding where their food comes from, are they, girls?"

Freda turned to look at Ava and Emily as she spoke.

"Do you remember that packet of quails your dad got us to try from the supermarket?" She wrinkled her nose in disgust.

"Yes," replied Emily. "They looked like really miniature chickens in the packet. When he took the wrapper off, they still had their legs and heads on!" She shivered at the memory.

"Oh my God!" said Penny. "Really? Can you imagine that happening over here? People would go mad. What did your dad do?" she asked.

Freda took over.

"Richard didn't like that at all. He wasn't prepared to have to start butchering them. But it didn't bother me. I grew up just after the war. I often had to help me mam pluck chickens or skin rabbits. It's what you did in them days," Freda said.

"Len's mam used to get a full sheep's head from the butcher and boil it up. Him and his sister used to fight over who was picking its brains out. They had them on toast."

She looked at Ava, who was turning a shade of green.

"Sorry, love," she apologised. "You probably think that's terrible, but we grew up with rationing so we took what we could get. Len used to shoot wood pigeons to help his mam out. But me mam drew the line at that. She said they were vermin. Covered in fleas, they were too."

"Can't imagine there's much on one of them anyhow," said Penny. "Wouldn't have filled you lot up."

"No. That's why she always gave us loads of bread and butter with everything. She grew up in Yorkshire where they had Yorkshire pudding before their meals."

"We have Yorkshire pudding," said Emily, "but it's with our Sunday dinner."

"Yes, that's how I like it too," said Freda, "but they used to give it you first so you weren't as hungry and you didn't ask for much meat."

"Well they had to, I suppose," said Penny. "Times were hard back then. Me mam told me." Penny looked at Ava and Emily. "You don't know how lucky you are having so much food and a dad who used to be a chef. I bet he loved being in France trying everything out. Guess he saw loads of unusual things."

"Yes," replied Emily. "Ava, do you remember that packet Mum picked up in the supermarket which just look like a mask? It was basically a big piece of fat - a pig's face apparently. I don't know what you were supposed to do with that."

"Was it Halloween?" said Penny. "Maybe you could cook it, wear it all night, then eat it! Two for the price of one - an outfit and a meal. They're resourceful those Frenchies!"

The girls both laughed.

"Tell her about that market you went to," Freda chipped in. "The one with all the live animals for sale. Listen to this Penny!" she said, leaning back into her cushion.

Ava and Emily looked at each other knowingly. Their nana was always getting them to recount this story.

"Yes," said Emily. "There were all these lovely ducks and geese and fluffy rabbits in cages. I thought they were selling them as pets. I was only four."

"And what were they doing with them?" Penny enquired.

"Apparently they were for eating," Ava explained.

"Really?" said Penny.

" Yes. Or so we learned later. You had to pick the one you wanted and they killed it for you."

"Did they kill it quickly by wringing its neck or did they do it your nana's way and make sure it had a long lingering death?" Penny mocked, winking at Freda.

Freda rolled her eyes.

"I wasn't deliberately cruel!" she protested.

"Oh I know. I bet they did it like my Uncle Len did that rabbit of our Anna's! Did they hit it over the head with a rolling pin, Ava?" Penny was laughing now.

"What? Did my mum's dad really do that?" Ava was horrified. She'd never met her grandad as he'd died before she was even born. She'd heard enough about him however to consider such action a possibility.

"Yes, he did," replied Penny. "Killing things must run in their family. First your nana killing things, then your grandad."

"Well at least that was quick," said Freda defensively. "That's how I'd like to go. A quick hit over the head and have done with it. None of this taking weeks to fade away."

She looked momentarily pensive.

"What actually happened?" asked Ava, suddenly curious.

"Your mam's dad killed her pet rabbit then your nana dished it up for Sunday dinner! That's what happened, Ava!" replied Penny. "I remember me mam telling us all about it. It was awful. Like something out of a horror film!"

"Really?" said Emily. "Her own dad did that to her? Why? Were you short of food or something, Nana?" she asked.

"No, we weren't," said Freda. "We were off to Brownies

and I asked him to feed Big Bunny as we were running late."

Ava raised her eyebrows - her nana was always late. You had to tell her the wrong time or put it out by an hour to make sure she actually got there when you wanted her to.

"I told him he'd have to wear a glove 'cos it had a tendency to bite," said Freda. "But he just said, 'It won't bloody bite me, Freda!' "

She paused then said, "Well, obviously, it did and that was that!"

"It never bit anyone else again!" said Penny. "He hit it over the head with a rolling pin!"

"Oh my God!" said Ava.

"You see what grandparents you inherited, girls? One of them boils crabs to death and the other one bludgeons rabbits!" mocked Penny

She winked at Freda, who grinned back.

"That's not the worst, though, is it Freda? Tell them what your Peter and Jean did!" said Penny.

Freda bit at her lip. Then said, "Our Peter decided to make a glove out of its pelt."

"Yes. Stretched its skin out in a board and started 'curing' it with linseed oil and all that lot," said Penny. "And Jean took its feet off to school and offered them round as lucky charms! That's our cousins for you! Mad buggers! We couldn't believe it, me and our Gillian when we heard. And then you served it up for dinner, Freda!"

"Well there was no point wasting it, was there?" Freda said defensively.

"No point wasting it! You make me giggle, Freda," said Penny. "Me mam would've said the same. It's that thrifty Kendall streak coming out! The same one that makes you save buttons and collect margarine tubs! A throwback from the war! Your poor daughter - she should've had therapy after that! She had nightmares for years afterwards, you know, dreaming that her dad was going to do the same to her pony, Trixie."

"Yes. What he did was deplorable,' said Freda. "I don't

want to defend him, but they were New Zealand Whites. They're bred for eating. And we had others. They were always breeding. I think we had about a dozen at one point. We couldn't give them away. They were costing a fortune in food, straw, hay and what have you. It's a good job our Michael's a joiner. At least we had hutches for them."

"I remember,' said Penny. "I think you might have palmed a couple of them off on us. As pets, mind, not for our tea!"

"Well yes, we had to do something as they were always getting out of the garden and eating next door's flowers. Myrtle and Harold used to go mad, especially when the kids kept going over the garage roof to get into their garden to retrieve them. Once or twice one or other of the kids put their foot through the roof. We couldn't afford to repair it. The neighbours weren't happy. They were always keeping a beady eye on what we got up to. Even our Shane got to watching the rabbits like a hawk when we let them out. He used to steer them back onto our side."

"What? Shane, as in the German Shepherd?" asked Penny. She smiled mischievously, as she added, "The Child Scarer?"

Freda opened her mouth and was about to react but chose to ignore that comment. Instead, she continued, "He was a very intelligent dog, you know. I always said he'd been here before, that one!"

Ava rolled her eyes. Her nana was obsessed with dogs. Freda noticed and reacted defensively,

"I know you think I idolise dogs, Ava, but I tell you he was something special. You know I adore Niko, but Shane was something else. I loved that dogs to bits."

"I remember him," said Penny. "Beautiful he was, Ava. Proper good looking. Sired some gorgeous pups too. Me mam had one - our Radar. Fabulous dog."

"Yes!" Freda was on form now, settling down to her tale.

"Our Anna got a local artist to draw a picture of him as a present for me. The woman was so impressed by him that she asked if she could use him on her merchandise. She said his head was that fantastic."

Ava was reminded of the drawing of a dog which hung over the fireplace in her nana's house. She'd always assumed it was Niko but now she understood.

Freda smiled. "He once got our Michael into trouble for picking up a woman's white dog! I swear to this day he thought it was one of the rabbits and was bringing it back."

"Your Michael told me about that," said Penny. "He was in the back field throwing a ball for him and Zaer. It went over the brow of the hill and out of sight and both dogs chased it. A couple of minutes later, your Shane appeared with a poodle in his mouth! He couldn't believe it. The woman was going mental at him!"

"He didn't hurt it!" said Freda.

"I guess that's not the point though is it, Freda?" laughed Penny. "If you see a bloody big dog pick your little dog up and bugger off with it, you think the worst. Poor woman! You're lucky she didn't have a heart attack!"

"Well he can't have been that intelligent really when you think about it, can he, Nana?" said Emily.

"What do you mean, love?"

"Well, even I know the difference between a rabbit and a poodle!" she scoffed.

"Hey you, don't be so cheeky!" said Penny. "You know what your nana's like about her dogs. No criticising!"

"I know she's kidding," said Freda, winking at Emily. She continued, "No. Seriously though, he was a cracking dog, Shane. We went through a lot together. When I was really down, before I left home, he kept me going. I remember going off driving one night after a big row with Len. I was crying so much I could hardly see. I was on the motorway and I thought 'You know what? I could just put my foot down and crash this car now' but then I looked in my mirror and saw him looking back at me and it stopped me. That dog saved my life!" she said gratefully. Ava and Emily looked at each other but said nothing.

"I was devastated when he got run over," she said, a lump in her throat.

"I'm not surprised," said Penny. "I would be too. Dogs are great. They're never in a shit mood and are always overjoyed to see you. What more could you ask for?"

They were interrupted by the arrival of Peter. Fresh from his soup-making duties, he breezed in, armed with a flask.

"Alright Penny,' he said. "Long time, no see."

"Yes. Hello Peter. How are you?"

"Not bad, flower." Then to Freda, he said, "Here's some more soup, Mother. Please eat it. Took me all night to make it."

"Thanks, love. I'll look forward to it. What flavour is it?"

"Potato and leek. I've wazzed it up so there are no lumps in it. It should be easy to get down your neck."

"Oh, thanks, love. That's really kind."

Freda turned to Penny who was tidying up as she prepared to leave.

"Right, well. Thanks for visiting, Penny. It's been lovely seeing you. Tell Barry I hope he gets better soon and I look forward to seeing him when he's feeling up to it."

"Will do," said Penny. She turned to Ava and Emily. "Come on girls. Time to go."

Both girls wandered back to their nana to say goodbye.

"Hey! Don't forget to send me a picture of that new boyfriend of yours, Emily," said Freda. "Carlton isn't it?"

"No. It's Callum, Nana!" said Emily. "Yes, I'll do it when I get home. Take care."

"Will do, love," replied Freda.

And with that, they all departed, leaving Peter holding the fort.

CHAPTER 12

Peter was worried. It wasn't like his mum to sleep so much. True, she'd always had problems waking up in the morning and, as a rule, had to be practically dragged out of bed, usually after several renditions of 'Just five more minutes!' but, once up, she was like a night owl, staying awake until the early hours, only falling asleep to the sound of her radio at her bedside. This was out of character. Now, she was dozing yet again and it had only just turned five o'clock in the evening. It seemed as if having visitors for the afternoon had worn her out.

He suspected his sister, Anna, was behind the rota for this one. She seemed to be the one who was in touch with his mother's friends so he wouldn't put it past her to be ensuring they all got time with her. It might seem a thoughtful thing to do, but what his mum needed was rest so she could get better. He'd be having words with her when he saw her.

This is what she'd done last time his mum was in hospital, of course, following her hip operation. She'd made sure there were plenty of people popping along to visit her and keep her up-to-date. But that was different as visiting times were shorter then and the four of them were all too busy to make it to the afternoon slots, so they'd been grateful for someone else to take up the opportunity. Although it had conveniently fallen during her half-term holiday, Anna, he remembered, had taken turns with Jean to look after the dogs and supervise the installation of a new boiler, so couldn't devote all her time to sitting at her mum's bedside.

Peter smiled as he thought about that week. Everything that could go wrong, did go wrong! The boiler people turned up on time but wouldn't touch the job.

"Lead pipes, love. We can't work with them. You need to have them replaced before we can start."

"Well, who can I get to do that then?" Jean had enquired.

"No idea, love. Not our problem. Give our boss a ring when you've had it done and he'll arrange for us to come back."

"But it's got to be finished this week! Our mum's in hospital having had a serious operation. She's due home and she'll need to have the heating working. She's a pensioner."

"Like I said, love, it's not our problem. Sort out the pipe work and we'll be happy to come back." And with that they'd departed, leaving Jean and Anna to sort it out.

You had to give his sisters their due. When they put their minds to it they could achieve anything. Jean had scoured high and low for someone to do it and had finally been saved by her partner, Joe, calling in a favour from his mate, Bob. He postponed the job he was on and came straight round to sort it out.

"Anything for a mate of mine," he'd said, adding, "as long as you pay in cash."

Jean had raided her savings to copper together the money needed which turned out was even more as the stop-tap broke and had to be replaced. Anna had got straight on the phone and insisted the boiler men returned before the end of the week. It had all turned out fine.

Peter had loved watching them squirm as they told fib after fib to their mother upon visiting her, in their desire not to let her get stressed. Like the wind-up merchant that he was, he had ensured that he kept asking them how it was going.

"Really well," said Jean.

"Does the boiler fit in the cupboard properly?" asked Freda. "Have they had to take any floorboards up? They've not left any mess, have they?"

Question after question was asked. Both sisters told their mother what she wanted to hear. "Yes Mother. No Mother. Yes Mother."

"Why don't you take some photos?" said Peter, knowing full well that there was nothing to take a photograph of since the job had been delayed by a week.

"Or a video? That'd be nice wouldn't it, Mum?' he'd teased, 'It'd make you feel like you were there!"

"Don't be daft," Anna replied.

"What's daft about it, Anna?" he asked. "You've got a phone that takes photos, haven't you? Or don't they have technology yet in that village you live in in the back of beyond?"

"Course I have!" she'd retorted. "But I don't want Mum to see it yet. I want it to be a surprise!"

"Oh yes, it'll be a surprise all right!" he'd joked.

Freda had continued her onslaught of questions.

"You're making sure they're not leaving doors open, aren't you? I don't want the dogs to get out. It only takes a second for them to be out and off down the street. That main road is busy you know. Mollie's never been off her lead 'cos she can't be trusted so she'll just leg it given half a chance. I don't want my dogs getting run over!"

Unbeknown to his mother, this is exactly what had happened to Mollie the day before. She had got out, but, luckily, she hadn't been hit by a car. Jean had been in the kitchen dutifully brewing up for the plumbers when one of them had nipped off to the van for some tools. He'd made sure Niko was in the front room and closed the door but hadn't noticed that Mollie had been in the hallway. She'd promptly waddled off down the street, wagging her tail, no doubt excited by her new-found freedom.

Jean had nearly had a heart attack when she'd discovered her missing.

"Oh my God, Anna. You won't believe what's happened!" she'd sobbed down the phone that afternoon. Anna knew it was something serious by the fact she had rung her at work. That just didn't happen as a rule.

"Calm down. Take some deep breaths."

Jean was hyperventilating, which, for someone with COPD was not good. She imagined her clutching her chest as she tried to get the words out between the sobs.

"Mollie's got out and I can't find her anywhere! What am I supposed to do? Me and Janice have looked everywhere. Mum will kill me! You know what she's like about her dogs. She goes mad if you let them anywhere near the front door."

This was true. You always had to lock them in the living room before answering the door. This had been drummed into them for years.

Anna thought about Jean and their sister-in-law walking up and down all the streets near their mum's, frantically searching high and low. One of them with chest problems and the other an asthmatic - what a pair they made! You had to admire their commitment.

"We've been at it for three hours. I don't know what else I can do," Jean said.

"Have you asked the neighbours?" replied Anna.

"Course I have!" replied Jean.

"What did they say? Have they seen anything?"

"Well, get this, right," Jean's voice was returning to normal now, "Tina next door said she saw a dog that looked just like Mollie crossing the road near the town hall at lunchtime."

"Really?" said Anna. "And she didn't do anything or

think to knock on and tell you?"

"No! Apparently, she thought that there's no way it could be Mollie as she's not allowed out on her own and Mum's too careful to let her get out. So, she just ignored it."

"Stupid woman!" said Anna. "Doesn't she know mum's in hospital and the workmen are round?"

"Evidently not, our kid. I guess people aren't as vigilant these days. No 'Myrtles' round that way nosing through the curtains!"

"So how long ago was that?" asked Anna.

"Two and a half hours ago," replied Jean. "She could be anywhere now. I know she's a fat little bugger but even she can waddle quite a way in three hours. I'm cursing those bloody workmen. I told them to be careful not to leave the door open. What am I going to do?"

"Ring our Michael and get him to come round after work. I'll come over too and we'll all have another look. In the meantime, get a photo of her off your phone and stick it on Facebook. I bet someone else has seen her."

"Oh my God I hope you're right! I can't take any more stress! I'm shaking like a leaf here."

"Don't worry. She'll turn up sooner or later. Look on the bright side."

"The bright side? What's that then?" Jean asked.

"At least it wasn't Niko who got out!" Anna joked.

Jean started to laugh.

"Can you imagine it?" she replied, "She'd never speak to me again!" And with that, Anna had rung off.

Fortunately, luck had been on their side on this occasion. Having been thrown out of the town hall, Mollie had crossed the road again and toddled off down the towpath by the canal, eventually ending up in the next town - Hyde - where a more concerned passer-by had picked her up and taken her to the vet's. A quick scan of her microchip had revealed her owner and thankfully, they had telephoned the house rather than their mother's mobile. Janice had been manning the phone whilst Jean and Michael had been out searching again so she was able to relay the message to them as soon as it came in. Jean had shot round to the vet's straight away to collect her, vowing never to let her out of her sight again. Their mother would be none the wiser, unless she cared to notice the state of the animal's paws which were shredded and sore. Hopefully she'd be too besotted with Niko to see this. It had all turned out okay on the whole. There was, of course, the additional expense of the vet's bill but it was a small price to pay considering what could have happened.

At least it was quiet on the ward now - the lull before the official visiting session commenced. Peter listened. He could hear the noise of the air keeping the mattress inflated and his mum breathing heavily. Ethel was snoring across the way. Chloe's mother, Barbara, seemed preoccupied with a large bag under the bed. She was rummaging about, furtively trying to tuck something away. He leaned forward to see what it could be that she was being so secretive about. Then he twigged what she was up to. Blankets! Every time he'd been on the ward at the same time as her, she had asked the nurses if she could change her daughter's bed. Now he realised why. It wasn't that she was being attentive at all - she was stealing hospital bedding! The nurses entrusted her with the key to the cupboard, no doubt thinking she was helping them out when in fact she was helping herself! *What a nerve!*

What she was doing with them?, he wondered. *Sticking them on eBay probably.* Although it riled him, he wouldn't say anything to her. He'd learned not to mess with people like that. Anything for a quiet life, he wouldn't get involved. No. He would bide his time and report her when his mum had left the ward and he was no longer visiting every day so she couldn't put two and two together.

He sighed and looked at his watch. He was in for a long night. At least he'd have company, though as Janice was joining him later. The nurse in charge of the unit had had words with the family yesterday and informed them that it wasn't acceptable to have men on an all-women's ward overnight.

"You'll need to be chaperoned, I'm afraid," Michelle had explained.

"That's fair enough, flower," Peter replied. "I have to be CRB checked for work. It doesn't bother me. In fact, it's a relief. Don't want anyone feeling uncomfortable. I'm only here to keep an eye on Mum. Anyway, it'll give Mum someone different to talk to."

The nurse smiled at this. She'd hardly heard a word out of him whilst he'd been here. But then with Freda talking non-stop, he hadn't really had chance to say much. He obviously hadn't inherited her ability to talk about anything and everything. Perhaps he took after his dad in that respect. He nodded his head occasionally or answered 'yes, Mother,' giving the impression he was engaged, which seemed to keep her placated.

Peter felt his phone vibrate in his pocket. He checked the screen - another email from work.

Will they ever stop mithering? he thought.

This was the third email he'd received since lunchtime. It seemed they couldn't cope without him. As one of only two electrical engineers in the company, he was in high demand. They were close to completing the electrics on a new swimming pool and needed his advice on some specifics. They wanted him to visit the site. Well, they'd have to wait. His mum took priority. He sent back a quick reply then switched off his phone. Hopefully his mum would be home soon and he could sort things out then.

"Is that work again?" Freda had woken up at last. "You're not in trouble for not going in, are you?"

"No!" said Peter. "It's nothing to worry about. They just wanted some information about that job I've been working on. The time's coming up for the pool to be commissioned, that's all. I've told you before, I can stay off as long as you need me," Peter lied.

"As long as you're sure? I don't want you missing deadlines on account of me."

"Yes, I'm sure, Mother."

Then, getting up, he fetched a carton of juice, put in the straw and passed it to her.

"Here you are, get that down your neck. You need to keep hydrated."

"Thanks, love. My mouth feels really dry."

Freda took a small sip, grimacing as she swallowed. Peter noticed small cracks at the corners of her mouth.

Just then, Michelle arrived with the medicine trolley.

"Is it that time again?" Freda asked.

"I'm afraid so," Michelle replied, preparing a syringe. "How are you feeling?"

"Not bad. But my mouth feels really sore."

"Let me have a look," she offered.

Michelle took a spatula from its packet, then manoeuvred around the bed to position herself at Freda's side.

"Open wide!" she said. She gently pressed down on her tongue and had a good look inside her mouth.

"I'm afraid you've got thrush, darling," she explained. "I'll get you some gel to put on it."

"How on earth have I got that?" Freda sighed. "I thought that was something babies got."

"It's quite common when you're on antibiotics. Also, you've had a lot of chemotherapy recently so a dry mouth isn't unusual," Michelle explained. Then noticing her dejection, added, "It's nothing to be ashamed of. We all carry the fungus in our mouths and have the potential to develop it. The important thing is that we treat it."

"It's one thing after another!" Freda complained.

Michelle proceeded to administer her medicine then returned to the trolley. She rummaged around then drew out a package which she passed to Peter.

"Here you are. You can make yourself useful whilst you're here. This is an oral care kit. It's got everything you need to keep your mum's mouth clean. You need to get some warm water then use it to wipe all around her mouth and tongue using the disposable swabs inside. Try to get rid of any build up in there but take care to be gentle."

Peter took a look inside the packet and emptied the contents out onto the table.

"Will do, flower," he said. "Our Janice's due any minute. I'll get her to do it. Give her something to do. She'll enjoy that."

He looked at his mum and grinned.

She smiled back, knowingly.

Janice was a very quiet person as a rule, preferring the company of an iPad to that of a person, but she came into her own when in the company of people who were ill. She had had a difficult time over the last few years overcoming breast cancer so was quite 'genned up' on procedures, treatments and hospitals. The subject transformed her from a meek and mild individual to a specialist orator. She'd also been going to on a regular basis to the local hospice so had met others who were going through similar experiences. Consequently, she could empathise with Freda's condition. She would be happy to be of use in this way.

"She's an angel," Freda commented.

"Anyway, it's teatime now," Peter said, changing the subject, as the orderly approached with the food trolley. He took the tray from him and put it on the table. He lifted the metal lid off the plate, revealing a purée of meat and vegetables.

"What's that supposed to be?" Freda asked.

"It says stew on the card," Peter replied.

"It's obviously been processed to make it soft. It's right up your street, this is. That's all you ever fed us when we were kids. Stew or derivatives thereof. I know you tried to disguise your offerings as something else - labelling them as meat and potato hash, hot pot, goulash and what have you.

But they were all basically the same dish. Stew! All that's lacking is the big plate of bread and butter!" he mocked.

"You cheeky sod! I made more than that!" Freda retorted as she took up her fork and half- heartedly began to eat.

"Oh yes. You made cheese soufflé occasionally even though you 'don't like cheese,' he said mimicking her voice.

"I made lots of things actually, Peter," she protested, "chow mein, chilli con carne, spaghetti Bolognese, chicken pie, paella with prawns - quite adventurous I'd say!"

"Er...yes but technically speaking, you didn't 'make them' - they were all from packets, courtesy of Colman's, Captain Birds Eye, or Vesta. Paella with prawns might sound exotic, Mother, but the truth was that it was really just a load of dried up bits - rehydrated peas like bullets in amongst fluorescent yellow rice and minuscule prawns which were more like shrimps. You had to shout 'whip' if you found any! And you were always getting stuff in tins - Goblin meat puddings and Fray Bentos pies."

"Well I never really enjoyed cooking. I always said I would happily clear up and wash the pots if someone else was prepared to make the tea. Feeding four kids on the money your dad gave me was hard work. I didn't have time to make everything from scratch. I don't think your dad knew where the kitchen was in our house!"

Peter chuckled at this. It was true. He never saw his dad in the kitchen. Not even to brew up. Usually, when he got in from work, he parked himself in the armchair directly in front of the telly and didn't move until pub opening time. He would hold out his hand and shout "Fetch me a cup of tea!" and one or other of them would dutifully oblige. He even remained in his chair to eat his meal, expecting waitress service, in his rightful position as head of the house. Once, he had failed to touch his meal but instead scowled all the way through the six o'clock news until their mum had dared to ask him what was wrong.

"You didn't give me a knife and fork!" he shouted

loudly. "I can't be expected to eat a meal without a knife and fork!"

Obviously he couldn't be expected to walk the two yards to the table to get his own cutlery either. Peter was surprised he hadn't taken root over the years, he'd been stationed in that chair for so long!

"I'm only pulling your leg, Mother," Peter apologised. "We all know you could put on a good spread, especially in the pudding department." He winked then added, "You were a dab hand at opening packets of Mr Kipling and tins of Del Monte!"

Freda laughed, then added, "Well, 'Mr Kipling does make exceedingly good cakes', Peter. Anyway, I actually baked quite a lot when you were little, if you remember? Lemon meringue, parkin, jam tarts. We often baked bread together and I made the Christmas cake every year. It was me who taught you how to make that fruit cake you're always doing."

"Oh yes. I'd forgotten that. You used to make your cake in September and wrap it up 'til Christmas week when you put on the almond paste and snow scene."

"There! Told you! I'm surprised you'd forgotten that, seeing as how you lot always tried to find it and pinch bits off it. You cut a whole inch layer off the bottom of it one year thinking I wouldn't notice and another year you hollowed out its middle. You must've thought I was born yesterday! I wasn't so much storing it as hiding it. I had to come up with ever-inventive places to put it. In the end, I had to take it to your nana's. It was ridiculous."

Freda put down her fork. She'd barely eaten anything.

"Is that all you're having?" Peter was incredulous. He was used to her tucking away large portions of food as a rule, the product of having been brought up with rationing. Nothing was ever wasted.

"Sorry, love, I've just no appetite. I haven't done anything all day, have I? I don't need much."

"Even our Janice's guinea pig eats more than that," Peter complained. "Be careful, Mum, else I'll be changing your name to Aunty Sarah," he mocked. "She ate like a mouse!"

"Not really," said Freda. "She just gave that impression 'cos of the measly portions she dished up on the rare occasion she offered to feed us," she said. "She and your uncle Martin both got discounts on meals at their staff canteen so they stuffed themselves up at dinnertime so they didn't have to cook in the evening. A proper thrifty pair they were!"

"Aye, I remember," said Peter. "We went for tea once - a salad - and all she put out on the plate was just one of everything - one slice of meat, one slice of egg, one slice of cucumber, one slice of tomato and a solitary lettuce leaf. Do you remember you had to get the chip pan out when we got home 'cos we were all starving?"

"I do," she replied.

She remembered how she peeled the potatoes with a Lancashire peeler as her mother had always done, then deep fried them in beef dripping and wrapped in newspaper lined with kitchen roll for that authentic 'Chippy' feel she knew they all liked.

"I had to count out the chips to ensure you all got exactly the same to save on arguments. You had 'previous' on arguing over portion sizes so I'd learned my lesson on that front," she recalled.

"Also, of course, you'd buttered a mountain of sliced bread which was on the table waiting with the salt and vinegar," Peter remembered. "I guess that was because you'd been brought up during the war by Nana. You were always trying to fill us up."

"Well I had to, didn't I? You were like a flock of gannets, descending on the table. You devoured the lot!"

Worried about her calorie intake, Peter switched the conversation back round to tonight's meal.

"What about a yogurt? I'm sure you've got room in your 'pudding place.' " he said.

This was a standing joke in the family. She had a soft spot for sweet things. Whenever she went round for tea, he'd spoil her by offering her several different options. This appealed to his sense of humour as he knew she couldn't cope with choices. She'd always settle for 'a bit of each'. Like his mum, Peter was 'a feeder' who was intent on making sure no one could ever say they went home from his house feeling hungry.

"Ok. I'll have a taste. What flavour is it?" Freda asked.

Peter examined the carton.

"Strawberry. You like strawberry, don't you?"

But then, "Oh, hang on. You can't have this. It's out of date! Bloody hell - it ran out a week ago. What are they playing at in this hospital?"

"I don't know about Aunty Sarah. This looks more like Uncle Eric's! He was always giving us out-of-date cakes."

"That's 'cos he was a tight sod too," explained Freda. "He deliberately bought them like that 'cos they were cheaper. It's always them that has money who skimp on the basics. That's how they get it. Him and Agnes were well suited. She was always cutting corners too. I remember when she made her downstairs curtains. She hemmed them in a completely different fabric so she could get away with buying an end-of-roll piece 'cos it was on offer. All to save a few pence. She got away with it 'cos she was a fantastic seamstress, but I saw through it! After she died, Eric became just like her. Jean and Anna went to stop with him once. He only had a one-bedroomed flat and he told them they could have his room and that he'd book himself into a hotel for the night. It got to eleven o'clock and he suddenly disappeared upstairs and returned with a sleeping bag to kip in the front room! They felt awful 'cos he was in his eighties and they'd taken his bed."

"Oh aye, they told me about that," said Peter. "They were woken up at six in the morning by a rattling sound. He suddenly appeared in the bedroom carrying a tray with a pot of tea and two cups. Jean said it was like something out of

Acorn Antiques. Just reminded her of Mrs Overall, he did. They couldn't stop laughing! It was accompanied by a five-day old malt loaf which he was trying to pass off as breakfast."

"Aw bless! He meant well," said Freda. "Blame it on the war. All those years of 'Make do and Mend' took their toll. Nothing went to waste. Your dad was the same. He once made a bedspread out of bits of old clothes. Lovely it was."

"What? My dad could sew?" Peter asked, genuinely surprised.

"Yes. He was quite good at it. Learned whilst doing his National Service. Believe it or not, he could cook too. When I first met him, he made me some lovely meals. He wasn't always the lazy sod you remember him as. He just morphed into that person when we got married. They should bring back National Service, in my opinion. Teach these teenagers we have nowadays how to look after themselves."

Peter nodded in agreement as he scanned the ward. He spotted Michelle.

"Hey flower! Check this out!"

She dutifully walked over. He passed her the carton.

"It's out of date," he said, pointing to the lid.

"You're right," she said. "That's way out of order. I'll make sure that it gets reported. I'm not having my patients put at risk. I'm very sorry." Then, to Freda, "Do you want me to fetch you one of your Angel Delights that Jean made for you, from the fridge?"

"No thanks, love, I'm not really hungry," Freda replied. "I'll just have this cup of tea."

"All right if you're sure? Just ask if you fancy something later."

"Will do," she replied, as she took out her iPad once more and settled down in the bed.

Peter shook his head and looked at her. Where had all her energy gone? The smallest activity seemed to wipe her out now. He worried about how she'd cope when she got home. Fiercely independent, she didn't like having to rely on others to do things for her. But she'd have to do so, for sure. He would just have to put his foot down and make sure she did as she was told. Now, however, that day seemed a very long way off.

CHAPTER 13

Anna arrived on the ward to find her mother sitting up in bed, wearing an oxygen mask. This was unusual. Up to now she had only had one on when taking her medicine through a nebuliser, but this was something different. More permanent. Jean was sitting by the bedside, tickling her feet for her. She looked up as Anna approached, giving her a warning look that said 'Don't ask'.

So, acting like this was nothing to worry about, Anna kissed her mother on the cheek then tidied up her table before joining her twin in a position by the bedside. Looking like a couple of bookends, Jean made light of the situation.

"Hiya our kid. Just tickling Mum's feet. You like this don't you, Mum? It's what we do to chillax."

Freda nodded and smiled. Briefly pulling down the mask, she said, "It's usually Mollie that tickles my feet by licking them!"

"Hey you! Never mind comparing me to that mutt of yours!" said Jean, "I'll have you know that I'm very good at tickling feet!" Then, to Anna, "Don't you get your Bobby to lick your toes for you?"

"No I don't!" Anna retorted. "He might have done it

122

once or twice by accident but not deliberately. You're thinking of one of Penny's Jack Russell Terriers - Angel - she's always licking Barry's feet for him."

"It's because of the salt," rasped Freda as she momentarily pulled down the mask. "Do you remember how our Sherry used to always lick your feet when you were kids?"

"I do," replied Anna. "Our Peter used to smear cheese spread on his toes to get her to do it!" She curled her nose up at the thought, then added. "Penny was telling me that Angel even went up to Barry the other day and began nudging his feet and whining! She wanted him to take off his shoes so she could do it again!"

"Aw bless!" said Jean. "I don't need a dog for that, though. I just ask Jessica."

"Ugh!" Anna feigned alarm. "Jessica licks your feet?"

"No! She tickles them for me! And my back. I love having my back tickled. I have to pay her, of course, but it's well worth it. Makes you feel all relaxed."

She turned to her mum. "Doesn't it, Mother?" she asked.

Having replaced her mask, Freda just nodded.

"I should set up a business tickling people," Jean continued. "They would pay a premium for it."

Anna rolled her eyes. "You'd have to watch that one. You'd get all sorts of dodgy people turning up!" she said.

"No I wouldn't! It'd be all above board and decent. I've even got a name for it - 'The Tickly Back Shack.' "

Freda and Anna both snorted with laughter. Only Jean could come up with a proposal like that.

"You may mock but I think it's a great idea," said Jean. "I've thought it through. Just need a small premises with a settee in it. I'd put candles around the room and everything. Nothing seedy. And a big sign outside. The Tickly Back Shack has a ring to it. Catchy. I reckon I could easily charge a fiver for half an hour. They'd be queuing to get in."

"Well best of luck with that one, Jean," laughed Anna. "Rather you than me. It's probably someone's fetish, you know."

Anna carried on talking. "Did you see that programme about those women in Sheffield who cater to the 'needs' of different men? They did all sorts of unusual things."

"Oh, I saw that!" Freda said. She pulled down her mask fully now so that it rested on her chest. Anna noticed the red lines etched down either side of her face where the straps had dug in and made a mental note to remind herself to adjust it later.

Freda commanded the conversation, "A mother and daughter had set up a business together. Basically, they were both on the game but were trying to pass it off as a legitimate enterprise. It was hilarious!"

"Yes it was," agreed Anna. "You've never seen anything like it, Jean. There was a guy who went every week to stand naked in a bath whilst this big woman in a basque threw baked beans at him! I've not seen anything so funny for ages!"

"Yes. They filmed her doing it," added Freda. "The room was scattered with empty tins of value beans!" Then, mimicking a thick northern accent, she continued, "Tha's no use wasting tha money on Heinz! These do the job just grand!"

"Yes! I couldn't stop laughing!" said Anna. "Did you see that one who turned up and just asked to be undressed? When she took his clothes off, he had his mother's clothes on underneath."

"Really?" said Jean. "Then did she have sex with him?"

"No. That was all he wanted. He was only a young man too - about twenty-five - I was surprised."

"Aw bless! He obviously had some issues."

"Well it's not as bad as that other programme I watched," said Freda, "where that woman was paid to treat men like they were babies."

"I saw that too," said Anna. "She was earning a fortune."

"Why? What did she do?" asked Jean.

"She undressed and bathed them and then dried them and doused them in talc, then she put a big incontinence pad on them to act like a nappy, fed them a bottle and put them in a giant cot for the afternoon!" said Anna.

"What? Left them to sleep whilst she got paid for it? That's a good earner. What did she charge for that?"

"One hundred and fifty pounds a session," replied Anna.

"Really?" said Jean. Then, winking at her mum, added, "I'll have to put my prices up!"

"It was double if they wanted to be breast fed," said Freda.

"Ugh! Where did she get the milk from?" asked Jean.

"She had a new baby," replied Anna.

"Well you wouldn't catch me doing owt like that!"

"I should hope not," said Freda. "All of them were prostitutes!"

"Well, technically speaking, this one wasn't," said Anna. "She wasn't having sex with them. Just earning some cash on the side to make up her statutory maternity pay!"

"But the ones in Sheffield were, weren't they, Anna?" said Freda. "It showed them going to buy a camper van to use as another premises since business was booming and they couldn't afford to rent anywhere. It showed them discussing how they would use the living area with the bed made up whilst a colleague sat in the driving seat keeping an eye out!"

"What?" remarked Jean. "You mean one of them was at it with a bloke whilst another listened in?"

"She put the radio on to drown out any noise," said Freda.

"Wow! I bet that made all the difference!" Jean spoke sarcastically.

"Well, Jean, it's only like that time you went on holiday with that girl from the pub - Julie something or other," said Anna.

"Slapper Julie? Oh, I'd forgotten about her. Yes, she was terrible. Talk about not knowing someone! We only went for a week and she copped off with a bloke almost straight away. It was terrible as we had a twin room and she brought him back to ours for a bit of 'How's your father'. I couldn't stand it."

"Well I would've told her!" said Freda. "I wouldn't have put up with that. It was your holiday too!"

"Didn't you say anything to her?" asked Anna.

"I didn't know she was going to actually do it with him!" said Jean. "I was in my bed asleep and I heard a noise. I put my hands over my ears and my head under the covers to block it out. When she'd finished, she shouted me to pass her a fag. When I turned round, she was lying buck-naked on top of him. I didn't know where to look!"

"Shame on her!" remarked Freda.

"So, what happened to the business in Sheffield?" asked Jean, switching the conversation back quickly. "Surely, they couldn't make a programme about running a brothel and get away with it?"

"Apparently it's been closed down," said Anna

"Has it?" asked Freda. "Just when they've shelled out for a camper van too. They're not cheap them things you know!"

Jean and Anna looked at each other and burst out laughing. Trust their mother to come up with that!

Freda snorted, and was immediately overcome with a fit of coughing. Jean sprang up and began to rub her back urgently whilst Anna fiddled with the oxygen mask, keen to replace it as soon as possible. Once the coughing had subsided, she gently placed it over her nose and mouth and adjusted the straps one more time. Satisfied that it was comfortable, she sat back in her chair and relaxed.

"Anyway, how did you get on sleeping at Mum's last night, our kid?" Jean said, changing the subject.

"I didn't," said Anna

"What!" Freda mouthed behind the plastic mask. "You were supposed to be looking after the dogs!" She pulled down her mask again, determined to join in the conversation. Anna tutted.

"I did! What I meant was that I didn't get any sleep. You know I've always been scared of sleeping at your house on account of those ghosts you've got there," said Anna.

"Oh, give over!" said Freda. "They're harmless!"

"Really, Mother?" said Jean. "Aren't they the same ghosts who booted Ben down the stairs when you first got him? And terrorised our Michael? He woke up in that back room surrounded by carefully placed suitcases! Why do you think he used to always get comatose when he lived at yours? It's so he could tolerate what went on!"

"Well that's one excuse for drinking, I guess!" replied Freda. Then she added, "But they've never done me any harm. I passed a bloke on the landing just the other week when I got up to go to the toilet in the middle of the night."

"You're kidding me!" said Jean, mouth open.

"I just walked past him and said 'How do' and he stared back."

"I wonder if that's the one that blew smoke in my face when I slept over at New Year?" said Anna. "It was well scary. I buried my head under the duvet hoping it'd go away. I was too frightened to get out of bed. That's why I only sleep upstairs if I have Bobby with me. But then I don't sleep 'cos he spends all night woofing at everyone who passes outside the house on their way home from the pub on the corner."

"Oh yes. Your Bobby's lovely but that's his one downfall - barking!" said Freda. "I tried everything to stop him from doing it when he used to stay with me when you went on holiday. I even got a water pistol since the dog trainer said if you squirted him with it, he would be surprised and he'd stop."

"And was he surprised?" asked Jean.

"Oh yes! For all of about ten seconds! Then he treated it like a game. He loved catching the water and barked even more to get me to do it. I couldn't win!"

Freda coughed again. Both girls looked at each other anxiously, but said nothing. Then Jean spoke up.

"I have to admit, Mum, things have got a bit mad at yours since you came in here. It's like they've taken over! You know me, I don't get frightened like our Anna, but even I was scared the other day."

Listening to this reminded Anna of the episode when Jean had visited her mum at Aunty Sandra's house. Freda had been looking after the shop for her sister whilst she was living it up on the QE2. This necessitated her sleeping there as she had to get up at five in the morning to do the papers, as well as look after Henry, Sandra's German Shepherd. Jean had gone round to keep her company and had been sitting at the table opposite her reading the paper when suddenly she felt something falling down her face. She'd reached up to discover lots of petals all over her head!

"What did you do that for, Mother?" Jean asked.

"I didn't do anything!" replied Freda. "Believe it or not, the head of that chrysanthemum just came off and travelled through the air to your head! It was as if someone had snapped it off and crumbled it over your hair! It must've been your uncle Terry."

Jean's favourite uncle had recently passed away and Freda was adamant that he was haunting the place.

"He'll be having a laugh with you. He always had a funny sense of humour!" she said.

But Jean was far from laughing. She was nervous. Earlier in the week, she knew, her mum had overslept and switched off her alarm. Minutes later, another alarm had gone off louder than ever. She'd been forced to get out of bed to find the source of the noise and discovered a disused electronic alarm clock radio in the corner. It wasn't even plugged in! Freda had thought how it was typical of her brother-in-law to make sure his business was still being run smoothly in his absence! These thoughts sent a shiver down Anna's spine. She refocused on the conversation taking place now.

"What happened at my house, then, which made you so scared?' Freda enquired of Jean.

"It's what I saw in your kitchen," she replied. "I was watching *'Corrie'* when Niko started growling. It's not like him to behave like that. All his hackles were up and everything and he was staring at something near the cooker. I looked over and there was this 'thing' suspended in the air!"

"What 'thing'?" asked Freda, grinning.

"Well, it was what I can only describe as a kind of vapour, like steam in the outline of a person. You know like you see in horror films?"

Freda sniggered. Anna didn't want to believe this story since it freaked her out.

"And how much weed had you smoked by that point, Jean?" Anna asked.

"Honest to God, Anna, I know I like a joint but I hadn't touched one. Cross my heart! I kid you not. It was really scary!"

"Had you just had the kettle on?" asked Freda.

"No, Mother! It wasn't steam like that! It definitely looked like a spirit of some kind. Niko was proper growling too. He wouldn't let me go in there. He was protecting me from something."

"Well, how did Mollie react?" asked Freda. "If it was a ghost, I'm sure she would've noticed too."

"You're joking, aren't you? She was upside down on the rocking chair away with the fairies!" said Jean. "Fat, lazy sod she is! She wouldn't notice owt!"

"Aw! You're always dissing her!" lamented Freda. "No-one seems to like our Mollie!"

"Including you!" muttered Anna under her breath.

"Anyway, Jean," asked Anna, "what happened with the ghost in the kitchen? Did it just go away?"

"Well it did and it didn't," she replied. "I got Niko to sit next to me on the settee and watched TV to distract myself but then this noise started in the hallway."

"What kind of noise?"

"Running. And banging. You know, like someone was charging down the stairs and then jumping off the bottom step? I thought one of the kids was coming down. I was expecting them to come into the living room any minute. Only, they didn't. They just kept doing it over and over again. I was all comfy by this point so I wasn't getting up to sort it out so I shouted them to stop buggering about. But they just ignored me. In the end, I whipped open the door, hoping to catch 'em at it. But there was no one there. Upstairs was in total darkness. Niko shot off the chair and stood in front of me growling and showing his teeth."

Anna looked at her mother who was rummaging up her sleeve in search of a tissue. She caught her attention briefly and they both grinned. Anna rolled her eyes.

"Oh, I bet it was the kids winding you up," Anna said. "It would be just like them to play a trick on you."

"No, they were both fast asleep in bed. All the doors were shut and everything."

"It'd be the visitors," said Freda matter-of-factly. It must be 'cos I'm not there. What did you do?"

"I was bricking it! I ran back into the living room and shut the door. Niko sat there like a sentry constantly growling. I lit a joint to calm myself down."

"And did the noise stop?" asked Anna.

"No! I phoned our Michael and asked him to come round. He was only in The Red Lion on the corner so he came straight away."

Having successfully located her tissue, Freda straightened it out before spitting something into it. She hastily scrunched it up.

"So, did Michael hear it too?" Anna asked her sister.

"No! The second he put his key in the door, the noise ended!" said Jean.

"That'll be because they know him," said Freda, who

unlike the girls was not a bit perturbed by these events. Anna and Jean looked at each other.

Then Jean continued, "He came in the living room and said 'What's up, our kid? Why've you got me out of the pub on a Saturday night?' So, I told him all about the vapour and the jumping off the stairs and everything. He could see for himself that Niko was standing guard."

"And what did he say? Did he believe you?"

"Yes! Of course he did, Anna! I was proper shaking and everything."

"So, what did he do?"

"Well, he went upstairs and checked on the kids who were both out for the count in their beds, rolled himself a joint, then said 'Welcome to my world, Jean! Why do you think I moved out?!' "

"Fat lot of use he was then!" said Anna

"I know!" said Jean. "He was like: 'Well Jean, there's nowt I can do about it. I've just got a pint in. If I don't hurry back some thieving bugger will drink it. See you later!' Then he went off."

"That was that, then, presumably?" asked Anna.

"No it wasn't," replied Jean. "As soon as the door shut behind him, it started again!"

"Oh my God. I would've been out of there," said Anna. She shuddered at the thought of it then casually reached her hand out towards her mother, grimacing as she tentatively took the used tissue off her and made for the bin by the sink.

"Believe me, our kid, I wanted to get gone but I couldn't so very well go out and leave the kids on their own, could I?" Jean continued. "And there was no way I was going into the hallway in a hurry. Niko wouldn't have let me past him even if I'd wanted to."

"So, what did you do?" Anna asked, as she disposed of the tissue in the bin, shrivelling her nose up in distaste at the thought of its contents.

"I turned the TV up!" Jean replied. "I figured that if I

drowned out the noise, I wouldn't have to think about it. Then I prayed I didn't need the toilet! I smoked a couple of joints to chillax. Eventually the noise stopped. They must've had enough!"

"Did you sleep upstairs?' "asked Freda.

"Yes, I got in with Jessica. But I switched like every light on in the house!"

"That's exactly why I don't like sleeping there," said Anna, as she sanitised her hands. She returned to her chair to re-join the conversation.

"It's like that film, *Poltergeist*" she remarked.

"Give over!" said Freda. "It's not that bad!"

"Mum! It's freaky!" said Anna. "I swear things move about on their own. I used to think it was you moving things about and forgetting that you'd done it. Like you were getting dementia or something."

"Charming!" said Freda, as she absent-mindedly played with the cuffs on her sleeve.

"Well, you are getting on a bit!" Jean joked.

Anna carried on, "But then when I stopped there to look after the dogs that time you went on holiday, I saw it for myself. Things moved and I knew damn well I hadn't done it."

"What? Like Ava's iPod which Mollie chewed up and I had to pay for?" asked Freda.

"Yes! We definitely left it on the mantelpiece where she couldn't get it. Believe me, Mother, after that first night when Mollie nicked Emily's headphones, the kids had it drilled into them not to leave anything where she could reach. We checked and double-checked every time we went out. There's no way that it was on the table. That wasn't the worst, though, it was that puffy teddy you keep on the chair in your bedroom."

"That one I brought back for her from Bognor Regis?" asked Jean, sitting up with renewed interest. She'd always loved that teddy. "What happened?"

"Well, it was sitting on the chair as usual, whilst I was

tidying up. I remember because it was covered in clothes and I put them in the washing basket and apologised to it as I straightened it up."

"Ha! That's what Mum would've done,' said Jean, "talk to toys!"

"I know! I laughed at myself for doing it. I talk out loud to stop me being so scared up there. I went out of the room and when I came back it was gone!"

"Get away with you!" laughed Freda. "Had one of the girls moved it?"

"No. I was on my own. I went into the other bedroom and it was sitting on the bed!"

"That's definitely like *Poltergeist!*" said Jean. "You know that scene with the clown. Do you remember? Where it sits on a chair in the corner with a dodgy grin on its face? There's a storm and the boy checks under the bed, comes back up and looks relieved, then turns round and the clown is sitting right next to him!"

"Yes! That's exactly what it was like!" exclaimed Anna, remembering the scene only too vividly from when she'd watched the film years before. It had shaken her up then just as the memory disturbed her now.

"I tell you, I couldn't get out of that room quick enough! I nearly fell running down the stairs. I was terrified. Ask Penny next time you see her. I phoned her up and she calmed me down."

"They don't come downstairs as a rule," said Freda, trying to reach for the box of tissues off the bedside cabinet. To her, the paranormal was fascinating rather than frightening.

"Well they did the other day, Mother!" said Jean, picking up the box and passing it to her. "They locked our Jessica out of the house!"

"Really?" asked Anna. "I didn't know that."

"Yes," Jean said, stressing the point.

"I left her at Mum's on her own for ten minutes whilst I nipped out with the dogs. She wouldn't come with me so I said she could stay in on condition she just watched TV. When I came back, she came out of next door's house with Caroline. She said she'd heard a knock at the door and assumed it was me coming back without my key. She'd opened the door and stepped outside for a minute to look for me. Then the door slammed behind her."

"Was it windy?" asked Freda, pulling several tissues out of the box and pushing them up her sleeve.

"I know you don't believe me, Mother, but there's no way the wind blew that door shut. You know how heavy it is. I kid you not. I swear on Niko's life and everything. Something pushed it."

"Well, knowing your Jessica, she probably decided to go out and shut the door behind her," said Anna. "She probably went next door so she didn't get cold waiting for you."

"No," said Jean. "I know she's a little sod an' all but she didn't do that. She definitely heard someone at the door and went to answer it. She was proper shook up when I got back."

Noticing her mother had finished with the box of tissues, Anna took the box and placed it on the table within reach.

"Well our Ava reckoned something like that happened to her that night we brought you in here, Mum," Anna said directly to her mother.

"She said she heard a noise downstairs and then the bedroom door flew open. She assumed it was me coming back, she said. Only no-one came into the room. Thinking it was odd, she called downstairs and then went down to find me. Only I wasn't there, of course. The house was still in darkness and the dogs were on their own."

"Aw! Poor Ava," said Jean. Then to her mother, "See, I told you! Do you believe me now? Ava never lies about stuff."

"Well, it's odd, that's all," Freda said. She motioned to Anna to pass her the carton of juice from the side and took a big sip. Then she passed her tongue over her lips in an attempt to moisten them.

"Well, didn't our Penny say that something happened when she was there too?" asked Jean. "She told me she went upstairs to the toilet and heard someone running along the landing. She assumed it was Jason or Jessica but neither of them was there."

"Ah yes, she told me that," said Freda, still licking her lips.

"To be honest, she did look a bit shook up when she came downstairs. But they can't do you any harm you know!" She continued, keen to find out what had gone on, "So what happened last night then, Anna, that stopped you sleeping? Was it a 'visitor' downstairs?"

"No, actually, it wasn't."

Freda looked surprised.

"It was Niko! He kept me awake wandering up and down all night! Backwards and forwards he was. Did my head in!"

"Well, just out of interest, whereabouts on the settee did you sleep?" asked Freda.

"On the end nearest the hall door. Why? What difference does that make?" asked Anna.

Freda passed a knowing look to Jean, who nodded back.

"Why?" asked Anna again.

"That's Niko's side of the settee!" said Jean. "Mum sits at the side nearest the kitchen and Niko sits at the other end nearest the hall."

"He'd be upset 'cos you nicked his bed!" explained Freda.

"Oh my God, I've heard it all now!" said Anna. "You and your dogs!"

Jean smirked. "Anyway, I need to get going. Didn't you say you needed to go to the drinks machine, our kid?" she said.

"What?" replied Anna.

Jean cast her a look.

"Oh yes. I can't risk drinking any of that tea or coffee they do in here. Our Peter says him and Janice couldn't get off the toilet all last week because of that. Come on, then."

They both got up to leave.

"See you later, Mum," said Jean.

"Back in a minute, Mum," said Anna, exiting the ward after her sister.

Jean took Anna into the day room.

"I didn't want to tell you in front of Mum, our kid, but she was proper upset when I got there this morning. Janice said she'd had a panic attack in the night. You know like she did that night when she was banging on the wall and I didn't hear her?"

Anna nodded. She remembered this all too well. Her mum had been fighting for breath and Jean had slept through it all. She frowned.

"Janice said she'd been proper distressed," Jean explained. She talked her through it and managed to calm her down. Mum said she was an angel. We'll have to keep an eye on her more. I'm going to get some answers from them doctors next time they come round. I'm really worried about what this means. Seems like we're going backwards not forwards."

"I agree," said Anna.

"Don't say owt to her about it though, Anna. Just keep her mind off it."

"Will do. See you later."

Anna returned to the ward, where Freda was tapping on her iPad.

"You're good at jigsaws aren't you, love?" Freda said.

"I certainly am!"

"Well, see if you can help me this one."

Anna sat down where she could see the screen clearly. *Typical!* she thought. It was a picture of a dog

CHAPTER 14

Peter arrived on the ward.

"Blummin 'eck, what have you been up to?" said Freda.

Anna looked up from her book, to see her brother, looking dishevelled and tired. Clearly, he was nursing a hangover. "Been out on the bevvy?" she asked.

"Aye, something like that," he said. "Andy turned up on my doorstep last night so we had one or two cans. And maybe some whiskey."

"Snork?" asked Anna. "I thought he lived in Thailand or some such place. Last I heard he'd got himself some woman over there. What was he doing in your neck of the woods?

Andy was an old friend of Peter's from school. He earned his nickname from the fact he snored incredibly loudly. He'd not really had much of a home life as his mum passed away when he was little and his dad had shacked up with a much older woman. Once he became a teenager, there wasn't really a place for him, so he'd resorted to staying out a lot. He'd spent many a night at their house, kipping on the settee and Freda had treated him like one of the family. Even Len had tolerated him, largely on account of the fact that they both smoked Benson and Hedges and liked a pint. Also, Snork didn't seem to mind that Len got up really early at weekends to watch old black and white films. He got used to being woken from his drunken slumber by the sound of cowboys and Indians fighting.

"He just turned up last night," continued Peter. "He's back in England trying to earn some money before heading back. I guess he was hoping I'd have some contacts to get him some work as a casual labourer."

"Blimey!" said Freda, temporarily removing her oxygen mask. "Who would've thought? That's a turn up for the books. I wasn't sure he was still alive! What with his high blood pressure an' all. Haven't seen him for years."

"Well yes, me too," said Peter. "Mind you, he looked a bit rum! He turned up in some kind of kaftan and sandals! I'm surprised he got through security at Manchester airport - he'd easily pass for a terrorist!"

"Well, he always said he was going to bag himself a Thai bride," said Anna. "Said he wanted a woman who was good in the kitchen and the bedroom and was always grateful! Is that what he's got, then, Peter?" She laughed.

"Aye. Something on those lines. He lives out in the middle of nowhere surrounded by paddy fields. By his reckoning, he's treated like some kind of chief over there on account of the fact he is the only one with a plumbed-in toilet and a herd of goats!"

"Blimey!" Freda repeated. Peter noticed that her voice was sounding croaky.

"Who would've thought that he'd end up there? Did he look any different?" she asked.

"Oh aye- short, fat and going bald! And hardly any teeth!" Peter laughed loudly. "I barely recognised him at first. I thought he was one of those 'Jo Jobbers' or something after converting me!"

"So, did he spend the night at your house then?" asked Anna.

"Yes. He bunked down on the settee."

"Like the old days!" Anna said. "Nothing changes."

"Well it's a luxury, apparently. His home is a one-room building where they all sleep on the floor!"

"I guess you had a lot of catching up to do. Is he stopping with you now?"

"No! He's at his sister's. I dropped him off on the way here. He sends his best wishes to you, Mum," Peter said, as he took up a chair by the bedside.

"Aw. That's nice," she replied. Freda always had a soft spot for Andy. He was good to her, and had even gone out walking the dogs with her on several occasions. He didn't even mind escorting them in his van - unless, that is, they were particularly dirty... She thought about the time she had Kyle, a golden retriever who had the unfortunate affliction of loving mud! The wetter, the better. They'd gone up Werneth Low one afternoon and he'd somehow found the deepest pile of cow slurry he could. Submerging himself in it, he was having a ball. This was all within sight of the guests at a posh restaurant. Freda had been mortified and had had to do a walk of shame all the way home, as there was no way he could get inside a vehicle in that state. It had taken an age to clean him up as well as the bathroom afterwards. It was a good job she lived in her own house then and didn't have anyone else to worry about. She smiled at the memory.

"So, no wonder you look wrecked, Peter," continued Anna. "Andy was always one for knocking them back. Bet you got through some drink, then?"

"You might say that, yes. One or two," he smirked.

"I don't know how you do it, you lot, drinking all the time," said Freda. "I've never seen the attraction in it. Your dad was in the pub every night and all weekend, drinking away his wages. We never had any money on account of it. Drank his life away, he did. I don't want any of you going down that road."

"Give over, Mother!" said Peter. "I don't drink like dad did. Our Michael might though!"

"That's what I mean," she lamented.

Freda always worried about everything.

"Well, you're not averse to a glass or two yourself, Mother!" said Peter.

"Hardly!" She coughed slightly. The oxygen was making her voice quite hoarse.

It was Anna's turn to come to her mother's defence now.

"Peter, you can't call the odd glass of wine with her lunch on a Sunday every once in a while, a sign that she's a drinker!" she said. "She never even finishes a glass when she comes to mine."

"That's because you serve crap wine, Anna. She has several at mine!" Peter retorted.

"Well yes, that's because you keep topping her glass up when she's not looking, then telling her to get drinking. You do that with everyone. I've been banned from drinking at yours by Richard on account of the state I get into!"

"Aw. Give over! You're a lightweight!"

"Well I'd rather be that than comatosed and not know what I've been up to! I'm not the one who jumped off the bar at the train station and broke all the bones in my feet, then had to stop off work because I couldn't walk!" Anna reminded him.

Peter looked momentarily embarrassed then started laughing as he recalled that night: They'd all been out for a drink on Christmas Eve - him, Michael, Anna and Andy - and had stayed in after hours. The music was on full blast and they'd been dancing around the bar when Peter had clambered up, shouting "Look what I can do!" He'd launched himself off the bar, landing on both feet, received a round of applause then turned to Anna and complained that his feet hurt. She'd thought nothing of it, and had left not long afterwards with Andy who was nodding off, leaving Peter and Michael there for a lock-in.

The pub was on the railway platform, and at about six in the morning, feeling the cold, the lads had woken up and decided to come home. But they'd been unable to wake the landlord, who was passed out in the back room. Michael, being a joiner, had resorted to taking out the window so they could escape the confines of the pub. At that point he'd discovered that Peter really couldn't walk, so he'd requisitioned a trolley from the waiting room in which to push him up the hill to their house. Their mum had gone mad when she saw them arrive. It wasn't the sort of present she'd expected on Christmas morning and she could feel the eyes of the neighbours on her as they hid behind their twitching net curtains.

Reaching for an empty cup, Peter poured himself some water from the jug on the table and downed it in one.

"And there was that time we all went for a Chinese meal for our Michael's birthday. Peter, and you got so drunk you fell down your stairs," Anna continued. "You sent us a text saying you'd pooed your pants as I remember!"

"Oh my God, I'd forgotten about that," said Freda. She was looking directly at her son. "That was the night you kept plying us all with drink and then ordered champagne. Jean brought me home drunk and I was throwing up in the bathroom. Then I flushed the toilet before realising I'd dropped my false teeth in the bowl!"

Peter started laughing. Then Anna joined in.

"I've never seen our Michael laugh so much in his life," Anna recalled. "You just stood there in the living room, all bedraggled and sobbing. Then you opened your mouth to show us your teeth had gone. You just had a space full of gums. You like something out of *Fraggle Rock*!"

"Aw! It wasn't funny, Anna! I'd had those teeth for years! What was I going to do?"

Anna was giggling like mad.

"Our Michael turned round and said 'Don't worry, Mother, you'll be able to do that gurning now like Les Dawson!' " Peter said, tears running down his face.

"That wasn't even the best of it," said Anna. "Our Jean went into the kitchen to make her a brew to calm her down and noticed that old cup on the side with a lid on it. She opened it up and found Mum's teeth inside! It turned out she'd not chucked them up down the toilet after all but in fact had never even had them in in the first place! Jean was ecstatic but Mum just burst into floods of tears. I remember her saying, 'That's even worse! I've been out all night without my teeth!' "

"Well yes, I must've been," Freda recalled.

"Unless you took them out before you went to the bathroom, Mother," said Anna. "You were so drunk you wouldn't have remembered. I'm sure we would've noticed at the restaurant if we were sharing a table with an old toothless woman!"

"Yes. That'd be right," added Peter. "There's no way you could've caved in those spare ribs without your pegs in!"

"No, I wouldn't," said Freda. "I'm not like my dad was, eating anything with only one tooth to his name. That must've been what happened. I'll never get like that again! That's why I never drink. Something similar happened when I went to Majorca with my friend, Veronica, years ago."

"What? You spat your false teeth down the loo?" joked Peter.

"No! I got drunk and didn't know where I was," Freda continued. "It was the night before we came home. One minute I was drinking a big glass of something because I was thirsty and the next, I was waking up on the plane. I don't remember packing or boarding or anything. I swore it'd never happen again."

"Well that'll teach you not to drink, Mother!" Peter sounded virtuous. "You don't get like that on halves of pale-ale and lime. What on earth were you drinking?"

"That's it. I don't know," she answered. "We were celebrating with some cricket team or other. One of the blokes - Cecil Pepper was his name - thought it would be funny to go along the optics and fill up a pint glass then give it to me to quench my thirst. I had no idea what he'd done. Good job I had Veronica watching out for me."

"Oh yes! She was doing a sterling job by the sound of it," Anna said sarcastically.

"Well, she didn't see him do that of course! She looked after me when she found me passed out in the toilets."

"And you call us!" mocked Peter.

"Cecil Pepper? I'm sure I've heard of him somewhere. Wasn't he quite famous?" asked Anna. She got out her phone to google him.

"I've no idea," said Freda. "I know it's not a name I've ever forgotten! I definitely know he was Australian and that he liked a drink! He lived in Yorkshire somewhere. He invited us all to his house for a party after we got back. My dad drove me up there. I didn't stop long."

"Yes, here it is," said Anna, reading from her phone. "It says here that he was a professional in league cricket. He could've been 'One of the greatest all-rounders the world has ever seen. But he missed out due to his attitude and over-ripe language'. Sounds like you, Peter. You're always swearing like a trooper." Anna dug her brother in the ribs.

"Like fuck, I am!" he joked, winking at his mum. "Whatever gave you that fucking idea?"

"Peter!" Freda chastened him.

She quickly scanned the ward to make sure no-one had heard him. Luckily, Sylvia was asleep, and Ethel was too absorbed folding her pairs of knickers again. Not that she would've heard anyhow, judging by how the staff had to shout whenever they spoke to her. And Chloe didn't really count, living in her own little world across the way.

"Well, you're better off not drinking, in my opinion, Mother," said Anna. "Alcohol obviously doesn't agree with you."

"Not when you're throwing it down your neck, no!" said Peter.

"I seem to remember you getting drunk once before though," said Anna, "when we were kids. You and Elaine

Smith. You drank Ian's home-made nettle wine."

"Oh, that was an accident," said Freda. "I went round to hers for the afternoon before I came to pick you lot up from school and she suggested we try a glass. I had no idea it was that strong. Before I knew it, we'd finished a bottle. Don't know how I managed to get to school. We nearly didn't make it on time."

"Well it wouldn't be the first time you didn't turn up for us, would it?" said Anna. "I believe you once left me and Jean outside Marjorie's shop in Mottram."

"Aw! That was just a mistake. She used to let me leave the two of you in your pram outside her shop whilst I walked the lads up to school. It saved me having to push you up that big hill. I took a shortcut home down the 'gibble gabble'. I thought there was something missing when I got home!"

"Nice to see you took your mothering duties so seriously!" Peter was winding her up again. "That's what happens when you have so many kids!"

"You take no notice of 'em, Freda," said Michelle, the staff nurse, who had just appeared on the ward. Freda smiled at her. "How are you doing today?" she asked.

"Not bad," Freda replied. "I'm losing my voice, though. My throat still feels sore."

"That'll be the oxygen, darling. It dries out your throat."

"Or the fact you never stop talking, Mother!" joked Peter.

"Hey! Leave her alone!" said Michelle. "We love listening to her talking."

Then, walking to the bed, she added, "Just let me check your mouth, darling."

Michelle took a small wooden spatula from her breast pocket. Gently, she moved the oxygen mask out of the way then asked her to open her mouth. Pressing the spatula down on her tongue, she carefully inspected inside.

"Yes, your mouth's looking really dry," she noted. "It

looks like you've still got a bit of thrush too. I'll get you some more drops."

Freda rolled her eyes. Nothing seemed to be getting better. Only worse. It seemed like her whole day was punctuated by procedures, potions and tablets. She'd no idea what half of them were for! She felt like a medicine cabinet. Pick her up and she was sure she'd rattle!

"I'm also going to get you another mouth cleaning kit," Michelle continued, "as you've nearly exhausted the supplies in the last one."

Michelle turned to Anna. "I'll fetch it now so your brother can show you how to use it," she said.

"All right, flower," Peter acknowledged, as she left the ward. He got up and went over to his mother.

"This mask needs adjusting too," he said. "It's digging in your face at the side." He took hold of the straps and carefully altered them, then fit the mask back on her face. "You should try and keep it on more, so it can do its job properly. Better?"

Freda nodded dutifully.

Peter stroked his finger affectionately down her cheek.

"We'll make a storm trooper of you yet, Mother!" he laughed.

He turned to Anna.

"I'd best be off now. I only popped in to pick up the flask and drop off a clean nightie. Got a few errands to run."

Picking up his keys and phone, he turned to leave.

"Off home to make you some of that soup you keep leaving, Mother!" he said. Freda looked chastened. Her eyes glistened slightly.

"I'll be back tonight. See you later, our Anna."

Anna nodded. Freda acknowledged with a wave.

As he was leaving, Michelle was returning with the mouth kit.

"See you later, flower," he said. Then added, "You can give that kit to our Anna. She'll use it on Mum. She's done that sort of thing before when she worked on the old people's ward."

"Will do," she replied.

Peter passed the nursing station. It was a hive of activity. Staff nurses were answering the phones, filling in paperwork and dealing with a variety of orderlies and auxiliary nurses whom they were directing to various tasks around the unit. He marvelled at how hard these people all worked. They never seemed to take a break. As he exited through the security door, he noticed two doctors arriving. He recognised one instantly - 'Dr Death' Jean called him - and hoped that he wasn't on his way to see their mother. That was the last thing she needed just now.

Mind you, if he knew our Anna well, he thought, he'd avoid going anywhere near. She'd soon give him sharp shrift!

As he emerged up the steps into the car park, the sun glared in his eyes. It was like an entirely different world out there.

CHAPTER 15

Freda was the first to admit that she had always been a talker. She loved nothing better than a good gab and would literally converse with anybody and everybody. But there was someone else who beat her hands down - Pauline.

Pauline, whom she'd known since moving to Dukinfield years ago, didn't live far away from Freda - just a few streets - and spoke to her regularly on the phone, often late at night and frequently into the early hours of the morning. Now in her eighties, her skills were well honed, and getting a word in edgeways was difficult for anybody. There used to be a joke told years ago about what were the fastest three ways to communicate, the punchline being telephone, television and tell-a-woman. Pauline personified the latter. There was nothing in the neighbourhood that escaped her attention and she saw it as her duty to keep everyone up-to-date with the various goings on.

So it was that she was now visiting Freda to ensure she wasn't missing out on any news. Having talked at length about next door's cat needing an operation, the price of milk going up at the corner shop, and Mrs Higginbottom's nephew's son passing his exams, she was now in full flow on the subject of their mutual friend, June.

Oblivious to the fact that Freda was finding it difficult to keep her eyes open, on account of her medication, she insisted on recounting the exact detail of a trip they'd made together by public transport earlier in the week. Never having learned to drive, and having lost her husband many years before, she'd become dependent on buses to get about. Also, being a pensioner in possession of a free bus pass, she was determined to make the most of the facility, often engineering days out just to get her money's worth.

Pauline talked at length about the bus times, who got on and off at each stop and what they saw on the way. Freda zoned in and out, occasionally catching a snippet of what was being said and feigning an interest by smiling politely. Ordinarily, she would have interjected and brought the conversation around to something more interesting, but she just didn't have the inclination today. She was too tired and fed up. So, instead, she let Pauline warble on and on to her heart's content.

Meanwhile, she took the opportunity to scan the ward to see what was going on. Chloe was curled up fast asleep, sucking her thumb in a manner reminiscent of a toddler; Ethel was reading a magazine upside down; and Sylvia was sitting up in bed staring inanely at her husband, who, as usual, had nothing to say. She took note of the time on the clock. Visiting time would soon be over, and she could be relieved of her duty to listen to her friend. It wasn't that she wasn't grateful to see Pauline - it was always nice to see a familiar face - but her presence reminded her of the fact that the world continued as normal outside these four walls and made her feel the desire to go home. To her own house. To her own bed. To her dogs.

She missed Niko and Mollie greeting her every morning; playing ball or just snuggling up on the settee watching *'Corrie'*. She'd not even watched any soap operas in a while, now. Jean was still dutifully recording them for her on the iPad, but she found herself viewing them half-heartedly.

She was no longer bothered about the characters or where the storylines were heading. They didn't matter. Usually she'd be reading in advance in the TV Quick about what was going to happen, but not anymore. Who cared?

Just then, to Freda's relief, Anna returned.

"Hello, Pauline. Nice to see you. How are you?" Anna asked politely.

"Oh I can't complain, love. I was just telling your mum about me and June going on the bus the other day."

Before she could launch into another rendition of her epic journey, Anna seized the chance to cut her short.

"Sorry to interrupt you, Pauline," she said. Then, turning to the bed, "Dr Bennett and another doctor are on their way to see you, Mother."

Pauline's ears pricked up. She was on red-alert, anticipating hearing something before anyone else from their locality. She could be the first to relay any news back to the neighbours, corner shop and window cleaner.

Dr Bennett breezed in. Tall and handsome, he cut an elegant figure in contrast to the short, bespectacled man who accompanied him. Freda smiled broadly as she instantly took a shine to him. He had a nice air about him.

"Good afternoon, Freda. I'm very pleased to meet you," he said, as he unclipped her medical chart from its position at the end of the bed and glanced through the charts.

"How are you?"

Freda pulled down the oxygen mask and croaked, "I'm losing my voice, doctor."

"Yes that'll be the oxygen doing that," he remarked. "But apart from that? How are you?"

"Her blood counts were low this morning," said Anna. "The consultant says they need to start rising."

"Oh, we don't worry about blood counts!" he scoffed. "It's what goes on here!" he said, pointing to the eyes and circling his fingers. "And I can see that you're a fighter! There's a twinkling in your eyes which tells me you're not giving up! That's what we want to see. That's what matters."

"She was hoping she might visit Silver Birch," Anna explained. Silver Birch Hospice was the local hospice for which he was the resident consultant.

"Janice, my sister-in-law, went there a few times as a day patient when she had breast cancer. Mum always liked the sound of it."

"Well, to be honest, I don't want to see you there," he replied. "It's not the place for you yet! I'm looking at you and I'm not seeing someone who needs to go there. But when you are ready to go, you'll know and of course we will look after you. As it is at the moment, you should continue to work on getting better, and, who knows, you might even be looking at going home."

"Is that a possibility?" she asked.

"Of course," he replied. "We're not giving up!"

Dr Bennett turned to his colleague, "What do you think, Dr Barber?"

"I agree," he said. "We're all working towards getting you home."

Freda smiled, then beckoned Anna towards her. Her voice hoarse, almost a whisper, she said, "Ask him how that will work in practice. I mean, how will I look after myself?"

Anna relayed her concerns to the two of them.

Dr Barber spoke up - "Well, we can arrange for nurses to call round several times a day to help you wash and dress and give you your meals. I assume you live in a house, so we can have your bed brought downstairs and provide you with a commode and such like."

Freda's face was dropping. She had helped to nurse her own father in a similar set-up years before and had always sworn that she would never end up like that - living in one room dependent on everyone else. That was no life at all. And what about her dogs?

Anticipating her obvious concern for the dogs, Anna spoke up.

"We'd all chip in to help, Mother," she said. Then, to the doctors, "She's got two dogs. She's concerned about them being looked after too."

"Well, I'm afraid we only look after people, not animals," said Dr Barber.

Freda rolled her eyes as if to say 'Well I know that, Stupid!' She would hardly expect nurses to walk the dogs. But she would be concerned about the disruption to Niko and Mollie's routine.

Noting her anxiety, Dr Bennett spoke up again.

"I want you to work on getting better, Freda, and not worry about anything."

"But I'm worried about my voice," she croaked, hardly audible. "I've always been a bit of a gabber, you see. If I can't talk, then I might as well hang up my boots!"

Dr Bennett listened attentively, then walked over to the side of the bed and took hold of her hand.

"Listen. I don't want you thinking about blood levels, or home-helps or anything. I just want you to concentrate on fighting this infection. Mind over matter!"

She gripped his arm back and gave him another big smile.

"Yes, Doctor. I will," she promised.

Squeezing her hand, he winked before turning to leave.

"Come on, Dr Barber!" he said. "There's no rest for the wicked!"

After he'd left, Anna remarked, "What a lovely man!" Freda nodded in agreement.

"Sounds like good news to me, Freda," said Pauline. "Anyway, love, I'll have to get going. The bus comes at ten past. If I get that one, I won't need to change at Ashton."

"I'll give you a lift, Pauline," offered Anna. "You can't be getting two buses, like that. It's only ten minutes in the car."

"Oh that's very kind of you, love. Are you sure? I don't want to put you to any bother."

"Of course I'm sure," said Anna. She looked at her mother. "I'll just take Pauline back then call and take the dogs out for a nice walk. I'll see you later. OK?"

"Yes," whispered Freda. She appreciated being offered time alone. Time to think.

"Come on then, Pauline," said Anna.

"I'm ever so grateful for the lift, love. I didn't tell you about mine and June's recent trip on the bus, did I?"

No, thought Anna. She had a feeling she was about to get every detail.

Freda watched them leave. It was good of Pauline to come all this way on the bus. As a driver herself, she hated the thought of having to hang about all the time waiting for buses, then having to keep stopping and starting. It took an age to get anywhere. When the kids were little, Len had control of the car and rarely let her drive it. Every Sunday she took two buses to her mam and dad's to visit, taking all four of them whilst Len slept off his dinnertime drinking session. They didn't run very often and it wasn't easy with a double buggy. Once or twice she'd taken the car, only to be shouted at when she returned. Selfish sod! It wasn't as if he needed it - the pub was only half a mile away and he shouldn't be drinking and driving anyway - but there was no telling him. Anything for a quiet life, in her opinion.

She thought about that time he had taken the rotor arm out of the engine to disable it and ensure it wouldn't go anywhere - he took it to bed with him! Her dad had gone mad, buying her another rotor arm so she could take the car. But then Len went one further, taking all the leads out of the engine!

"You should wrap them around his neck!" her mother had shouted.

But that was Len - he did what he wanted, when he wanted - sod everyone else.

But she didn't let it get to her. She saved and saved to get her own car - an old green Maxi. True, it wasn't very good looking and it certainly wasn't speedy - she had to lean forward when going uphill! - but it nevertheless got her from A to B and saved her hours in travel time. It did the job. She smiled with pride at the memory.

She still did more than enough walking, of course. For years, the girls used to go to Pony Club every week which was a good few miles away. They took turns to ride there on the mare, Trixie, and needed to be accompanied. She'd spent many an hour walking alongside them to ensure they were safe on the main roads. Rain or shine, she was there. At least she had Jack for company. The bandy-legged Jack Russell Terrier, purportedly belonging to the notorious 'Twinnies' from the local council estate, frequently hung around at the farm, killing off the rats. Fiercely independent, he seemed to know when it was weekend and always turned up to follow her on her journey. His little legs would be going like the clappers as he tried to keep up with them all. He was as fit as a butcher's dog that one! There was more resilience in that little terrier than she'd seen in many a person over the years.

Not that Jack was averse to other modes of transport! She remembered how he regularly took the bus down to Hyde, plodded around the market then got the bus home again completely unaccompanied. All the bus drivers knew him well and didn't bat an eyelid at him bus-hopping. Freda chuckled at the memory. He wasn't dissimilar to Pauline on that score! He'd mastered the skill of travelling for free. She wondered what had become of him.

"Penny for them?" It was Joan from the bed opposite, who was talking now, breaking the spell and bringing Freda back to the reality of the ward. "You looked like you were remembering something nice," she continued.

"Yes, I was," Freda replied quietly.

"I saw your Jean, earlier," Joan said. "She was going into the kitchen with a load of bowls of Angel Delight. I reckon she's made every flavour there is! You'll be spoilt for choice!"

"Sounds about right," Freda replied. "She's determined to make me eat."

"She's looking after you, love."

"I know. She means well," Freda's voice was straining now. "But it's really difficult to swallow anything. Breathing and eating at the same time is a real chore."

"I know," said Joan. "I overheard Michelle telling your Anna. She told her to pinch her nose and then try swallowing. She found it hard. I think it made her appreciate what it's like for you."

"Aw bless! They're good kids," said Freda. "It's just that sometimes they get a bit bossy with it!"

"Yes. I know what you mean. They just want you back to normal, though. It's hard for them to see you suffering."

"I know," replied Freda. "I'll try harder!"

She smiled at Joan who smiled back.

"Ah, here comes Jean now," she said. "Looks like she's brought cakes too."

"They'll be for the nurses," said Freda.

They watched through the glass partition as she placed a large box of cakes on the nursing station, before turning and heading towards them.

"And don't let them doctors have any of them!" Jean shouted back over her shoulder.

"Hello Mother! You'll be pleased to know I've been home and made you three different flavours of Angel Delight - put them in little pots and everything. They're in the fridge when you want them. All you have to do is ask a nurse and they'll fetch you one, or two, or three."

"Oh I won't be able to manage more than one, Jean," said Freda.

"I know that, Mother. I'm not expecting you to. But you won't be able to make your mind up either. This way, you can do your usual."

"What's 'your usual'?" quizzed Joan.

"A bit of each!" said Freda and Jean simultaneously.

They both laughed.

Sylvia looked over in earnest from the neighbouring bed, clearly wishing to join in. Her husband was slumped in the chair, eyes shut, having nodded off. She frowned. Embarrassed, she turned her back on him and caught Freda's eye. A look of recognition passed between them. Noticing this, Jean invited her into the conversation.

"How's it going?" she laughed as she pointed her finger at Sylvia's sleeping spouse.

His mouth was open now and his tongue lolled about sending a dribble of spittle onto his chin. Sylvia pursed her lips and tutted

"Give me strength!" she muttered.

"Glad I don't have one of them anymore!" Freda rasped, adjusting her oxygen mask so Sylvia could hear her properly.

"Lucky you!" she replied, shaking her head in disbelief that she was married to such a thing. Then, changing the subject, added, "I heard you might be going home. Bet you're glad about that, aren't you?"

"Hey you never told me that, Mother!" Jean chipped in, clearly offended.

"Give me a chance!" Freda mouthed. "You've only just got here!"

Joan came to her defence. "It was just something that nice doctor from Silver Birch said earlier," she commented.

"What did he say?" Jean enquired.

Sylvia now took up the duty of explaining - "That she should concentrate on fighting the infection and getting home, rather than worrying about whether she can get a place in the hospice."

"Oh, and I bet you asked about your dogs, didn't you, Mother?" said Jean. She raised her eyebrows and gave her mother a knowing stare.

Wearing the expression of a child who had been caught pinching sweets, Freda avoided her gaze.

Jean slapped her hand on the table in triumph. "Thought so!"

Freda looked chastened. Never mind being concerned about Pauline telling all and sundry about what was going on, it seemed everybody on the ward was party to her conversations. You couldn't keep anything private in here! You only got this with women. Men wouldn't give a monkey's. Sylvia's husband, oblivious to what was going on, and now dribbling more than ever, she observed, was a perfect example of this. Even if he had been awake, he would've taken no notice.

Not wishing to upset her mother by dwelling on the subject, Jean changed tack. What she needed, she surmised, was a bit of reassurance.

"Well, you'll be pleased to know, Mother, that the dogs are doing absolutely fine," she said. She rummaged in her bag and took out her mother's iPad.

"They're getting plenty of exercise and will continue to do so when you're home, so there's no need to worry on that front."

Opening the cover and propping it up on the bed, Jean switched it on.

"Now," she laughed, "I can't be saying the same about your farm!"

Freda looked at the screen as the game opened up. Frowning at the sight, she sat up straight and started tapping away in earnest. Jean settled back in her chair and took out her phone. At last she would have some time to herself. She wasn't going to waste it.

CHAPTER 16

Jean was sitting by her mother's bedside, engrossed in her phone.

"What day is it today?" she asked, looking up.

Freda mouthed the number eighteen then raised her eyebrows in a quizzical look to ask why.

"Because Christine has just texted to say her area has won the postcode lottery, that's why! I don't believe it!"

Jean used to live next door to Christine but had recently moved house.

Freda croaked, "Oh no!"

"I know! Twelve years I've been doing that lottery and haven't won so much as a pound, and then the minute I cancel it, they go and win! I wouldn't mind but I only stopped paying last month. They rang me up asking me if I wanted to keep it going. I said 'No way! That house has been nothing but bad luck. I want out!' And then this goes and happens!"

Jean was properly upset. Freda gave her a sympathetic look.

"I hope to God they don't win the big jackpot," said Jean. "That would be all!"

Just then, Anna returned from the café. Jean told her

the news.

"Well, it's the eighteenth isn't it? What did you expect?" she said, "Something always happens on a date with an eight in it."

"Oh God it is! Yes, you're right. That explains it," said Jean. "That number will be the death of us."

"Aw, it's not always unlucky, Jean," said Anna. "Don't you remember that time when I was living in France, and Mum phoned me up to tell me about winning £1800 on Dickinson's Real Deal?"

"Of course! How could I forget? We never heard the end of it!" laughed Jean.

"You had to guess the price some antiques would fetch at auction, didn't you, Mum?" continued Anna.

Freda nodded.

"You guessed £1800 as it was the tenth anniversary of dad's death and he'd been born on the 18th of September, so you put two and two together," explained Anna. "I remember 'cos you phoned me up 'specially. You turned the volume down whilst you hoovered up and then you saw your name appear on the TV screen! You were well excited weren't you, Mum?"

Freda nodded and smiled. She pulled down her mask. "I used it to get some work done in the garden. Made it nice for the dogs to sit outside."

"Well, it's not lucky this time!" ranted Jean. "I won't be getting bugger all done in the garden!"

"You'll have to ask June for some help with yours, Jean," said Anna. "She's good at designing things. She knows all the plants to put in and everything."

"Who? Fat June? Pauline's best mate?" said Jean. "The one who got stuck in the squeezer gate?"

Freda grimaced at her. June shared a love of dogs and they'd been walking together many a time. They'd go out for hours on end. She was a big woman, it was true, but she was also very kind. She'd never got married or had children of her own so she'd invested all her time in her dogs and in

Pauline's grandchildren. Indeed, when Freda's grandchildren had come along, she'd knitted lots of clothes for them all. Freda didn't like her being berated in this way.

Jean looked at Anna, who was similarly offended.

"What? It's true isn't it? She was too big to go through the gate. Wedged in it she was! Took an age to prise her free."

"She was really hurt by that you know, Jean," Anna said.

"Why? 'Cos she couldn't get home in time to get her pies!" Jean cackled. Then added, "Well, she should've known her limits! Fancy thinking she could get through it when she's built like a brick shithouse!"

"Well, she wanted to finish the walk with Mum,' said Anna. "She couldn't climb over the wall so they'd gone a different route. Luckily, some people came along who were able to help. On a previous occasion she'd not been so fortunate. She'd bent down to pick a flower and fallen over and couldn't get back up. It was a remote area and she was there for several hours before she got any assistance."

"See! She should lay off the pies then, shouldn't she!" laughed Jean.

Anna rolled her eyes. There was no convincing Jean once she got a bee in her bonnet about something.

"Anyway, my point is that June could help you plan out your garden," said Anna.

"Well I'll bear it in mind," Jean conceded. She gave a wry smirk, paused for effect, then continued, "should I need any grass flattening!"

"Jean!" Freda chastened. She held the mask away from her face as she spoke, "June's not well at the moment, actually. She's on a ward at this hospital with a very bad knee. Pauline told me yesterday. Before she visited me, she called in to see how she was."

"It's all that pressure she puts on it!" Jean retorted.

The conversation was interrupted by Ethel shouting from across the ward.

"Nurse! Nurse! What's wrong with this telly? I can't get the channel to turn over. I don't want to watch this rubbish that's on!"

Anna and Jean both looked across at the old woman, then looked at each other and burst out laughing. Holding a remote control aloft, she was pointing it at the television on the wall, frantically pressing every button on it. But rather than swapping the channels, it was altering the bed! One minute it was going up higher and higher and the next it was plummeting down, throwing the poor woman about as it went. They hadn't seen anything so funny for ages! Next, the press of another button sent her tipping right up so her legs were pointing to the sky, revealing her rather ample naked bottom. The giggling was infectious. Soon, all three of them were raucously laughing. Snorting, Freda started coughing, prompting Jean to pat her on the back, whilst Anna went to Ethel's rescue. Returning the bed to its rightful position, and tucking the old lady in, Anna handed her the correct remote, making sure to hang up the one for the bed at the back of the headboard out of her reach.

"God bless you!" Ethel said, then proceeded to go through the full repertoire of channels. Squinting as she did so, Anna doubted that Ethel could actually see what was on anyhow. Sure enough, she soon decided that the TV was a waste of time and switched it off completely, settled down under the covers and was quickly fast asleep.

"Aw, bless!" said Jean.

"I'm surprised she was interested in the first place," said Anna. "It's not as if she'd be able to hear it anyway. Not unless she put it on full blast and then we'd all have to hear it."

"Like our grandad," said Jean. "Do you remember how loud his TV was? You could hear it as you approached the cul-de-sac! God knows what the neighbours thought."

"I know. He wouldn't admit he needed a hearing aid, would he? Mind you, Happy was nearly as bad. He used to get up dead early on a Saturday morning and put on Cowboy and Indian films full blast."

"I remember that, yes," replied Jean. "Poor Andy was on the settee where he'd passed out the night before. Got woken up. Bet he didn't know what had hit him!"

"I know. Happy did that every week and didn't bat an eyelid about who he woke up and yet woe betide anyone else who had the telly on loud when he was trying to sleep!"

Freda chipped in now, " Do you remember that time we were all watching that film that night - you four and Andy - and he kept banging on the floor from upstairs to tell us to turn it down?"

"I do!" said Anna, laughing. "Eventually he came down the stairs in a temper and switched it off."

"Yes!" said Jean. "The banging had stopped and we assumed he'd got fed up and gone to sleep. We were all sitting quietly, enjoying the film, when, all of a sudden, the door was flung open and in he flew!" She clutched at her belly as she laughed.

"His eyes were like organ stops!" Freda laughed. "We all just sat there in disbelief. Do you remember what he did next?" She could hardly control the giggles.

"Aw, yes I do!" said Jean. "Our Peter switched it back on. It had been on about ten minutes or so when all of a sudden, all the electricity went off!"

"Yes! He'd taken the fuse out of the box and gone back to bed with it!" said Freda.

"He was always doing stuff like that," said Anna. "Didn't he tamper with the phone to stop you using it?"

"Yes. He took the mouthpiece out so no-one could hear me," Freda replied.

"Miserable bugger!" said Jean. Then, "Hey! Speaking of mouths, has anyone swabbed your mouth to clean it today, Mother?"

Freda shook her head.

"Our Anna'll do it for you then, won't you, our kid?" asked Jean. "You know I don't do mouths!"

"Oh, right. Is that going on the list along with toenails then," mocked Anna, "of things you don't do?"

"Hey you! I'll remind you that I've been going round to Mum's for months now giving her injections! You know I don't do needles - always been terrified of them. Don't you remember? That's why I always had to have gas when I had any teeth out."

"Oh aye, yes, I remember. You were always at the dentist's!"

Jean chose to ignore that comment and continued, "I had to overcome my phobia, so don't you go criticising me! I've done my bit thank you very much!"

This was true of course. But for her, her mum wouldn't have received the injection within the necessary two-hour window each day. It had taken a lot of willpower on Jean's behalf.

"I'm only pulling your leg, Jean. Of course, I'll do it," said Anna.

She turned to her mother.

"I'll also squirt some of this liquid on your tongue, Mother - this one for the thrush. Judging by what's left in this bottle, you've not been doing that either."

Anna picked up the bottle and tipped it back and forth, inspecting its contents.

Freda groaned. She was fed up of being messed with. Jean clocked the look she gave Anna, then made ready to leave.

"Good luck with that then, our kid." She winked as Anna grimaced back.

"See you tomorrow, Mother!"

"Bye love," Freda replied. Anna took a deep breath and braced herself for the ordeal.

CHAPTER 17

Michelle entered the ward. Jean looked up. She was used to seeing her rushing around doing ward rounds, distributing medicines or giving injections, but this time she was armed only with a hairbrush. She watched as she went over to Chloe who had just woken up. Her mother had left several minutes earlier, carrying a bulging bag which Jean thought was a tad suspicious.

"Hello sweetheart," Michelle said. "I've got a spare moment so I'm going to have a go at your hair. See if I can't make something nice out of it."

With that, she proceeded to lift her up the bed, straighten her legs and make sure she was comfortable, all the while taking care to explain everything that she was doing. Jean went back to her travel brochure on America which she'd picked up earlier this morning whilst doing her Saturday big-shop at the local supermarket.

"Why are you reading that?" rasped Freda, from behind her oxygen mask. "Are you planning a holiday?"

"I'm just looking," Jean replied. "Jessica's mithering to go to Florida - Disney World - so I said I'd have a look. I'm hoping to get our Anna to come with me."

Freda raised her eyebrows. There was no way that Anna

would ever contemplate going on holiday with Jean's kids in tow. She'd accompanied her on a day out to Southport when Jessica was only little and that had been enough. They'd done her head in. It had the Jack Russell, Bobby's, first day out. The kids had not only let him off the lead which had led to a mad chase across the sands to retrieve him, but then they'd fed him endless cakes and biscuits when Anna wasn't looking, which made him throw up. Anna was as fastidious in her treatment of dogs as she was, so Freda understood where she was coming from.

Jessica had gone missing at one point too - whilst Jean was busy admiring two German Shepherds - and then Jake and Jason had thought it funny to hurl her into the sea repeatedly whilst Jean had her back turned, smoking a cigarette. They were lucky she didn't drown. Jean had gone ballistic since she had no spare clothes or even a towel. It was fortunate that Anna had a towel in the car for Bobby, and Ava and Emily had willingly given up some of their layers to help keep her covered up.

It had taken all of Anna's patience not to just pack up and go home, especially as Jean was continually having to holler at the kids to try to keep them in order. She'd thought that supplying the lads with kites apiece would've kept them out of mischief but this had backfired, since all they did was argue over getting in each other's way - a whole beach wasn't a big enough space for two kites it seemed - and they'd ended up tangling them up together. Jean had repeatedly shouted "Don't cross the streams!" in a line taken from *Ghostbusters* but to no avail. Both soon abandoned the new toys in a pile on the sand for Jean to deal with, and reverted to stone skimming and whining endlessly about needing ice-cream. Despite her insistence that they would "no way be getting a chuffing Ice- cream," and her stomping off up the dunes back to the car, Jean had nevertheless relented and bought them each a 99 cornet.

This was much to the annoyance of Anna who, as a teacher, was programmed not to give in. Standards never slipped. Ava and Emily both knew this and were equally annoyed by Jean's lack of resilience. They'd found it hard to believe that their aunty was such a pushover. Jean, of course, just wanted anything for a quiet life. Suitably appeased, the lads had taken up base in the car, playing noiselessly on their various devices and leaving Jean be. She could enjoy an all-girls walk on the beach, accompanied by the puppy, without anyone "pecking her head". She looked forward to the day when the kids would prefer to stay at home rather than insist on being taken out for the day.

Jean was in a world of her own again now, poring over the resort information. Across the way, Michelle was painstakingly brushing out all the lugs from Chloe's hair, strand by strand. For a mother who harped on so much about her daughter's welfare, Freda thought, Barbara had failed to meet her needs. It wasn't the nurse's job to sort out the girl's hair. She watched as Michelle French plaited it and fastened the ends off. Then she fetched a mirror and showed Chloe what she'd done. Eyes open wide, Chloe whooped in glee and clapped her hands. Michelle beamed. It was nice to be appreciated.

"That looks lovely," said Freda. She was barely audible, but Michelle understood. Jean looked up.

"You've done a cracking job of that," she said, "it looks tons better. I'll have to get you to do our Jessica's for her. She's got lovely long hair. I've tried doing that but I just haven't got the knack. Have you had plenty of practice?"

"Not really. I've got three lads, so there's no call for it at our house," she replied. "Don't get the opportunity but for doing my own. It's been nice doing that. I've been itching to get over here and sort her hair out all week. But this is the first chance I've had."

"Can you cut hair as well, love?" a voice boomed out from behind Michelle, making her turn around quickly. She put her hand to her chest and blew out her breath as she recognised Michael who had just arrived on the ward. He was wearing an old pair of jeans and must have come straight from work.

"Only, I could do with a trim!" he continued.

"Don't push your luck, sunshine," Michelle answered.

"Hiya Mum,' he said. "Sorry I'm late, Jean. I got here on time but didn't have any change for the car park. I've had to rummage about the car looking for coins to use. Good job I'm always dropping them! They're dead keen patrolling the car parks 'round here. Didn't want to get another fine."

He proceeded to clear up the bed of all Jean's paraphernalia - magazines, empty Slush Puppie cup, handbag and iPad. He wasn't one for mess.

"You should've said if you had no money, our kid. I can lend you some if you're skint again," Jean said, as she continued to flick through the travel brochure.

"No! You're all right, Jean. I've got the wrong trousers on, that's all! I usually have pockets full of change."

Jean mimicked Wallace from the TV – "The wrong trousers, Gromit!"

Both of them laughed.

He pointed at the brochure, and remarked, "You're not seriously thinking of taking your kids to Florida, are you?"

"Not all of them, no. I was thinking just me and Jessica and then our Anna and Ava and Emily. Make it a proper girls' holiday."

"You're having a laugh, aren't you?" Michael harrumphed. "Our Anna won't agree to go on holiday with your lot. One day at Southport was enough for her. She swore she'd never go again!"

Freda looked on. Michael was saying everything she'd been thinking. Trust him to pull no punches.

"I'll have you know that my kids can be very well behaved when they want to!" Jean retorted.

Freda threw Michael a warning look but he carried on regardless.

"That's my point!" he said, jabbing his finger as he

spoke. "When they want to. But they never really want to, do they?" he chuckled.

"And your Jessica's the worst one of all! Proper little madam she can be! It's hard enough going out for a meal together once every blue moon, let alone trying to spend a week full-time in each other's company. That's the equation, Jean!"

Jean knew this was true. They'd once been asked to leave a restaurant for behaving poorly, and she must be the only mother going who'd actually been barred from Asda's café! Mind you, that was more to do with Joe shouting at the kids than it was with the kids themselves, she recalled.

She pretended to look crestfallen.

"I was thinking more like a fortnight, actually," she said, "It's too far to go for a week."

They looked at each other, then at Freda, who was chuckling to herself. They both burst out laughing.

"Think of it like this," said Michael, "you won't have to put up with Anna's 'routines'. You know what she's like. She'll have everybody up at six to 'seize the day' (Michael made inverted comma gestures with his hands as he spoke) then she'll have it all mapped out like a military operation - where you're going, what you're doing, when you're eating. You'll need another holiday to get over that one! Best stick to what you usually do. Stay at home!"

He took the brochure from her and placed it in the pile of magazines at the side of the bed. "Cheeky sod!" Jean protested. "I'll have you know that we've been on three holidays in the last four years. All to five-star hotels. A bedroom each, several balconies, private swimming pool, and all that lot. Pushed the boat out and went all-inclusive, we did. Ask Mum. She came with us a couple of times, didn't you, Mum?"

Jean looked directly at her mother as she sought to get her on her side.

Freda pulled herself up the bed and nodded in Jean's direction. Jean stood up and began rearranging her mother's pillows so she was propped up. Satisfied that she was comfortable, she continued to defend herself.

"We've been to Greece together and Bulgaria!" she said.

Freda nodded in confirmation.

"We could have travelled to America too. We always said we'd go on a horse-riding holiday - me, Mum and our Anna - like Cowboys. We were going to camp on a ranch and herd cattle, sleep under the stars, eat beans and everything. But we never got 'round to it." Jean paused. Her eyes betrayed a sadness at not pursuing this dream. "Guess we'll never do it now," she lamented.

Freda shook her head. She used to love horse-riding. When the girls were little, she'd saved up like mad to buy them a pony of their own, a bay mare called Trixie, to save them from having to keep following Tracy Jones round on the off-chance they might get a go on her pony, Sovereign. Later, she'd bought herself an ex-riding school horse, Caltah, and spent many a day out trekking with one or other of them as they took it in turns to share Trixie. Of course, they outgrew the mare and then she'd had to re-home Caltah. She'd decided to leave Len and just didn't have the money for his upkeep. By that point, it was only Anna who bothered with him as she herself was busy with the dogs. Anna was off to university anyway. It broke Freda's heart to sell him after so long. He was a cracking horse, a true friend. She smiled as she thought about him.

Michael broke the silence.

"You'd never do it now even if you wanted to, Jean," he said. "You couldn't sit in a saddle all day and camp outside. You're not built for it."

"I know," admitted Jean, "there's not enough fat on my arse anymore to cushion me! Wouldn't want to get saddle sore!"

"Our Anna'd be all right on that score!" Michael laughed. Jean joined in. She turned back towards her mother.

"We like our five-star holidays, don't we, Mum? Doing

nowt but lying by a pool all day stuffing our faces with food. It's the only time I get to eat properly when we go all-inclusive. I even eat salad, don't I, Mum?"

Freda smiled. Jean wasn't a big eater as a rule. Lived on a diet of convenience food, takeaways and cigarettes most of the time. It worried Freda how little she ate, so she really enjoyed going on holiday with her and watching her tucking into proper food, for a change. They'd had a fabulous time last year in Greece. Jake had stayed at home, so they only had Jason and Jessica to look after. They'd made friends with some other kids and so they had great fun playing in the pool each day which gave Jean time to relax. Freda had enjoyed their company.

"Aw, do you remember, Mum? We nearly lost our Jessica?"

Freda nodded. Michael laughed.

"Aw it wasn't funny, our kid." she continued. "We were seeing off her new friend who was going home before us. One minute, Jessica was by my side and the next she'd gone! I shouted to Mum. Then I looked up to see her waving from the back seat of the coach as it was driving away!"

"Really? You're joking?" said Michael, raising his eyebrows.

"No!" Jean replied, "I had to run after the coach to try to get it to stop. You know me, I don't do running! I just about manage walking and breathing at the same time! But I was proper legging it! Can you imagine?"

Freda conjured up the image of Jean trying to run after the coach in her flip flops, screaming at the driver whilst everyone looked on. It was a priceless memory.

"I don't know what I would've done if the coach driver hadn't stopped the coach. We weren't leaving 'til the evening. Mind you, I blame the reps myself. They should check who they've got on board their coaches. It should be routine to count them on and off. I always took my role seriously when I was doing the coach tours with Kirsty."

Michael smiled at this. It was typical of Jean to blame

someone else. She would never have admitted that she should've been watching what Jessica was up to. No doubt, she thought their mum would be keeping an eye on her, as usual.

"Would that be the coach tours you did to Spain, where you took about fifty people but only ever paid for about twenty?" Michael recalled. He had wet some paper towels and was now wiping down the table. "Called for good counting skills, that one did! Some clever accounting! I'm surprised you got away with it!"

"Aw, I know! It was well embarrassing," said Jean. "You'd get to the ferry with this coach stuffed with people and be asked how many passengers you had. You'd look at the ticket and it was always for less than half! We just used to smile and act daft like we didn't know anything about it. We were just two young women to them who didn't know any better! They always let us get on with them all too. Just used to bribe the officials with plenty of duty free!"

Michael had finished cleaning the table. He threw the paper towels into the nearby bin as he spoke.

"That's shocking!" He squeezed some hand sanitiser from the dispenser on the wall and rubbed his hands together. "But at least you could've lost one or two and not been blamed since the evidence was in your favour!"

"Always a bright side!" Jean laughed. "I could happily have left some of them too! They were a right lot of scumbags. We were supposed to make our money selling them food and drink on the journey but they all brought their own. We couldn't say owt to them since we were outnumbered! The only thing they ever asked for was hot drinks. They drew the line at bringing flasks with them. I remember just trying to nod off after being awake for eighteen hours and being woken up at three in the morning by a bloke wanting a hot chocolate. I could've killed him! I was exhausted."

"I'm surprised you made it for him, Jean," said Michael.

"Of course I did! I'll have you know I'm very

professional. I got up and made it and took it to him. I smiled through gritted teeth and told him very politely that if he ever asked me for a drink at that time again, he'd get it over his head!"

Michael laughed. That was more like the Jean he knew! Freda tried to speak from behind the mask.

"What's that, Mum? You're all muffled," Jean said.

She pulled her mask down so that it rested on her chin.

"I said tell him about how you left loads of them stranded over there, Jean." She grinned.

"Aw, that wasn't me! That was Kirsty. I was in the office in Manchester. She got them to the hotel and they didn't have the rooms for them. Turned out that the company director, Geoff, hadn't paid the bills for months so they'd pulled the plug on it all. Kirsty had all these people 'doing one' on her. I wouldn't mind but she'd not even taken the full cohort! I'd had people phoning me up at the office saying the coach hadn't turned up. Where was it? They were standing at the side of the road with their suitcases, inflatables, sandwiches and everything with nowhere to go! It was terrible."

"What did you do about it, our kid?"

"Well I took the phone off the hook, didn't I!"

"Great customer service!" said Michael.

"Well, there was nowt I could do about it, was there?" she replied.

"Poor sods!" mouthed Freda. She thought about the people who always went on that kind of holiday. They never had much money and it would've taken them all year to save up to afford it. It was such a shame.

"Don't look at me like that, Mother!" Jean said as she clocked the expression on her face. "It wasn't my fault. It was Geoff's. Don't forget, I was losing my job as a result of it too, they weren't the only victims."

Jean shuffled forward in her seat until she was perched on the edge of it, then rearranged her cardigan so it covered her knees.

"What happened to him?" asked Michael. Did he get prosecuted?"

"No. He should've done - would've got a few years too according to Kirsty. They throw the book at you if you commit fraud on the scale he did. He hadn't even insured them or anything. He was up to his neck in it," said Jean. She picked some dog hairs off her leggings and flicked them on the floor.

"No. He was really lucky, actually," she continued. "The day before he was up in court, he had a massive heart attack and dropped dead."

Michael winced in disbelief as he parked a chair by the bedside. Lucky! Only his sister could think that was lucky. She made him laugh.

"Anyway, Jean. Let's get back to the original equation. You had to take our mum on holiday with you and the kids 'cos Joe wouldn't go," said Michael. "That must tell you something when even the kids' own dad won't go on holiday with them! And..." he dragged the last point out, "you never went back to the same place, did you? For all you said it was amazing."

"Well it doesn't do to go on the same holiday twice, Michael. Variety is the spice of life!" Jean continued to focus on picking at her clothes.

"Anyway, we preferred it without him. He just wanted to get up at the crack of dawn, frogmarch us for miles, then eat and go to sleep. We don't do mornings as a rule. He used to bugger off to bed every afternoon and leave me with them all so I might as well have been a single parent. It was much better with Mum."

Freda still held the mask in her hand. She held it to one side, taking care to move the straps so that they didn't dig into her cheeks then cleared her throat before speaking,

"You should always go somewhere twice." She paused then added, "The second time to apologise!" She started laughing.

Michael sniggered. Freda laughed even more. Then

more. Soon, she was in fits of laughter. They all were. But then she was laughing so hard that she started to wheeze. Turning red, she began to struggle for breath. Soon, she was gasping for air.

Jean shot out of her chair and began rubbing her back frantically whilst Michael manoeuvred the oxygen mask back onto her face. In a soothing voice, he encouraged her to breathe steadily, as he'd seen the physio do, stroking her hand gently while Jean continued to rub her back. Eventually, he managed to calm her down to the point where her breathing once more became steady and regular. Her eyes were red and watering. He took out a tissue and wiped them carefully. Then he sat down, relieved.

"Bloody hell, Mother! Don't do that to me!" Jean screeched. "You nearly gave me a heart attack! My nerves can't take it!"

"I was only laughing," Freda rasped. "Laughing's supposed to be a tonic."

"Well you can stick to Lucozade from now on," said Michael. "No more laughing out loud!"

"What's this then?" Michelle was back on the ward, alerted by the loud coughing noises which had emanated from the room.

"Are you ok, sweetheart?" she enquired. She took Freda's wrist and looked at her fob-watch, whilst she measured her pulse rate. Freda smiled weakly.

"You need a rest," Michelle continued. She took hold of the mask. "This needs to be on all the time," she said as she gently adjusted the straps. "I'm going to do your stats then give you your nebuliser. You're about due anyway. Then I'm going to get you an injection."

She turned to Jean as she said this. A knowing look passed between them.

"That's enough frivolity for today!" Michelle warned.

"Well, I'd best be off now anyway," said Jean, reaching for her coat. She put it on and fastened up all the buttons but for the top one. Then she leaned over to kiss her mum, ruffling her hair as she did so.

"I'll see you tomorrow, Mother. Bright eyed and bushy tailed!"

Freda squeezed her hand. "Thanks, love."

"See you our kid," said Jean as she made for the doorway.

"Yes, see you tomorrow, love," Michael replied.

He sat down. Then, looking at Michelle, he asked, "When's the drinks trolley coming round, love? I've got a thirst on!"

CHAPTER 18

The afternoon had started off well. Michael had managed to get his mum to eat some of the home-made soup which Peter had left in a flask for her. This time, he'd taken into consideration her difficulty in swallowing and made it of a thinner consistency with no bits in. She'd been reluctant at first since each mouthful was a real effort, necessitating as it did a struggle to breathe at the same time, but Michael had gone to town with his discourse on how much effort his brother must have gone to in order to produce it.

"It's not easy getting fresh ingredients late at night, Mum," he'd said. "He left here and went straight to the supermarket, so he could make that. Not only that, but after he'd cooked it, he had to sieve it so you didn't get any lumps. Slaving away into the early hours, he was."

Michael had "laid it on thick," as Freda would say, and this had done the trick - Peter was number one son after all and could never put a foot wrong in his mother's eyes - so she'd dutifully obliged and tried to swallow some of it.

It was unusual for Michael to talk much - he was generally a listener - but more recently he found he needed to fill in the silences more.

After that, he'd chatted to Mark, the physio, whilst his mum was being encouraged to do her breathing exercises to enable her to cough up various bits of gunge to help clear her chest. This reminded him of his dad, who, as a heavy smoker, had spent every morning in the bathroom making retching noises. Michael had got used to hearing it and it didn't bother him.

"It's a good job it's me that's here and not our Anna," he said to Mark. "She can't cope with anyone coughing up or being sick. When she was at university she worked as an auxiliary nurse on a chest ward in her holidays and that was the one thing that really got to her. She had to assist the nurses in suctioning green stuff out of the throats of the patients who had had strokes. Had to watch it all travelling up the tube and into the canister. It made her heave."

"It did me at first," said Mark, "but I've got used to it now." He pummelled Freda's back with his knuckles.

"She had to stop on the way to The Christie the other week too," Michael continued, "because mum was throwing up in the passenger seat. She gave her a vessel to vomit in then stood outside the car 'til she'd finished."

Freda nodded in recollection of this.

Freda was no longer bothered by anything like that. Having had four kids, she'd trained herself so she was accustomed to people vomiting. She came from strong stock, his mum! Blood, bones, gore - none of it seemed to bother her. In fact, she enjoyed nothing more than watching an operation on the television or even, more recently, a post-mortem. She relished in the opportunity to observe any surgeon at work, adding numerous programmes on the subject to her list of things to record.

Better still, she loved to recount these stories to anyone who was prepared to listen. She had a whole repertoire of tales to draw on in her conversations. Her sister, Aubrey, had been just the same. Both of them could recall in minute detail the ins and outs of countless operations they'd seen on the telly, often at the most inopportune moments as far as any squeamish guests were concerned!

Michael remembered his cousin, Penny, telling him about when her mum had been in hospital following an emergency operation to remove a large part of her bowel. She hadn't eaten any proper food for what seemed like days, not having felt up to it. Penny's husband, Barry, had called to visit her and had been pleased to see her having a go at some pea soup. A tall man, of strong stature, you'd be forgiven for thinking that nothing would faze him. But you'd be wrong. Part way into the soup, and having been deprived of a good natter for ages on account of feeling so terrible, Aubrey had begun to relay the details of her operation as she understood them. In full flow, there was no stopping her. To be honest, he may as well have been a cardboard cut-out for all she cared, oblivious as she was to his presence, such was her desire to talk to anyone prepared to listen.

Ravenous, she was devouring the green liquid. The more she ate, the more she talked between spoonfuls, the more details she gave. There were no holds barred.

As such, she failed to notice how uncomfortable she was making him feel. She failed to notice the colour draining from his face. She failed to notice his eyes glazing over - until it was too late…

Smack! His head whacked the floor as he toppled from his chair. Instantly, hospital staff were legging it over to deal with him. Forget all the other poorly patients in their charge. Forget that most of them needed constant supervision. Here was a visitor in need of urgent assistance!

So, when Penny turned up five minutes later, having taken the afternoon off to spend time with her mother, she'd found herself having to deal with her husband instead. Far from sympathetic - having been ordered by the doctors to escort Barry to A&E - she'd only had time to say a quick hello to her mother, before having to depart to another part of the hospital. She was livid. Barry found himself being frogmarched out of the ward and being given an ear-bashing by his enraged spouse. Michael chuckled to himself, as he remembered what she'd said. Penny didn't take any messing from 'soft' people. Once Barry had been triaged and she'd learned he might have to wait up to four hours to be seen, she'd quickly persuaded him that he'd "be fine!" and taken him home.

So, now, on the ward, everything was going smoothly, 'ticking over nicely' as his mother would say. But then, enter stage right, like a pantomime villain, the young doctor who had admitted his mum in the first place - the one Jean had nicknamed 'Dr Death'. Flying onto the ward like a whirling dervish, he'd rushed up to the bed, and, without so much as a 'hello', told Freda she was having an X-ray. "Now!"

Feeling sleepy after her medicines, Freda was caught off guard. But she had no time to prepare as he already had a machine in the wings, ready to go. Having commandeered two auxiliaries to lift and move her into the correct position on the bed, without any explanation of what he was doing, he proceeded to draw the curtains around her and impatiently continued with the procedure, only taking the time for everyone to stand out of harm's way whilst the X-ray was taken. All the while he was ranting about how it was "ridiculous" that this hadn't been done already, and it was "a bit late in the day to be doing it now since everyone knew that she was dying."

Michael was incredulous. How dare he come out with this! He looked at his mum. She might not be able to speak much but there was nothing wrong with her hearing. She stared at the doctor in disbelief. What had he just said? She was crestfallen. Michael watched on in horror as his mum's face changed. No longer the rosy cheeks. No longer the mischievous smile. No longer the twinkling eyes. Just blankness. It was like her light had just been switched off. In one moment, in one tactless word, this doctor had delivered a death blow to his mum. His lovely, kind mum, who never wished any harm on anyone, was now lying in a shrunken state, bottom lip trembling. It broke his heart to witness this.

Apparatus removed, auxiliaries departed and the doctor having moved onto his next victim, Michael was left to pick up the pieces of his broken mother, now just lying there and staring into space. He was lost for words. He knew there was nothing he could say to comfort her and he felt utterly helpless. He wanted to march after the doctor and give him a piece of his mind. He wanted to ask him who he thought he was bullying patients in this manner and treating them with so little respect. He just wanted to scream!

But he wouldn't do that, of course. He couldn't. His mum needed him. So, fighting any inclination to chase after the doctor, Michael returned to his mother's bedside, and carefully took hold of her hand, squeezing it gently, to tell her he understood. She responded by gripping his hand. He noticed the tears in her eyes and resisted the temptation to shed tears of his own. He had to be strong. They sat quietly together, comfortable in each other's company, no one speaking. Eventually, she succumbed to tiredness and drifted off into a fitful sleep. Michael kept watch.

The afternoon wore on. The nurses bustled about. The cleaners continued with their chores. Various specialists did their ward rounds then left. The next shift of nurses arrived and received updates on the patients from those going off duty. Michael continued to sit there. Thinking.

He saw it was starting to go dark outside. He checked his watch. The nights were drawing in. Summer was coming to an end, it seemed. He waited patiently for his sister to arrive, so he could tell her what had happened. All the while, he never let go of his mum's hand, just as he knew she would never want to let go of his. And he wracked his brain as to what he was going to do.

CHAPTER 19

Anna arrived to find Michael walking out of the unit, clearly keen to intercept her before she got onto the ward. Seeing the immediate panic on her face, he was quick to reassure her.

"Don't worry, Mum's sleeping," he said. "I've only left her for a minute. I wanted to speak to you before you got in there. It's been awful."

He proceeded to tell her all about the visit from Dr Death. Anna had never seen him so upset. By the time he'd finished, she too was really angry.

"You've got to do something about it, our kid. He can't go round treating people like that," said Michael. "Honestly, I've never heard anything like it! When he'd finished with Mum he went off but then came back to start on Ethel!"

"What do you mean?" asked Anna.

"Well he told her she needed an X-ray and she told him to 'get lost' as she 'wasn't having a bloody X-ray!' She was well confused. But he hadn't even introduced himself or anything. He never even put the curtains 'round the bed."

Anna understood why he might not put the curtains around a patient if he was on his own with her. But she should've been chaperoned anyway. She remembered seeing him on a previous occasion and recalled his impatience. The nurses were probably too busy but he wouldn't have wanted to wait.

"Poor sod probably wondered who the hell he was," Anna said.

"I know!" said Michael. "And you know how deaf she is, right? Well, he was shouting out at her - 'You need to cooperate or you're going to die! You're going to die!' "

Anna was horrified. Although Ethel was none of her business, she felt obliged to stick up for her. She'd only had one visitor in all the time she'd been there - a grand-daughter - and she hadn't stopped long as she had a small child with her who kept running off. Anna wondered why some people bothered visiting when it was clear they couldn't invest any quality time in the experience. A sense of duty wasn't always justified.

"Where is he now?" Anna enquired.

"Gone off to persecute someone else, I expect," replied Michael. "I overheard him say he was coming back later. Keep an eye out for him and don't let him near our mum again."

"How is she?" asked Anna.

"Not good. It's like all the hope just went out of her. I've never seen her like that before. She's gone to sleep now. Hopefully the rest will give her chance to think things through more clearly."

"Did Mum say anything? After he'd gone, I mean?" asked Anna.

"No. Nothing. She just stared into space. I couldn't say anything to him in front of her, could I? And I didn't want to leave her on her own after that."

"No. You did right, Michael," Anna reassured him.

"It's a good job our Jean wasn't here, I can tell you!" said Michael.

"You're right. She would've gone ballistic at him. Or hit him!" Anna laughed.

"Yes. Then this would be another one to add to her list of places from which she's banned!" Michael smiled.

"Perish the thought!" said Anna.

"Right, well, I'd best be going now. I need a fag after all this! When Mum wakes up tell her I'll be back tomorrow."

"Will do. See you later."

Anna took a moment to sit down and think. It was obvious that her mother's health was deteriorating. Since she'd been admitted to hospital, she'd had to be given a special mattress, had stopped walking to the toilet by herself and had had to be catheterised. The oxygen mask was worn constantly now and the percentage levels had been increased. Moreover, she'd been written up for morphine and was being given regular injections during the day. She knew from her experience on the Care of the Elderly unit that this wasn't a good sign. It was something done near the end of life to keep someone comfortable. Up to this point, however, she'd wanted to believe that all this was somehow reversible. As Dr Bennett had said, it was all about hope and spirit, not necessarily the mechanics and statistics. Human nature defies medicine. And her mum had lots of spirit. Or used to have.

Her thoughts were interrupted by the sound of footsteps. There he was! Passing by in front of her was the man who had so rudely taken hope away from her mother. This was her opportunity to strike.

"Excuse me, Doctor. Please can I have a word?" she asked.

"Oh, hello. I'm just on my way to see your mother. Shall we talk by her bedside?" he said, continuing to walk briskly.

"No. I really don't think that's a good idea. Can we talk in private, please?"

"Of course. I'll just ask the staff nurse to come along too," he replied.

He opened the door to a small room on the left usually reserved for visitors. It was unoccupied.

"I shan't be a minute," he said, as he held the door open for her.

Anna wandered in and perched on the end of a seat. A couple of minutes later, the doctor came in, followed by Michelle. Anna was relieved to see a familiar and friendly face. She rose to formally introduce herself and shake his hand, determined to model how to be professional in one's conduct. She said 'hi' to Michelle, then they all took seats across from each other.

"I'd like to talk to you about your mother," he started. "We've taken an X-ray this afternoon and the results aren't good. Your mother is not responding to treatment in the way we had hoped."

He was so matter-of-fact, it made Anna cringe. Believing he was coming to apologise for his outburst this afternoon, she was completely mistaken. Rather, he just wanted to lay out the facts as he saw them. He could have been talking about any inanimate object, rather than her lovely mum. She took a deep breath, then began,

"Forgive me, Doctor, but have you any idea how you have come across this afternoon? Do you know what you've said to our mother? Do you know how much you've upset her and my family?"

He looked perplexed.

"I've just told her the truth, that's all," he explained. "It's my job to diagnose patients and tell them what's happening. I believe in being honest."

"Really?" said Anna. She felt her voice going up an octave and tried to control it.

She continued, "So you think that telling someone they are going to die, out loud, on the ward, in front of everyone else, is appropriate? Could you not have thought about how best to break the news? That's my mother in there. She knows she's terminally ill, of course she does. But she's a hopeful person full of spirit. And my brother's just witnessed you knock all that out of her!"

"I just tell it how it is," he said, calmly. "There's no use pretending it's any different. I'm not here to deceive people. I wouldn't be doing my job properly if I told you lies."

"I appreciate that, Doctor, but there are ways and means," replied Anna. "We've been in here for weeks now and we know the score. We know our mum isn't going to get better, and she does too. But she doesn't need it shoving down her throat in the manner you did this afternoon. You destroyed her today. How would you feel if someone treated your mother like that? Like an object of no importance? Just another old woman taking up a hospital bed? What would you say to that?"

The doctor opened his mouth to reply but Anna wouldn't let him speak. She was getting more and more angry and upset.

"You'd want to do what I'm doing now!" she continued. "You'd want to take that doctor to one side and tell him what you think of him. Remind him of his duty to the patient. Remind him that this is your mother. She's fragile and vulnerable enough. She doesn't need knocking down by the very person whose job it is to take care of her."

Anna stopped. She could feel the tears running down her face. She wiped them on her sleeve. She had wanted to be brave and not cry. She'd failed. Michelle picked up a box of tissues from the coffee table and passed them to her. Taking one, she wiped her eyes and thanked her, before returning the box. She took some deep breaths.

The doctor looked at her straight on.

"I'm sorry if I've upset your family," he said, "but I've always been a pragmatist. I tell it like it is. Some truths are harder to swallow than others. There's no easy way of telling people these things, so I just come out with it."

"Yes. Well I'm a pragmatist too," said Anna. "I call a spade a spade. I don't pussyfoot around like you seem to infer. But I'm also able to empathise with people. I structure my response to meet their needs and think before I speak. There are better ways of getting the message across. You didn't have to do it like that. What you did was cruel."

"With hindsight, I suppose I could have discussed it with the family first," he admitted.

"Yes. You should have. We know our mum best and we know how to approach matters with her. We could have broken it to her gently and let her prepare - parried the blow. You've taken that away from us now. She's devastated."

"Once again. Apologies. Is there anything you'd like to know about her prognosis? Would you like me to speak to your brother? And haven't you got a sister? Would you like me to speak to her too?"

"I've two brothers and a twin sister," said Anna. "And, no, I don't think you should speak to any of them. My brother, Michael, wouldn't thank you for it, and Peter is still in denial so he's best left to us. As for Jean! Well, let's just say she is the less calm one out of the two of us. You'd best keep out of her way. She's already marked your card. You're not on her list of favourite people."

She looked across to Michelle, who smiled at her knowingly.

"Well, I'll take my leave of you, then, Mrs Croft," he said, standing up to shake her hand. "If there's anything you need to know then please don't hesitate to ask."

"Oh I think you've said enough actually, Doctor. Good afternoon," Anna said, taking a deep breath and drawing herself up to her full height.

Looking chastened, he exited the room. Michelle stayed behind.

"Are you all right, darling?' Michelle asked. Putting down her clipboard, she came over and hugged Anna close. Anna began to sob on her shoulder.

"Go on darling. You let it all out. It's a shock, I know. No-one wants to be told they're going to lose someone. I know how you feel. I love your mum to bits even though I've only known her a short amount of time. She's a great character and I'll miss her. From when we are born, our death is the one absolute certainty in life. But nobody ever talks about. It's daft really. No one can avoid it! It happens to everyone whether they want it to or not. This is why we all need to make our lives the best they can be before it's too late. Make the most of the time that's left with your mum. Tell her how you feel about her. It's what you've all been doing so well these last few weeks. It's marvellous to see how much you all care for her."

"We do," Anna cried. "That's why I got so upset about that doctor's manner. He didn't seem to care like we do."

"I know, darling. He seems to lack a bedside manner."

"He was awful to Ethel too!" Anna said.

"I heard. But don't worry about it. What's done is done. I'll be having words with the ward sister about his conduct," replied Michelle.

"It is what it is, as our Peter would say!" Anna joked. She pulled herself away from Michelle and wiped her eyes.

"Oh God, look at your uniform! It's all wet now. Sorry."

"Oh, it's had worse things than tears on it, believe me!" Michelle smiled. Her eyes were damp too.

"I'd best be off to see to the patients," she said. "Make sure that doctor's not causing any more trouble! You go and freshen up. Take your time. You don't want your mum seeing you like this."

"I will. Thanks Michelle."

"You're welcome, darling. You did really well to speak to the doctor like you did. You were very professional."

"Despite my blubbering?" said Anna.

"Well he didn't see all of that, did he? You kept it together. Well done."

With that she left, leaving Anna to ponder on what to do next.

CHAPTER 20

There was an elephant in the room. Not just any old elephant but a huge, great giant of an elephant. Everyone tried to ignore it, pretending it was invisible. But it wasn't going away...

Freda was lying in the bed, surrounded by all four of her offspring. When was the last time they'd got together as a family? Certainly not for Christmas or Easter for many years now. They each had families of their own - one or other of them always had somewhere else they had to be. Even on the occasion of her 70th, just three years ago, when Jean had thrown a surprise party for her at the local restaurant, Peter had been unable to come since he was working away. She worried about the amount of time he spent at work to the detriment of everything else. It wasn't healthy.

Thinking about it, it was probably Aubrey's funeral when they last met up as a group, unless you counted that one time when they'd gone for the Chinese and she'd got drunk and lost her teeth. She smiled recalling the memory. But now, here they all were, when she needed them the most. She wished the circumstances were different.

Lorna, the Macmillan nurse, was on her way to see her.

She was bringing along a friendly lady doctor she knew who could explain matters clearly. Conscious of how heavily she was breathing into her oxygen mask, Freda made a determined effort to regulate her breath using the exercises which Mark had taught her. In, out. In, out. She could feel her pulse slowing down to a more normal beat. In, out. In, out. It was working. In, out. In, out. She'd never really thought about her breathing in this way before - for seventy-three years, she'd just taken it for granted. That's what your body did automatically. How times changed.

The only saving grace was that the mask filtered out the smell of the ward. She'd never liked that smell. Old people. Stale urine. Disinfectant. The only exception was the maternity ward. The smell of new babies. Talcum powder. Life. She loved that smell!

From her position of hiding, behind the mask, she took a moment to survey her surroundings. Anna, she observed, was sitting slightly back from the bed, just out of her direct line of vision. Like herself, she was no doubt deliberately avoiding engaging in any eye contact that would give away her feelings. Peter was also pretending to look busy, staring at his phone. Only Jean and Michael were speaking, about anything and everything, rambling in their need to fill the silence.

"What you been up to, our kid?" Michael asked.

"Tidying Mum's house," she replied.

Catching her name, Freda instinctively tuned in on the conversation. She raised her eyebrows, in mock disbelief.

Noticing this, Jean teased, "Hey you! I'll have you know I've been keeping your house super tidy whilst you've been in here. Washed up and everything. I've even ironed the bedding."

Freda found this hard to believe. She knew for a fact that the only things Jean ever ironed were those items she had to, like the kids' school shirts and her own work clothes. She was lucky if her duvets had covers on, let alone ironed covers! Still, she appreciated that Jean was trying. Both she and Anna had been stopping there on and off over the last few weeks so they could look after the dogs. She didn't know what she would have done without them. She felt a tinge of sadness as she thought about Mollie and Niko.

"As a matter of fact, Mother, I also tidied your hallway. And I discovered a shedload of Our Dog magazines," Jean continued.

"Yes, I have a subscription. Been buying it for years," Freda croaked.

"I know!" Jean replied. "But you haven't been reading them! Most of them still had the cellophane on."

"I haven't got round to it yet," Freda rasped, then added, "Don't throw them away!"

"Don't worry," replied Jean. "Tempted though I was to fill up your recycling bin, I resisted and stacked them all neatly for you."

"She likes to collect things," explained Michael. "Like those people in that programme on TV about hoarding. You're one of them, aren't you, Mother? You should be on it!"

Then, looking at Jean, he added, "If you think that's bad, you ought to try looking in the cupboard under the stairs - it's a war zone! There's stuff in there that she's not seen for years! Letters, cards, and all sorts. It looks like she's never thrown any post away."

Freda looked sheepish. It was true, in part. Lacking Anna's disciplined approach to mail, she never bothered sorting through it and separating out the junk. Rather, she put letters in carrier bags meaning to do it at a later date, then put these out of sight, and out of mind. Before she knew it, they had built up into quite a stockpile. But this had only happened since she took ill. She lacked any motivation to tackle it.

"Well at least they're tidied away, Jean," said Anna. "It's more usual to see opened envelopes behind the clock on the mantelpiece, bearing messages." She leant forward and nudged her mother, giving her a surreptitious wink. Freda

189

gave her a playful poke her in the arm.

"Recycling!" Freda mouthed. She was well aware of how many lists she regularly produced. They were always useful. And she frequently scribbled numbers onto the back of envelopes which happened to be handy when she was on the phone.

"Yes, right!" Jean said. "Is that what you're calling it? I'm surprised that Mollie has never ripped up your post. Bobby chews up Anna's post all the time. It's a terrier thing. You know how much she likes shredding paper."

"Not as much as she enjoys eating iPods apparently!" Peter interjected, looking at Anna.

"Mollie's got taste, actually, Peter," Anna continued. "She doesn't like any old paper." She paused for effect - "She prefers banknotes!"

"Banknotes?" asked Michael.

"Yes. Don't you remember? Mum was on the phone in the hallway…"

"Isn't she always?" Peter interrupted. Anna ignored this.

"…and when she went back in the living room, £30 had gone off the table!"

"Are you sure it wasn't our Michael borrowing it?" Peter asked.

"Hey! Get lost, our kid. I don't take stuff without asking!" Michael looked insulted.

"No, it wasn't," Anna replied. "Mollie was in the corner with one of the notes between her paws chewing it up. Mum was gutted. It was the last of her pension which she needed for her shopping."

Freda nodded in agreement.

"Well, you will have stupid dogs, Mother!" Peter said. "You should stick to guinea pigs like our Janice has. A lot less trouble."

"Taste nice too," Anna added, having tried one out on a trip to Ecuador. "You should try barbecuing it, Peter."

"Aye. I would do, but there's not much meat on it. Not

like your rabbit," he smirked.

Anna continued, ignoring his jibe, "Well it was all right in the end. She phoned the bank and they said that as long as she could find the serial numbers to each note, they'd honour them and reimburse her."

"Really?" said Michael.

"Yes. They paid up. But Mum was mortified going up to the counter with little bits of notes!"

"I'm not surprised," said Jean, then, "Hey, do you think she nicks cigarette packets too, 'cos I've had a few disappear in the last few days. I've literally just gone upstairs and when I've returned, they've vanished."

"That'll be your Jessica," said Peter. "Never mind blaming an innocent dog!"

"No it won't, Peter! Jessica's never touched a cigarette in her life. There's only Jake out of my three kids who smokes, actually, and he wasn't in the house at the time."

"It's Mum's 'guests' " Michael offered by way of explanation. "They're always moving stuff around. It happened when I lived there. Did my head in."

He was referring once again to the two ghosts who apparently lived upstairs in the house. It sent a shiver up Anna's spine. She was stopping there on her own later and wasn't looking forward to it. The last thing she wanted was a reminder of how scary it was.

"Not that old mumbo jumbo again!" said Peter, who had never believed a word of any of it. He wasn't one for superstition and paranormal activity. "Just take our kid with you, Anna. He reckons he can draw them and they'll disappear!"

Michael looked at his mum, then Jean. When he'd been living at the house, he had experienced many odd things such as waking up in the early hours to find himself covered in suitcases, but the incident with the head in a box floating in front of him was the weirdest of all. It had really frightened him. He'd picked up a pencil and sketched it quickly on one of his mum's used envelopes to show her.

It had promptly vanished.

"Cross my heart, our kid. I saw what I saw. That's the equation," Michael said defensively. "Ask Mum. She saw the colour drain from my face and came over to see what I was doing then saw it for herself."

Freda nodded. Anna looked a bit freaked out. Noticing this, Jean chipped in, "That's nothing, our Anna. You should hear about the fly!"

She started to laugh. Michael joined in.

"Oh my God. Now that was weird!" said Michael.

"Oh. Don't tell me. I've heard this one," Peter joked. "There was a fly that came to visit you and Mum every night after tea. It sat on your hand and you both stared at it! What you fail to mention is that you'd been on the pop all day, and smoking that wacky backy of our Jean's in the house. You were probably both off your heads and made it up!"

"No! Not a word of a lie, our Peter," said Jean. "I saw it."

"And what do you suppose it was, then, Jean?" asked Peter.

"I've no idea but flies don't do that," she replied.

"It was probably a different fly every night," he retorted.

"No it wasn't! I know that 'cos it had a blob of white paint on it. It was definitely the same one every night. I don't know what it wanted but it was dead chilled out. It sat there proper still on our Michael's hand like it was a pet. In fact, Peter, when our Michael tapped his hand, it rolled over and played dead."

"Yeah, right! Likely story!" Peter mocked. "So, where is it now then?"

"I don't know," Jean answered. "What happened to it, Michael?"

"I don't know, Jean," he replied. "But it was definitely a sign for something."

"Yes it was," chuckled Peter. "It was a sign that our mother's house needed spraying for insects!"

"Don't joke!" implored Michael. He was really quite

serious.

Just then, they were interrupted by the arrival of Lorna and her friend whom she introduced to everyone as Dr Morris. Peter stood up and pointed to his chair.

"There you go, flower," he said. "Park yourself there."

He went off to fetch two more chairs. On the way back, he paused briefly and took a deep breath to steel himself for what was to come.

Once everyone was seated around the bed, the curtains were partly drawn. This gave an illusion of privacy to the meeting. Lorna went first.

"Freda, this is Dr Morris, who I was telling you about. She's here to answer any questions you might have."

Freda mouthed "Hello" and offered a smile as the smartly dressed woman to her right took hold of her hand and squeezed it gently.

"I've read your notes and I see that you were diagnosed with lung cancer just a short while ago," Dr Morris began.

"It was only five months ago!" Jean interjected.

"Well, it appears from your recent X-ray that the tumour is embedded around your lungs. You've had an infection for many days now, too, which isn't responding to any of the antibiotics they've tried giving you."

"All them bugs still having a picnic, Mother!" Jean added, trying to keep the tone light and stave off the news which she knew was coming.

"Have they been giving her enough medication, though, Doctor?" Peter enquired. "Only, when I was here the other day, they didn't seem to have a scooby doo what they were doing. They asked me to guess how much she weighed as they were unsure of the dosage."

"Usually they would have weighed you, Freda," Lorna explained, ignoring the criticism, "but you are quite weak now, aren't you?"

Freda nodded almost imperceptibly.

Lorna turned to Peter. "They will have given her

enough, Peter. The drugs just aren't working."

"There's a song in there somewhere," Michael joked nervously. Lorna smiled at him.

"Are there no other treatments they could try, Doctor?" asked Anna.

"I'm afraid not," she replied.

"I never understood why they didn't just cut the tumour out in the first place," Anna commented, "instead of all that chemotherapy they put mum through."

"It was inoperable," Lorna explained. "Chemotherapy was the best option to try and destroy it."

"We always knew that it wasn't going to cure her, Anna," Jean said, looking her straight in the eye. "We've just been fighting time."

Time. That word again. So little and yet so precious. The word resonated in Anna's ears reminding her once again of the day - that day - when her mum had received the results of her scan. When the devastating blow had been delivered.

Fighting back a tear, Anna was taken back to *that day*. The 8th of March. A Wednesday. The day that marked the turning point. The day would be etched in her mind forever.

She recalled a small room in the hospital. Four chairs. Herself and Jean seated by a door, their mother seated opposite by a window, Lorna, newly introduced as the Macmillan nurse, seated to the side between a second door and a small metal bed draped in a white sheet. Dr Kane arrived, perching herself on the edge of the bed. Casually dressed in jeans and a checked shirt, she wasn't what Anna had been expecting the consultant in charge to look like. She'd had a small brown bag clipped around her waist which looked very similar to the one she'd seen her mother wearing when she took the dogs out for a walk. She remembered wondering if it too was stuffed with dog treats and poo bags and sharing a look with her mum which suggested they were thinking the same thing.

She'd watched her mother relax a little at the sight of such an ordinary looking individual. A woman not unlike herself. Yet different in one very important respect. She had power - because she had answers. And for that, she deserved respect.

Formalities quickly dispensed with, the inevitable could be delayed no more. The day they'd learn their mother's fate. The day they'd learn what form of cancer she had and how far it had spread. The room was silent. Everyone waited, until Freda broke the silence:

"Is it bad news?"

Dr Kane looked Freda directly in the eye, "Yes, I'm afraid so."

Jean and Anna looked at each other. Freda stared at the doctor and she bit down on her lip. Her left hand reached up to her neck as she sought out the crucifix she always wore. She wrapped her fingers around it and gripped it tightly, bracing herself.

The doctor continued, "Mrs Simpson, I'm afraid to say that your scan revealed that you have Stage Four lung cancer."

"Stage Four? But? How many stages are there, Doctor?" Freda asked.

"Four."

"Four? But...? How long have I got?" Freda asked.

"Six to eighteen months."

"Months? I thought you'd say years! Our Aubrey had two types of cancer and she got five years. I'd be happy with five years. I thought you were going to say years..."

Her voice trailed off as she realised what was being said. Her bottom lip began to tremble. No-one spoke a word.

A shaft of light shone through the window, illuminating the myriad dust specks dancing in the air. Nobody moved.

Dr Kane continued to hold Freda's gaze. Jean and Anna just stared in disbelief, trying to process what they'd just heard. Ordinarily they might have run over to their mother who looked so vulnerable now. Ordinarily they might have hugged her and told her that it would all be all right. But this wasn't ordinary and their response wasn't either. The weight of the situation kept them both locked in their chairs, unable to move. Unable to offer any comfort.

The doctor broke the silence: "Well, I'm not God and it's not an exact science. I could be wrong. I'd be hoping for eighteen months rather than six. Let's try some treatments and see if we can't improve your situation."

That was that. It had been a lot to take in - about chemotherapy and radiotherapy and such like. The only thing Anna clearly remembered was that her mother's pressing concern had been about her hair!

"Will my hair fall out?" she'd asked. "Will I have to have a wig? That's what happened with our Aubrey, you know, my sister. She lost all of it - even her eyebrows disappeared! I don't want to lose my hair. You wear a headscarf and you advertise your fate to all and sundry. I don't want everyone knowing my business!'

"Your hair won't fall out," the consultant replied.

"Are you sure? Our Aubrey's did. She had bowel cancer."

"It definitely won't," the consultant reiterated. "Not with this type of treatment."

Freda took a sigh of relief.

"Good. That's one saving grace then. One less thing to worry about."

The consultant stood up to leave.

"Well, I'll leave you with Lorna then, Mrs Simpson. You can ask her anything you want. Take your time to consider the options. No rush. Let her know what you want and she'll set it all up. Lovely to meet you."

She shook Freda's hand, nodded at everyone else and left.

Freda took a long sigh. For once she was stuck for words. Her mind was blank.

Ever the practical one, but feeling too overwhelmed to

ask any questions, Anna obtained some leaflets from Lorna along with her business card so she could contact her when she felt ready.

They'd walked out of the hospital saying nothing about it, exchanging mere banalities. But it had been their way of coping.

Anna had the day off school and Jean didn't need to go back to work, so they'd taken themselves off to the garden centre - a large piece of lemon meringue and a cup of tea was in order to assuage the pain. They'd even bought extra slices to take away. Pushed the boat out. Bought a whimsical ornament for the garden. A large stick with an owl's head on it. On any other day they would have ignored it. It was expensive for what it was. But that didn't matter today. Freda loved owls and she loved gardens. She could have anything she wanted.

"We can talk about this another time if you prefer?" Anna heard Dr Morris and zoned back into the conversation which was taking place today. She felt the all too familiar knot in her chest tighten. Shuffling in her seat, she tried to get comfortable. She needed to pay attention. As ready as she was ever going to be, she looked at the doctor and got ready to join back in

.

CHAPTER 21

Dr Morris was still seated at Freda's bedside. Little else was going on in the ward. The physios had been and gone and the tea lady was clearing away cups and saucers onto her trolley. With her eyes firmly trained on her patient, Dr Morris gently rubbed her hand between her own as she spoke.

"Freda, we both know the prognosis here. We know what the outcome is going to be. Is there anything you wish to discuss?"

"You don't have to speak in front of everyone here, if you don't want to," added Lorna, "I'm sure your family will understand if you want to speak privately later." She cast her eyes around all four of Freda's offspring, gauging their feelings. None of them spoke but just gazed at their mother.

Freda reclaimed her hand from the doctor's grasp and fiddled with her mask, drawing it down so it rested on her chin. Clearing her throat, she looked her in the eye then spoke in a rasp,

"They've all been really good to me, Doctor. I can say what I need to in front of them. They know the score."

She tried to smile but quickly turned her head back

towards the doctor.

"I do have one question for you, though," she added.

Freda paused then rummaged around in the bed as she searched for the words. Locating the top of the bedsheet, she gathered its edges up towards her before letting it go. She began to carefully fold it. Once. Twice.

All was still. Everyone was watching her intently, mesmerised by her actions. Using the flats of both hands, she gently smoothed out the crisp, white sheet. Satisfied that she was ready, she spoke directly and assertively.

"My only question, Doctor, is what will it be like? I've always hoped I'd just go to sleep one day and not wake up. It's just that I'm scared I won't be able to get my breath. That happened to me before I came in here and it proper frightened me. I don't want to suffocate. It won't be like that, will it?"

Nobody spoke. Nobody could speak. The room was so silent.

Jean looked at Michael but then quickly looked away and focused instead on the pile of magazines at the bottom of Ethel's bed. She began to count them. Michael continued to stare into space. Peter stared at his iPhone. Anna looked down at her mother's hand which was now once again sandwiched between those of the doctor. It looked so soft and warm.

Memories of her childhood flooded back - she was a little girl again, clutching her mother's hand as they crossed the busy road; she felt safe as she remembered those hands keeping her afloat in the swimming pool; as they held the reins of her determined pony preventing it from running away with her. She was a teenager again being propped up at the side of the car the first time she'd ever got drunk, being given a leg up over a wall when they were out walking, being pushed and pulled as they jived together at a club in Corfu. She recalled her mother looking down at her hands frequently and remarking "Look at my hands! I've got hands like a navvy! I should've been a fella!"

A strong pair of hands. A safe pair of hands. Such a contrast to the hands she now saw which seemed so much smaller. Delicate, the skin paper-thin.

Anna allowed her eyes to slowly venture upwards. Up past the folded down sheet, past the oxygen mask now hanging by her mother's chest and up towards her face. Although her body gave her an air of composure, her face betrayed her. Her cheeks were red. Her eyes were watery. Her whole demeanour had changed. She looked fragile.

Anna heard Dr Morris take a deep breath, in preparation for her response. All eyes were on her. She spoke slowly and deliberately, choosing every word with care.

"We'll do everything we can to make you comfortable," she said. "But I can't promise you that you'll just go to sleep. I don't know what it will be like."

Freda bit down on her lip.

Lorna tried to reassure her, "It won't be like it was that night, Freda. You've not experienced any panic attacks like that since you've been on the oxygen. I promise you that we won't take it off you. We will write you up a care plan with plenty of morphine. We won't let you suffer."

Peter spoke next - "This is your fault, Anna!" he shouted. His eyes bulged and the veins on his neck stood out. "I told you not to let her have radiotherapy! I told you that Tim had it and it finished him off! I don't know anyone who it's worked for. But you wouldn't listen. You always think you know best."

"Hey! Don't blame our Anna!" Jean spoke up. "We all discussed the options and Mum made up her own mind about the treatment she wanted. Actually, she was advised to have the radiotherapy first, whilst she was still strong. If anything, it was you who persuaded her to have chemotherapy instead. And not just one lot either, but two rounds of the stuff. Then you said she should hang fire before considering the radiotherapy so treatment was delayed. Therefore, the risk of infection was higher. So, don't you go pointing the blame at anyone!"

"Can we all stop arguing, please?" Michael looked straight at his mother as he continued, "No one's to blame here. It is what it is. That's the equation."

Freda looked back at her son and nodded. She turned to Peter,

"It's nobody's fault, love. It's one of those things. I chose my own treatment, so don't blame anyone else. I've always said that when your number's up, your number's up. If He opens the book and your name's on the page, you're going. Nobody can do anything to change that. It is what it is."

Peter didn't reply.

Dr Morris broke the tension. She got up from her chair but kept hold of Freda's hand.

"Well, it's been lovely meeting you, Freda," she said, "and your family."

She looked and nodded at each one in turn.

"If you wish to speak to me again, just ask Lorna." She squeezed Freda's hand in both of hers, then gently placed it on the bed. She smiled.

Lorna got up too.

"Yes. That goes for me too," said Lorna. "I'll be visiting you every day. Feel free to ask me anything you think of," she said as she looked at each of them.

Peter got up and turned his back on his siblings. He shook hands with Dr Morris then Lorna.

"Thanks for coming, flower," he said.

"You're welcome."

As they both left, Peter made himself busy putting the chairs away. He patted his mum on the head and then swiftly exited the room. It had been as much as he could take. He needed to get out of there and think clearly.

Anna got up and began tidying around. Unused to this level of silence, Michael piped up,

"Well, Mother, look at it this way, you won't have to be here for Christmas. You've always hated Christmas."

"Michael!" Anna and Jean shouted at him together.

Then they all quickly looked at their mum. She was tugging at the mask which she'd just replaced as she laughed out loud.

"Typical of you, that!" she exclaimed.

Jean got in on the joke - "Well, he has a point, I suppose," she said, "Every cloud has a silver lining and all that lot. Once you're up there, Mother, you can come back to your house and get rid of them buggers who've been haunting it for God knows how long. Make yourself useful!"

They were all laughing now.

"No Gorsey Brow then?" Freda asked.

It had been a standing joke she'd had with them since they were little. Resenting the fact that she would get old one day, she had always maintained that when she got too elderly and decrepit, rather than being put in an old people's home, she wanted to be put in a wheelchair and pushed down the steepest hill in Broadbottom.

They all looked at each other.

"I'd forgotten about that one," laughed Anna.

"I thought you wanted your head mounting on a piece of wood over the top of the telly," said Jean.

"Yes, you told me that too," said Michael. "You said you'd wink at Happy when he least expected it and frighten the life out of him."

"Yes, like that time we popped a balloon under him when he was asleep in the armchair after drinking down the pub all afternoon," Jean continued.

The mood was lightening.

"Aw! I remember that," said Anna. "He jumped about ten feet into the air. He went ballistic."

"Not as much as he did when you bought Zaer as a puppy for our Michael and didn't tell him!" said Jean. "You just opened the living room door and casually let her in, then went back to making the tea!"

"As if he wouldn't notice!" added Anna. "I can still see

his face now!"

"Oh God!" said Freda, suddenly serious.

"What?" they asked in unison.

"I'll have to meet him again, won't I?"

"I wouldn't worry about that, Mother," Jean replied. "He'll be right at the back of the queue. You'll have hundreds of friends and family to get through first."

"And don't forget the hundreds of dogs, our kid!" Michael chuckled.

"Oh aye, of course! And all them cats, horses and rabbits we used to have," she said.

"Yes, after Happy bumped some of them off," Anna added, thinking of Big Bunny.

"Anyway, Dad won't come to see you, Mother," Anna added. "He'll be sitting in an armchair waiting for you to come to him!"

"Yes, all you'll hear is him hollering," said Michael as he mimicked, "Freda! Fetch me a cup of tea!"

With that, all three of them began to laugh loudly again.

"What's going on here, then?" Michelle had just come onto the ward for her shift, "Family meeting?"

"Something like that, love," Michael replied. "Anyway, I'm starving," he said. "Do you do a bacon butty, love? To go with that nice cup of coffee you usually make for me?"

"Watch it, sunshine," replied Michelle.

"Well, I know where I'm not wanted! I'll be on my way," Michael replied. He leaned over to kiss his mum, gave Jean and Anna a quick hug and walked off.

"Time for your injection, darling," Michelle said.

She beckoned to Karen to assist her. She wasn't allowed to give morphine without the consent of another senior nurse. Karen unclipped her keys from her belt and unlocked the medicine cabinet located just above the bed.

"Partners in crime, hey?" Jean remarked.

"Yeah, something like that," Michelle replied.

"Well, I'll be off too, Mum. Let you get some rest," said Anna. She couldn't give her a kiss as the two nurses were in the way.

"Hope so!" Freda mouthed. "Give Mollie and Niko a kiss each from me!"

"Will do," she replied. She walked away.

"Well, if you're going to nod off, I'll get myself off to the canteen for a Slush Puppie," said Jean. "Do either of you two lovely ladies want anything whilst I'm there?" she asked Michelle and Karen. "They do a lovely chocolate brownie."

"No you're all right, Jean. Thanks."

"See you in a bit then, Mother," she called.

Jean exited the ward and made a conscious effort not to look back. As she rounded the corner, out of sight, she suddenly burst into tears and had to sit down.

"Oh my God, what am I going to do?" she sobbed.

CHAPTER 22

Peter looked up from his iPad as a voice called out to him.

"Hey up, Peter, I didn't expect to see you here this morning! I thought it was Anna's turn to do the night shift?" Penny was working from home, so had taken the opportunity to call in to visit. There was only so much sitting in front of a computer screen she could take. The customers she dealt with seemed to be getting more awkward and had driven her round the bend so she'd come out to get away from it all and clear her head.

"Our Anna doesn't really do nights, flower," Peter explained. "Me and our Janice stayed here last night. You've just missed her, actually. She's gone to the canteen to fetch some coffee. You can't drink the stuff they give you in here. Gives you the squirts!"

"You've got her well trained!" Penny remarked.

"Well, you don't have a dog and bark yourself!" he joked. He added a wink. He liked to tease people. It was the sort of thing his dad used to say all the time when they were growing up. He knew Penny would see that he was kidding.

"How is she?" asked Penny.

"She's fine. Just tired from being awake all night."

"Not Janice, you flake! I meant your mum!"

"Oh! She's been out for the count. Hasn't really moved much. Just been snoring like a good 'un!"

"Aw, bless. Well I won't wake her. Me mam always said that you only sleep if you really need it."

"Or if you've been drugged up with morphine!" Peter replied.

Penny drew up a chair, put her car keys in her bag and placed it on the floor, before switching her phone to silent and putting it in her pocket.

"What are you doing there? Answering emails again?" Penny said. She pointed to Peter's iPad.

"No! Work can sod off. They're always mithering me about when I'm coming back in. They can't seem to cope without me. They're not happy that I'm not in, especially when I've had so much time off recently looking after Janice."

Janice suffered a lot with her health. She'd recovered from breast cancer and a mastectomy and then developed a whole host of related secondary medical issues which had kept her busy going to appointments. It didn't help that she was asthmatic either, which complicated her condition. Penny was quite glad she was at the canteen at this moment in time. Much as she liked her, she wasn't sure she could endure another full explanation of her various ailments.

"I was just playing a game on the iPad," Peter continued. "I've nearly finished all forty levels. I've had to search various lands for parts for a robot and he's nearly complete."

"Blummin' 'eck! You sound like our Nick," said Penny. "He's into strategy games and all that lot. When he's not on his Xbox, he's out catching Pokémon on his phone. He's obsessed."

"Oh it's only a bit of fun," said Peter. "I don't usually have time for such things but I've had a lot of stretches sitting here with nothing to do so it whiles away the hours. The young lads at work are all into that Pokémon GO stuff too, but I don't see the attraction myself."

"Me neither," said Penny. "You won't believe this, right, but you know Nick's just gone on holiday with his girlfriend?"

"I didn't actually, no," said Peter.

"Well, he has, right. Gone to Portugal. Anyway, that's by the by. But he comes 'round the other night just before he was setting off for the airport and gives me his phone, right? And he says, 'Mum, do me a favour whilst I'm away, will you? Here's my phone. There's a Pokémon been seen over in Denton. Drive over, will you, and catch it for me, it's the last one in a set."

"Really? So, did you go then?" asked Peter.

"Are you joking?" replied Penny. "I said to him 'Do you think I've got time in my busy day, with work and the house and three dogs and a cat, to go buggering about collecting fictitious beasts or whatever they are?' I told him he had no chance."

"What did he say?"

"Oh my God, right. He begged me! He pleaded with me! He even offered me the petrol money! It was absolutely ridiculous! I said to him, 'Look, you're nearly thirty! You're a grown man. Get a life!'"

"What did he say to that?"

"Well, he sulked, didn't he? Like all blokes do when they don't get their way. He's like a big kid!"

"So, have you driven to Denton this week?" Peter teased.

"Well, yes, actually I have,' she said sheepishly. "I've zapped it or whatever it is they call it. It's captured in his phone somehow. I felt like I was in *Ghostbusters*! He'll be chuffed to bits when he gets back. But don't you go telling him about it! If he asks, I was over that way anyway, dealing with a client!"

"Don't worry, your secret's safe with me," said Peter.

He knew what Penny was like. She only had one son and she idolised him. If he wanted her to do something for him, then nine times out of ten she'd see that it was done. He was the same with his own son, Daniel. Let him have whatever he wanted.

"So, how's life treating you, then?" asked Peter

"Oh. It's just all work and no play at the moment," she replied. "I feel like I'm on a roller coaster and can't get off. We've had a change of management at work and they're trying to make their mark. They want blood. I'm a bit sick of it to be honest."

"I know how you feel," said Peter. "My bosses are like that. No matter what I do, they want more. They expect me to just be at their beck and call all the time. Send me up and down the country at all times of the day and night. That's why it's been difficult being in here. There's no one else who does what I do in the company, so, when I'm not there, it all goes tits up. I've been keeping on top of emails and talking people through what to do but it's hard. But I told them my mum comes first!"

"Quite right!" replied Penny. "It was the same when my mam got bowel cancer. I was off for weeks."

"And what were they like with you?"

"You know what, Peter, I have to say that they were brilliant. They never questioned it. Sent me flowers. But, even if I say so myself, I'm damn good at my job and they know it. I make them a fortune every year selling their computer systems. It's only recently that they've become gits. And you're like me. You're brilliant at what you do. Don't let them force you to go to work. This time with your mum is too important."

"I know. I've told them. It's bad timing really. First our Janice had cancer and now my mum. They don't believe it. They've asked for evidence that she's poorly!"

"Really?" said Penny. "Really! Are they having a laugh? Oh my God, I wouldn't put up with it. That's terrible!"

"Well, I'm in the process of changing jobs. I'm hoping to leave them soon," said Peter.

"Good for you! Sounds like they don't appreciate you.

Tell them to sling their hook! Fancy not just taking your word for it! Who in their right mind would make something like this up? I wouldn't wish it on anyone."

"I know. I'll bide my time for now. But it looks like I may have to go and do a job this week, all the same."

"Well, I hope not, Peter," replied Penny.

Just then they heard a cough. They both turned round to see Freda awake. Neither were sure how long she'd been listening to them.

"Hiya, Freda!" said Penny. "How are you feeling?"

"A bit fed up," Freda rasped. "No Barry with you today?"

"No! Don't be silly! He's still got the man flu. I've left him in bed with a bottle of All-in-One and a hot water bottle. There's no way I'm letting him near you with all his germs. But he sends his love and says he's sorry he can't visit."

"What's he up to these days?" asked Peter.

"He's working at the airport. Meet and Greet. He loves it. Far better than putting up fences all day for that tight-arsed brother-in-law of mine. Can you believe he expected him to work outside in all weathers and wouldn't even give him an electric saw to cut the wood?"

"What? He expected him to saw everything by hand? Bet that took ages."

"Of course it did! And there were miles of the stuff. He had the contract for a huge estate. You should've seen the state of his hands when he got home. I told him to pack it in. I don't care if our Carol isn't happy about it. I'm not having my husband used like that!"

"Good for you!" Peter agreed.

"Anyway, Freda," Penny said, turning her attention to her aunty, "I've brought you those birthday cards you asked me to get for you. There's one here for Emily and another for Jake."

"When are their birthdays?" Peter asked.

"Next week," Freda mouthed. "Emily's is the 9th of

September and Jake's the 10th."

"Right. You'd best tell our Janice. She deals with stuff like that."

Penny and Freda both rolled their eyes. It was typical of Peter to leave things for Janice to do. His dad had been like that too. Never bought a card or a present for any of them when they were little.

Penny put the cards on the bedside cupboard where Freda could reach them when she felt up to writing them out. Freda smiled and said 'thank you'. She was barely audible.

The clanging of a metal buckle as it met with the end of the bed, told them that Jean had arrived. She placed her coat on top of the handbag.

"Carry on like that and we'll have to get you on Lip Sync Battle Mother!" she joked. Then, to Penny and Peter, "Hello you two. Sorry I'm late, but I got stuck behind some stupid woman driving here. Going about twenty miles an hour, she was. I blasted my horn at her a few times but she took no notice!"

Freda smiled. This reminded her of Len. He was always an impatient driver. He used to go right up to people's car bumpers and try and intimidate them. He would've been bibbing too and swearing! Many a time she'd had to pick him up from the pub and endure his endless rants and raves as he insisted on telling her how to drive. "Put your foot down! Don't let him get in front of you! Blast him!" He'd be leaning over the steering wheel trying to press the horn. It did her head in. She was a damn good driver and hated his interference.

Of course, she never told him how she felt - just put up with it until they got home. He'd usually only last half an hour or so in front of the TV before going off to bed anyway. So, it was never that long to wait for a bit of peace and quiet.

"Where's our Anna?" Peter asked. "She was supposed

to be here now, not you. Have you got the timetable wrong again or what?"

Jean laughed - "No! Let's just say that she's a bit incapacitated at the moment. She won't be able to make it until this evening."

"What? Is she hungover?" Penny asked.

"Oh aye!" Jean replied, chuckling. "I spoke to her on the phone earlier. Had a big night out last night and daren't drive her car for fear of still being over the limit!"

"What? Our Anna?" said Peter. He raised his eyebrows. "Give over! What's she had? A couple of Shandies? She's a lightweight."

Penny nodded in agreement. Her cousin was noted for not being able to drink much, unlike the rest of the clan. A couple of glasses of wine and she was usually done in.

"Oh, I think she had a bit more than that, our kid!" Jean laughed. "According to Emily, she spent most of the night with her head down the bog chucking up and saying she felt dizzy. Apparently, she'd already binned up all over the kitchen floor when she got in and then slipped in it! Her dress was covered in vomit."

"Charming!" Freda spoke up. She shook her head in despair. Both her sons took after Len in many respects when it came to drinking - Peter always had a few pints or a bottle of wine each evening, and Michael practically lived in the pub - but the girls weren't really like that as a rule. She must've had a good reason to drink. Maybe the stress of everything was getting to her.

"Well, at least she did it at home!" Penny remarked. "It could've been worse, couldn't it? She could have thrown up at the do and showed herself up in front of Richard's boss. I remember now - she was telling me she was going to a barbecue with all the fellas from Richard's work. It's an annual event but the wives aren't invited but Richard was going to take her anyway. He was hoping to act daft if they said owt and pretend he didn't know it was just for men. That's if they noticed!"

"Oh, I think they noticed our kid all right!" laughed Jean. "Richard told me that she got so drunk that she fell over playing tennis and couldn't get back up! She was rolling about on the floor laughing and showing her knickers to everyone!"

"Aw!" Freda remarked. She imagined how distressed Anna would be to learn that she had behaved so disgracefully - she was usually so prim and proper!

It wasn't this behaviour which surprised Peter, however, but the fact that Anna had been playing tennis! She wasn't a sporty person at all. And Richard's boss must be pretty posh to have his own tennis court which said something about the kind of do it was. She'd be mortified all right!

"Oh! That's not all!" Jean continued. She was revelling in recounting the details of the evening. "Having got pissed as a fart, she started talking to the boss's dogs and then got in the dog bed and was falling asleep!"

"Dogs?" Freda perked up now.

"Yes, Mother. You'll like this bit. He has two blummin' big German Shepherds." Then added, "Neither of them is a patch on Niko of course!"

"Of course!" Penny added.

Freda smiled proudly.

"What did Richard do then?" asked Penny. She knew he'd be really embarrassed by her behaviour. He hated being the centre of attention.

"Well, luckily, his friend Sophie noticed. She advised him to take her home before everyone else saw her in that state."

"So that's what he did, then?" asked Penny.

"Well, he tried," replied Jean. "He got as far as the gate without anyone noticing they'd left but then realised he needed a code to get out! He left her and went to find out the code and when he got back, she had disappeared!"

"Oh my God! Where was she?" asked Penny, laughing.

"In the bushes!" Jean chortled. "She'd fallen down. He just saw her feet sticking out! He had to try and prop her up whilst he opened the gates. He said she was a dead weight."

Freda smiled, remembering the first time Anna had got drunk. Accompanying her to her friend's wine party at the age of seventeen, she'd had to bring her home and try and get her out of the car and up into bed. She'd propped her up at the side of the road whilst she locked the car up and watched her slide onto the pavement! It had taken all her strength to drag her up the path and clamber up the steps to the front door before depositing her on the settee.

"So, how did Richard get Anna home, then?" asked Peter. "A taxi?"

"No! He couldn't call one as there's no signal around there and he didn't want to draw attention to her by asking to use the landline so he walked her back along the canal. Well, I say 'walked'. I mean 'carried' of course!"

"Blummin' heck!" Penny remarked. She'd walked along that canal herself with her dogs and Anna and Bobby - the towpath wasn't very wide. It certainly wasn't the sort of place to be travelling on in the dark.

"I'm surprised she didn't fall in!" she said.

"She nearly did!" laughed Jean. "Took him over an hour to get home. One step forward and two steps back!"

"I would've just left her there!" Peter chipped in.

"He would an' all!" Jean confirmed.

"You tight sod, Peter!" Penny smirked. "Remind me never to have a night out with you!"

"You've no worries there!" Peter joked. "From what I've heard, I bet you could drink me under the table if you put your mind to it."

"If I put my mind to it!" Penny replied, winking at her cousin.

"Poor Anna, though!" Penny returned to the conversation, "I'll give her a ring later and see how she is."

Penny was interrupted as a nurse came up to the bed, carrying a nebuliser. Jean didn't recognise her as one of the usual staff.

"No Michelle today, love?" she asked.

"No. She's off today, duck," the nurse replied. "I'm Hilary. I'm covering the ward for the night shift as they're short of staff. I've just brought your mum's medicine."

Hilary walked over towards the wall where the oxygen tank was fitted and began to turn it off.

"What're you doing?" Jean asked, alarmed.

"I'm just giving your mum her nebuliser. So I need to turn off the oxygen whilst she breathes it in," she said.

"Mum always keeps the oxygen on whilst she takes her medicine," Jean explained, "Michelle says so. She needs it."

Hilary continued adjusting the machinery.

"We always give nebulisers on their own," she insisted.

"But hasn't Michelle left instructions for you?" asked Jean. She began to dig a thumb into her palm. She didn't like the thought of her mum being without her oxygen.

"I'm in charge," Hilary replied. "This is how it's done. Otherwise, you lose the benefits."

Jean wasn't sure. She watched as the nurse continued to move the machine out of the way and set up the nebuliser, gently placing the new mask on her mum's face. The oxygen was switched off. Its loud and constant noise was suddenly replaced by the much less obvious and very slight hissing sound. Everyone stared at it, keeping their fingers crossed that she was right and praying for the procedure to be quickly over so that they could get Freda back onto the oxygen and be reassured that she was safe again. Jean, in particular, could not avert her stare. Having witnessed first-hand several occasions when her mum had struggled for breath, she was keen to make sure that she wasn't without her oxygen a second longer than was absolutely necessary. As the last of the cloudy mixture dispersed, she called Hilary back and instructed her to reset the levels on the machine. Only then could she sit down, satisfied that all was in order.

It was Penny who broke the silence.

"Well, I'd best be making tracks," she said.

"Me too," said Peter. "I'd best see where our Janice has got to!"

He quickly tidied up the table, throwing away the carton of juice which had been standing there all morning, barely touched.

"Order Mum another one of these, will you, our kid?" he requested. "And try and get her to drink some of it."

"Will do!" replied Jean.

"I'll try and visit later in the week, Freda," said Penny. "I've got to go all the sodding way to London, tomorrow, so I can't come then."

"What? On the quest for another Pokémon, are you?" Peter jested.

"Hey! I told you that in confidence!" Penny replied. Then, approaching the bed, she leant down and gave her aunty a big hug.

"Give us a cuddle," she said. "And make sure you drink something!"

Peter hovered at the foot of the bed. He wasn't comfortable showing his affections like Penny was. Instead, he gave a simple wave then departed, Penny following closely behind.

Jean got up and rummaged through her bag. Taking out three small tubs, she placed them one by one on the table.

"Right! Here's your Angel Delight. You've got strawberry, chocolate and butterscotch to choose from. I'll go and put them in the fridge and order us a round of drinks! You might not be thirsty but I'm as dry as a nun's crotch!"

And with that, she scooped up the pots and whisked off to the staff kitchen, leaving Freda smiling to herself.

CHAPTER 23

It was seven o'clock in the morning and Freda was awake. This was unusual. What's more, it was a Saturday. Even more unusual. As a rule, she never got up before at least ten at the weekend. Mind you, that part wasn't any different! She couldn't remember the last time she'd got out of bed. There was no reason to. It wasn't as if she could go to the day room - by all accounts that was just for visitors - and, since she'd been catheterised, there was no need to go to the toilet either. When was the last time she'd been for a number two? She didn't know. She smiled as she recalled what her sister, Aubrey, had said about this once, when she had just had her bowel taken away and a bag fitted. She had bemoaned the fact that she could no longer just sit on the toilet and "have a good poo!" It was funny how the little things in life could be so missed.

Once again, she felt a flood of admiration for her and the way she had battled against her cancer so stoically. Even when she'd had to have a second bag fitted on her back due to a failing kidney, she'd not given up. She had just given it a name - Ethel - to go with the first one which she called Cyril. Sounded like a double-Act! "And tonight, for one night only! Ethel and Cyril!"

It meant she could talk more openly about her toilet issues, instead of sounding clinical. It was "You won't believe what Ethel did today, Freda! I woke up and she'd come off in the night. You've never seen anything like it!" Or "Cyril has decided he doesn't like peas. They give him shocking wind and he can't fart. You should've seen him last night. All blown up like a balloon he was! I prayed he didn't pop! Can you imagine?"

Freda could. And she was certain she couldn't have coped with it. *But then, that's what makes people so different and unique.* She heard her mother's words in her head – "It wouldn't be doing if we were all the same, Freda!"

Aubrey's troubles had been vast. She'd had most of her bowel removed, and then the chemotherapy had made all her hair fall out and her taste buds act up. But she'd coped and adjusted. Freda was now having to do the same but with a different set of problems - all associated with her lungs instead of her bowels. She too, was having to adapt and adjust to an ever-evolving set of circumstances. Wear an oxygen mask 24-7, put up with staying in bed all the time, use a pen and paper to write down what she was trying to say.

It was this which really upset her. She could cope with the mask and the chest issues - after all, she had medication for that, and, let's face it, she was asleep most of the time anyway, so she was blissfully unaware, but she detested not being able to articulate what she wanted to say. It wasn't the same writing it down. The kids humoured her, of course, joking about her inability to lip synch as she tried to rasp her words out.

She looked out of the window. It looked cold and crisp - 'fresh' - just the sort of morning she liked. Niko and Mollie loved it when it was like this. No mud or rain to spoil it. She thought of them longingly. How she wished she was able to take them out. Crunch through the leaves around Dovestone Reservoir, watch Niko chase the ball. Of course, he wouldn't bring it back! She needed Anna's dog,

Bobby, to do that. He'd run after Niko and wait for him to get bored and let go of it, then he'd nick it off him and charge back to her and drop it at her feet, all the while bouncing! She smiled. Mollie wouldn't even chase it. She'd just plod along sniffing at everything. She should've been a dog instead of a bitch.

That's where they'd be now - out and about with Anna. She was due to visit later, so she'd be making sure they got a good bout of exercise before she left them in the house on their own. Freda hoped she remembered to give them a chew stick and put the radio on for them. Dogs, like children, need routines.

Jean was due back any minute. She'd had to leave to use her phone. No doubt she was arranging the timetable for them all for the next few days. She was good at that. Hopefully she wouldn't allow too many visitors to come this week. It was tiring seeing so many people. Representatives from the 'Canal Eight', as Michael nicknamed them, had been twice now. It was a nice surprise the first time and she'd enjoyed catching up on all their news but there had been a noticeable change in their demeanour recently. They'd been far more serious and empathetic, which unnerved her. She didn't like the sympathy vote. Ever since she'd been told her prognosis, she'd feared that it might change the way people saw her. And, to some extent, it had. Some people avoided her altogether which made her sad. She was still the same person.

At least her kids weren't like that. They acted no differently but carried on as usual, telling her their stories which often made her laugh. That's what she needed. To feel normal. At least 'normal' in the sense of her family! She looked forward to hearing their laughter. Perked her up no end.

She was just wondering where Jean had got to, when she heard a raucous laugh. There she was, approaching the ward with Anna, no doubt ribbing her about her drunken night out.

"Hey up, Mother!" Jean shouted. "Still awake?"

She breezed in, plonking her mobile phone down on the table. then paused to take a big slurp of a Slushie drink. Anna approached the bed and drew up a chair.

"Hiya, Mum. How are you?" Anna asked.

Freda gave her a thumbs up.

"Right, Mother," said Jean, who was in 'organising' mode. "Our Anna's staying 'til this evening then I'm coming back, then it should be our Peter, then probably Michael. Pauline's on her way too. I bumped into her outside. She's visiting June. Apparently, she's thumped one of the nurses and had to be restrained. There's only Pauline that can handle her so they've asked her to come in."

Freda shook her head. Poor Pauline. She was in her eighties now and had never learned to drive so she had to go everywhere on the bus. It was commendable how devoted she was to looking after their friend. Who would've thought that June could deteriorate so quickly? This time last year she had been so active and normal. Then dementia had set in, on top of her ill health. It changed her. She'd punched a woman in Morrisons just for getting to the meat counter before her! And lashed out at a nurse in Outpatients who was changing the dressings on her leg. It was tragic.

As if reading her thoughts, Anna commented, "It's unbelievable isn't it? Who would've thought June could behave like that? When I took Pauline home the other day, she was telling me how aggressive June's become. They've had to medicate her. Last time I took them both home she wouldn't keep her seatbelt on and kept telling me she was getting out of the car when we were moving! I was glad to get rid of her. Poor Pauline! That woman is an angel!"

"Yes!" agreed Jean. Then, laughing, "A gassing angel! She never shut up when I saw her the other day. I'd nipped into Asda for one or two bits and bobs ahead of my Saturday big-shop. I told Joe I wouldn't be long, so he asked me to pick him up some scratch cards. But then I bumped into Pauline and I couldn't escape. She was going on about one of her neighbours, Craig, who had collapsed in the street. It was she who had called for an ambulance. Turns out he'd had a heart attack. He had to be blue-lighted to Ashton hospital.

Freda's ears pricked up and she raised her eyebrows in surprise. Evidently, she knew him. Jean looked at her, awaiting a comment. Freda mouthed the words "Border Collie". Jean rolled her eyes, before continuing, "Well, yes Mother. I expect you know everyone around there with a dog!"

"Bet you wish you'd been there, don't you, Mum?" Anna laughed. "You know how much you like to ride in an ambulance!"

Anna thought back to when she'd been hit by a car as a child, right outside their house. Her mum hadn't shut up talking about the ride to the hospital. She'd 'dined out' on that story for months afterwards. Of course, she'd neglected to mention how, Anna, having been carried into the house (quite wrongly by the way) by a 'do-gooder', she herself had panicked about the state of the living room and started to tidy up! She could see her now, ordering the dogs to be locked away in the kitchen and Jean to side the table whilst she frantically pushed the hoover round the carpet! As if the ambulance drivers could care less! She smiled.

"Well that's not all, Mother!" Jean carried on the tale, "When she got back from the hospital, she called round to see another neighbour, John. You know the one with the manky dog he claims is a German Shepherd?"

Freda nodded enthusiastically. There was no way, in her opinion, it was anything but a cross-breed. It might be large and black and tan but that was where the resemblance ended. It wasn't a patch on Niko - one of its ears didn't even stand up!

"Well, turns out he was really poorly with some kind of chest infection," said Jean. "Pauline had to call the doctor out and everything."

"Blimey! Poor Pauline," said Anna. "First June, then Craig, and then John."

"Poor Pauline?" said Jean. "Poor neighbours I'd say! She's a right Jonah! Everyone she goes near ends up in need of treatment! Never mind an Angel, she's a devil in disguise! Beelzebub they ought to call her. I'm keeping well away!"

"You'd best be quick then, Jean, as here she comes now!" said Anna.

Jean spun round in time to see the little old lady coming towards them. Freda was trying to stifle a laugh, which made her cough. Anna automatically rubbed her back, until it passed.

"Well, on that note..." Jean chuckled then began to hurriedly collect her things ready to leave. "It's time I made a move."

While Pauline was saying 'Hello' to each of the other patients on her way up the ward, Jean took the opportunity to say goodbye, planting a kiss on her mother's cheek.

"Now! Be good!" she instructed. Then, throwing a wink to Anna, she whispered, "Whatever you do, don't let her touch you! Unclean! Unclean!" She waved her hands in the air as she giggled.

Jean departed, apologising quickly to Pauline as she passed, "Got to dash, Pauline. Things to do!" Then, as she got out of her line of vision, she turned and mouthed "Jonah!" to her sister and mother who were trying their hardest to keep their faces straight.

"Here you are, love. I've brought you some bits and bobs," said Pauline to Freda, as she placed a bottle of nail varnish on the bed.

"Isn't it a nice colour? Here's some perfume too. I thought it might cheer you up."

She turned to Anna, "I didn't know what to bring really. I know your mum likes flowers but they're not allowed on this ward. No point bringing grapes, either. We don't eat grapes, do we, at our age? What, with our false teeth and such like. Bits get stuck under your palette, you know?

There's only June who eats grapes. I took her some last week. But they've been banned now after she threw them all over the ward. She was chucking them at the nurses! I didn't know what to do." She paused to take a breath, then added, "I felt awful leaving her on that ward. But I couldn't cope with her at my house. She was always wandering off somewhere. I couldn't leave her for a minute. Up and down the stairs she was. Well, I'm eighty-six, you know. I couldn't keep following her everywhere. I was exhausted."

This reminded Anna of having babies. Her friends had been quite competitive about whose offspring would crawl first, or, better still, walk. She'd never forgotten the time she went to John Lewis and met Sarah's daughter walking about in her first pair of shoes. Eleven months old was all she was - six months younger than her Ava but already ahead! This wasn't fair.

She'd felt the heat rising in her face and her heart-rate quickening as she grappled with the feeling of inferiority. As she looked down at the pushchair, it was evident that Ava, resembling as she did the Michelin Man, was no way capable of getting up, let alone being actively mobile. Taking a deep breath, Anna had forced herself to smile as she congratulated her friend.

They all walk in the end of course, as her mother had quite rightly pointed out. At least it meant that she could leave her briefly unattended and not worry about her going off anywhere as she was always still where she'd left her. This wasn't the same for Sarah. She was always running round like a blue-arsed fly! Recalling this made Anna have an empathy for Pauline.

Pauline was still talking of course - "I phoned her sisters and asked them if they'd help me. You know, give me a bit of respite, but they weren't interested."

Freda shook her head in disbelief.

"I always thought June was an only child," said Anna.

"No!" replied Pauline. Freda shook her head again.

"She's got three sisters!" continued Pauline, "But they

don't bother. I wouldn't mind, but one of them's a nun. You'd think she would want to help, wouldn't you? I don't understand folk sometimes. It wasn't like I was asking them to have her for any length of time. A day off, that's all I wanted. But they turned me down."

Anna noticed a tear roll down Pauline's cheek, so quickly interjected, "Well, don't feel guilty. June's lucky to have a friend as kind as you. There's not many as would look after someone like you've looked after her. You deserve a pat on the back. And even more so now - coming up here every day to see her."

Freda nodded in agreement, as Pauline took out a tissue and wiped her eyes.

"I'm all she's got!" Pauline whimpered.

"Here, take my chair and have a sit down," offered Anna. "I'll go off and get some tea. You stay here with my mum and have a good chinwag."

Anna made to go, leaving Pauline to change the subject to something else. She was just firing up on her tale of "that woman from Smith Street. Remember? The one that ran off with that bloke who was married to what's-her-face?"

Anna had to give it to Pauline - she certainly had the gift of the gab! She looked fleetingly at her mother, resigned to listen rather than join in the conversation, and suddenly felt overcome by a profound sense of sadness. Her poor mother.

Anna fetched Pauline a cup of tea, then made her way to the day room to catch up on her work emails and check in with Richard and the girls. School was due to start soon and they both needed new shoes and such like, so they were off to Manchester for the day. They'd each made a video to show their nana as they couldn't visit. Anna made a mental note to show this to her after Pauline had left. She also took the opportunity to ring her niece, Melissa. The day room was empty so it was fine to speak out loud. She'd visited the other day but Freda had been asleep for the entire time.

Melissa had sat quietly embroidering for a couple of hours, just content to be in her nana's company. It was a shame as she'd had to get two buses to get there. Anna was trying to see when she might next be free, so she could arrange a lift for her.

After that, she organised a delivery of dog food to her mum's - it was running low again - and some more duck food. In her mother's absence, Jean and herself had taken up the duty of walking to the canal and scattering the food for the ducks that lived there. Admittedly, it wasn't on the daily basis their mother expected, but at least they were still doing it. Personally, Anna thought it wasteful, especially considering Freda didn't have any money. The ducks had been declining in number in recent months. Rumour had it that they were being bumped off for food by some locals. Not surprising, she thought, considering how well fed they were! It horrified her mother that someone could do this. She loved a bit of duck, of course, but she never made the connection between these and the ones served up on her dinner plate. To her, they were like her pets. It was a double-edged sword - the more she fed them, the more appealing they were to the ravenous! Anna smiled at the thought that her mother was not only helping the duck population, but she was inadvertently aiding the impoverished too! If that was any consolation.

It was typical of her mother of course, to want to give what she had to others. The tree in her back garden was full of a myriad of different bird feeders, designed to take both seed and fat balls - another regular expense. Forget *Birdman of Alcatraz*, she was 'Birdwoman of Dukinfield'! Squirrel-proof and durable, they attracted a wealth of birds to the garden. It gave Freda a lot of pleasure to watch them. She'd even had a water fountain installed so they could take baths. She marvelled at how there really was a 'pecking order' as tens of birds queued up in an orderly fashion, on its different levels, awaiting their turn.

Her generosity didn't stop there either. Freda regularly

gave money to charity and sponsored a dog from Dogs Trust. A proper 'Heinz 57', it sent her a birthday card and Christmas card each year which she proudly displayed on her mantelpiece. It was about the fifth such dog she had sponsored in her lifetime. She was a sucker for a sob story!

Anna's thoughts were interrupted by the dulcet tones of Pauline who had appeared at the doorway of the day room asking for help. Anna panicked, thinking something bad had happened and immediately sprung to her feet, ready to rush to her mother's bedside.

"It's nothing to worry about!" Pauline reassured her, having sensed the fear in Anna's demeanour. "It's just that your mum is trying to tell me something and I don't know what she's saying. I've tried listening really hard but I can't make out what it is she wants and I'm hoping you can help. She doesn't want to write it down."

Feeling a sense of relief, Anna promptly followed the old lady back onto the ward. Her mum was sitting up in bed, shaking her head and waving as if to say that whatever it was, she had wanted to say to Pauline, it really didn't matter anymore. But Pauline was persistent. She went up to her friend and stroked her hand.

"I've fetched your Anna to help me work out what you want to say, love," said Pauline. "Go on, say it again."

Freda tried to mouth the words to Pauline alone.

"She wants to ask me someone's name, I think," explained Pauline. "I got that much. But I don't know what it's in connection with. I think she's saying 'Edith'."

Anna knew exactly what her mother wanted to know, and the realisation made her share the awkwardness which her mother was feeling right now. Edith had been a friend of her mum's who had passed away last year. She recalled how, recently, they'd had a conversation about her funeral do which had been at a local hotel. Freda had earmarked it for her own funeral buffet. They'd had a discussion about the female funeral director who had been used and whom she and Pauline had bumped into a few weeks earlier. Anna had promised to find out her name and details from Pauline but it had slipped her mind. She took a deep breath and drew up the courage to ask her mum what she wanted to know.

Freda looked sheepish and was clearly embarrassed about asking this in front of Anna. She repeated the question to her friend, who, for once, was speechless. Pauline's bottom lip trembling, all she could do was shake her head. Clearly, it had dawned on her that Freda did not envisage making a recovery.

Anna too, felt a lump in her throat. She picked up the notepad and passed it to Pauline who dutifully scribbled down the name. All the while, Anna held her mother's gaze. A feeling of understanding passed between them.

Pauline looked at her friend sympathetically and gripped her hand. Anna felt like all the air in the room had just been taken away.

"You are a dear, dear friend," said Pauline. "We've had some good times together, haven't we? You, me and June. You've always been there for me. When I lost Reg, and then when I had to have Monty put down."

Typical! thought Anna, Trust Pauline to put her husband's passing in the same sentence as her dog's! Anna caught her mum smiling and returned the gesture, but was feeling more and more overwhelmed. She needed to get away.

"I'll give you a lift home, Pauline. Save you catching the bus," Anna offered.

"Oh, you don't have to, love. I'll ring for a taxi."

"You'll do no such thing!" Anna remarked. "It'll only take me ten minutes! Now I'm not taking no for an answer!"

"Aw, thanks love. I've got to come back later to see June, so that'll really help me out. You are kind."

"No probs," replied Anna. She shifted her weight from foot to foot.

Reluctantly, Pauline let go of her friend's hand.

"Take care, love," she said. Freda nodded.

"See you in a bit, Mum," said Anna, matter-of-factly. She deliberately avoided eye contact, and instead quickly rushed out of the ward. As she rounded the corner, out of sight, she burst into tears. She sat down in a chair.

Pauline sat down beside her and took her in her arms. Anna sobbed onto her shoulder.

"Go on, love. It's all right," Pauline said, as she rubbed her back. "You let it all out! I know how you feel. She's your mum and you love her to bits. We all do. No one wants to lose her. Look! You've set me off now!"

Pauline briefly let go of her and rummaged in her pockets. Finding two tissues, she passed one to Anna. Then she used hers to blow her nose loudly.

"There you go!" said Pauline. "What are we like, eh? It's better out than in!"

"That's what Mum would say," Anna said. "I'm sorry for crying like this."

"Don't ever say sorry for crying over your mum! Everyone needs somebody to confide in. I will always be here for you, too. You can ring me up whenever you want. Me and your mum have always chatted on the phone. On many occasions she's listened to me until the early hours of the morning. I'll do the same for you. Don't hesitate to call. I mean that."

She squeezed Anna's hand. Both of them smiled.

"Thanks," said Anna. She took a deep breath before saying, "Come on then, Pauline! Let's get going or we'll no sooner get you home than it'll be time for you to come back again."

The old lady stood up and followed Anna out of the ward, into the bright sunshine.

CHAPTER 24

Anna arrived on the ward.

"Is it raining?" Freda mouthed.

Looking like a drowned rat, it was pretty obvious that it was, in fact, pissing it down, but Anna resisted the urge to be sarcastic, and instead, replied, "Just a tad, Mother!"

Peeling off her soaked coat and placing it over the back of a chair, she took care to manoeuvre it so that any drips were out of the way. Ava followed her in and promptly did the same.

Freda smiled warmly, and rasped, "Nice to see you."

Anna fetched some paper towels and began to place them on the floor.

"What are you doing?" asked Ava.

"Making sure I don't leave a puddle," Anna replied. "We don't want anyone slipping in here."

"They're hardly going to be walking under our chairs, Mother!" replied Ava, taking up the seat nearest to her nana.

Anna carried on, then joined her by the bedside. She looked around. The ward seemed much quieter than usual. Noticing her concern, Freda indicated with her eyes towards Sylvia in the next bed, drew her hand up to her chest and patted at her heart, whispering, "Problems. Being monitored. No stress." She put her fingers towards where her lips were behind her mask.

Anna nodded in understanding as she looked at the woman who was quietly dozing. That might explain why the head of her bed was raised up. Perhaps they were trying to improve her breathing. She turned to Ava, "Are you still thirsty? You can go and get a drink from the canteen if you want."

"I am but I don't want to go out in the rain again," she replied. She turned to her nana - "Isn't there a drinks trolley for guests? Uncle Michael says he usually gets a drink off the nurses."

Freda raised her eyebrows, and looked at Anna knowingly.

"There is, yes, but you don't want to see what that leads to," Anna explained. "All I can say is that your uncle Michael's got a stronger constitution than most. If you take uncle Peter's advice, you'd leave well alone."

"Oh," said Ava.

"Whose is this bottle here, Mum?" Anna asked, picking up a glass bottle of sparkling grapefruit juice from the shelf at the back of the beds. She looked at her mother so she could tell what she was saying.

"Mine," Freda mouthed, waving her hand towards it to indicate she should take it, "Kirsty."

Anna remembered that Jean's boss had called this morning. She was a friend of the family's and had once lodged with their mum for many months before she got her own house. Anna was glad she'd taken the time to call. Her mother would've enjoyed seeing her after such a long time.

Ava looked sheepish.

"If you're sure, Nana?" she asked.

Freda nodded enthusiastically.

"Mum, will you open it please?" said Ava. "I'm not very good with those kinds of stoppers."

"Give over!" said Anna. "You can do that yourself. Give you some practice for when you're older and drinking

Prosecco!"

She passed Ava the bottle.

"You can pour me one too," she said, leaning over the bed and passing her two clean plastic cups.

Ava put the cups to the side and stood up with the bottle, away from the bed. Placing it between her knees in the way she'd seen her mother do, she grasped the stopper and twisted it hard. Feeling it move only slightly, she looked at her nana for reassurance that she was doing it right.

Freda nodded and smiled back at her.

"Give it some welly!" joked Anna.

Having moved it sufficiently to get some leverage, Ava placed her two thumbs up against its plastic head and pushed with all her might.

The force released the stopper with an almighty bang! Like a missile, it hurtled through the air in the direction of Sylvia, narrowly missing her head and waking her instantly from her slumber. She shot up in alarm wondering what the hell was happening. Juice spurted all over her bedspread.

Desperate, Ava put her fingers over the top of the bottle. The gushing jet became an even more violent spray.

"Mother! Help me!" Ava pleaded.

Anna grabbed a wedge of paper towels.

"Here you go!" she said as she tossed them towards her daughter. Ava turned and tried to catch them in the crook of her arms but in doing so momentarily lost her grip on the mouth of the bottle. The juice was redirected back towards the head of the bed just as a bewildered Sylvia was looking up. She received it full-on in the face.

Everything stopped. Ava looked on. The old lady's face was coated in pink juice. Her once-wispy fringe was now plastered back against her forehead. Numerous droplets were suspended from her eyelashes. One blink sent them rushing down her cheeks to join forces with the others which peppered her face. Gaining momentum, they cascaded onwards to her chin. Here they launched themselves off in a small waterfall which flowed onto her chest and guttered into the depths of her Winceyette nightie.

Ava continued to stare at what she'd done. Paralysed, it was left to Anna to try to rectify the damage before the nurses got wind of it. She was on it in an instant!

Armed with fists full of tissues, she rushed to Sylvia's aid, apologising profusely. Sylvia was grateful for the assistance. She took the tissues in both hands and used them like a towel to dredge the water from her face and neck. Eager to contain the situation, Anna went for reinforcements. Frantically pulling out more and more tissues from the box on the bedside table, she repeatedly swapped Sylvia's wet tissues for dry ones, each time disposing of the evidence in the nearby bin. Only when she was satisfied that the old lady was returning to normal, did she consider turning her attention to the bed. Too late. She had underestimated the perceptive nature of members of the NHS. Programmed not to miss anything, they were heading straight for her. In her head, she could hear the words of her grandad when he'd been temporarily placed in Barnes' hospital years before – "That lot can hear a mouse fart!" A rare and unusual measurement of being gifted, she'd thought, and only one which could have been conjured from inside the mind of the old fella. She gulped.

"What on earth is going on?" the tall bossy one Anna recognised as the Duty Nurse demanded to know. "This ward is supposed to being kept quiet today!"

She looked at the bottle which a red-faced Ava still held in her hand.

"What is it? Prosecco? What do you think this is? Some kind of social club? There are very sick patients in this medical unit!" she shouted, as she quickly commandeered an army of staff to clear up and hurried to check Sylvia's blood pressure.

Chastened, Ava looked at the ground. Freda smiled at her in sympathy and beckoned her to sit down. Anna took the bottle from her, poured out a small cupful from what was left of the drink and placed it in front of her.

"There you go!" she said. She hid the empty bottle behind some cards on the side.

Ava pushed the cup away.

"I'm not thirsty," she said.

Anna remained standing. She watched as two auxiliaries who had removed Sylvia's bedspread struggled to find a replacement in the usually overfilled bedding cupboard...

"Sorry!" she said to Sylvia.

"No worries, sweetheart," she replied. "I'm not that wet!"

"Well, your blood pressure has gone up," said the nurse. "Let's sit you up a bit more now."

She helped her to get upright and adjusted the bed back to its usual position. She departed, but not before shooting a warning look at Ava and Anna. Anyone would've thought they'd deliberately shook up the bottle and aimed it at the patients.

Anna looked at Ava. "Don't be upset. You've actually helped the situation. Sylvia's feeling better now, aren't you?" she said, addressing the old lady, who nodded in agreement.

Ava didn't look convinced.

Two domestics, armed with industrial-strength mops appeared and were skirting around the floor in an attempt to remove the sticky mess before it endangered anyone. You had to give it to the staff - they were very protective of their charges at least. Meanwhile, Ava's complexion had returned to its usual pale colour. She was no longer subdued but stared angrily at her mother.

"These things happen," Anna explained. "What's done is done."

"It wouldn't have happened if you hadn't made me open it in the first place!" Ava retorted. "I told you I couldn't open it but you wouldn't help me. As usual. I'm never listening to you again!"

Ava turned around, so that all Anna could see was her

back. Anna frowned. It didn't help that they were periodically reminded of the event every time someone entered the ward and noticed their shoes sticking to the floor. So much for the 'deep clean' they'd been critically informed they had prompted by their actions. It was no wonder the hospital was still in special measures.

Having washed, dried and sanitised her hands, Anna sat back down by the bedside. Her mother was now busy on her iPad. No doubt, she was on one or other of her games - planting crops - in a bid to outdo Jean in the farming stakes. She smiled at her competitiveness - a streak which ran through all of the family. She looked across to Ava. She had her head in a book and clearly didn't want to be disturbed either.

Anna decided she might as well join them. There was a copy of *The Sun* folded up on the table, between two barely-drunk Build Up drinks and a full bowl of soup which had gone cold. Michael would have bought the paper this morning when he'd gone for his cigarettes. Not that he read much. He would just have skimmed over the headlines, scanned a few of the pictures or maybe looked at the racing pages whilst drinking his morning brew. No doubt he'd thought his mum might like to catch up on the latest happenings and had left it for her. She hadn't touched it. Anna settled down to flick through the pages, glad of the opportunity to sit and escape from reality.

The familiar theme tune from *Downton Abbey* broke through the silence. Ethel had commandeered the remote again and was squinting at the screen at the end of the room.

Anna turned her attention to the TV.

"Oh look, Mum, it's *Downton*. Bet you're looking forward to this new series, aren't you?" Anna asked.

Freda diverted her attention momentarily from her game and pulled down her mask.

"What?" she rasped. She looked briefly at the advert then put her mask back on and returned to her game.

This was surprising. As a rule, she always idolised people

from her favourite soap. This was out of character. Somehow it disturbed Anna.

"What about this, then?" Anna nudged her mother as an advert for the new season of *Strictly* came on. This was sure to interest her. Freda took no notice.

Anna gave up. It was clear that television really didn't matter anymore. This was worrying.

Anna tried a different tack, in an attempt to engage her mother.

"So, how was Kirsty then?" she asked.

"Same," Freda replied nonchalantly. She continued to play her game.

Anna tried again, "Jean said she was trying for a baby."

Freda sighed. She stopped what she was doing, put the iPad down and picked up her pad and pen from the table. Her hand was shaking as she attempted to write. Anna waited patiently. After what seemed like an age, Freda turned the pad so Anna could read what she'd written. She'd managed one sentence.

Anna read it out loud, "She's planning a cruise? Well there's a bit of a difference between going on a cruise and having a baby!"

Freda gestured for her to return the pad to her. She wrote again.

This time Anna peered over her shoulder as she wrote 'tummy tuck' followed by lots of pound signs.

"Ah! I see. She's spent so much on that tummy tuck that she doesn't want to ruin it by getting pregnant!" Anna filled in the gaps in the conversation on her mother's behalf. "Well I'm not surprised really," she continued. "She's always put herself first. Likes the easy life. She's too selfish to have a child. It'd do her head in. She's better off just concentrating on her life with that gorgeous new husband of hers - Colin."

Freda nodded in agreement. She took up the pen again and wrote 'dog'

Anna read the message.

"What? He's a dog!" Anna laughed. "That can't be right! He's not a dog! He's well fit!" Ava looked up momentarily, shook her head and went back to her book.

Freda wagged her finger and pointed once again to the word 'dog'.

Anna thought again. "Oh, you mean she's got a dog?"

Freda's eyes told her that she was wrong again.

"She hasn't got a dog?" Anna queried.

Freda shook her head again.

She jabbed at the word on the page. At the same time, Anna could see her mask fogging up as she tried to speak.

"Yes. Dog. I see that," said Anna. "But you've said she hasn't got a dog!"

Freda rolled her eyes then took her pen and vigorously underlined the word 'dog'.

"I don't follow," said Anna. "Has she got a dog or has she not got a dog?" It was clear she was getting frustrated now.

Freda turned to her granddaughter who, having been alerted to the growing disagreement had finally given up reading and put down her book. Ava looked at her nana then tipped the pad of paper towards herself so she could get a good look. Freda stared back at her intently, and pulled down her mask and mouthed a word. Ava got it straight away.

"She's telling you that Kirsty wants a dog but isn't getting one," Ava explained.

Freda flopped back against the pillow and extended her arms in the air as if to say 'hallelujah!'

"Well how was I supposed to work that out?" cried Anna. "It's like Name that Tune. 'I'll name that tune in one, Tom,' " she mimicked. "I'd defy anyone to work that out!"

Freda tossed the pad of paper up the bed out of reach. She put her mask back on to make it clear that she was no longer playing this game.

The Duty Nurse appeared. Anna hoped she'd calmed down

since this afternoon's shenanigans.

"Hello, Mrs Simpson, time for your nebuliser," she said as she approached the oxygen machine by the bed. Unhooking another mask from where it was hanging, she injected some medicine into it before swapping it with the one on Freda's face and setting it to work with the oxygen source on the wall. She turned Freda's main machine off and then left the bay.

Anna sat down but kept her eyes trained on the lights on the monitor as each one went out. Then she and Ava stared at the vapours which swirled and danced around Freda's nose.

Ten minutes later the mask had cleared. Anna scanned the ward seeking out the Duty Nurse. There was no sign of her. She stood up and changed the masks back over, making sure not to catch her mum's hair in the elastic straps. Satisfied that it was on correctly, she switched off the oxygen tap on the wall as the nurses usually did. Next, she turned her attention to the main oxygen unit. But the dials and buttons baffled her. She looked at Ava.

"Don't ask me!" Ava protested. "I don't know how it works."

Anna hurried off to find someone who might know how to operate it. But she returned with just an auxiliary who explained that the handover was being conducted and so there were no nurses available.

"Is it this machine here?" the auxiliary asked, as she walked towards it. Not a good start. Anna watched as the nurse fumbled with the buttons.

"Oh, I don't really know how to do this," she explained as she pressed each one in turn. "But I'll give it a go."

Freda looked away from the auxiliary and towards Ava and Anna. Anna made eye contact and registered her mother's thoughts. This auxiliary knew no more about the machinery than they did. Anna shifted uncomfortably from one foot to the other. She was regretting having fetched this woman and fearful lest she mess up the settings. Mindful that every minute spent fiddling with it was another minute her mother was without oxygen, Anna was itching to tell her to 'Bugger off!' She was just about to suggest they wait until a staff nurse was available when she heard a hissing sound.

"Looks like that's done it," the auxiliary smiled, blissfully unaware of the looks which she'd been getting behind her back. "I'll get someone to pop back in a bit just to check on it," she said cheerfully as she departed.

"Too bloody right you will," Anna muttered under her breath. She made for the machine to see what it was set on. She wished she could remember what numbers had been on display before it had been switched off.

"Sorry, Mum. I'll keep an eye out and get someone over here as soon as I can."

"Anything I can help with, flower?"

Anna turned to see Peter approaching the bed. Freda's eyes lit up in surprise.

"Hiya," said Anna. She extended her hand to take the flask which he was holding out in front of him. At the same time, she made sure to move the newspaper so that it hid the untouched bowl of soup from his view.

"I thought you weren't coming until tomorrow?" she said, as she placed the flask on the bedside cabinet.

"Change of plan. Work are sending me to Nottingham first thing so I'm on a flying visit to see Mum before I go. I've brought more soup."

He smiled at his mum who gave him a thumbs up. The creases either side of her mask told him that she was grinning underneath it. Peter acknowledged Ava with a slight nod then went straight to the machine. His brow was furrowed as he checked out first that the tubing was correctly attached and then that the oxygen supply was turned on sufficiently. As a specialist in the machinery used to circulate chemicals around swimming pools, he could at the very least tell if it was operating properly. He shook his head.

"Summat's not right here," he said. "There's a pump in

this unit which should be oxygenating the air. Listen. Hear that?"

"I can't hear anything except a hissing," Anna replied.

"Exactly!" said Peter. "You should be able to hear the pump going. But you can't. This is doing diddly squat."

"Are you sure?" Ava said, putting down her book again and staring at her uncle.

"Yes, I'm sure, Ava," he replied. "Believe me I've heard it often enough times whilst I've been sitting where you are. Also, see these numbers here?" He pointed to the screen to the right of the machine.

Everyone peered more closely as he spoke.

"Well the reading should be on about seventy per cent. This isn't even displaying a reading."

Peter turned to Anna.

"Fetch a nurse back as soon as you can. Make sure you get one of the proper ones not one of those in a beige uniform. All they're fit for is fetching and carrying or giving you the shits with their cups of tea and coffee!"

Ava winced.

"Oh, I speak from experience, Ava, believe me. Don't go accepting any drinks from them."

Given the afternoon she'd had she wasn't about to accept any drinks from anyone.

"Well, I've got to dash, Mum," he said. He made towards the side of the bed and bent down. He kissed her quickly on the cheek and made to leave but she grasped his hand. She stared at him as she gripped his fingers with her own. Her eyes were watery. She held his gaze for more than a moment. A look passed between them. Peter shifted his feet then took a tighter grip of his mother's hand and gave it a decisive shake before letting go. Freda clasped both hands together across her tummy, her eyes momentarily downcast.

"I'll only be gone a couple of days," he announced. "Eat that soup I've made you, Mum, and concentrate on getting better. I'll see you when I get back."

Freda looked up but was silent. Peter waved as he turned to leave. She half-heartedly waved back as her eyes followed him to the end of the bed, down the ward, and around the corner. Only when he was out of sight, did she turn her attention back to Ava and Anna. With glistening eyes, she took a big sigh. Ava touched her nana's hands and smiled.

Anna checked her watch. Seven o'clock. Just three more hours until Jean would take over. Ava's phone beeped.

"It's a text from dad," she explained. "He's outside now."

She had school in the morning, whereas Anna was stopping at her mother's again.

Ava stood up and retrieved her coat from the back of the chair, but decided not to put it on. It was still dripping wet. She folded it over her arm then kissed her nana goodbye.

"Love you," she said.

Freda squeezed her hand. Ava squeezed it back and smiled warmly. Then she turned to leave.

"See you tomorrow, Mum," she said.

"Will do," Anna replied. Then instructed, "Don't you stay up too late. Make sure you have a good night's sleep! Don't forget you need to take a packed lunch!"

"Yes Mother! I will do, Mother! Anything you say, Mother!' she said as she departed.

Freda gave Anna a knowing look. She didn't need to write anything down this time. Anna knew exactly what she was thinking. Like mother, like daughter.

CHAPTER 25

Anna looked upon her mother. She'd dropped off to sleep almost the minute Ava had left and showed no sign of waking up anytime soon. The oxygen machine still wasn't making the noise it usually did but she didn't know who else she could ask about it. She'd already located the staff nurse in charge of the ward tonight and voiced her concerns to her and had been met with quite a stern reproach. The machine, she'd said, was working "just fine." They were short staffed and there were other patients on the ward with more pressing concerns. She should "stop worrying."

But she did worry. She worried all the time. She read in the paper every day about NHS staff getting things wrong. What if this was one of those times? What if the machine really wasn't working properly, as Peter had said, and her mother was being deprived of oxygen? The whole reason for being on it in the first place was to keep her alive. What if, whilst she was sitting here doing nothing, her mother was slowly dying? Anna looked again at her mum's face. It was really pale. No, it was grey...

Panicked, Anna took hold of her mother's wrist and checked for her pulse. It was still there but seemed faint.

She traced her fingers down over her hand. It felt cold to the touch. Fuck. Someone needed to see her. And quick.

She scanned the ward desperately seeking out someone in a blue uniform. No-one. She stood up so she could see clearly through the glass window at the end of the ward. Still no-one. She looked beyond the nursing station. A glimpse of blue...

As she shifted her weight from one foot to the other, she willed the nurse to come closer. "Come on! Turn around!"

Every moment seemed like an eternity.

At last she came into view! Anna waved frantically.

The staff nurse approached the bed. Just one look at Freda was enough.

"How long has she looked like this?" she asked as she began to time her pulse using her fob watch.

"A while," said Anna. "I told the other nurse that I thought the machine wasn't working properly but she insisted it was."

The nurse looked at the machine and frowned. She pressed some buttons and fiddled with the dial. She chewed at her bottom lip.

"Perhaps it was then but it isn't working now," she said. "Wait here!"

She left the bedside and sprinted to the desk where she picked up the phone. Anna saw her wave across to another member of staff. She promptly returned with a blood pressure gauge and placed it on the bed. Then she set about disconnecting Freda's oxygen tube from the machine and reconnecting it to another machine which an orderly had just plugged in. She unhooked a clip from it and placed it on Freda's index finger. Immediately, a reading appeared on a screen. She frowned.

"I'm just taking your blood pressure, Freda," she said, wrapping a sleeve around her arm and securing it with the Velcro. Anna stared at her mother who continued to sleep.

"She is going to be okay, isn't she? Only I told the other nurse I was worried about that machine and she said it was

241

all fine."

Anna felt like her heart was in her mouth. She twisted the rings on her finger as she tried to control her trembling. She looked at the nurse.

"Her blood pressure is always low," Anna explained.

"Yes, I know," the nurse replied. She removed the sleeve and put the machine to one side. Gently, she stroked her fingers down Freda's cheek.

"Freda, can you open your eyes for me, please?" she asked.

Anna stared as her mum's eyes flickered but remained shut.

The nurse asked again, still stroking Freda's cheek as she spoke.

"Freda? Freda?"

"Oh my God, Anna! What's happened?" It was Jean who spoke now. Having just arrived on the ward, she flung her handbag down on the bed, threw off her coat and shot to her mother's side, where she took hold of her hand.

"She's freezing cold, Anna!" Jean screeched. She began to rub her mother's hand between her own. "Mum, please wake up!" There was an urgency in her voice as she turned to Anna to seek out an explanation.

"The machine hasn't been working, Jean. I told them but they said it was fine," said Anna. Her bottom lip trembled as she spoke and she felt her cheeks going hot.

Jean didn't look convinced. "You should've got someone!" she said. "For God's sake, Anna, she's grey!" She rubbed her hand some more.

"I tried, but I couldn't find anyone."

"You don't need to 'find' anyone, Anna! There's a fucking big red button at the back of the bed which you press when you need help. There!" she shouted as she pointed at a remote-control dangling from the wall, "See it?"

Anna did see it. Yes. It seemed obvious now. That's what the patients were supposed to press when they needed assistance, although most of them on this ward had had theirs fastened away to stop them pestering all day long. Why hadn't she thought of that? Stupid! She could've kicked herself. She clenched her fists and dug her finger nails into her palms. She felt the pain. She squeezed them even harder as she held her breath.

Jean looked at the clip on her mother's finger. As she had COPD, she was used to using one of these on herself at the end of each day to measure her heart rate and oxygen levels to work out whether she needed to hook up to her oxygen tank for a while. The oxygen reading was creeping back up into the nineties. Thank God for that! Hopefully it would get closer to one hundred per cent but she was happy with that for now.

The nurse noticed Anna trying to puzzle out the meaning of the readings.

"She's getting enough oxygen in her bloodstream now," she explained. "For someone with her condition, anything over ninety per cent is good."

"What about the heart-rate?" Anna asked. The reading was one hundred and twenty. "What should that be?"

"Well, it can be anywhere between sixty and one hundred beats per minute in a person when they're resting," the nurse replied.

Anna frowned.

"Bearing in mind that your mum's lungs aren't working properly, her heart is having to work much harder to get the oxygen around her body," the nurse said. "It's what I'd expect it to be. There's no need to be concerned."

Huh! She'd heard that before: "No need to be concerned." It was easy for her to say. It wasn't her mother who was lying in a hospital bed struggling to breathe. It wasn't her mother who'd been deprived of the very oxygen that was keeping her alive and was now having to fight with every ounce of her reserve just to keep going. She hadn't had to sit and watch her own mother deteriorate in front of her eyes. She hadn't been the one sitting by the bedside for the past few weeks. She hadn't had to observe her mother as her weight plummeted and her skin sagged; console her as she lost the independence to go to the toilet and had to suffer the indignity of, first bedpans, and then a catheter and incontinence pads; reassure her that the physio she endured each morning would make some difference to her well-being; that the food she left untouched each day, since it hurt like hell to swallow, didn't matter; that the increasing doses of morphine each time weren't something to worry about. No. This wasn't her mother. Anna had every reason to be concerned.

Freda coughed, drawing everyone's attention to her face. Her eyes were open at last.

"There you are!" said the nurse, smiling. Jean let out a gasp of relief.

"Back in the room, Mother!" she joked nervously. She was grateful to see that the colour was returning to her cheeks.

The nurse smiled down at Freda, "Well, your blood pressure's back up, Freda, and your stats are within the boundaries of what they should be," she explained. "How are you feeling?"

Freda pulled down the mask.

"Tired," she mouthed. Then she beckoned towards a glass on the table and opened her mouth to indicate that she was thirsty. Jean picked up the glass. She placed her other hand gently on the back of her mum's head and raised the glass towards her mouth to help her to take a drink. Freda took two large gulps then rested back down against the pillows, exhausted. Anna passed her a tissue. She dabbed at her lips. They were cracked and looked sore. Anna imagined that the inside of her mouth wasn't dissimilar and made a mental note to remember to use the mouth care kit later and to fetch her some lip balm.

Noticing her staring, Freda smiled at her, her eyes twinkling.

"Come on, Mother, let's get your mask back on," said

Jean. "We don't want you turning that colour again! You proper scared me! You were whiter than our Jason and that's saying something. Don't do that to me! My nerves can't take it."

She helped her to put her mask back on and turned to the nurse. "This is working now isn't it?" she demanded.

"Yes, of course," she replied. She took the clipboard from the end of the bed and scribbled down some notes.

"I'll check on you later," she said. She left.

"Too right you will!" muttered Jean. "You've got to watch them in here, Anna. We're all right when Michelle or Karen are on the shift but you can't trust any of these other ones. They don't know their arse from their elbow. You've got to be on them at all times. God knows what would've happened if I hadn't turned up!"

"I did try you know. I told them several times I thought the machine wasn't working but they kept saying it was. I don't know what else I could've done," Anna protested.

"You shouldn't have let them switch it off in the first place, our kid. Michelle said to keep the oxygen on when Mum's having a nebuliser. That duty nurse has got it all wrong. She won't get away with it now I'm here. Anyway, you get off back to Mum's now for a rest. You're back here in the morning filling in for our Peter. You look terrible."

Jean turned her back on her, picked up the jug of water and approached the sink.

"Is it my imagination, Mother, or is this floor really sticky?" she said. "It's like I'm back in Yates' on a Saturday night."

Freda tried to grin.

"Remind me to tell that auxiliary when she turns up," Jean continued. "I'm not one for cleaning but even I know that this floor needs a good mopping. God knows when it was last done!"

Freda rolled her eyes. Placing the jug back on the table, Jean reached for her bag. She drew out her iPad and began to put in her password.

"Now! You've got to see this, Mother!"

Jean sat down and placed the screen in full view of them both.

"You'll be impressed with this. You've never seen a farm like it!"

CHAPTER 26

It was Saturday night and Jean was in Smokey's. Seated at a table near to the stage, she awaited the main act. She imagined that the room was packed as usual though she couldn't actually see as it was so dark. She wasn't sure who she was with but someone to her right was snoring loudly. No doubt they'd got tired of waiting. That wasn't surprising. She had an overwhelming desire to fall asleep herself. She couldn't remember the last time she'd felt like this. It was probably when she'd first had kids. Every muscle in her body ached. It was as if her legs had been glued to the floor. Her arms felt disconnected and heavy, like they belonged to someone else. It had taken all her energy just to fold them. She leant forward and rested them on the table so that they formed a kind of cradle. The table was soft like a feather bed. Inviting.

Jean's head was throbbing but much as she wanted to, she fought off the desire to nestle down in her arms. She must resist. She knew she had to stay awake. She knew it was important although she couldn't quite remember why.

Why was there no music? She'd heard the announcement for the main turn ages ago but she'd yet to see who it was. Come to think of it there wasn't much noise at all. Just some muttering in the background and that woman behind her doing her own kind of karaoke. She sounded like Eartha Kitt as she warbled her way through an out-of-tune rendition of an old Vera Lynn number. Well, not really 'through' it as such but more just singing the opening lyrics over and over again. Bluebirds were repeatedly flying over the white cliffs, the woman's rattly voice was getting louder and louder and Jean's eyelids were becoming heavier and heavier. Like garage doors when the remote was broken, they repeatedly opened and closed, until at last, despite her best efforts, they just slammed shut.

"For fuck's sake, will you stop singing that fucking song!"

Jean was awoken with a start. She squinted. She rubbed her eyes and blinked repeatedly as she tried to focus on her watch. What time was it? What day was it? Where was she?

She looked up. White walls, an array of machines, drip stands, that musty smell. Shit! She'd fallen asleep when she was supposed to be looking after her mother. She turned around. There she was, lying very still. Quickly she sought out her hand. It was warm. *Thank God for that.*

So, what was all that noise about? Her eyes swept the room. Sylvia and Joan were both sound asleep but Ethel was very much awake and clearly agitated. In the bed next door to her was a new woman. With long grey hair cascading down her wizened face, she was clutching a hairbrush in her hand and speaking into it like it was a microphone.

"And now, for one night only, it's.... Vera!" she announced, before starting to sing once more. "There'll be blue birds over..."

"Shut up! I can't take any more!" pleaded Ethel. "Nurse! Nurse! Anybody! Please shut her up!"

She screwed up her eyes and homed in on Jean as the old woman, having got to the end of the first line, restarted the song.

"Will you help me, love?" she begged.

Jean sighed and wondered how she'd managed to sleep

through this. She really must've been tired. Reluctantly, she got up and walked towards the old lady's bed.

The new woman stopped singing. Jean looked at the board above her bed, seeking out her name.

"Margery Smith. Dr Azura. Nil by mouth," she read.

"At last! You're here!" cried the new lady, dropping her hairbrush and clapping her hands together.

"I've been waiting all night for you!" she continued. "Come on, the band is all set up just over there." She pointed to the corner of the room by the window where a large mobile medicine cabinet was parked underneath the television.

Jean looked on, then back at the old dear. Margery's eyes were wide with wonder as she eagerly anticipated Jean's contribution to the evening entertainment. It was evident that this behaviour was more than the product of having been starved of food for a few hours. Clearly, the woman had dementia. This was going to take some effort.

"Hello, Margery!" Jean began.

"Who are you talking to, love?" the old woman asked.

Jean thought quickly.

"Hello, Vera!" she began again. The old woman grinned widely, revealing her gums. Jean smiled. She reminded her of a character from *Fraggle Rock*. No wonder she sounded so odd.

"Right. Well I've had a word with the band over there," said Jean, pointing in the direction of the medicine cabinet, "and they said that they've finished for the night and they'll see you tomorrow night, as usual."

"Finished? But it's still early!" the old lady replied. "We've got a whole set of songs to get through."

Jean checked her watch. It was approaching three o'clock in the morning. No wonder poor Ethel was going 'spare'. God knows how long Margery had been singing for. She wasn't even looking remotely tired. She was probably one of those women who slept all day and so could stay awake all night. Well, Jean wasn't going to put up with this.

249

Her mum needed to rest. She might be asleep now but she could easily be woken up if this continued. And poor Ethel didn't deserve this either. Jean decided to try a different tactic. She approached the bed, and leant down so she could speak directly into the old lady's ear.

"You see these ladies here?" she said, pointing to the beds of Sylvia and Joan. "Well, they absolutely love your singing."

"Really?" said Margery, beaming with pride.

"Yes. Really," replied Jean. "But they're asleep at the moment, so they're missing out."

"Let's wake them up!" shouted Margery.

Jean took a deep breath. Then continued, "If you wait until tomorrow, not only will you have these ladies to listen to you but, if you time it right, you'll have all their visitors too!"

Margery's eyes lit up.

Jean decided to 'lay it on thicker' - "And... get this, right? You'll have all the staff as well! So that's a full audience and the band to accompany you."

"Yes. You're right!"

Jean smiled as the old lady took the bait. Talking like this reminded her of when she used to have to persuade her kids to go back to bed when they got up too early on Christmas Day. "But you have to go to sleep first so you can be ready," she added.

"But I'm not ready for sleep! I need to practise," Margery replied.

"Good singers rest their voices," Jean continued, "and you can't practise without a band, and they've gone home."

Margery squinted into the corner once more where she believed the band to be sitting.

"Well, yes, they're very quiet,' she conceded.

"They are," replied Jean. "That's because they're resting."

"Resting?"

"Yes."

"For tomorrow?"

"For tomorrow."

"Then they'll play whilst I sing?" asked Margery.

" Yes," replied Jean. "They'll play all night. You can sing to your heart's content. There'll be a huge audience and everything. It'll be brilliant." She hoped she sounded convincing.

"And you'll be there too?" enquired Margery.

Jean remembered her role as backing singer in all this.

"Of course! I wouldn't miss it for the world!" she replied.

"Shall I go to sleep now?" asked Margery.

"Yes, sweetheart, you go to sleep," said Jean. The old lady began to shuffle down under her covers. Jean helped to tuck her in.

"Good night, dear," said Margery. "You won't forget to wake me up when the band's ready, will you?"

"Oh I won't forget, Vera," said Jean. "Goodnight."

And with that she blew out a sigh of relief and began to tiptoe back to her mum. Ethel looked up at her gratefully as she passed her bed and nodded at her. Jean held up both her hands with the fingers crossed. She prayed the trick had worked so they could all get some rest

.

CHAPTER 27

Anna noticed that the ward felt different today. And it wasn't because of the new long-haired old woman who had arrived on the ward, whose antics had been relayed by Jean. No. It was something else. She couldn't quite put her finger on it, but there was a definite change in atmosphere. There was a stillness. A calm. There wasn't the usual bustle of auxiliaries helping out patients, or nurses administering treatments. The physios who routinely visited at this time every day were conspicuously absent. Even the patients were quiet. Today there was no idle chatter. Everyone kept themselves to themselves. Each lay in their beds and just stared into space, content to be alone with their thoughts. Anna caught a glance at Sylvia. She returned only the slightest of nods in acknowledgement before turning quickly away. Something was going on. It was as if they were all harbouring some big secret between them. And what was certain was that they weren't about to let Anna in on it.

She took up a chair by her mother's bed and resigned herself to joining in the silence. She watched her as she slept. Even with the assistance of the oxygen, her breathing seemed laboured. Her chest was rising and falling too quickly for someone who was at rest. She felt the quickening of her own heartbeat as she thought about what this meant. So, in an attempt to distract herself from what was happening, she looked around for clues of what was going on.

The signs were visible enough. The three tubs of medication - untouched. The bowl of soup - uneaten. The cartons of juice - unopened. Even the iPad - uncharged. She took note of other pointers. A set of three birthday cards - one each for Emily, Jake and Peter - was propped up against a bottle on the bedside cabinet. Emily's birthday was only in two days' time on the 9th of September, followed by Jake's on the 10th of September and Peter's on the 18th of September. Her mother never wrote cards out this far in advance. She didn't even buy them until the day before they were needed...

Of course, these clues had been there all along for anyone who cared to look. But they were unseen for a reason. No one had dared to look. Looking meant admitting that things were changing, admitting that things were worsening. And no-one was prepared to do that. No-one was prepared...

"This is Mrs Simpson."

Anna was brought back to reality by a man's voice. She looked up to see the consultant, surrounded by a posse of medical students carrying clipboards. Dressed in pristine white coats, they stood in sharp contrast to him. Tall and tanned, and dressed casually in a checked shirt, only the stethoscope gave him away. He looked past Anna, took out a pen and addressed her mother who was now awake.

"How are you today, dear?" he said, his eyes downcast as he read her notes which had been passed to him by an enthusiastic bespectacled woman.

He repeated himself, shouting loudly and deliberately, "'How. Are. You. Today?"

Freda stared at him in bemusement. She might be old but she wasn't deaf and she wasn't stupid. She pulled down her mask and attempted to answer. But he wasn't looking. Instead he had turned his back and was talking to his charges, reeling off all kinds of numbers about various blood counts. They were nodding in understanding but it meant nothing to Freda or Anna.

"Excuse me, Doctor?" Anna interjected. The consultant turned around as if he had only just noticed her.

"Ah! Who might you be?" he asked.

"Anna Croft," she replied. "I'm Freda's daughter. Can you explain what's going on please?"

"Well your mother's blood counts aren't good," he said. He turned to Freda, and shouted again, "Your blood markers aren't good, my dear!"

Freda rolled her eyes.

"What does that mean, exactly?" asked Anna.

"Well, they should be going down in value by now," he explained. "Considering the amount of medication your mother has been receiving, we would expect them to be significantly lower but they've hardly moved since last week."

"And..?" said Anna.

He scratched his head. "Well, that's that really," he said, as he turned to leave, his mind already on the next patient.

Anna felt a tugging on her sleeve. She looked back at her mum.

"Ask him what's going on," Freda whispered.

"I just did," said Anna. "He says your blood markers are high and they should be much lower by now."

Freda looked none the wiser.

Anna tried again. "Excuse me, Doctor," she said.

He turned to look at her.

"What is the value of the blood markers?" she asked.

"Well one of them is down from ninety to fifty and the other one has gone from fifteen to ten," he answered.

"Well that's good surely?" replied Anna. "They're going down! What should they be?"

"Well, the first one needs to be less than ten and the

second less than three," he answered.

"Oh," replied Anna.

The doctor turned his attention to his trainees, "We'll leave things as they are for now and just wait and see. There's not much we can do here. Who's next?"

One of them consulted their list. "Mr Jones in the next bay," they said.

The consultant briefly turned to Anna and her mum. "All right. Well, good day to you both," he said. And with that, he walked briskly away.

Like Lorenz's goslings, the trainees followed him out. Anna turned to her mother. She looked weary.

"That's it then, isn't it?" Freda croaked.

"What do you mean?" said Anna. "You heard what Dr Bennett said the other day. It doesn't matter what your blood markers are. It's how you feel that matters. That consultant just sees facts and figures. Take no notice of him."

Freda pulled her mask all the way down, so that her face was clearly visible. She faced Anna square on and drew herself up. Mustering all her energy, it was obvious that she was making a determined effort to get herself heard. She looked her daughter straight in the eye, and, for the first time in what seemed like ages, Anna could actually tell what she was saying.

"I'm on my way out, aren't I?" Freda said.

The words hung in the air. Anna didn't know what to say but held onto her mother's gaze. Logic demanded the answer 'yes' but this was her mum and she couldn't bring herself to say anything. She just looked back.

Freda continued, "You've been here before, love. You've worked on a ward like this. You know how this goes. If I was a dog, you'd put me down. They can give me something, can't they? You've seen it done."

It was true, of course. Anna had seen many patients on their deathbeds given large doses of morphine to send them on their way. Her mother had already been given larger and larger doses of the stuff this week so she guessed it was only the next step, but she couldn't answer. She didn't want to be the one they all blamed for her mother's swift demise. It was Sod's law that all this would happen on her watch. By rights it should've been Peter sitting here now. If he hadn't gone to work, he would've been the one facing this dilemma. Just her luck.

Her mother continued to wait for a response. She looked like a small determined child appealing for permission to go and play out. She knew what answer she wanted and she wasn't going to move until she got it.

Anna knew when she'd been defeated. She gave the barest of nods. Her mother looked relieved. She smiled weakly.

"Now, go and get Michelle," Freda said, "and tell her it's time."

Dutifully, Anna got up, but she didn't need to go far. Like an actress who had been waiting in the wings, Michelle appeared.

"Are you ready, Freda?" she asked.

"Yes," she replied. She continued to look at Anna.

Michelle took her keys from her belt and momentarily left the bay. She returned almost immediately carrying a tray of packages which she placed on the bed. A folded piece of paper lay on the top. Michelle picked it up and checked the contents of the tray against this list.

"You soon got that lot ready, didn't you?" Anna joked. "Anyone would've thought you knew what was going to happen today!"

Michelle looked at Freda. A knowing look passed between them.

For Anna, the penny dropped. This was her mother's 'End of Life' care plan - signed, sealed and now to be delivered. That's what had been going on this morning. For the briefest of time her mother had been left on her own and she'd used it to conspire with Michelle. As if reading her thoughts, Michelle sought to explain.

"This is your mum's wish," she said. "She asked me to have the plan drawn up and authorised. You can see all the signatures if you like."

Michelle pointed to the foot of the paper, "Here's your mum's handwriting."

Anna didn't need to look. She knew this was her mother's doing.

Michelle turned back to Freda - "I'm just going set up this syringe feeder, Freda, so that we don't have to keep making you into a pincushion!"

She unwrapped a unit which looked like a small pencil case and placed it on the bed. She opened a packet of sterile gloves and put them on.

"What? No regular injections?" asked Anna.

"No," replied Michelle. "This unit will deliver a slow infusion of medication over the next few hours."

She pulled back the covers of the bed as she spoke.

"Freda, I'm putting this very small needle just under the skin here on your tummy. It won't hurt but you'll feel a small scratch. Sorry if my hands are cold!"

Freda smiled. "This is nothing compared to the amount of injections I've been having for the last few months for my blood clots," she rasped.

Michelle attached a thin piece of tubing to the needle. Then she took out a roll of tape and broke a piece off. Carefully, she swirled the tubing around the needle rather like a Catherine Wheel and fixed it in place with the tape. She added more tape to ensure it was secure then attached it to the unit which she placed next to Freda's side. Having set it up to work, she gently covered Freda back up and used the bed covers to hide the unit. She tucked Freda in.

"There. All done," she said. She leant forward and kissed her on the forehead then gave her a big hug. "There you go, darling. You take care."

Freda hugged her back. "Thank you, sweetheart."

Michelle stood up and straightened her uniform. She turned to Anna.

"Your mum will feel tired shortly as the medicines kick in. She won't be in any pain. I'll be here all evening so don't hesitate to call me over if there is anything at all that you need. I'm here for you."

"I will," said Anna. "Thank you."

Michelle walked away. As Anna watched her leave, she saw her hand reach into her pocket and pull out a tissue. She heard her blow her nose. Anna took a deep breath and turned her attention back to her mum. She knew she was going to have to conjure up a good deal of resolve to get through the next few hours...

CHAPTER 28

If there was ever a law that defined the Simpsons it was Sod's law. If something could go wrong it invariably did. Like that time Freda had left it until the last minute to put on her lottery numbers at the local shop, knowing she would be passing on her way home from her friend's. She'd always used the same numbers and she'd never missed a week. Then Jean had rung to say she'd got stuck in traffic and she needed her to pick the kids up - there was no one else and she was desperate. Freda had obliged, then driven at breakneck speed to the shop and arrived with five minutes to spare but then the pen at the desk wouldn't work and the shop assistant was busy. She'd scrambled around to find a pen at the bottom of her bag, filled in the card and got to the till in what she thought was just in time only to see that the time on the machine was a minute faster than her watch said it was and it wouldn't let her enter. She'd resigned herself to not taking part, bought some milk and gone to Jean's with the kids, thinking nothing more about it. She'd never won so much as a tenner so it wasn't the end of the world if she missed this once. Except that it turned out it would've been the start of a new world for her, as all six numbers came in...

Anna had heard this story many times and now felt a sense of déjà vu as the law now thwarted her attempts to get each of her siblings to the hospital as soon as possible. Of course, she knew Peter was in Nottingham, but she also knew that if he set off straight away, he could make it back in a couple of hours, so she contacted him first. But all she got was the computer-generated voice stating, "Sorry it has not been possible to connect you, please try again later."

Shit. She thought she'd had more luck with Michael as he answered immediately but he didn't have any petrol in his car and his card had just been declined at the cash point. He was on his way to the pub to seek out a friend to lend him some money. Jean wasn't answering her phone but then Anna remembered that it would be on silent as she'd gone back to their mum's for a sleep. It was all right as there was a phone by her mum's bedside so all she had to do was ring the landline. The volume on the ringer was set so high that she couldn't fail to pick up the call. Except she did fail to do so. Several times in fact. It just rang and rang and rang.

Anna bit her lips as she tried to think what to do next. But then she heard a ringing from the cupboard at the side of the bed. Her mum's mobile phone. Maybe Jean had heard the phone ring after all and for whatever reason was trying to contact Anna via her mother's device. She rushed over to the cupboard, sought out the handset and pressed the receive button.

"Jean?" she questioned.

A woman's voice came on the other end, "Good morning. Is this Mrs Simpson?"

Anna sighed and moved away towards the day room where she couldn't disturb anyone.

"No, it's her daughter, Anna," she replied.

"Oh. Well I'm just ringing from the doctor's surgery to check on your mother's health. I believe Doctor Smith made a home visit recently as she was quite poorly and we wanted to make sure she's all right now."

Anna felt angry. The emergency doctor had indeed been called out to check on her mother. He'd said a hospital visit wasn't necessary and instead had left a long list of prescribed medicines which Jean had had to go out and get. Less than twenty-four hours later, they had been rushing their mother in by ambulance. That was a month ago! A whole month had passed and here was his secretary now, only just doing a follow up call? It beggared belief.

"Hello? Are you still there?" the woman asked. "How is your mum doing? Is she better?"

"No. She's in hospital," Anna replied.

"Oh. I'm sorry to hear that. When was she admitted?" she asked.

"The day after your doctor visited," Anna replied. "She was brought in by ambulance in the middle of the night. She's been in here a month."

"Oh dear. I can only apologise for not following this up sooner, but I can assure you that once she's out, Dr Smith can visit her at home so she doesn't have to struggle to get to the surgery. Do you know when she's coming out?" the lady asked.

Anna felt her stomach churn. She took a deep breath before replying,

"She won't be coming out...She's dying."

There. She'd said it. Out loud. Anna felt her voice break as she spoke the words. She reached for the arm of a nearby chair and sat herself down, still holding the phone to her ear. There was a brief silence on the other end of the line.

"My dear, I am so very, very sorry," replied the lady.

She must've heard the falter in Anna's voice as she added, "Are you going to be all right?"

Anna tasted salt on her lips. She passed the handset to her other hand as she attempted to pull down her sleeve and wipe away her tears which were now streaming down her face.

"Yes. I'll be fine," she answered, her trembling voice

betraying her, as she thanked her for calling and switched off the phone. She placed it on her lap whilst she searched in her pockets for a tissue. Just an empty packet and some keys. She pulled both her sleeves down now and wiped each eye in turn. She couldn't let people see her like this. She had to be brave. Composing herself, she took several breaths. In. Out. In. Out. Confident she was ready, she pushed herself up from the chair and turned back towards the ward. With a determined stride, she walked back to the bedside where her mother still slept, swapped the phones over and in a moment of inspiration dialled Jean's landline on the off-chance she'd gone back to her own house instead of their mum's.

Jean answered almost immediately.

"All right our kid? I was just trying to get some sleep at my own house away from that stupid bloody dog of yours that you've left at Mum's. Does he ever stop barking? What's up?"

"It's time," Anna answered.

Silence.

"Jean?"

"Yes, I heard you. I'm on my way."

CHAPTER 29

It seemed strange being in such a small room after having spent so long in one of the main wards. It was only around the corner but it could've been anywhere in the hospital such was its isolation. It was for the best of course. No patient wanted to watch another patient die in the bed next to them and neither did the family want their affairs to be on show to the public. They'd willingly agreed to move their mother to this more private location out of the sight of others. Away from prying eyes.

And it didn't seem as if they were any more out of mind than usual. The staff still called in to make regular checks - more on them than on their mother - but they had been almost part of the furniture for the past month or so, so they were not at all put out by the interruptions. In fact, it would've been more upsetting if people hadn't been dropping by. It was only sad that the visits were under such circumstances and that, as yet, no place had become available at Silver Birch Hospice.

Jean was fighting tooth and nail to get her mother to the hospice before it was too late. It had spacious, warmly decorated rooms, big comfortable armchairs for visitors, large beds looking out through patio doors to beautiful gardens. And, of course, the dogs were allowed in so her mum would get to see Niko and Mollie one final time. That, more than anything was worth fighting for.

Jean couldn't bear the thought of her mum passing away in this hospital instead. All she saw was white walls, and white furniture - even the blind was an off-white colour. There was just about enough room for chairs for the four of them. It was fine as long as no-one needed to leave and no-one was trying to get in. Otherwise, the position of the door meant they had to pass one of the chairs from one side of the bed to the other and hold it in the air temporarily whilst they all shuffled along sideways and out of the room to allow someone access. It was worse still when a pair of auxiliaries needed to come in see to their mother's bedding and freshen her up a bit. In that case, they had to remove the chairs from the room altogether and they all had to wait outside. It was reminiscent of a game of musical chairs but without the nice music. No. This wasn't the end Jean had imagined for her mum at all. It was altogether too clinical.

The sad truth, of course, was that the only way a place would become available at the hospice was if someone who was occupying one of the beds was to vacate it. Or, in other words, die. Jean was acutely aware of this fact and ordinarily wouldn't have wished such a thing on anyone but, as she told herself, they were in there to die anyway so what difference would a few hours make? She prayed that someone hurried up their journey to the afterlife so her mum could get a shot at departing from a more comfortable place which wasn't tainted with the smell of stale sweat and urine.

Her thoughts were interrupted by knocking followed by the door swinging open and banging against the leg of one of the chairs. Luckily, it was empty as Michael had only just left. He'd had to leave quickly as he'd realised that the parking ticket had already run out on his car. Anna was sitting beside the head of the bed, holding her mother's hand. Janice, Peter's other half, sat next to her staring into space. They all looked up as Peter made his way into the room.

He was stopped in his tracks by the sight of his mother. Propped up in the bed and still wearing her oxygen mask, her eyes were wide open but she acted to all intents and purposes as if she was asleep. She made no attempt to move and did not acknowledge his presence.

Peter stood transfixed for a moment, his hands holding onto the metal frame of the bed. He blinked. Then, he swallowed hard before speaking,

"Right! So, she's given up has she? She's not going to fight it?" he said. His knuckles turned white as he tightened his grip. No one replied.

He continued, "So, who sanctioned all this then?" He looked at each of his sisters in turn.

"Your Anna, of course. Who else could it have been?" came the reply from Janice.

Peter stared at Anna as he dared her to deny it.

Anna didn't meet his gaze but chose to stare straight at Janice instead.

"I didn't sanction anything, Janice. It was nothing to do with me. Mum had already made her mind up and signed the paperwork," she said.

"Well it's funny that she should choose to do that when you were looking after her, isn't it?" Janice retorted. "That's some coincidence don't you think?"

She spat out the last words as she actively sought out Peter's response. He didn't get chance to say anything as Jean butted in:

"Hey! Don't you go blaming our Anna! You haven't been here the last couple of days so you haven't seen how Mum's deteriorated since that night when the oxygen wasn't working properly. If you want to blame someone then blame the staff nurse who was on duty who said it was working when it wasn't. She started all this. It just so happened that our Anna was here this morning when Mum asked for her care plan to be put into operation. It's not something that they just do, Janice. These things take time and a lot of consultation before they're drawn up. I thought you of all people would know that. You're always spouting off about all the people you've met at Silver Birch who've subsequently died there. Don't pretend you don't know how these things work. Any one of us could've been here this morning, so you leave our Anna alone!"

Jean took her inhaler out of her bag and took a couple of puffs before resting back in the chair. Janice kept quiet.

"Right! Well I'm here now," said Peter, "so we'll have some order."

He pointed at two empty cups on the bedside cabinet and spoke to Anna.

"Pass those to Jean! She can make herself useful and return them to the kitchen. You can take one of these chairs away, Anna. There's not enough room as it is in here, let alone having extra chairs cluttering up the place."

Anna was in half a mind whether to respond to this or not but quickly decided against it. Biting her lip, she did as she was instructed and exited the room with Jean. She waited until she was out of earshot, before saying,

"Let's leave him to it. He needs some time with Mum on his own."

"Yes. He looked proper shocked when he saw her, didn't he?" replied Jean.

"Yes" said Anna as she stacked the chair away. She followed Jean to the kitchen to return the cups.

"Bet you've not eaten anything today, either, have you?" asked Jean. She knew full well what the answer was, so didn't wait for a reply.

"Come on! I'll take you to the café before it closes. What you need is one of those red Slushie drinks and a chocolate muffin. My treat. They're très delish!"

Anna smiled. Trust her sister to think that these were the most important substitutes for three square meals! She followed her through the doors and up the stairs to the outside of the building where it was going dark. The sharp cold made her shudder.

"Follow me, our kid!" ordered Jean. "I know exactly how to get there!"

"So you should!" said Anna. "You've been enough times!"

"I know. They'll be thinking I live at this hospital!" she laughed.

That's how Anna felt already but said nothing. She joined her sister's side and linked arms with her. It made her feel stronger. And she was going to need all the strength she could muster to get through the next few hours.

CHAPTER 30

Freda felt something wet and cold on her face. It reminded her of when she was a child - her mum giving her a wash before bedtime. "A lick and a promise" she called it. But it wasn't the roughness of a flannel she felt, nor the smell of carbolic soap which made her nostrils twitch but rather a much softer cloth and the faint aroma of aloe vera. If she wasn't mistaken, this was more like one of those wipes she used to use on the grandchildren when she was changing their nappies. But who would use one of them on the face? No-one. No. It must be a make-up wipe. Maybe she'd been out for the night? She couldn't remember. Although, now she thought about it, she did feel a bit giddy, like she'd had a few. She lifted her hand up to her face, seeking out her glasses. But they weren't there. She hoped she hadn't lost them. That would be all, wouldn't it? How would she explain that to the kids?

"Ah! You're awake! Wondering where your glasses are?"

Someone had read her thoughts.

"Don't worry, Freda. They're just on the cupboard there."

Freda turned her head towards the voice. A large

woman in a beige checked dress and a plastic apron was pointing past her.

"We'll leave them there for now, shall we? Whilst we sort you out."

The door opened and another similarly-dressed woman entered, carrying a set of fresh linen.

"Need a hand, Julie?"

"Yes please, Janet."

Janet placed the bedding at the foot of the bed whilst she pulled on a pair of plastic gloves.

"Right. Where are you up to?" she asked.

"Well, I've done her face," Julie said. She disposed of the wipe into a refuse sack. "I just need a hand changing her nightie and sorting out down below. Did you bring a pad?"

"Yes, I've got everything," she replied.

She smiled down at Freda.

"Let's get you freshened up, shall we?"

Together, the two auxiliaries manoeuvred Freda's nightie over her head, taking care to ensure the oxygen mask, which was currently dangling by her chest, was fed through. They paused momentarily to give her chest and armpits a quick wash and dry, before re-dressing her in a clean nightie. They rolled this down just as far as her abdomen whilst they cleaned up her lower half and dusted her with talcum powder to ensure she was dry. Julie placed her hands on Freda's shoulder and bottom.

"I'm just going to roll you towards me whilst we change your draw sheet, Freda," she explained.

Freda was rolled briskly to one side. Her nose rested briefly on the plastic apron. She felt the old cloth being tucked up against her and the softness of the clean sheet as it was put in place. Then she was rolled onto her other side. The first nurse dragged the old sheet out and disposed of it on the floor before pulling the clean sheet through. Both nurses helped lift Freda into a comfortable position up the bed and replaced her oxygen mask, before tucking in the covers once more.

"There. All done and dusted," said Julie.

Freda could feel the thickness of the incontinence pad beneath her like a big nappy. She giggled to herself. It was a long time since she'd been treated like a baby and there was something really comforting about it. She'd always loved it when the bed was changed. The feel of crisp, freshly-laundered bedding was a treat. She smiled warmly as she watched the two women tidying up and listened to their idle chat.

"I can't believe I saw Beth tonight," said Janet. "She asked me if I wanted to see Rosie's photographs of the wedding. I didn't even know she'd got married!"

"Rosie?" replied Julie. "The girl with the Border Collie dog?"

Freda's ears pricked up.

"Yes. You remember, don't you?" said Janet. "Well he's a singer as well."

"What? The dog?" Julie joked as she gathered up the dirty bedding from the floor.

"No! The fiancé!" laughed Janet, poking Julie in the ribs as she passed her. Freda laughed along.

"Look at her laughing at us!" said Julie.

"Aw! Bless!" replied Janet. "It's a pity she can't talk, isn't it? She was so chatty when she first came in."

Freda wondered what she meant. She'd not stopped talking since they'd woken her up. Couldn't they hear her or something?

She tried to ask them, but they evidently weren't listening. She settled back in the bed and frowned as she watched them leave the room.

CHAPTER 31

It's funny how the body can stay awake for a long period of time when it really has to. Anna calculated she hadn't slept for over twenty-four hours. She had briefly tried to get her head down about three-thirty in the morning in the day room, reclining in the chair which had been bought specifically for visitors to nap in, but had found it difficult to get comfortable. She'd only just drifted off when she'd been awoken by Peter shouting her name. Instantly panicked, she'd jumped up out of the chair, fearing the worst. But he was only calling in to tell her that he and Janice were going home for some sleep and they'd return after breakfast. Brilliant. Why he couldn't have let her rest, she didn't know. Jean was still keeping a vigil by her mother's bedside so she would've alerted her to any change in her condition. She'd found it impossible to settle after that so had returned to the room to keep her sister company.

They'd sat either side of the bed in silence for most of the night, just exchanging the occasional comment, whilst their mother slept on, oblivious to their presence. It was now past eight o'clock in the morning and they could hear the ward coming to life.

Jean yawned and stretched. "Jesus, I'm knackered," she said.

"Me too," said Anna. "It's amazing how doing nothing can make you so tired."

Just then, the door opened. Peter breezed in, carrying a coffee. He walked straight over to the window and pulled up the blind. The room was instantly flooded with light. Both Jean and Anna shielded their eyes.

"What are you sitting in the dark for?" Peter asked. "It's morning time. The day's begun. You can't still be sleeping now."

"Neither of us have been to sleep, actually, Peter," said Jean.

"Oh, give over!" Peter replied. "When I left, you were nodding off at the bedside and our Anna was asleep in the day room!"

"Yes, I *was* asleep," retorted Anna, "but a certain somebody woke me up to tell me he was going home to bed! Thanks for that, Peter."

"You're welcome," he replied sarcastically.

"Right, well you can get yourselves off now. Me and Janice will take over - give you both a break."

Anna looked at Jean. She rolled her eyes.

"Come on, Anna. We know where we're not wanted. Let's wait outside. Our Michael said he'd meet us at 8.30 and it's getting on for that time now."

She stood up and moved the chair against the wall. Anna offered her chair to Janice who sat down straight away. She felt her phone vibrate in her pocket and took it out to see who was texting.

"It's our Michael," she explained. "He says he's just made us some bacon butties and a flask of tea. He'll be outside in five minutes so can we go and grab them off him so he doesn't have to park up?"

"Top result!" said Jean. "Let's get out there. I'm that hungry, I could eat a scabby dog!"

For a moment, Anna thought she saw her mother's eyes

flicker at the word 'dog' but she couldn't be sure. She planted a kiss on her forehead before retrieving her coat from the back of the chair. Then they both left the ward.

Outside, the cold air was a welcome contrast to the stifling heat of the ward. In a move reminiscent of a drug drop off, Michael paused briefly on the double yellow lines to deliver the breakfast before moving swiftly off. He had something 'important' to do but would see them later at Silver Birch. Anna admired his optimism. She really hoped he was right and that her mum could hang on until a place became available.

There was nowhere suitable to sit outside - not even a step - so they had to make do with sitting on the flagged floor. They took care to keep out of the way of the main doors and instead rested their backs against the wall of the building to one side, before tucking into their food. Michael had used plenty of foil to ensure the butties were still hot and hadn't skimped on the bacon either. He'd even remembered to bring along some kitchen roll. This was soon being put to good use as they both mopped up the butter and brown sauce which, in their haste to devour their breakfast, oozed from the sides of the bread and ran down their chins.

Jean finished first. "God, I was ready for that," she said. "I think that's the best bacon butty I've ever had."

"Me too," Anna agreed. "That is just what I needed. Our Michael's a star."

"Yes. He can be a pain in the arse sometimes but he always comes up trumps when it matters. There's no way I could've lasted 'til the hospital café opens. That'll keep me going for the day."

"Yes, me too. All I need now is that mug of tea. Are you cracking open that flask or what, Jean?"

"Yes. I'll be Mum, shall I?" she answered. Her voice faltered. Silently, she placed the two mugs on the ground and began to pour out the tea.

"Well, if you're going to be Mum, you have to walk over

there and start up a random conversation with one of those people," Anna joked.

Jean looked across to the doorway where some patients had gathered. A fat woman in a pink dressing gown and a pair of fluffy slippers was leaning against a post. She had one hand on her drip-stand and was using the other to hold her cigarette. She took long drags, each one savoured, as she stared into space. Jean eyed her with envy, recalling the pleasure brought about by the first cigarette of the day.

The hacking cough of an elderly gentleman to her side, soon brought her back to reality and reminded her of why she tried not to smoke these days. Accompanied by a younger woman who Jean guessed was probably his daughter, he was hunched forward in a wheelchair attempting to smoke a cigarette. Each puff made him wheeze and forced him to take up the mask which lay in his lap, attached to a canister at his side. His hands trembled as he applied it to his face and hungrily drank in the oxygen.

"Poor bastard," Anna commented. "He looks worse than Mum."

"Yes," replied Jean. She watched him as he yet again coughed and retched. He beckoned to the woman for the tissue which she held in her hand. Dutifully, she obliged, waited patiently whilst he spat into it, then took it back from him and put it into the nearby bin. The old man, noticing that the cigarette had burnt right down to the end, cast it to the ground. Half-heartedly, he tried to brush off the deposits of ash which littered his pyjama bottoms, before indicating that he wanted to go back indoors.

"Jesus," said Jean. "He reminded me of our dad, then. Do you remember what he was like at the end? Always coughing up stuff? Yuk!"

"Unfortunately, I do, yes," said Anna. "The sad thing was that he wasn't anywhere near as old as that bloke was. He was only fifty-eight when he died."

"Yes, I remember," said Jean. "But he looked just as old. He couldn't even stand up on his own! I still think they let him out of hospital just so he could die at home. They even hastened his demise by failing to send sufficient oxygen home with him. I played hell with the doctors for that. I'll never forget finding him dead in his chair. It was an awful sight."

Anna recalled that day only too clearly. It wasn't something you ever forgot.

"Well, let's be glad that the same mistake isn't going to happen today," she said.

"Damn right it isn't!" Jean replied. She stood up and stretched. "Come on, our kid. Let's get back to Mum. She's been left on her own long enough with Peter and Janice. She's probably woken up by now and if all she sees is their miserable faces, she'll think she's already dead!"

Anna laughed. You had to give it to Jean - even on a day like this, she could make someone smile. She took out her phone and sent a quick text to Richard and the girls to assure them she was fine, then followed her sister back into the darkness of the hospital.

CHAPTER 32

Dedication. If there was one word, thought Peter, to describe the quality which was most obvious today amongst the staff on this ward, this was it. They couldn't do enough for his mum and family. He smiled as he was reminded of Roy Castle's song and imagined him singing it full blast in the middle of the room, accompanied by his trumpet. It would be a fitting tribute at this moment, given that he, too, had battled against lung cancer. The staff might not have been out to break any records but they were certainly out to do the best job they could with the resources they had.

Peter looked out of the door at the nursing station which was just across the way. Michelle was back on duty again, just hours after clocking off last night. She never took a break, it seemed. She sat at the desk, trying to balance the receiver of the phone under her chin whilst making notes and taking bites out of her toast which she washed down with gulps of tea. No doubt she was now contacting Silver Birch as promised, to chase up a bed for his mother. He really hoped she was successful. Much as the nurses attended to his mum's needs and kept her clean and comfortable, he knew from visiting his friend, Tim, that the hospice would be a much better place. And he was certain that this is what his mum was hanging on for. She wasn't going until she'd seen her dogs.

Peter looked back at his mum and tried to guess what was going through her mind. Her lips were moving behind her oxygen mask and she was gesticulating with her hands. She paused every now and then as if listening to someone before starting up again. He had absolutely no idea what she was saying or who she imagined she was talking to. Anyone could've been forgiven for thinking there was another person in the room besides Peter. But there wasn't.

Peter thought back to what Anna had said their grandad had told her just days before he died - "They've all been here, you know, Anna. My old pals. Visiting me. They stand around the bed and keep asking me when I'm going to join them."

He wondered if that was what was happening now. If there was someone in the room who had passed on and was talking to her. But he quickly put it out of his mind. He wasn't like Michael and his sisters. He'd never believed in all that nonsense about ghosts and the like. No. The only logical answer was that it was the drugs that were doing this to her. Pure and simple.

He sighed. How he wished he could be the one engaging in a conversation with her now. It wouldn't matter what they talked about. She could witter on to her heart's content. He'd even listen to endless chat about dogs. He wouldn't mind at all. He just wanted to hear her voice properly and for her to make eye contact with him as she spoke. He'd never felt so left out. He shouldn't have gone back to work when he did. He should have put his foot down and refused. That way he could've been here when she decided it was time to go and could've spoken to her properly. He bent forward in his chair and ran both of his hands through his hair over and over again. He took several deep breaths. He had to get through this.

"Penny for them?" Penny was at the door.

Peter turned around just in time to see her expression completely change as she cast her eyes from his, over to his mother. Penny froze. A redness crept up from her chest and made its way into her cheeks. Instinctively, she clutched at the chain around her neck.

Peter knew she'd been here before. It wasn't that long ago since she'd watched her own mother die and now here she was again. He got up and manoeuvred his chair to behind her legs, then gently encouraged her to sit down. She didn't speak but began to rummage about in her pockets. She emptied the contents out onto the bed in front of her. In amongst the half-eaten packet of mints, a door key and some loose change, she found a tissue. She blew her nose loudly then wiped her eyes with the back of her sleeve. Peter could still see the traces of the tears which had run down her face, like the trails of slugs on a patio. She drew in her breath then spoke.

"Sorry, Peter," she said. "The last thing you need is me blubbering."

She made herself busy putting things back in her pockets.

Peter composed himself. "You're all right, flower," he said. He looked at the way she was dressed. She was wearing an oversized jumper on top of some baggy jogging bottoms. Very different from her usual smart attire. He joked, "Well I guess you're not in work today, then?"

"Course not!" she said, before realising he was taking the mick.

She added, "I couldn't bring myself to go. Not after speaking to your Anna last night. And it's the eighth today, isn't it? So, I figured this was my last chance to see your mum."

"Not you as well!" said Peter. "I thought it was only my brother and sisters who believed in all that eight nonsense."

"Well, I don't generally believe in it," replied Penny, "but, on this occasion it makes sense. Your mum's always put others before herself, and that's what she's doing now."

She took hold of her aunty's hand and squeezed it. "Aren't you, Freda?" she said.

Peter smiled at the look of admiration in Penny's face.

Penny continued, "You're making sure you don't spoil the grandchildren's birthdays, aren't you?" She pointed at the birthday cards on the bedside table.

"See, Peter?" she said. "When have you ever known your mum to be that organised?"

Peter looked at the envelopes. He nodded.

"That's the Kendall gene working it's magic," Penny said. "They're all selfless. Your mum has known for a while now that she wasn't going to beat this cancer, so she's been sorting things out. You've not noticed whilst you've been here because you've chosen not to."

Peter had to agree. He thought about everything she'd done for him - the days she'd sacrificed to help him out with childcare or housework or lifts for Janice. She'd even come out in the early hours of the morning to drive him and his mates home when they were pissed up and couldn't find a taxi. She'd never once complained. He was going to really miss her...

His thoughts were interrupted by a rap on the door. Michelle appeared accompanied by a man in glasses.

"Peter, this is Dr Bennett from Silver Birch Hospice,' she explained. Peter stood up and shook his hand.

"Pleased to meet you," he said. "This is my cousin, Penny."

Dr Bennett turned around to acknowledge Penny before looking over at Freda in the bed.

"Hello," he said. She stopped muttering. Peter couldn't be certain but he thought he saw her eyes twinkle for just the briefest of moments. Dr Bennett picked his way through the chairs, over to her, drew the stethoscope from around his neck, and gently placed it on her chest, as he explained, "I'm just going to listen to your heart, Freda."

Nobody spoke.

Dr Bennett removed the stethoscope then placed it back around his neck. He patted the bed covers then gestured to Peter and Michelle to follow him outside the room, leaving Penny the opportunity to hold Freda's hand and whisper her goodbyes.

Once outside the door, Dr Bennett's voice took on a very serious tone.

"Your mother is very weak," he explained to Peter. "We have an ambulance waiting outside to take her to the hospice but I have to warn you that she might not make it there."

Peter gulped but remained silent.

"I will need one of you to accompany her in the ambulance," he continued. "Is that all right?"

Peter looked over at Anna. She was with Mark, the physio. She was sobbing uncontrollably onto his shoulder. Jean was next to her, trying to hold herself together. He looked back at Dr Bennett.

"I'll do it," he said.

"Are you sure?" said Dr Bennett. "You do fully understand what I'm saying, don't you?"

"Yes, I do," replied Peter, "and I'm confident she'll get there. It's what she's been hanging on for."

"Right. Well let's get moving then," he said.

Peter watched him commandeer some staff and head back towards the room. Penny was walking over. Her eyes were red.

"I guess this is it, then?" she said to Peter. She went up to him and gave him a big hug. "You take care of yourself," she said. "I hope it all works out."

"I hope so," Peter replied nervously.

He watched her go over to his sisters. He took a deep breath and exhaled slowly. He was as ready as he was ever going to be.

CHAPTER 33

To anyone walking past the door to Freda's room in the hospice, it might have seemed odd that people were laughing. After all, this was a place where people had been brought to die. Just a glance down the corridor was a sufficient reminder of this fact as several of the doors were partially open, revealing serene scenes of families waiting silently at their loved one's bedsides. But it couldn't be helped.

The first thing that set them off giggling was Jean recounting her drive from the hospital to the hospice. It was only a short journey - literally, a couple of streets away - but they'd each taken their own cars to make it. They'd left the ward together in great haste, conscious of the need to get there as soon as they could since there was the danger that their mother might die in the ambulance. Indeed, Dr Bennett had organised a 'signal' should this happen, which was that the ambulance driver would park at the front of Silver Birch if everything was okay and at the back entrance otherwise

So it was that like robbers fleeing the scene of a crime, Anna, Jean and Janice 'legged it' from the ward. Or, rather, Anna, who had parked the furthest away in the cheaper car park, legged it. Like Speedy Gonzalez, she sprinted away. Janice, being asthmatic, just about managed a fast walk and Jean, who found it difficult to breathe and walk with any kind of pace at the same time, was way behind. But she only had to cross the road to get to her car so she was confident she would arrive at the same time as the others. But, of course, she hadn't factored in getting out of the car park...

She'd recently bought a kind of 'season ticket' for her car to enable her to visit the hospital without taking out a mortgage, but, in the stress of getting to the ward quickly yesterday morning, had failed to check on its expiry date and time, the 8th of September at 0800 hours. The digital display at the exit was showing 1705. This was typical of her luck! Jean was regaling the tale of how she'd pleaded into the intercom at the barrier to get the security guards to open it up. She'd made every promise to them under the sun, but they hadn't taken her up on any of them. Her distress was evidence enough of her sincerity and they'd willingly obliged and waived any fees.

What was making the others laugh was the way she was telling the story now. For someone who had difficulty breathing, she hadn't yet taken a breath and was talking like someone who'd taken Speed. What's more, she was blaming her dying mother for the whole episode!

"It's your fault, Mother," she joked. "You and that bloody number eight! I can understand you wanting to leave this mortal earth before all the birthdays which are coming up but you could've chosen the day before so I wouldn't have to renew my car park ticket!"

Freda was propped up in bed attached to an oxygen machine on one side and an automated syringe-driver on the other. She stared ahead as Jean continued,

"You might look like you're not listening but I know you are!" she said.

Just then, the door flung open to reveal Michael being dragged in by Niko. The large German Shepherd strained at his lead as he sniffed at the air in search of his owner. He stopped in his tracks; his eyes fixed upon the bed. Everyone looked from him to their mother and back again. Nobody spoke. It was as if the pair of them - owner and dog - were locked in a private conversation from which they were all excluded. After a minute, which felt distinctly longer, Niko walked forward and sat down obediently at the bedside. He rested his head on the covers and nuzzled Freda's hand.

"Aw!" said Jean. "Look at that! He knows, doesn't he?" Her voice faltered. She looked down at Mollie who had waddled up to the bed and was now waiting attentively for Freda to take notice of her. Anna went over and scooped her up in her arms then lifted her up so she could see clearly. Mollie scrambled to get closer. Niko took a sideways look at her then reverted his gaze to Freda.

"Don't let go of her, Anna," said Peter. "We don't want her jumping on Mum."

"Don't worry, I won't," she replied. She gently placed her on the bed but took care to keep hold of her collar. Mollie sniffed the air and tried to break free. Jean also kept a tight grip. Mollie strained but then accepted defeat. She lay down and rested her head on her paws. Anna stroked her fur. It felt soft and silky. She bent her head down and sniffed her coat. It smelt lovely. Clean. In fact, Niko was the same. Both dogs were immaculate. So, that's what Michael had been doing all day. She turned to Michael,

"Ah! So that's what you've been up to - bathing the dogs."

"Well It needed to be done, our kid," Michael replied. "I couldn't have brought them in as they were. They stank to high heaven!"

Jean laughed. "Rather you than me, Michael," she said. "Mollie had dried shit all over her arse when I saw her last!"

"Charming!" said Peter. "Trust you to lower the tone."

"Well, there was that," said Michael, "but the real issue wasn't poo - they both reeked of pot! Your Jake has been smoking it all week at Mum's. We'd never have lived it down if the people in here got wafted with that scent."

"Oh, I don't know. It's better than some smells you can get in places like this. And imagine how chilled out everyone would be!" said Jean.

"Actually, thinking about it, I could've done with something like that when I walked up the corridor a minute ago," said Michael. "This old bloke was walking in front of me, dead slow. He turned briefly and saw Mollie, so stopped and bent down to say hello. But he mustn't have noticed Niko 'cos he was on the other side of him. He was making a fuss of Mollie when Niko tried to get in on the act, pushing his nose into the man's face. You know what he's like, Jean, don't you?" He looked directly at his sister.

"I do, yes. He's a right jealous sod! Aren't you, boy?" Jean said. She got down to Niko's level and ran both her hands over his head and down through his thick fur on his chest. He automatically gave her his paw. She continued to tickle his chest.

"You like that, don't you?" she said. She turned to Anna. "You know, he'd let me do that all day!"

Anna laughed.

Michael continued, "Honestly right, I thought this bloke was going to have a cardiac! He shot in the air and jumped back against the wall with his hands above his head. You know, like he was under arrest or something?"

"Are you surprised?" said Peter.

"No, but he obviously was!" quipped Jean. She looked at Michael and grinned. They both started laughing.

"Aw! Imagine the headline," she went on, "Man in hospice dies of fright! It'd be all over the news."

Peter joined in the laughing now. "We could start a new business," he said, "hiring him out to people who want to bump off their elderly relatives!"

"Yes, that's a great idea," said Jean. "All we'd need is a few unsuspecting codgers with dicky hearts and dodgy legs and we'd be sorted."

"Well, it beats having to run up behind them and shout 'Boo!' " added Michael. "We could do a roaring trade."

"You lot are terrible," said Anna. She turned to Michael. "I hope you apologised to him."

"Yes Miss. Sorry Miss. It won't happen again, Miss," he answered.

He looked at Jean and winked. "Ever the school teacher!" he said.

"Well you need to be careful," said Anna. "We don't want them banning dogs from coming in on account of ours. It's very good that they let them in."

"I know, love. I know," said Michael. "Don't worry. It's all fine. He still lives."

"I can vouch for that!" said a voice from behind Michael. It was Dr Bennett. He took big strides across the room towards Niko.

"So, who's this lovely fella?" he asked as he squatted down to his level and began to stroke him.

"Niko," beamed Jean. "Isn't he just gorgeous? He's my mum's pride and joy."

She cast a glance at her mother. Although still not speaking, she had moved her head and was looking in their general direction. Jean was certain she knew what was going on.

"He certainly is!" continued Dr Bennett.

He ran his hands over both of Niko's velvety ears as he spoke to him directly.

"So, you're the one causing all the commotion in our hospice, are you?" he said.

"Sorry about that, Doctor," said Michael, rather sheepishly. "He was only saying hello."

"It's fine," he replied. "It's not often we get dogs in here. It's a bit of a novelty, to be honest. The staff are itching to get in here and say hello to him."

He turned to the side, noticing Mollie for the first time.

"And who might this be?" he asked.

"Mollie," said Jean. "Mum got her to keep Niko company."

He stood up and patted her on the head.

"And what breed is she, then?" he asked. "Is she a mongrel?"

There was a sharp intake of breath. Everyone looked at Freda. Did they imagine it or did their mother just roll her eyes?

Jean interjected, "She's a Cairn Terrier, actually, Doctor. She's very highly bred. Won prizes and everything. You probably just don't know the breed very well."

"Oh I do," he said. "My friend has a Cairn. Looks nothing like that though."

Again, they looked at their mother. Yes. There was no doubt about it. She was definitely throwing daggers at the good doctor.

Anna noticed and felt the need to explain.

"Well, Mollie's a bit heavier than she ought to be as Mum's not been able to exercise her as much as she'd like to," she said.

"Ah, I see," he replied though he didn't look convinced. "Well, there's a lovely garden out there," he said, pointing to the patio doors. "Every room backs out onto it. Feel free to let the dogs go out. The sun's still shining. It'll do you good to take a little time out."

He looked at Anna as he said that. He'd already taken her to one side when she'd arrived and expressed his concern about her wellbeing.

"It's a difficult time for everyone," he'd said. "You've not had much rest. You need to be strong and that means taking care of yourself. Your mum knows you are all here with her. You are allowed to leave her side."

His reassurance had meant a lot to her. She'd felt comforted by his words. Unlike the doctors at the hospital, he was genuinely concerned about everyone involved here - not just the patient. How glad she was that her mother had been given the opportunity to come here. It was so much better for all of them.

Dr Bennett turned to leave. "You might not see me

again," he said. "You all take care of yourselves and don't hesitate to ask for anything. Just press that buzzer on the wall and a member of staff will come along to assist."

Jean looked at Anna, "See that? A buzzer. You press it when needed," she said sarcastically.

"Does it do room service?" asked Michael. "Only I could do with a bite to eat."

"Michael!" said Anna.

"Well if you don't ask you don't get!" he said.

Dr Bennett laughed along.

"No, it doesn't, I'm afraid," he said. "But there's a café just down the corridor which is run by volunteers. They do lovely sandwiches." He looked at his watch.

"They're still open," he said. "They close in half an hour."

"Right, well I'll get down there and see what they've got left," said Peter. He headed for the door, seemingly pleased to have a new sense of purpose.

"I'll come with you," said Jean. "No offence but I don't want you choosing my food, our kid. God knows what you'll bring back."

"Me too," said Anna. "Give my legs a stretch. Michael, you can take over from me and hold Mollie."

"Will do," he replied, moving to the bedside.

"The nurse will make you some hot drinks," said Dr Bennett. "She'll be along shortly to ask what you'd like."

"Thanks," they all said.

Everyone left the room. Michael sat down at the side of his mum. This was the last time he would be with her on his own so he wanted to make sure that he told her everything she needed to hear

CHAPTER 34

When they were growing up, the four children used to spend many a Saturday evening snuggled up on the sofa with their mum. Their dad, having slept off his afternoon session of drinking, would be down the pub as usual. In his absence, they could relax, safe in the knowledge that he wouldn't return before closing time.

It was treats all round. With a budget of twenty pence per person, they would each have a chocolate bar, a 'mix up' or two ounces of sweets from the corner shop. At least two of them would go on the errand, taking the dogs for some exercise at the same time. They loved the sight of all the jars lined up on the shelf - an array of colours - displaying lemon sherbets, fizz bombs, rhubarb and custards and many more. They'd walk home happily, clutching their paper bags and wouldn't touch them until everyone had theirs and they'd settled down to watch telly. Their mum would always have something like a Fry's Chocolate Cream bar or a Turkish Delight, or, if she was really pushing the boat out, a bar of Old Jamaica. Those were happy days.

Tonight they weren't at home and it wasn't Saturday but Tuesday. There was no sofa, but a set of comfortable armchairs around a bed; a television on the wall instead of on a stand. It had more channels than you could shake a stick at and no Radio Rentals' sticker to declare to the world that you couldn't afford to buy. It even had a remote control. Very different to their childhood experience but nonetheless the same in one very important way. They were all together.

The dogs had been taken home. It was going dark outside now. Peter had drawn the heavy curtains across the patio doors. With the garden no longer in view, all eyes stared banally at the television. It was some programme or other about people catching giant fish. No-one was really watching it. The noise of the oxygen machine was still playing in the background. A nurse had asked if they wanted to remove the mask now that it wasn't actually doing anything but they'd all said "No." It was, strangely, comforting. Whilst they could hear that gentle hissing, they could believe their mum was still with them. No-one wanted to imagine the alternative of the occasional breath being gasped. Least of all Anna. She'd been here before with patients when she'd worked in the Care of the Elderly unit and she didn't want to be reminded of the inevitable. She still held her mother's hand even though there was no sense of response in it any more. It felt cold and clammy to the touch.

Periodically, Anna rubbed her mother's fingers between the palms of her hand in the way that she had rubbed her hands as a child when she'd come in from the cold. A vain attempt to instil some warmth into them. Some life.

Anna continued to quietly chat away to her mum, explaining everything that they were talking about. It was like someone did when they had a deaf aunt who needed to be kept in the conversation. Except she wasn't shouting out but whispering very softly. Her mother might have lost many of her faculties over the last few hours but Anna felt sure her hearing was not yet one of them. She'd always loved a good conversation and she wasn't going to deny her any opportunity to be involved - even if it was only as a passive bystander.

Anna felt a nudge on her arm.

"This is that film I was telling you about, Anna!" Jean said, as she pointed at the television, having switched the channel over. She continued, "The one me and Mum watched that night when I was stopping over at hers after she first came out of hospital following her hip replacement. Do you remember me telling you about it?"

"Oh, I've seen this," interrupted Michael. "It's that one with Will Smith where he's the only one left in New York trying to find a cure for a virus that's wiped out billions of people."

Anna looked up at the screen. Will Smith was being chased by a band of grey, bloodied men and was running for his life. Every now and then he stopped to fire a machine gun at them.

"What? You watched *this* with Mum?" asked Anna. "That can't be right! She's like me," she said, "she doesn't do zombie films. They're too scary."

Anna remembered being taken to see *Dawn of the Dead* years ago by an old boyfriend. It had scared the life out of her and she'd avoided them ever since. Her mother shared the same aversion.

"It's not a zombie film," said Jean.

"Well, what are *they* then?" asked Anna. Will Smith had now taken refuge behind a glass screen which was being bashed repeatedly by the ringleader. A man resembling one of the dancers from Michael Jackson's *Thriller* video, he growled and snarled as he tried to head-butt his way into the laboratory. A dozen or so others, similarly rabid, followed his example. Blood and flesh smeared the glass as it began to crack in all directions. Anna shuddered.

"Well, technically-speaking, I suppose it is a bit of a zombie film," admitted Jean. "But that's not why we watched it. We watched it for the dog."

"For Niko?" Anna was puzzled.

Peter laughed.

"Bloody hell it's like explaining something to Mum," he said. "What Jean means is that it's got a dog in the film. A German Shepherd. It's his only companion. Looks like Niko."

"Well I can't see any dog with him," said Anna, "but I can see two other people there. I thought you said the dog was his only companion?"

Will Smith was now hiding a woman and a small boy in a tunnel at the back of the room.

"That's 'cos the dog's dead!" said Peter. "And he's only just discovered those other two exist." He pursed his lips in frustration.

"Ok! Keep your hair on!" said Anna. Then added, "Bloody hell, spoiler alert!"

"Well you're not exactly going to watch it, are you?" said Peter.

"Not now, I'm not!" replied Anna. Peter rolled his eyes.

"Made Mum cry it did!" said Jean. "His dog got bitten by a pack of infected wild dogs so he had to put it to sleep. It was well sad."

Michael laughed. "Trust Mum! She'd watch any old crap if it had a dog in it."

"Well, you know, don't knock it," said Jean. "She said she wanted to watch films with dogs in, so that's what we did!"

"An odd choice, though, Jean," laughed Anna.

"Well, she'd watched pretty much everything else," said Jean, *Marley and Me, Greyfriars Bobby, Turner and Hooch, Hachi: A Dog's Tale.* You name it, she'd seen it. We had to look further afield. Try new genders, so to speak."

"I think you mean genres," said Anna.

"Yeah, well, that an' all," replied Jean. Then "What's up, our kid?"

Jean looked at Peter who was staring at the bed. All of them followed his line of vision. Their eyes all rested on their mum. She had been lying with her head to one side but now she lifted her chin and very slowly and methodically moved her head. As she turned from one side to the other, she seemed to look at each of her children, one by one. She took a deep gasp. Her head rolled so that her face now came to rest on the other side of the pillow. Beneath the mask, her mouth was clearly open.

No one moved. For what seemed like an age, they all just stood there, looking at her.

"Is this it, then?" asked Jean, presently. "Has she gone?"

"I guess so," said Anna.

"What should we do now?" asked Michael.

All four of them just looked at each other. Anna still held onto her mother's hand,

"Call the doctor," said Peter. He pointed to the red button at the side of the bed. Jean leant forward and pressed it. She looked at Anna.

"That's how it's done," she said. She smiled nervously.

Within a minute there was a soft tap at the door. Michael answered it.

"Is everything all right?" asked a middle-aged lady.

"We think she's gone," said Jean. She stood up to allow the doctor to take her space at the side of the bed.

The doctor took the head of her stethoscope and placed it gently on Freda's chest. She put the tips of the headset into her ears and listened carefully.

"She's still with us," she said, "but it won't be long now. Shall I switch off the oxygen?"

"Yes, please," said Jean.

"Can we take the mask off too?" asked Anna.

"Of course," she replied.

She got up and switched off the cylinder then carefully removed the oxygen mask which she placed on the bedside cabinet. Then she indicated to Jean to sit back down.

"I'll be just outside when you need me," she said. She folded her stethoscope into her hand and walked away from the bed.

"Thanks, love," said Michael. She smiled back at him. All watched as she closed the door. It made just the slightest of clicks. Then they were left alone in the silent room.

CHAPTER 35

It wasn't much longer after the doctor left that Freda passed away. There was to be no mistaking it this time. It was obvious to all that she'd gone. There'd been one final gasp and that was that. Her mouth lolled open and her eyes stared out vacantly. No. She definitely wasn't in there anymore.

Time of death: 9.18pm, Tuesday the 8th of September 2015. That number again - eight. Even the digits of the year added up to eight.

Freda had gone out of the world on the same date of the month as she had come into it, and, judging by her appearance now, with the same spirited effort. The area around the bed smelt strongly of sweat. Beads of moisture ran down Freda's brow and her hair was matted against her forehead. All visible signs of her final battle. The war was over.

Anna released her grip on her mother's hand, allowing her arm to fall back to its natural position by her side. She looked upon her face. There were red indentations which carved out where the mask had been. Anna put her hand out and traced around them. Her mother's skin was soft but mottled. She let her fingers linger a moment, hoping that their touch might somehow erase the marks. But, stubbornly, they remained. She stood up and kissed her on the cheek.

"You can stay with her as long as you like." It was the doctor who spoke now. "There's no need to rush," she said as she made to leave.

"Thanks," said Anna, "but that's not my mum anymore. I've said all I need to."

Anna found she could hardly bear to look. She moved to the side as first Michael, and then Peter, took turns to say their goodbyes.

Michael whispered something in his mother's ear before backing off. Peter laid the lightest of touches on her hand but said nothing. He turned, eager to get away.

In her lifetime, Anna had never seen either of her brothers cry in public and it was to be no different today. Stoic as ever, she knew they'd bottle it all up until they were by themselves. Only Jean was visibly upset. Tears streamed down her face as she stood trance-like and stared at the bed. Peter rummaged in his pocket. He passed Jean a tissue.

"Thanks our kid," she said. She blotted each eye, blew her nose and then took a deep breath.

"I knew it would be today," she said, as her bottom lip trembled. "I just knew it. Mum planned it this way. I'm just so relieved that she got to die here and not in that hospital bed. I couldn't have coped with that. And, she got to see her dogs too. We didn't do too bad did we?"

She sniffed and looked around. Michael moved forward and put his arm around her shoulder. He drew her into a hug.

"You did well, Sis. Mum got the death she wanted, surrounded by all her family. You couldn't have done any more for her."

He kissed the top of her head.

"Yes, I know but it hurts, that's all," said Jean. "I feel like I've lost everything."

"I know," said Michael, "but you've still got us."

Peter walked over and patted her on the shoulder.

"We'll make sure she gets a good send off, Jean," he said. "It's what she deserves."

"Yes. Nothing will be too much trouble," agreed Michael. "It'll be her last day out after all."

Jean smiled.

"You do know that she expects her coffin to be drawn on a cart pulled by four German Shepherds, don't you, Michael?" Jean laughed.

"Led by Niko," added Anna.

"Oh I don't doubt it," Michael replied.

"Yes. And you will be the one making the cart, our kid," mocked Peter, "seeing as you're so good with wood."

"Peter, I can make anything out of wood. Don't worry. But I won't be making a cart."

"Is that because you know you'll never get it past Lillian?" Anna asked, referring to the undertaker her mother had chosen.

"No. Obviously it's because you can't take dogs to a funeral!" said Peter.

"Actually it's neither of those things," said Michael. "I know the equation." He looked at Jean and started laughing. "It's because I'd never find another three German Shepherds good enough for the role!"

They all started laughing now. How true!

"But don't worry, there'll be a dog at the funeral in one form or another. I've got it all worked out. You just leave it to me. I'll do her proud."

None of them doubted Michael. They all knew that he would put one hundred per cent into whatever he was planning and that the end result would be something special. Different. Unique. And solely for their mum. No one else would ever get the same.

Anna felt a warm glow inside. She looked fondly at her siblings. Here they all were, a family once again. It felt like old times. Like when they were younger. Before they had families of their own and moved apart.

If there was one positive to come out of all this, Anna thought, it was that the past few weeks had given them the opportunity to reconnect as brothers and sisters. To spend time together. To talk to each other every day. To reminisce about the past and rediscover their shared sense of humour. Their mother's illness, albeit tragic, had united them once more. Each one of them had answered her call for help. No questions asked. They'd willingly put their lives on hold for her sake. It was a testament to the immense love they had for her that she could command such devotion.

They finally left the room and said their goodbyes in the car park sometime after ten, agreeing to meet up the day after. Zipping up her coat against the cold breeze, Anna rummaged instinctively in her pocket for her car keys and pressed on the fob. The headlights flashed twice and she reached out for the door handle and opened the door. Placing one foot on the jamb of the door, she didn't get in but instead remained standing, one hand on the door and the other on the roof of the car as she surveyed the exit. She watched as first Peter, and then Michael departed. It was as if Peter couldn't get away fast enough. Driving one handed, as always, his tyres threw up bits of gravel and water as he drove through a large puddle. The windows were up and his eyes were firmly focused on the road ahead. He gave only a perfunctory wave in her general direction, before speeding off. In contrast, Michael, following just behind him, had put down all the windows and was waving a hand about. Having just finished a cigarette in the shadows of the bushes at the front, he was no doubt trying to get rid of the smell which had followed him into his car. Anna saw him pop a mint into his mouth before putting his hands back on the steering wheel and changing up a gear. Soon, he too, was gone. Only Jean still remained.

Rain began to fall, forcing Anna to finally get in her car. She switched on the ignition so that she could put on the wipers and afford herself a clearer view of her twin seated in the small grey Nissan in the far corner of the car park. Like Michael, Jean too had just had a cigarette before getting in her car. Anna knew that, like their mother, Jean always kept a packet of cigarettes stashed in the glove box in case of emergency. She didn't blame her giving in to her craving tonight. Anna had never smoked herself, but had seen enough people smoking in her lifetime to understand the calming effect a cigarette could have. She imagined how Jean's hands might have shaken as she fumbled with the packet in her haste, then the relief as she took that first drag.

Anna's chest felt tight. In the silence of the car, she could hear her heart beating in her ears. She switched on the blowers to mask the sound and watched as two clear patches of glass at the bottom of the windscreen began to grow upwards to meet each other. Still, she could not bring herself to start the car. There was a reluctance to leave this place. It was a reluctance which she knew she shared with her sister, judging by her behaviour now. Anna looked across at Jean's car, still quietly sitting on the tarmac. This was the end of a chapter in their lives. A chapter which had revolved around the lynchpin that was their mum. She had been the one constant in their lives which had held them all together and Anna knew that life could never be the same again. She knew it was more than the loss of her mother which she mourned - it was the loss of her siblings too. Leaving now would mean having to admit this. And accept it.

Anna decided to take her lead from Jean. She waited until she saw the headlights on the Nissan light up and reckoned that Jean had finally managed to compose herself. Seeing her buckle up her seatbelt, she did the same. Anna checked her mirrors. She paused momentarily as she caught her reflection. Her face looked so tired and drawn! What she needed more than anything was a good night's sleep. She imagined what her mother would say now. She would no doubt tell her to get herself home and into the warmth.

"I know, Mother," Anna spoke out loud, conceding that it was time to go.

Her thoughts turned to Richard and the girls. She hadn't been in touch with them since earlier this evening, when they had been very upset. She felt a pang of guilt that they were waiting up for her. It would take an hour to get back. It was Emily's birthday tomorrow and a school day too. Anna took a deep breath, drew herself up and started the car. Putting it in gear, she moved away from the hospice and home to her family.

ACKNOWLEDGEMENTS

A huge thank you to my cousin, Jacqueline Evans, for encouraging me to write this book and for her patience in reading and re-reading the drafts. Without her persistence, it would never have been completed!

Also, to Nik Perring, author and creative writing teacher for inviting me to join the Bollington Library Writing Group - the support of Nik and the group members is much appreciated. In particular, I would like to thank Jenny Martin, and my colleagues, Paul Norris and Wesley Royle who unhesitatingly and generously gave up their time to proof-read my work and offer suggestions.

Thanks also to my daughter Amber, my sister Jaine, and my friend Stella Johnston, for reading the story and offering their ideas.

My grateful thanks to Christina Neuman for capturing the essence of my mum so well in her design for the front cover.

Printed in Great Britain
by Amazon